Things Falling Apart

BY J.W. SCHNARR

To Kay,
Thanks for the
Support!
Aug 11/2012

PUBLISHED BY
FIVE RIVERS PUBLISHING
WWW.5RIVERS.ORG

Published by Five Rivers Chapmanry, 704 Queen Street, P.O. Box 293, Neustadt, ON N0G 2M0, Canada www.5rivers.org

Edited by Lorina Stephens.

Interior design and layout by Lorina Stephens.

Title set in The Unseen

Byline set in SF Movie Poster

Text set in Adobe Garamond Pro

Published in Canada

Library and Archives Canada Cataloguing in Publication

Schnarr, James, 1976-

Things falling apart / James Schnarr.

Short stories.

Also issued in electronic format.

ISBN 978-1-927400-03-6

I. Title.

PS8637.C4496T55 2012 C813'.6 C2012-900992-X

For Jessica. For everything.

Contents

Dredging up the Dead

October 25. Days at sea: 9

Another accident on the tow today. The Frenchman we picked up in Halifax this time. Robert Denis (ROBE AIR if you ask him). Not paying attention, as usual. Honestly I don't know why he spends so much time talking when he's the only one on the crew who understands his accent. Anyway, he busted a couple of his fingers on the trawling line because he wasn't watching where his hands were. (~~I wonder how pissed he'll be when he finds out~~) I'm putting him on gaff and knife for now I guess, if he can hold a blade. Let him bleed cod for a few days. That'll teach him to watch what he's doing maybe. Jesus, we're not equipped to handle this kind of stupidity.

The sea was calm. We had a good haul today, low by-catch. I miss you, Maggie.

October 27. Days at sea: 10

No trawl today. A storm came up last night, and we were in the middle of bad swells all day. Normally I'd make the boys work through it, but it was raining and the deck gets like a slide when the boat is rocking. Gotta be extra careful, with my *problem* I can't afford any injuries at all. There may be some hell to pay with Denis as it is, he complained loudly that he couldn't even handle the knife yesterday, and the flopping cod tails were making things worse. If I'd known what a baby he was I would have left him in bloody Halifax.

Oh and to top it all off, somebody on the ship has been smoking pot. I can smell it in the cabin but nobody is confessing. I swear to Christ if one of them drowns because they're stoned and fall off the deck I won't be held responsible. Idiots, in the finest sense of the word.

The sea was choppy. No haul, so I'm heading north early. I miss you, Maggie.

October 28. Days at sea: 11

Picked up something weird in the nets today. Two yellow barrels of...something. We couldn't tell what it was. They had Russian all over them, and a poison symbol, so that's a double strike in my book. Thing is, it was in the middle of a decent haul of cod. We dropped the net and these two barrels came clunking out of there. One of them had been ripped open by the trawling door. It was leaking this black shit all over the fish. All over the trawl line too. Smelled like car exhaust a little. (~~Probably nuclear waste~~.) It had this really filmy texture like dish soap. If the Russians DID do a wholesale dump of some chemical shit around here, the entire area could be contaminated. Cod are like sponges when it comes to that stuff. I can't come back to port with a hold full of contaminated fish. Not now.

Fuckin' dumpers. It's like the old man always said. "The ocean is big enough to hide any man's mistakes."

I ordered the boys to hose the deck, and we pitched the barrels back where we found 'em (after we got a sample, of course, I'm not a total bastard). I marked the spot we picked 'em up, and I relayed it to the Coast Guard. Not that they're much use out here, but maybe they'll send the Canadian Navy out to take a look at it. Either way, their problem now, not mine.

The sea was calm today. Good haul. Count two barrels as by-catch. I was thinking of your blue and white dress today, Maggie, and the last time I saw you wear it. Church. Never had much use for God before that day.

October 29. Days at sea: 12

~~The hold is definitely contaminated~~.

October 30. Days at sea: 13

OK, I'm writing this down because it's just a little too

fucked up for me to keep in my head. I can't talk about it with the men because they're already freaked out. *Did we all touch that shit*? I can't remember now for sure. I know I did.

The hold is definitely contaminated. We're sitting on half a ton of gaffed and bled cod, and I'm probably going to have to dump the whole lot of it. Some of that Russian toxic waste got in there, and it...caused a reaction when it came in contact with the fish. I don't know how, but (~~the haul we put in there yesterday is still alive~~.) the cargo has had their nervous systems affected by the substance from the drums. They dance and flop like they're alive. We brought some out because at first we thought they were missed bleeds, and that can make your hold stink to high hell. They *were* bled though. I double checked the cuts myself.

Denis went off in mostly French about how we were all contaminated, and I swear I almost threw him off the ship. Last thing I need right now is some jackass going off half cocked and freaking everyone out. I *did* wash my hands again though, just to be sure.

I sent this in to the Coast Guard. I told them I'm dumping my hold, too. We'll do that the next two days and then flush it out with seawater. That's five days work lost, but it's a lot better than having my damn boat taken away for bringing in a hold full of toxic waste. They're pissed, of course. They don't want *me* dumping toxic waste either. Too damn bad.

The sea was calm today. No trawl. I miss you, Maggie; I miss simpler times.

October 31. Days at sea: 14

This is totally fucked. I got the Canadian Navy telling me to come home, and I got the Russian Navy telling me to meet up with a science ship they dispatched to try and figure out what the hell is in those canisters. I told them both they were contradicting each other, and now I'm being told to "stand by for further instructions." In the meantime, we dumped our hold. The smell was unbelievable. And the fish...if I didn't see the bleed cuts and knew for a fact that some of those fish have been out of water for days, I might think differently about them. The fact is they *are alive* to some extent. They actually swim in the water, though kind of lazy and half-assed. Like they're air sick maybe.

It really unnerved the crew watching thousands of cod swimming like that in the water, away from the boat. Especially Robert Denis, who cut most of those fish himself. I was happy to see them go. There was a pod of sperm whales about a thousand feet off the bow when we made our dump. It didn't concern me at the time, but now I'm thinking: *what would happen if they got into those sick fish?* Seems like an easy meal. If they're smart, they'll steer clear.

I hope they're that smart.

The seas were calm today. No trawl (obviously). I'm thinking of the time when you and I went to Churchill for your sister's wedding, and we ended up spending the weekend in the jet tub at the hotel. I miss you, Maggie. God love you.

November 1. Days at sea: 15

I moved the boat. I know we weren't supposed to, but those fuckin ~~(zombie)~~ fish (~~There! I finally said it! And I~~

~~feel like an idiot now, thanks!~~) were lolling around still, swimming on their sides, or upside down. It's like they have nowhere to go, so they just swim around the boat. Some got into the rudders, so when I started the engine I was chopping the hell out of them. Worse, they seem to not even notice the damage. I saw fish chopped in half with both sides trying to swim. I get the head, maybe, *but the tail end?* How is that possible?

That pod of whales is still in the area, and that has me worried. There are a couple of bulls in that pack, must be thirty feet long. There's nothing you can do to scare 'em off either. Looks like they're taking me up on that easy meal.

I hope they're fine; Maggie, I remember how much you loved whale watching from the bow of the ship. Denis was actually laughing and pretending to shoot them with a harpoon gun. I told him to get his shit together. It's going to be no end of problems with that man, I know it now. I don't care anymore if he drops an insurance claim on me or not. I don't have any. Let him sue me.

The hold is clean. We trawl tomorrow!

I'm expecting word from the Russians soon. I hope they brought a translator.

The seas were calm today. No trawl. Thinking of whale watching with you, Maggie. I wish you could see this pod!

November 2. Days at sea 16

Two men are dead. Ray Stevens and John Kruthers. I'm not really sure what to write, but I need to write something. Lately the act of writing in this book you gave me is the only thing that's been stable in the world. I'm a little drunk, so I apologize for the melodrama. How selfish am I? Two men with families are dead today and all I can think about is how shitty my own life is. Well, John Kruther's wife was always a bitch, but I am still hurting for her. Nobody deserves this. Hell, I don't deserve this either.

We were halfway through our second trawl when something got snagged in the trawling net. It was huge. It rocked the boat. Almost threw a rudder. I ordered a full stop, and we tried to raise the net. It's not unheard of to get snagged on an underwater rock or even a wreck down there that the GPS missed. Hell, I figured that's what it was. I was dead wrong.

We cranked the hoists and started pulling this damn net out of the water, but it was really slow going. It was coming though, so I had hope that there wasn't too much damage to the net. That's all I would have needed, you know? Those things are expensive to replace.

Denis saw it first. He shouted at me to come look. By the time I'd gotten to the back of the boat everyone was standing around, and I pushed through to the front. I couldn't believe what I saw when I looked down into the blue-black Atlantic.

I swear if I hadn't seen it myself I wouldn't believe it.

One of those goddamn whales had pushed into the net. We couldn't haul the thing up because it had wedged itself in there. Chasing cod maybe. Thing is, we were scraping the bottom of the ocean floor, and I've never heard of whales just sitting down there getting in the way. I've been out here over thirty years.

So the net comes up and this whale is halfway down the cod net. Just kind of sitting there. I figure the only thing we can do is turn the net and try to push him out. Otherwise we cut the lines and we are out a net. I'm still carrying the spare, but like I said, those things are expensive. Money was on my mind. So I guess that's why I decided to be stupid instead of just cutting those lines. Now they're dead and I'm getting drunk in my cabin.

We got the net up to surface and even managed to turn it a bit. Then the whale decided he'd had enough. His tail came up and thrashed the side of the boat. Just once. Once was enough to angle the net down and he pushed what must be twelve tons of weight toward the bottom of the ocean. Those trawl lines can't stand up to that. They handle a ton, ton and a half at most. This was *twelve tons* of whale.

The cables snapped. They came back at the ship. Same time, almost identical strikes. Of course, they were both standing there as lead lines, so it's not a surprise. Kruthers caught the damn line across the throat. Actually took his head right off. Ray Stevens, well, I'm not sure where he took his hit. It was somewhere on the chest, cuz he just grabbed at his heart like he'd been shot and toppled into the water. The whale swam away with the net. We managed to gaff Kruthers body. (~~His fuckin head is long gone though.~~) We couldn't find anything else. There's a mile of water under us right now.

I'm very sorry to both families.

The seas were red. The trawl is gone. I wish I was with you right now, Maggie. You've never felt farther away than you do right now.

November 3. Days at sea: who gives a fuck

We're heading home.

I'm a total failure. I'm sorry everyone. I'm sorry for the

dead men. I'm sorry, Maggie. I'm not sorry to you, Robert Denis. You're still an arrogant prick. And I know it was you smoking pot in the lower deck, I just can't prove it. Lucky for you we're leaving. I'll drop your ass in a hundred feet of Canadian water and you can swim to shore.

As an added punishment for this damned trip, the sperm whales are sick. It was those goddamned fish. You know there are still a couple swimming around the boat? Denis gaffed one and tossed it on board for shits and giggles. The damn thing was still flopping on the deck some four hours later. *Four hours.* It was missing scales, and its eyes were all milky white. It *is* a dead fish. I swear my life on this. And after we tossed it in the water it just swam in a lazy little circle. Its air bladder must have been totally full of air, because it couldn't straighten itself out no matter how hard it tried.

But the whales ate those dead fish, and now they are all sick. I could see them rolling on the surface all day. That's a sure sign of a sick whale. God, this area is like a damn charnel pit. Everything is either dead or dying.

So we're going home. Maybe if they don't take my boat we'll have a chance to go out one more time before it gets too cold. If they do take my boat, well, I'll spend the winter getting drunk. Maybe take a walk in the snow and look for you, Maggie. You never know, I might be able to find you yet.

The sea was dead today. Trawling is out of the question. I love you, Maggie. I'm coming home.

November 5. Days at sea:

The Russians sent some kind of military ship to deal with

us. We've been stopped for about two hours now. They were already aboard and looked over the rig. Thankfully the soldiers speak English, so we can understand what they want when they point their fuckin' rifles at us. The Captain had me aboard to discuss exactly what I had seen. He wouldn't tell me what was in the barrels. He claims he doesn't know anything, but I know he's lying about that.

I told him about the fish and then the sick whales. He responded by turning their 12.7mm DShk guns on the damn things. Double machine guns. The noise was terrific. There was whale meat everywhere. If it hadn't been for all the shit that's been going on here the last week or so, I might have actually been upset about seeing that. I know you would have, Maggie. There was something awful about those whales though. I swear. They were turning, just like the fish.

(~~The soldiers are leaving now, so we might be able to get underway in a bit. I'll come back later and finish this~~)

November 6ish.

I can't believe I found this. It's some kind of fate.

The Russians didn't want to help. They turned those fuckin' guns on us the minute the last soldier left the ship. There were holes everywhere. We took on water so fast...

The *Aurora Brite* is gone to the bottom of the ocean.

Everyone is dead, as far as I can tell. I'm stuck in this stupid orange emergency boat out on the high sea. I *will* die out here. I had to smash my emergency beacon in case the Russians picked it up and swung back for another go.

I had the book in my hands when they opened fire. I guess in my panic I managed to hold onto it. I should count myself grateful: I now have something to do to take my mind off the fact that I am four hundred miles away from shore. The emergency boat has a built in water filter underneath me somewhere, so I'm good there, and I have a stack of protein crackers to eat. I also have a little orange hood to keep the sun off my head.

It's the vacation I always wanted, I tell you!

Now when the Russians come back they'll have a nice orange target to shoot at, and they can blow my fucking head off and end this sad joke of a life once and for all.

For the record, I'm sad the *Aurora Brite* is lost but it wasn't my boat to lose. The bank was going to take it when we docked, full hold or not. Fish money would have helped stave them off for one more trip, maybe two, but so what? What would have happened when the season was over?

Now, when the bank asks, I can tell them to come find it. Maybe they'll run into the Russians too. Ahh, I'm such an idiot for calling those barrels in!

Am I sad about losing my crew? I suppose I am. They didn't deserve their fates. Even the Frenchman, who I couldn't stand. I'm sure he has a family somewhere who miss him even now. Truth is, so little of my heart wasn't broken by you, Maggie. I miss you so much that I can't begin to add to the pain with the loss of mere men. Employees. My heart is a cup filled over with tears for you, my love.

That's poetic. I think you would have liked that, but I think you would have slapped my arm and told me how silly I was. I bet you would have smiled though.

In my mind you are frozen as you were that Sunday we went to church, with your little blue and white dress. That's how I choose to remember you. But there is another you, lurking in my nightmares, the you that is bald and frail and sickly; the you that vomits on yourself because you are too weak to turn your head.

If God made all things, then He made your cancer, and He took you from me, and I will curse Him when I see Him. I fantasize about burning churches, so when they ask me why I can tell them, "I am mad at God. I rage because He crushed my life."

The Sea is my grave. I'm going to be with you soon, my love.

November.

Those whales surfaced today.

I'd resigned myself to a long agonizing death. I wasn't going to write again, but the whales surfaced.

One of them is about twenty feet from my raft. God, he stinks to high Hell! I can see the oozing bullet holes along the length of his body. He becomes visible every time the sun ducks behind a cloud. His huge white eyes blindly staring back and forth, as though he's hunting something nearby. It's probably me. Maybe he can smell me, but he can't see me.

He's just like those fish. I knew it. *I fucking knew it holy christ you would not believe it, Maggie.*

I need to calm down. Just looking at that huge, rotted thing, rolling over in the water like some giant piece of shit floating in a toilet bowl...it makes my chest flutter. I'm going to go insane watching this dead thing try to swim around. It's just so big.

It just blew its blowhole. I puked on my raft. The smell

inside is so much worse. A spout of black slime and blood and meat chunks blew from the top of the whale, out into the water. Like he'd just blown his brains all over himself. It reminded me of cancer, Maggie, a little. The sick girl I hate to think about.

Thought: If these are zombie whales, and that big bastard just blew his brains out, shouldn't he stop moving now?

Well he isn't.

He rolls over, shows me his belly, then flops back to right side up; sometimes he swims on his side. A little while ago, he nearly sank. Only the tip of his head was visible in the water. Like he was coming straight up from the bottom of the ocean. Shit. I'd drown myself but I'm terrified to get into the water with that thing nearby. I can see him grabbing hold of my leg and dragging me to the bottom of the ocean.

I'll be long dead by then. The speed he swims, it could take hours to get down there. Plus the weight of the water down there, and the cold...and the black. Glowing fish monsters and giant squid are all you find down there. And me, with my leg stuck in some damn whale.

I need to stop for a while. I'm losing it.

The sea is fuck you God today. Kill me please.

November.

I'm out of food now.

November.

I brok the pensil. i bit a hole in my hand and Im writing in blood. The whales are all around. they are losing their skin.

i see greasy fat and grey meat in the splits of their flesh. I have never touched a whale, but I look at that bone white fat and all i can think is that running my hands through it would be like squeezing lard through my fingers. I kno its not true. theyr meat. they arent lard covered in skin. Its a stupid thought. one that I can't seem to shake. I'm a stupid man.

Im coming soon I think maggs. The filter is broken. I taste sea water in my stores now. cant be much longr. i think i taste whalestink in the water too, but maybe its just cuz i smell them and they smell so fuckin bad i cant help but taste them to.

If I do taste them

Can i die?

If they make me sick that would be something huh? if it happens im stepping off the raft and sinking to the bottom of the ocean. its were i belong anyway. maybe ill grab a handful of grease off that whale before i go down. have a snack.

I'll just lay on the bottom of the ocean, bones crushed, eyes popped like rotting grapes, surrounded by the long cold death of the sea. how long? forever maybe. yes. forever.

Goodbye maggie. I wont write again. I hope I see you soon. If not, please know I love you. I hope I see you.

Good You

Frogger

We both grew up in the Eighties.

I was a big fan of video games even then. I loved my Atari. Little black joystick, bright red button on the top. I remember it cost my mother a fortune when it first came out.

We had to turn the controller sideways when we wanted

to play Q-Bert. You remember that little round guy who jumped on the pyramid?

My sister wouldn't play that one. She always said it was too hard to figure out where to go.

It's *easy*, I'd tell her, and then we would fight about it. There were a lot of games, though, so eventually we'd find something to play. Pac-Man. Combat. Mouse Trap.

I loved Frogger more than anything.

You remember that game, don't you?

You were the frog at the bottom of the screen. You had to get to the top of the screen where four little frog-holes were waiting. Your home in the swamp.

You only had four lives, so you couldn't die even once if you wanted to make high score.

And there was traffic. A lot of it.

Large multi-coloured rectangles for cars and trucks. Even bigger ones that represented semi-trailers. Four long lanes of traffic, bumper to bumper, humming along at a steady pace. Everybody was watching the car in front of him, and nobody was watching the side of the road for the little frog.

He only wanted to get home.

So busy, these commuters, always driving in one direction, or another. Never watching what was going on around them.

There were little gaps. Tiny spaces where a smart frog could gain some ground.

And so he'd begin.

If he was smart enough, and quick enough, he would make it out onto that first lane.

If he could make it through two lanes, he might even catch a breather in a thin little strip of grass between the two sections of busy commuters.

Eventually, though, he would have to go on.

So he'd jump.

Sometimes he'd be crushed flat under the rolling tires of the traffic.

Sometimes his head would hit the windshield of a commuter car and burst like a melon. His broken body would sail through the air as the shocked driver hit the brakes and swear to God that the little frog hadn't been there but a moment before.

Of course, there were times when he made it.

He would be so close to the swamp that he could smell it. He knew once he got there he would face other problems, of course. Like logs in the water, and crocodiles.

None of that mattered at this point.

So he'd watch. And he'd wait. Eventually, it all came down to guts.

Was this little frog fast enough to take the plunge and jump into traffic? Of course he was. Even stuck in that little frog position like that, he could move as fast as he wanted. Was he smart enough? That's tough to say. Certainly he was clever enough to recognize the patterns in the traffic and react accordingly.

But was he brave enough?

That's the big kicker, isn't it? That's all the tomatoes, right there. Eventually it all comes down to whether you have the guts to hold your breath, close your eyes, and step out into that wall of speeding cars.

Could you take that step knowing full well that you might end up in the grille of some speeding commuter with a big fancy truck? How about being mashed under the tires of a semi-trailer, with twenty thousand pounds of speeding weight mashing you into a pulp?

Sounds like hell, doesn't it?

Doesn't it?

You should have thought of that before you made her break my heart. Fourteen years together, and my heart broke like a hot glass filled with ice. I cupped the pieces in my hands and they bled and bled. Now stop talking about her or I'll pull out a blindfold.

There's no sense crying about it, my friend. There is absolutely nothing you can do now. Those ropes on your hands and feet aren't going to let you escape, and this shiny nickel-plated handgun is going to make sure you don't try anything stupid.

Because if you are thinking of being a hero, I'm going to put a bullet in your head right here by the side of the road.

Then I'm going to go to your house and shoot your wife and children, before putting the gun in my mouth and pulling the trigger.

Maybe I *am* crazy. Maybe I've just had enough of this place to keep me full for a good long while. Maybe she was the only thing in the whole world that mattered to me, and you took that away when I found you two in bed together.

It's just about time for you to start your journey. The ropes on your feet are so tight, aren't they? You'll have to hop, just like the little frog.

You never know. You could make it across all those lanes

of traffic safely. Do that, well, and I might just let you walk away.

Why not?

You'll be free to get back to your little frog-hole in the swamp. Sounds fair to me. Are you feeling brave?

Good.

It's almost time to go.

And don't ask about her again.

Let's just say that this time I won't be getting a high score.

Anna's Jar of Hurts

It was the biggest pickle jar Marie had ever seen, and when her mother suggested they give it to Anna as a special gift, she thought it was a fine idea. They scraped all the pickle paper off and her mother scrubbed it with lots of soap to get the smell out. Afterwards, it still kinda smelled like pickles, but Marie didn't think Anna would mind too much.

"She'll like it, won't she, Momma?" Marie said.

"I think she will," Momma said. "This will be a special jar. A magic one, to make her feel better."

So they put a little bow on it and Marie made a special sign with crayons and glue and glitter that said *Anna* on it and she pasted it over the glue marks where the pickle paper used to be and they took it upstairs to Anna's room where she was sleeping. Her oxygen machine and heart monitor bleeped quietly beside her, and Marie was careful as always to only stand on the side of the bed that didn't have any wires.

"Anna!" Marie said. "We have a present for you!"

Anna's eyes flickered open, and it took her a moment to recognize the faces in front of her. Then she smiled.

"You do?" she said. "What is it?"

Momma handed the jar over to Marie who pushed it up onto the bed beside her sister.

"It's a magic jar!" Marie exclaimed. "It's just for you!"

"I see!" Anna said happily. "It has my name on it and everything!"

"I also got you a pad of paper and a pencil," Momma said. "I was thinking that anytime you have a bad feeling, or a sad one, or you hurt, you can write it down. Then you can keep them in this jar, and you won't have to feel them anymore."

"That sounds like a good idea," Anna said. "*Anna's Jar of Hurts*. Pandora reborn. I love it."

"Open it!" Marie said excitedly. "It smells like pickles!"

Anna opened the jar. She tilted her elfin face so she could take a good deep breath of the air inside. It made her cough. "It *does* smell like pickles," Anna said, smiling at her younger sister. "I *really* love it."

"I knew it," Marie said.

Anna coughed again, wincing as she did. Then she looked up at Momma and smiled. "Let's see if this thing works," she said.

She quickly wrote down the words *chest cough*, folded the paper and dropped it into the jar. She paused, her pencil hovering over the paper. Then having made up her mind, she wrote the word *Leukemia* and dropped that one in there too.

Momma sucked in a breath but didn't say anything.

"It works!" Anna said, smiling down at Marie. "I feel better already."

They put the jar on a little table beside Anna's bed, on the wire side so it wouldn't get in Marie's way when she came to visit. Anna kept her glittery name facing the bed at all times, and whenever Marie was around she made a big show of adding aches and pains to the jar. She added *headaches* and *sore throats, stiff backs, upset tummies,* and she even added a sneeze once to make Marie giggle.

"There," Anna said, sniffling. "No more sneezes."

After Marie went to bed, and Anna's mother would sit with her, she would add words like *Lymphatic Infection* and *Anaemia*. After a check with her doctor about her failing eyesight, she added *Roth Spots*.

When Anna was alone, she added words like *Sad* and *Afraid*, and more than once she added the word *Burden*. Some of them she triple folded, and those ones said *God kill me now please.*

Within a few weeks the jar had a good padding of notes in it. By the end of a month, the jar was half full, and Marie looked over at it one day while they were dressing dollies on Anna's bed.

"You have a lot of pains," she observed.

"I also have a lot of joys," Anna said, though her face darkened when she glanced at the jar. The *Anna* sparkles had lost a little glitter and the jar looked as though it was sporting a fine layer of dust.

"Are you gonna die?" Marie asked calmly.

"I certainly hope not."

The look on Marie's face told Anna that wasn't the answer she was looking for. "Of course not, silly bunny," she said. She ran her finger along the top of Marie's nose. The girl giggled and shook her hand away.

"I don't want you to die."

"Well that's good," Anna said. "I don't want you to die either."

The notes in the jar continued to grow, a few at a time. One day, while the doctor was examining her, he happened to look over at it. By now the sparkles were mostly worn off and the walls of the jar looked like they were dusted with carbon. Filth tinted the glass, making it an ugly yellow-black. It reminded Anna of a smoker's breath.

"What is that?" the doctor said. "Some kind of ashtray?"

"I put all my bad thoughts in there," Anna said awkwardly. "It's supposed to take everything away. It's *Anna's Jar of Hurts.*"

"Pandora's Misery," he said.

"It was Marie and my mother's idea," she said.

"Well, whatever it is, it seems to be working," the doctor smiled. "You're as strong as I've seen you in months."

"I feel better," Anna said.

"That's always a good sign."

After he left, Anna pulled out her notebook and wrote the word *Embarrassed* on a sheet of paper, folded it, and slipped it into her jar. She was surprised to find the glass warm to the touch, like a spreading infection.

A few weeks later, when spring awoke from its winter slumber, Anna was ready for it. She sat out on the front porch, soaking up rays of warm sunshine and pulling in as many fresh springtime smells as she could. She watched Marie make a hopscotch board on the sidewalk with new chalk she got for Christmas. She listened to birds in the trees and watched the cat's futile attempts to hunt them. She got tired all too quickly, however, and soon had to get her mother to help her back up to her room to lie down.

She was awakened sometime later by a tearful Marie looking up at her from the wireless side of the bed.

"What is it?" Anna said. "What happened?"

"I tripped on the *hopscotch*," Marie whimpered. "I fell down and made my knee bleed." She was clutching a large, folded sheet of paper in her hand.

"You wanted to use my jar?" Anna said. Marie nodded viciously.

"You can use my jar," Anna said. It was now mostly full. The sparkles were all gone off Anna's name, leaving behind Marie's childlike outline in crayon and some yellowed globs of paper glue. The inside of the jar was caked in black and yellow tar, like the inside of a cigarette filter. A thin crust had formed under the lid; it cracked and flaked away when

Anna twisted it. A fine grey mist escaped when she lifted it from the jar.

"Eww," Marie said. "It stinks like eggs." She put her hand close to the jar, and then stopped. Anna could feel the angry heat radiating off it.

"I liked it better when it smelled like pickles," Marie said. "Is it safe?"

"Oh sure," Anna said. "It's just a pickle jar."

"Not anymore," Marie said as she slipped the folded paper into the jar. It was nearly full now, and the paper stuck out of the top. "Now it's a yucky jar."

"Yeah," Anna said. She quickly tightened the lid back on and then pushed it as far away from her bed as she could.

One day toward the end of spring they came home from the Hospital cheering, all of them; Marie, Anna, and Momma. Anna's latest screen had come back cancer-negative with a strong white blood cell count. Her leukemia was in complete remission. The doctor had congratulated her with a mile-wide grin and a handshake, saying they hadn't found a single trace of the disease in any of their scans. Anna thanked him with a big hug. Momma wouldn't stop smiling and crying at the same time. Once inside the house Momma set to order pizza to celebrate while Marie and Anna went up to Anna's room.

"Does this mean you'll get to throw away all these machines?" Marie said.

"We'll give them back to the hospital I think," Anna said. "Someone else can use them."

"Even your gross jar?" Marie said. She pointed over to where it sat on the edge of the little night table, its glass completely fogged by sickly yellow-black sludge.

"*That* can't go back to the hospital," Anna said.

"We should do something with it," Momma said, coming into the room behind them. "It's pretty awful looking."

"What is it?" Anna said.

"Chemical reaction to something on the paper maybe," Momma said. "Something to do with the vinegar left in the jar no doubt. I should have cleaned it a little better."

"Can we bury it?" Anna said suddenly, turning to her mother.

There was something fearful in her eyes that made Momma immediately say yes. She walked over to the jar and picked it up gingerly in her arms, like a sick baby.

"It's really warm," she said.

"Let's bury it in the back garden," Anna said.

The three of them went downstairs, grabbed their shoes, and filed out the back door. The garden in the back yard was a long brown strip of earth that ran along the house. Lonely weeds waved at them as they passed. At the end of the garden, on the corner of the house, Anna stopped.

"Here?" she said, and her mother nodded yes.

"We need something to dig a hole," Momma said. The tool shed was across the lawn at the very back of the yard. She put the jar down and walked to it. After a minute of fighting with the door she turned around. "It's stuck!" she said.

"I'll help," Anna said. "You have to *lift* the door."

She turned and pointed a finger at Marie. "Don't you touch that thing," Anna said, quick and soft.

"I won't," Marie said. Her eyes were big enough that Anna believed her.

The two women were struggling with the shed door and Marie was staring down at the blackened jar. It was so gross and smoky, but she could see clear as day that the top paper was the one she'd made that day after falling on the hopscotch and skinning her knee. It was such a little hurt; it didn't really belong in there with all the things her sister had placed in it. She felt kind of silly about it now.

Maybe it would be best if she took her note back.

She twisted the lid on the pickle jar. It creaked open, slowly at first, and then black flecks of corruption fluttered down and the lid spun. That sickly, egg smell was stronger than before, and a dusting of grey mist wafted out of the top of the jar. Marie was transfixed by the smoke, but a moment later it was gone and she was looking down at a plain old smelly jar filled with folded up paper.

She reached down and plucked hers from the top of the pile.

She opened it delicately. It was yellowed and egg-smelly like the jar. The words *My knee is scraped and bleeding* were there in Marie's own red crayon. As she watched, the waxen letters turned black and flaked off the page. At the same time, a healed scrape on her knee opened up and blood splashed out.

Marie screeched and fell back. She clutched at her knee. Blood dribbled from between her fingers.

"*Marie!*" Momma shouted. She turned and sprinted across the field toward her daughter.

"*Owwwwwie!*" Marie wailed.

Momma reached down and swept her crying baby up in her arms. In her panic, she kicked over the jar, spilling dozens of little folded up notes onto the yard. The egg stink followed them. The ones on the bottom were little more than yellow husks of greasy onion paper. They were the oldest hurts.

"You're okay," Momma said, soothing the child. "It's just a little scraped knee."

"What happened?" Anna said. She stopped short when she saw the jar kicked over, and the little notes fluttering on the grass like cancerous butterflies. "*Mom?*"

"She must have cut herself on the jar," Momma said. She looked down at the papers and sighed. "*So many hurts in there.*"

"A lifetime's worth," Anna said.

"Can you hold her for a minute?" Momma said, handing off Marie to Anna.

Anna was looking down at the paper by Momma's feet. Marie's scraped knee hurt.

"I just wanted my *hopscotch* hurt," Marie whimpered into Anna's shoulder, as Momma bent down and started sweeping the folded notes back into the jar.

"What did you say?" Anna said, looking at the little girl. She suddenly felt like a slipping cog, just a bit out of step with everything around her. The word *Don't* bubbled from her throat and caught against her teeth.

"So many of these things," Momma said. She picked up a brittle yellow note that had been triple folded.

She looked down at Anna's delicate, perfect writing. The words *God kill me now please* began to turn black and flutter in the warm still air.

And suddenly Anna was shrieking, but Momma couldn't hear it.

Sunlight and Shadows

with John Sunseri

Laci had come to the ocean looking for ghosts, and the old lighthouse at Frenchman's Head was the perfect place to start.

The car was back a few hundred yards, alone on the roadside turn-off. She'd dragged herself over the guard rail, climbed down into the low forest and fought her way through the muddy earth, cold rain water hitting her in huge drops as it fell from the branches. The sun was still clawing its way toward the ocean, bloating as it grew lower and larger, and she'd only have another half-hour of light to play with. There was little time to look for a better vantage.

She wrestled her way up the tallest spruce she could find, making filthy her clothes in the process. Her head throbbed, and she stopped fifteen feet up to dry-swallow another couple of Advil. They hadn't been helping much, but she didn't want to think about the pain that would result if she stopped taking them altogether. She sucked the water from her lips, grimaced, and fought upwards ten more feet before settling into a sturdy crotch.

There was the lighthouse, all right. She'd found her clear shot.

A promontory of rocky land stretched northward and out into the choppy grey of the sea. The lighthouse at Frenchman's Head stood on its tip, stark and sentinel. The building caught the dying light of the falling sun, but only on its western flank—the other side was shadowed and hidden.

Perfect.

She snapped a couple of quick shots to capture the chiaroscuro, using the spruce needles around her to frame the pictures. Whoever viewed them would sense the surrounding flora, would feel like a lurker in the woods peering out at the half-shadowed building as if in ambush.

She slowed down and started playing with the digital settings. The machine was the closest thing she had to a lover, and she touched it with knowledge born of long experience, caressing and coaxing and prodding all the right places. Like a lover, she knew how to produce what she wanted from the Canon, and the two of them moved in perfect, primal rhythm.

Lightning flared in the distance over the ocean and Laci cursed. Halfway up the tallest tree in the short forest wasn't where she wanted to be if the storm hit in earnest. She started to inch her sneaker down to the next branch. Her head throbbed as a roll of thunder swept in over the beach, over her. Rain fell harder, hitting her exposed face like the sting of a wet towel. Looking out over the water, she decided she had time for one more shot before it was time to pack it in.

She raised the Canon to her eyes, scrolling back over the pictures she had just taken. At frame seven she stopped.

She squinted through the mist. Another explosion of lightning out at sea, and then a sweep of thunder. She ignored the flash and the shadowed darkness that followed, peering intently at the little view screen on her camera.

Something—someone—stood there, on her screen. Atop the empty lighthouse, half a mile distant. A black silhouette.

She pressed closer to the slick bark of the spruce's trunk and started pushing the zoom buttons. She enlarged, enlarged again, clicked on the upper-right quadrant to focus; enlarged again.

Two faces, not one. Young faces, grainy with distance and low resolution. Black eyes moist, peering across the rocks, over the trees.

Four arms, two of them lightly grasping the rail outside the lamp chamber, two held in the air at odd angles. Wind whipped their hair into a spider web around them. Their clothes were strange, archaic.

The two boys were joined at the hip.

They stared straight at her, solid black eyes making the hundreds of yards of space disappear.

They hadn't been in the previous frame, taken only a second before.

She managed to get to the ground and shook the water from her hair. When she did, pain hit her with stiletto sharpness, and an involuntary cry left her mouth as she whipped her hand up to the side of her head, cradling the small scar above her ear. She massaged the bulge, born of scar tissue and healing bone, and forced her breath into controlled bursts until the light behind her eyes receded.

Eventually, she opened her eyes. She could see the lighthouse through the trees, but it was still dim February and whoever was in charge of the historic lighthouses of the coast hadn't started the season yet. The distant building was now fully shrouded in gloom as the sun shimmered weakly on the horizon, an old man going to bed. She moved through the slick leaves and greedy, slurping mud of the little forest toward Frenchman's Head.

There were two young boys atop the lighthouse in the storm. They might need help.

But that wasn't it—not really. She was sensitive to phenomena, and she knew a little about the spirit world. It was why she was on this trip, after all—she normally photographed auras and haunts, and she'd only stopped to shoot the lighthouse on a whim. And in her deep places, she knew that the boys weren't going to need help when she got there.

But she needed help, all right. She needed this, whatever

it was. She moved a little faster. If she hurried, she could make it there in twenty minutes.

The lighthouse was monolithic; a great pale erection jabbing out of the earth and thrusting toward the sky. It loomed over Laci as she struggled through the wet tangle of trees and brush that covered the gorge below the cliffs. Far below, the ocean surf spasmed and released onto the rocks.

As Laci approached the sentinel, her stomach churned. There was energy here. It danced along her spine and tickled the back of her neck.

"Hello?" she called, blocking the rain from her eyes with her hand. She held her camera in her other hand and as she rounded the side of the building she instinctively pulled it close, like a shield.

The children loomed over her, not speaking, barely breathing.

The two boys, identical twins, watched as Laci approached. Their black hollow eyes stared down at her from the promenade of the lamp room. They were attached at the hip, their old-fashioned schoolboy uniforms perfectly stitched to allow for the disfiguration.

Their black hair seemed as kerosene dripping from their pale brows. They barely moved as they clutched the guard rail. The wind tugged at their clothes, but if the driving February rain was cold on them their faces didn't register it.

"Hello?" Laci said again, but more quietly, more hesitantly. Acting on instinct, she drew the camera to her face and pressed the trigger. The Canon fluttered, snapping off a flurry of shots.

The boys said nothing.

She framed her shots and bled the last bit of light from the sky. Then she opened her cell phone and called 911.

The Sheriff's car was quickly followed by a camera crew from the local news station, and when Laci saw it coming she looked at Officer Danton.

He shrugged. "They scan the police band." He wore his rain slicks and had his flashlight out. Adjusting his hat, he clicked the light on and flipped it toward the third level of the lighthouse.

"Jesus *Christ*," he said, taking a half-step back toward his car.

Two pairs of black eyes shone down at him. The boys stared at Laci, ignoring the cop. They were soaked to their pale skin.

"Conjoined twins," Laci said, snapping a slow-shutter picture in Danton's light. "I have no idea where they came from. They weren't there—then they were."

"Hello?" Danton asked. He kept the light on their faces. The stark, bright beam elongated the shadows on their cheeks, under their eyes. "You…*kids* all right?"

The boys said nothing. They briefly swivelled their heads, looked at the source of the light, then turned back in tandem to stare again at Laci.

"I think they could be deaf," she said, shuddering in the chill rain. "They don't respond to me. I don't know that they can hear us."

The television crew parked their van several metres back from the squad car. Laci watched as a young woman got out and unloaded some camera gear while a man checked himself in a side mirror.

"Can you hear me?" Danton suddenly yelled. "How did you get up there?"

"The door on the side is locked," Laci said. "I already tried it."

"Maybe they locked it when they went up there?"

"Doubt it," said Laci. "It's a big old padlock. Looks like it's been there a while."

Danton turned to Laci. "Guess you thought of everything, then, didn't you?"

"Sorry," Laci said. "I'll let you do your job."

"Thank you kindly, ma'am," said Danton. "Since you're so eager to help, you want to hold this flash for me while I grab some my lock tools out of my trunk?" He smiled disarmingly at her, showing perfect teeth. *No hard feelings,* the smile said.

"Glad to, Sheriff." She took the flashlight from him and held it on the boys.

They said nothing. They did nothing.

All along the coast, windows were shuttered and doors locked as the wind picked up and the rain intensified. A storm was on the way, and there was no telling what it was going to bring with it.

Eventually they got the children off the balcony, and Sheriff Danton called an ambulance to come get them. Aside from their bizarre condition, they appeared to be physically fine. They were pale and thin, but the medics announced that their hearts were healthy and all their vital signs stable.

The children refused to speak, however, and because they hadn't appeared in any missing person reports, the sheriff decided that they would go to the children's hospital in Calamity Falls until the proper authorities could be determined and contacted.

Laci, meanwhile, spoke to the local TV crew about finding the boys and what she had been doing in the woods. They offered her five hundred dollars for her photos, which she accepted, and then the Sheriff gave her a ride back to her car.

She checked into a Motel 6 with strict instructions that she was not to leave town until the Sheriff had talked to her again, and the police department paid for her room. She waved as the Sheriff drove away, but as soon as he was out of the parking lot she ducked behind her car and vomited until there was nothing left in her stomach.

She was exhausted from her exertions and the miserable weather, and her head pounded flashes of blinding light behind her eyes with every beat of her pulse. She massaged the tender flesh behind her ear and it relieved a bit of the pressure, but not as much as some Percocet and a hot shower would.

The Percocet she had in her handbag. The shower was waiting for her in her rented room. She stood there for another few seconds, in the antiseptic glare of the vapour lights of the parking lot, then slowly began to walk toward the motel and warmth.

She awoke to the sound of knocking, and for a few

moments was disoriented—she wasn't in her bed, she wasn't in her apartment, and she couldn't hear the normal morning noises of traffic and the upstairs neighbours arguing about money.

And then it came back to her—the boys on the balcony. That strange silhouette, the gently waving arms, the spider web hair.

Those black, black eyes.

She heard the knock again, and looked toward the door of her room. It would be Sheriff Danton, she was sure, ready to continue the interrogation of the night before.

"Just a minute," she called, and frowned at the sound of her own voice. Before the operation and all the treatments, she had sounded like a robust young woman. Now her voice was that of a much older person—a frail person, a weak person.

"Just gotta put some clothes on," she told the door, and she forced herself to put some strength into it. She rolled off the bed and looked for her slacks and shirt, found them in a crumpled heap and shrugged into them. She checked the night table, saw the camera and her keys, nodded, and dragged herself over to the door. In some odd way she was looking forward to this, the questions and answers. Her attention, her imagination, had been completely captured by the twins at the lighthouse, and maybe she could learn more about them from the policeman.

But when she opened the door, it wasn't Sheriff Danton standing there on the other side. It was an old man, seventy or eighty maybe, with a face lined like ancient parchment, hands gnarled by arthritis and a shock of white hair over each ear.

"I'm sorry, miss," he said, his voice hesitant, his posture uncertain. "You don't know me, but I got your name from the folks at the newspaper, and I figured you'd be staying here, so I thought…"

They both stood there for a moment, the man holding one hand in the other, not looking straight at her, Laci confused and feeling rumpled in her already-worn clothes. Then he spoke again.

"You took those pictures of the boys at Frenchman's Head yesterday," he said, "and I'd be obliged if I could ask you a few questions about them."

"You—who are you?" she asked finally.

"I'm sorry," he said again. "No manners at all! My name's Caleb Mears, and I'm from here in Calamity Falls. I used to be the keeper at the lighthouse, back in the fifties, after the war."

"Oh my," she said, a rush of interest shooting through her. "*Absolutely* you can come in—sorry I look like this, but I didn't get much sleep last night, and I was too tired to get my stuff out of the trunk…"

"Oh, no need to apologize," said Mears, smiling. And now he looked at her, and she felt a frisson as she saw his eyes—they were clear and black, and for a moment she had a vertiginous sense that it was the twins standing there before her, in their schoolboy outfits and mussed hair—but the moment quickly passed as she stood aside and let the old man enter. "I've been married to three women, and they were none of 'em fashion models straight out of bed. You look a damn sight better than most early risers."

"Thank you," she said, and motioned toward the chair next to the bed. Then she laughed.

"Something funny?" he asked, his smile slipping. She could see his teeth white and strong—dentures, probably.

"Oh, I was just going to ask you if you wanted something to drink," she said. "Forgot I wasn't home. All I can offer you is water."

"Never drink the stuff," he said sombrely. "Takes years off your life."

Instantly, the smile returned to his face.

"All right, then," she said, dropping to sit on the side of the bed, looking at her guest. "What can I do for you, Mr. Mears?"

"Caleb," he said. "You can call me Caleb, if you want."

"Caleb, then," she said. "You said you had some questions?"

"Yep," he said. "Just a few. But the most important one is—can I look at those pictures you took yesterday? They ran one of 'em on the news last night, but it was only on the TV for a second, and when the paper came out this morning they only had a picture of the boys being taken away in the ambulance. I'd…I'd like to see those boys, if I may."

Laci sat there motionless for a moment, then nodded her head. "I suppose that'd be okay," she said, leaning over and reaching for the Canon. "Mind if I ask why you're so interested?"

"If I could just look at them for a minute," he said, "I'll tell you the whole story. I promise—on my honour."

"All right," she said, bemused. "Here, lean over a little so you can see the screen." He complied, and she could smell the old man's cologne—something cheap and manly, something a grandchild would give him for Christmas, maybe. Old Spice.

"These are all just shots of the lighthouse from that little forest down by the viewpoint…"

"Right above Corpse Cove," murmured the old man. "I know exactly where you were."

"Corpse Cove?" she asked. "It's not called that on the map."

"Bodies used to wash up there," he said. "Every time a ship wrecked, you'd get half the dead sailors washed up on the beach a few days later. The ones the sharks didn't get, that is. And, no. The official name is Beaulieu's Cove, named after the same French fellow the cape is. Nice pictures, by the way—pretty enough to be in a book."

"I've had my stuff in books," she murmured, clicking the finder forward. "But not this kind of stuff."

"You a, *whaddyacallit*, photojournalist?" he asked.

"I take pictures of auras and spirits," she said. She used to be self-conscious when she told people what she did, but she eventually grew a shell. Mostly, people just nodded and changed the subject, or asked asinine questions, but occasionally she got sarcasm or hostility. None of that mattered anymore, though—after all the suffering she'd been through, she could handle idiocy from the Philistines.

But Caleb just nodded, intently peering at the view screen. "Yeah," he said. "Yeah, that makes sense."

She was going to ask him what he meant, but then they got to the money shot, and he gasped and stiffened beside her. Alarmed, she whipped her head around, fearing that the old man was suffering a heart attack next to her, and what she saw didn't comfort her at all—Caleb had gone completely pale, his black eyes were open so wide she could see the little veins on their sides, and he shook silently.

"Mr. Mears?" she asked. "Are you all right?"

"My Lord," he breathed, and she sensed those two words were more prayer than ejaculation. "They've come back."

"Who?" she asked, fear warring with excitement in her brain. Whatever was coming, whatever had come with the storm, was going to reveal itself to her. She knew it as surely as she knew that she was meant to be here right now, in a cheap room at the Motel 6 next to this old lighthouse keeper. "Who's come back?"

"My sons," he whispered, and tears began to roll down that ancient face.

"My first wife's name was Sarah," he said after they'd ordered down for whiskey and soda, "but everyone called her Sally. I married her before I went off to Europe in '43, and when I got back we bumped around Oregon for a while before we decided to settle back on the coast. They were lighting the lighthouses up again—you know a Japanese sub got all the way over here, once? Happened in '42, and the Lighthouse Service shut 'em all off for the duration of the war, but in '45 they needed families to run the things again, and there I was, looking for work." He smiled. "It was a dream, young lady. We had a nice little house, plenty of privacy, and it wasn't too far to town in case Sally wanted to shop or something. And every nine months or so, the USLS would drop off another tank full of coal oil and boxes of books for us to read."

"Sounds…maybe a little boring?" said Laci.

"Sometimes it was," said Mears. "Sometimes it was

indeed. But we were young and in love, and Sally and I weren't really all that sociable a couple, anyway. It's why we were vagabonding around in the first place. I got my fill of people during the war in Italy—don't like being too close to anyone, you know? Foxholes and such…"

His voice trailed off, and he closed his eyes momentarily, lost in memory. But he soon reopened them and looked again at the picture on the view screen, the twins standing there in the gloom, their hair whipped by the wind and rain.

"And Sally came from a big *Eye*-talian family up in Portland, and they had about a thousand kids, you know? She loved the idea of having her own bathroom, having her own clothes without having three older sisters wearing 'em first. It was a stroke of luck, this job was."

"And you had kids?" Laci prompted.

"*And* we had two sons," he said quietly, nodding as he looked at the camera. "We didn't know we was having twins when she caught pregnant, nor during the pregnancy itself. Sally was huge, all right, but what did we know? Tom Foster came out from town every month or so, make sure Sally was eating enough, check her blood and such, but they didn't have them ultrasounds or anything back then, and Doc Foster was a bit of a drunk anyway, so we never knew. Not 'til they came, anyway...."

"The twins," said Laci. "The boys on the balcony."

"We never let 'em up there," said Mears. "Too dangerous. The house is only about fifty feet tall, but the winds you get up there will whip you right off, if you're not careful. And Jed and Jerry weren't all that coordinated sometimes."

"Those are their names?" she asked softly. She was enrapt

in the tale, and her questions were all lubricant for the story, meant to oil it along. It was working, too.

"Jedidiah and Jeremiah," he said. "Lucky they have names at all, you know. I ended up delivering 'em myself—they came a few weeks early, and we couldn't get to town for the birth. I had an old Packard, and it wouldn't run half the time without you taking apart the whole engine and putting it back together, and when the twins came it was dead on the drive, so there we were. There was a storm going, just like there is right now, and they hadn't electrified all the way out to Frenchman's head, so we were in the dark, there in the Keeper's house." He stopped for a second, and wiped his eyes.

"You know, I'd fought at Monte Casino and Rome in the Big One, I'd had a ship torpedoed from under me and had to swim for six hours to get to land. But that night—well, it was the hardest thing I'd ever gone through. Sally—poor, beautiful Sally—had a hell of a time with the birth. She was a small woman, and we were both little more than kids, you know? We didn't know what we was doing at all, and when Jed's head came out, I was so scared I think I would've rather faced a whole squadron of Krauts right at that moment."

A knock came on the door. Laci took a second to come out of her entranced state, gave Mears an apologetic look and stood.

"You wanted room service?" asked the man at the door, his look signalling what he thought of customers who wanted whiskey at ten in the morning. Laci ignored him, signed for the booze and shut the door.

"Soda?" she asked Mears.

"No thank you, ma'am," he said. "If you're gonna drink good whiskey, I see no point in watering it down."

"How about if you throw up easily?" she asked, moving to the bathroom to get the plastic cup that was there.

"Then maybe you shouldn't be drinking at all," he said, standing to join her as she unwrapped the sanitary protection on the glass. "I appreciate the whiskey, and you letting me look at the pictures, Miss Powell. You don't need to drink with me."

"I'm alive right now when I should be dead, Mr. Mears," she said, setting the cup down so that she could unscrew the cap on the Maker's Mark (a forty-dollar extra on the police department's hotel room tab). She poured herself a couple of fingers, handed the bottle to Caleb and opened the soda water. "I'm not going to worry about what I should and shouldn't do anymore."

He looked at her curiously. "You've got a story, too, don't you?"

"A boring one," she said, pouring club soda into her drink. "Cancer's not nearly as exciting as delivering conjoined twins in the dark in a rainstorm."

"Exciting," he snorted. "Yeah, it was exciting, all right. You got a glass for me?"

"Just take the bottle," Laci said. "What I've got should do me fine."

He shrugged and lifted the bottle to his lips, drank. He swallowed, the Adam's apple on his neck jiggling as the fiery liquid went down, set the whiskey on the bed table and sighed contentedly.

"I almost killed them right then," he said.

Laci looked at him.

"I stood there in the flickering candlelight, looking at Sally, who was near unconscious by then, been ripped apart and was bleeding so strongly that I thought I'd never be able to stop the flow. And in my hands, covered with blood and slime, I had…I had this thing, this freakish spidery-looking tangle of limbs and heads and squalling screams, and my first impulse was to take them and throw them as hard as I could against the wall. You believe that?"

Laci took a long pull of her drink and didn't speak. She moved past Mears, back to the bed, and sat down. He stayed in the doorway of the bathroom, looking at her with his black eyes. Finally, she answered.

"I think that's natural," she said. "Last night, when I saw them up there on the lighthouse, saw them staring down at me, I wanted to…I wanted them to be gone. I didn't want them to exist. They scare me, Mr. Mears, and even though they're at the hospital right now, they scare me still. And I don't know why."

"They went to that hospital before," he said. "After Sally killed herself."

Laci looked up at him.

"They were nine, just like they are in those pictures you showed me," he said. "We kept them at the lighthouse because people were scared of 'em, and because they were *odd*." He used the word carefully, as if he'd said it before a million times in reference to his sons. "They didn't talk much. Not to us, anyway. When they were alone, and they thought we couldn't hear 'em, they'd chitter like jaybirds in a cornfield—but as soon as they saw their mother or me coming, they'd clam up again. And you know what? It was scary, Miss Powell. Those children scared the living Jesus out of me. And Sally felt the same way—we'd be in our room at the Keeper's house, and the twins were in the next room over, and it would be pitch black. I'd be lying there next to my wife, both of us awake though it was the middle of the night, neither of us saying a word but both of us knowing we were still conscious. And the boys never cried, never screamed, were always perfectly quiet throughout the night...

"Except sometimes, every few nights, they'd make a noise."

"What noise?" asked Laci, gripping the plastic cup in her palms so tightly the material was bent.

"A scrabbling noise," said Mears. "A noise like they was slowly, carefully crawling out of their crib in the middle of the night. A noise like one of them maybe slipped a little on the way down to the floor, had to grab for one of the slats real quick, and then it would be silent—me and Sally lying still and quiet in our bed, Sally crying without making any noise, and Jed and Jerry hanging there in the blackness, waiting to see if I'd get up, light a lantern and come see what they were doing. Sometimes, that stillness would go on for hours."

"Did you ever go check?" Laci asked.

"No," whispered Mears. "No, I never did. But I thought about it all the time. I'd be in the lantern room, changing the wick, and that image would come to me. And I'm sure Sally thought about it, too—she'd be back in the house with the boys, feeding 'em, changing 'em, watching 'em grow up into what you saw last night—and they never talked to her. Never told her they loved her. When they got old enough, they'd start to just disappear, go rambling in the woods for hours, come back all burrs and smudges and skinned knees, never say a word.

"Once, they disappeared all day. I got back to the house, Sally was frantic. She hadn't seen them since breakfast, and she was about ready to bust a gut, she was so incoherent and terrified.

"Well, we went looking, and guess where we found them?"

Laci was startled. As if she would know…

But she did. Somehow, she did.

"Corpse Cove," she said.

"Bingo," whispered Caleb, and took another long pull from the bottle. "There'd been a wreck that I didn't know about—some pleasure boat on a long fishing trip from Astoria. They hadn't bothered to let anyone know where they were going, so none of us were on the lookout for 'em or anything. But they wrecked, all right, and the five people on board all washed up in the cove that day. And Jed and Jerry—they were there."

"What were they doing?" asked Laci querulously. Her weak voice was back, and she didn't care.

"Standing over those poor men, chittering," said Caleb. "Standing over them, waving their arms, gabbling to each other in that language they had. I didn't find 'em—Sally did. I just heard all about it that night, in bed. How they would sometimes kneel down, stroke the bloated skin of the dead men, smile and chant, and how Sally screamed at them while she spent ten minutes picking her way down the slope to get to 'em. But they never heard her, or just plain ignored her."

He stopped again. Looked at Laci.

"You haven't asked me how it's possible," he said.

"What do you mean?" she asked.

"My boys," he said. "They're still nine years old. You saw 'em. But they was nine in the early sixties, and they haven't aged any since then."

"Maybe I've got a better perspective on some things than your normal girl," she said. "I took a picture of a ghost once in a dressing room at a strip club. It was a murdered stripper, and she only showed up after the club closed. I spent two weeks there, and finally she showed herself. Your boys—they don't shock me."

"They're not ghosts," said Caleb. "It's like they stepped out of the past, if the past wasn't just a memory. Like it was an *actual place*, and they finally made their way back."

"I know," she whispered. "They're…I don't know what they are. But they're not dead. I like that analogy. Time travellers."

"Not dead," he said quietly, "but their mother is. Sally—I woke up one morning and Sally was gone. The boys were in their room, looking at a picture magazine I'd brought back from my last trip to the Falls, looking at it upside-down, like it didn't matter. And I knew.

"She was dead at the base of the cliff," he said, looking at the bottle before him as if judging how long it would take him to kill it. "She'd climbed up to the lantern room, let herself out onto the balcony, and jumped off the cliff side. I ran down both sets of ladders, fought my way down the hill to where she was, but the tide had come in by the time I got there, and I couldn't even find a body to bury."

"I'm so sorry," said Laci. "Truly, Caleb—I'm sorry."

"No call for that," he said. "No call at all. You had nothing to do with it."

"I've got something to do with this," she said. "I just don't know what."

The phone blazed in its cradle, startling both of them. Laci put a hand to her chest and let out a little laugh.

"I see we're both jumpy," Caleb said, chuckling into the bottle.

"A little," Laci said. "I should get this; it might be the Sheriff. They wanted me to stay in town."

Caleb waved a permissive gesture at her.

"I'll just sit here with my bottle quietly," he said. "Maybe you shouldn't tell him I'm here. I don't really want to talk to anyone else about this."

Laci nodded, then reached out to pick up the receiver.

"Hello?" she said.

"Ms. Powell?"

"Yes—is this Sheriff Danton?"

"Yeah," he said. "Listen, Ms. Powell. You need to turn on your television right now. Jesus Christ—you're never gonna believe this. Channel 10. I'll wait."

"Okay," Laci said. She shot a puzzled look toward Caleb, who was watching her intently. Then she walked over to the TV and clicked it on.

"...again, the twin boys, apparently from eight to ten years old and as yet unnamed, managing to somehow get outside *their room on the third floor of the Calamity Falls Children's Hospital, and are now considered to be missing somewhere in the vicinity of the Falls....*"

"What the hell?" Laci asked, putting her hand to her mouth and dropping onto the chair.

Caleb put the bottle down and crossed his arms over his chest, holding himself.

"...you're going to see this amazing Channel 10 exclusive one more time, Diane, and I have to say this is probably the most amazing thing I've seen in my fourteen years as a broadcast journalist. This footage was captured just a short time ago by our own cameraman John Davis while we were waiting outside the hospital for word on the mystery twins that had been found on the lighthouse...."

The screen went blank for a moment, then Laci gasped.

Caleb sucked in his breath.

The screen showed the outside wall of the Children's Hospital. It was old grey stone with rows of double-paned windows on each floor. About thirty feet up, battered by wind and lashing rain, Jedidiah and Jeremiah were carefully making their way down the side of the building. The cameraman was talking off-screen, but the noise of the storm whipped away his words.

The children *scuttled* down the grey bricks, moving headfirst toward the ground. Their arms and legs were somehow able to find minuscule perches, keeping them from falling, and they worked in perfect harmony. It gave a gangly, over-jointed impression to their movement.

"Oh my God," Laci whispered.

The children stopped their downward scuttle for a moment about halfway to the ground and looked directly at the camera. Even through the rain their eyes shone like black diamonds. Lightning crashed overhead and they tensed, as though they might fall.

"So that's how they did it," muttered Caleb. He began to rub his arm self-consciously.

Jedidiah and Jeremiah looked at each other, and Laci could see that they were talking to themselves—*chittering*, Caleb had called it. Then they swivelled their heads in unison toward one of the tall pines standing nearby.

They tensed their legs and leapt into space.

Laci gasped.

They sailed into the darkness, their arms and legs spread as though they were making snow angels. When they hit the tree, they bounced, disappearing briefly into the dense green foliage. There was a crash as they hit the branches and off-camera several onlookers screamed.

The boys were lost for a moment as the tree shook, then they reappeared, crawling spider-like down the trunk. When they got to the ground, they leapt to their feet and scurried off into the deeper darkness of the woods.

"Holy shit," Laci breathed.

On the screen lightning flashed again, and as the thunder pealed across the sky there was a brief, dazzling instant where the twins were perfectly outlined, their loping gait caught in the final frames of film, their arms waving like an anemone in the rain. The light gone, the screen went black.

"…Sheriff Danton has asked people to be on the lookout…."

"Oh, *crap!*" Laci said. She got up and stumbled to the phone, her feet unstable. She picked it up with two hands and held it to her ear.

"Hello?"

"Laci, *goddammit*," Danton said. His voice was angry. "I don't have time to sit on the phone all night...."

"Sorry," she said. There was a moment of silence.

"So did you see it?" Danton asked. The anger was gone—now there was something in his voice that sounded dangerously like *fear*.

"I saw it," said Laci. "I can't believe it."

"Well, I didn't either. But it happened. Any idea where they might be headed?"

"No, I...." she stopped, then, as Caleb put a hand on her shoulder. Then she nodded.

"I have no idea, Sheriff." She turned and looked into Caleb's pale, frightened face. He looked a hundred years old.

"Do you think they might be going back to the lighthouse?"

"Do *I* think they're going to the lighthouse?" she repeated, making sure Caleb could hear. He immediately shook his head *no*.

"No, Sheriff," she said quietly, her eyes fixed on the old man's. "Why would they? I think they probably just ran off into the storm. If they don't die of exposure, I'm sure someone will see them and call it in."

"That pair would be hard not to notice, I guess," Danton said. "Okay, Ms. Powell. If I have time, I'll keep you informed about what's going on here. I still need to talk to you, though, so don't go anywhere. I'll call you by tomorrow at the latest."

"Good afternoon, Sheriff, and thank you for calling me," Laci said.

"Good afternoon, Ms. Powell." There was a pause, then a click.

The lights flickered, once, as she put the phone down.

"We have to go," said Caleb. He reached for his coat, began to slip into it.

"To the lighthouse, right?" Laci asked.

"That's the only place they could be going. It's where they went before."

"What did you mean when you said 'so that's how they did it', Caleb?" Laci grabbed her coat, and picked up a ball cap to keep the rain out of her face.

"Come on," Caleb said, picking up the Maker's Mark. "I'll tell you in the car."

The rain made driving more than twenty miles per hour impossible. It blasted the windshield of her car, and she could barely see a couple of feet in front of her. The wipers worked overtime, but they may as well have been shut off for all the good they were doing.

"Take a left up here," Caleb said. He took a swig from the whiskey bottle.

Laci almost said something when she smelled the tang of the booze, but decided against it. The old man had been through several varieties of hell tonight, and she figured she wouldn't add to his problems. Instead, she decided to get back to the story.

"You gonna tell me what they did?"

Caleb shook the whiskey sting away.

"They were at that hospital before," he said. "After Sally died, I couldn't handle it. I blamed the boys for her death.

Oh, they didn't *push* her off that ledge, but it was their weird ways that drove her to jumping.

"So after we had an empty-casket service for her, I arranged to have the kids sent to the sanatorium. Cedar Pine, the place was called back then."

Laci took her eyes off the torrents cascading down the windshield and looked over at him. He nodded, staring straight ahead.

"Yep," he said. "I put 'em in the crazy house. I couldn't stand to think about just me and them in the house together, way out in the middle of nowhere. No one to help me, should they ever decide that I was in their way, too."

"*I guess*...I guess that's understandable," Laci said.

"I put 'em up, then moved the hell away from here. All the way to California, where I had some kin. Got a job working' in a shoe factory. Mostly, I just tried to forget about Jed and Jerry."

Laci pulled off the highway and crept onto a lonely stretch of road that led further up the coast. It had been the original highway before the four-lane road had been built. Now it was a scenic route—or would have been, could they see ten feet past their windshield.

"One day about six months after I moved, I got a phone call from Cedar Pine," Caleb said. He took another sip of whiskey. "Seems my boys somehow managed to find their way out of a locked room on the fourth floor of the place. Just up and walked off into the woods, like that. Nobody knew where they'd gone. *I* didn't know for a long time, neither—'til I got a letter from John Newman, the fellow the USLS put in charge of the lighthouse after I left."

"He'd seen them?" Laci asked.

"He'd seen *somethin'*," Caleb said. "He wrote me a letter and asked if I ever saw anything weird out near Corpse Cove—some strange wild animal or somethin'. Some kind of creature that lived in the trees, ate dead animals off the highway and things like that. He also said there'd been a couple more wrecks offshore, and hardly any bodies had washed ashore—or, if they had, something had gotten to 'em before the authorities could. Wanted my advice on how to deal with the situation."

"What did you do?" Laci asked.

"I called him up," Caleb said. "Asked him to go into details about this…creature, but before he'd even said two sentences I knew it was my boys. Said whatever was living in Corpse Cove was coming up into the balcony of the lighthouse at night when the lamp was on. Couple times he'd seen it from the Keeper's house, standing in the night like a giant spider or somethin'. Poor bastard thought he might be going crazy."

"What did you tell him?"

"Nuthin'," said Caleb. "He told me he'd been out there with his binoculars one night in a rainstorm—like tonight's—and he could see them outlined every time the lamp swung round inside the lighthouse. So he decided to take their picture. Ran inside, grabbed his camera, snapped a shot or two, then *bam!* They was gone.

"He said the light was on 'em, then it wasn't. He couldn't figure it out. Decided to track me down and ask me about it and got my address from the USLS."

"What do you think happened?" Laci asked.

They were coming up the road that would lead them

around the cove and up to Frenchman's Head. It was an access road, and Laci remembered the Sheriff taking her up it after last night's excitement, taking her back to her car.

"I don't rightly know," Caleb said slowly. "I've thought about it, though, and I've got kind of an idea."

He took a long pull from the bottle, then capped it tightly and tossed it into the backseat of the car.

"Imagine I've had about enough of that for the night," he said. Then he went on.

"I think those boys weren't never meant for this world. It sounds strange, but it also sounds true. I think they found themselves here, for whatever reason, but they didn't belong here and they realized it. Well, maybe once they figured out where they *was* supposed to be, they just...went there."

"You mean like another dimension or something?" Laci asked. She'd slowed the car down to ten miles per hour on the road and she could still feel it slipping in the mud. The rain was relentless. Lightning crashed overhead and the wind blew hard off the ocean. Impossible as it seemed, the storm was getting worse.

"Maybe," Caleb said. "Maybe not. I don't rightly know *exactly* where they came from. *Hell*, maybe. Or maybe they've just been living in the past all these years. Time travellers, like you said. At any rate, I think they found a way to get back there, and that's why they disappeared like that. It's also why they just appeared suddenly on your camera, because they decided to come back. And I think I know why."

"You came home," Laci said. Another flash of lightning illuminated the lighthouse some ways ahead of them. They were nearly there.

"Exactly," Caleb said. "They slipped away when they realized I wasn't coming back to the lighthouse, but the day I make it back to Calamity Falls, they show up. Just lucky you was out here when they appeared, or I might not have known. Or maybe I would have, when I finally made it out to look at the old girl one last time."

"Why *did* you come back?" Laci asked. This conversation felt more like an interview, but she was too wrapped up in the story at this point to care.

"I'm dying," Caleb said, without a pause. "Or, I *will* die. I've got early-stage Alzheimer's. I'm going to die, but I'm gonna be a mental baby first. I just wanted to say goodbye to my hometown again before I got too messed up to enjoy it."

"I'm so sorry," Laci said.

"Don't be," said Caleb. "I'm an old man now. That's what old men do—we get old and we die. Except…I think my boys are here to take me with them when they go back to wherever it is they came from. It's the only thing I can think of."

Laci stopped the car. They were there, the lighthouse towering above them. She turned and met the old man's eye.

"Maybe we shouldn't get out of the car," she said. "Maybe we ought to just turn around and go back to town, let Sheriff Danton deal with this."

"No," Caleb said. "I want to see them one more time before I go. They were scary as hell, my boys, but I *did* love them in my own way. Guess I want to show 'em I'm man enough to come back and face 'em after all that I done, after all the years that've passed."

Laci looked at the man for a moment, then slowly nodded.

"We're going to need flashlights," she said.

"There's a breaker inside. If the storm hasn't wiped out all the power in town, I'll turn on some lights," Caleb replied. He opened the car door and stepped out into the blinding rain. Ahead of him, weathering the storm like a stone titan, the lighthouse at Frenchman's Head suddenly blazed to life.

"They're here," Caleb said, watching as the beam shot out from the top of the lighthouse, out into the ocean. The rain caught it and gave it near-solid form, a tube of brilliance stretching out as far as the eye could see.

"How do you know that?" Laci asked, pulling herself out from the back seat of the car. She stopped short, looked up and saw the light. Her face dropped.

"Oh," she said in a small voice. Then she held up the little flashlight she'd dug out of the camera bag. "I guess this is going to be useless in there."

"Keep it," said Caleb, his eyes never leaving the roving beam of light. "Never know when you're going to need a little extra light, even in a place like this."

"Got it," Laci said.

Caleb turned to her.

"You ready?" he asked.

"No," she replied, then smiled weakly. "I imagine you *can't* be ready for something like this. But we've got to do it anyway."

Caleb nodded and walked toward the door to the lighthouse, Laci falling in behind him. When they got to the entrance, she looked down at the padlock and sighed.

"I don't have anything in the car that can get us through that," she said. "I thought maybe they would have left the door open for us."

"What, and risk having some stranger find them first?" Caleb asked. "My boys are smarter than that."

"So how are we going to get in?"

"Simple," Caleb said. He reached into his pocket and pulled out a set of keys. He jangled them in Laci's face.

"How did you…" she began.

"Honey, I used to work here, remember? I always kept a spare set on me, just in case." He reached down and fit the key into the lock.

"But they never changed the lock in all those years since you've been gone?" Laci asked. She watched him fiddle with the device, half-expecting the old key to fail.

The lock snapped open, and Caleb smiled.

"Why would they?" he asked, pushing open the door.

"Good point," Laci said.

The pair stepped out of the howling storm, and back in time.

"It looks like nobody's been here since last season," Caleb said. "Jesus—it looks like it did when I left."

They stood in a small round room with a desk and fold-down bed. There was a little bookshelf, some sea charts and old green beer bottles in its ranks. The walls were lined with paintings of ships and the ocean. Everything was covered with a thin layer of dust. They could hear, two stories above them, the groaning machinery of the lantern, grumbling its displeasure at having been woken up so early in the year.

Along the far wall was a simple iron ladder that ran up

to the next level. The ladder ended at a trap door in the ceiling.

"Up?" Laci asked.

Caleb nodded. "It's the only direction to go in a lighthouse."

The pair shuffled over to the ladder, dripping rainwater onto the dusty floor, and then Caleb rubbed his hands together and gripped the ladder. He climbed up to the portal in the ceiling—it was heavy and rusted and didn't give easily. Laci was amazed at how well the old man still navigated. She'd known plenty of men half his age who couldn't bounce up a ladder like that. His movement spoke volumes about how long he'd worked in this place.

Finally the door gave with a groan and a shower of rust particles, and Caleb disappeared through the hole in the ceiling. Laci followed. Halfway up, though, she had to stop. A spear of pain lanced through her head, causing her knees to buckle. She gasped. Squeezing her eyes shut, she laced her hands through a rung on the ladder and waited for the agony to subside.

"You alright down there?" Caleb asked from above, peering down through the trap. "You don't look so good."

"Fine," Laci said, her eyes pressed shut. When she opened them, her vision was blurry. She could barely make out the white face of Caleb above her.

"It's a side effect of the tumour," she said. "The treatment was…unique. I'm the experiment that worked."

Caleb looked at her quizzically.

Laci smiled.

"It was the size of a pool ball, and it had invaded my entire limbic system. The doctors gave me a zero percent chance of being alive in six months." The pain finally receding, she began to climb again. "So when these surgeons in San Diego approached me about an experimental procedure, I said 'why not?'. The only place I was going to was an early grave."

"And it worked," said Caleb. "That's amazing."

"Yeah, well," Laci said. She reached the top of the ladder and pulled herself into the next room. "They used pulses of radiation and a vacuum to get rid of the tumour. Some special laser thing they'd been working on, wanted a willing guinea pig. They said there was probably only a five percent chance that it would work. I died four times on the operating table, but they managed to revive me each time, and kept going. Something to do with tachyons. Pretty much right outta *Star Trek* or something."

"Incredible," Caleb said. He looked at Laci with no small measure of awe.

"So now I have a hole in my brain and it gives me these terrific headaches. A nice scar behind my ear, too. I spent six months in rehab, learning how to speak and walk again." She paused for a moment, trying to focus in the dim light given off by the small, dirty light bulbs on the walls around them. "What is this place?"

"Storage room," Caleb said, looking around at the boxes surrounding them. There were crates of lenses, bulbs, mechanical equipment, all bearing the stamp of the USLS. "Do you need to rest? I imagine we can stop here for a while."

"No, I'll be fine," Laci said. "It comes and goes in waves. The doctors said it might take years to fully recover—it's like my brain's been rewired."

"Sounds like a lot of work ahead of you," Caleb said, his face solemn. He pointed to another ladder, a smaller one, against the wall.

"That one's gonna take us up into the lantern room. If they're not up there, they'll be out on the railing. You sure you're ready to do this? I don't know what's gonna happen when we see them."

"I'm ready, Caleb," she said. "Really, I'm fine. If I can die four times and come back, I'm sure I can handle whatever your sons throw at us."

Caleb nodded and walked to the base of the ladder. He stopped suddenly, staring intently at the little trap door above him.

"What is it?" Laci asked.

"It's nuthin'," Caleb said. "Just that I haven't been up here since Sally died."

"You all right to go on?" she asked, placing a reassuring hand on his shoulder. "Like I said, we could just turn around and go home. Let the Sheriff take care of it."

"No, I'll be fine," Caleb said. He patted her hand, then stepped onto the ladder. Laci followed close behind.

Outside, the wind howled in rage as the sea pummelled the shoreline. Lightning struck like artillery up and down the coast as the front moved inland, bringing armies of rain to the defenceless shore. It was going to get much worse before it got any better.

The lantern room was only twenty feet across, much smaller than the rooms below it. The immensity of the lamp mechanism in the centre of the chamber made the size deceptive—in reality, there was only five feet or so on either side of the massive rotating contraption.

Half the room was walled with large glass panes while the other half was stone, like the rest of the building. The beam of screamingly bright light spun slowly on its axis, clockwise across the horizon, letting ships know exactly where the shoreline was.

Caleb crawled into the room, then offered a hand to Laci.

"Make sure you don't look into the lantern, whatever you do," he said. "The light's bright enough to burn the eyes outta your head."

Laci climbed into the room with Caleb's help, then squinted her eyes as the beam of light went by. Even with her eyes clamped shut, the lantern washed her eyelids with white hot light, sending pain through the side of her head. She grabbed for her skull, then stopped.

A sound floated across the threshold of pain, a soft dry sound.

Chittering.

"Jed? Jerry?" Caleb called, swinging around. "It's me, boys. Poppa's come back."

The chittering grew louder on the opposite side of the lamp mechanism, near the front of the lighthouse. Now that she could see again, Laci saw the small door that led out onto the balcony.

Caleb stepped around the side of the lantern.

"Boys?" he asked again, cautiously. The chittering noise stopped. All they could hear was the steady, monstrous *THRUM… THRUM… THRUM* of the lantern machinery. It came around again, and Laci turned her head away.

THRUM... THRUM... THRUM...

Caleb disappeared around the side of the light, leaving Laci alone. The shadows up here, such as they were, were in constant motion due to the shifting light source. It was difficult to judge where *anything* was.

"*Jedidiah!*" Caleb barked. "*Jeremiah!*"

Outside, the frenzied wind beat fat heavy raindrops like bullets against the glass wall of the room.

Inside, Laci scanned the living shadows for movement. It had gotten hideously quiet all of the sudden, which unnerved her.

"Caleb?" she asked. She took a step around the side of the lantern. The beam blasted the far wall, away from her. She took another step.

"Caleb?" she asked again.

As she rounded the machine to the front of the lighthouse, she saw Caleb standing there quietly, his face in his hands. He looked as though he wept.

She took another step toward the man.

Jed and Jerry were there, arms waving horribly above their heads. They stood before Caleb, but they paid no attention to him.

They stared at Laci.

One of the boys raised a hand toward her, pointing a long gnarled finger in her direction. It took Laci a moment to realize the finger dripped with blood.

"Oh my God," she whispered.

The light struck the twins then, lighting them up against the glass of the windows. Blood covered them. It was on their hands and arms; it flowed across their faces in crimson runnels. One of the boys chewed something slowly. Blood rimmed his mouth.

"Caleb!" Laci screamed.

The old man turned toward the sound of her voice, and she saw that he bled horribly through his fingers. When he raised his head, she had a brief moment of clarity.

The twins had taken his eyes.

"*GET OUUUUUT!*" he screamed at her, reaching out blindly. Blood poured from the claw marks on his face, the black pits where his eyes had been.

The twins reacted to the noise by reaching out and grabbing Caleb around the chest and throat. Using all four of their arms, they easily lifted the old man off the ground.

He struggled against his sons, but weakened as he was by blood loss and shock, it was all he could do to kick feebly at them.

The twins' large black eyes bored across the beam of light at Laci. Contemptuously, easily, they flung the old man against the windows. He let out an agonized gasp and collapsed in a heap.

Laci gaped at them. They had resumed the slow, rhythmic waving of their arms over their heads, and they rocked back and forth. One of them opened his mouth, revealing jagged, uneven teeth.

And then the chittering began again in earnest.

They began to move toward Laci just as the beam of lantern light hit her full on the face. She'd been so paralyzed by the sight of the boys she'd forgotten to cover her eyes.

She was remembering now.

The beam blasted her face like a bludgeon and there was

a terrible moment of excruciating white brilliance followed by a clear blue after-image of the scene before her. Laci staggered under the blow, clutching at her eyes and falling back against the wall. The intense heat of the beam bathed her as it passed.

The chittering grew louder, more excited.

Laci dug at her eyes with the palms of her hands. They itched horribly. The blue after-image began to fade, leaving only the malformed faces of the twins. She needed to get up and moving.

She opened her eyes, and amid the shifting, ever-changing shadows she saw grainy black spots. Somewhere amidst all that confusion and movement Jedidiah and Jeremiah were coming for her.

Laci rolled over to her side. The shock of the lantern light had brought on a staggering pain in her temple, but she tried to blink through it and crawl to her feet. She fell back against the wall, shuffling along it one step at a time. She was nearly blind and her head pounded with a nuclear throb.

The chittering grew louder yet. The twins were somewhere off to her right.

"Stay away from me!" she screamed, lashing out futilely with her fists.

"You don't belong here," came a leathery, insect-like voice out of the shadows.

She stopped dead where she stood.

"Keep back," she said.

"We are here for you," came the reply. "You called us, and we came."

"*What?*" Laci stumbled against the wall again. She came to a point where the wall suddenly became very cold, and it took her a moment to realize that she had come all the way around to the front of the building.

"We were not here for him," another voice said. It was softer than the first, but just as rough, just as buzzing, just as alien.

The lantern mechanism grumbled as the light once again passed by Laci. When she opened her eyes, she could barely make out the form of the twins before her.

Lightning crashed outside in the maelstrom and for one moment the room was lit up in electric blue light. The twins had resumed their waving, but they made no further moves toward Laci.

"Come with us," they said together, their voices one.

"Where?" whispered Laci. She backed several steps away from them and nearly fell over a soft obstacle resting against the window.

It was Caleb. He hadn't moved from where his sons had hurled him. His eye sockets oozed slow, thick blood onto the metal floor.

Laci bit her lip to keep from screaming.

"Come with us," they chanted again.

"*I'm not going anywhere with you!*" she shouted. "*Just leave me alone!*"

"You don't belong here, Laci," one of them said, and the other said: "They wait for you on the other side. We saw your light. We *followed* your light."

"Fuck you," she said, sobbing, her brain reeling with what they had said. Could it be true? Had they come back, come from whatever realm of shadow and darkness they'd been lost in for so many decades, to collect *her? What exactly had that tachyon laser done?* She looked down, sidestepped Caleb's body and resumed her slow shuffle along the wall. She saw the balcony door only feet away and decided that was going to be her exit.

She took three quick steps then, grabbing the handle of the door. The twins hissed at the sudden movement. Arms raised like an angry tarantula, they scuttled toward Laci.

She turned the knob and yanked hard.

It didn't budge.

"*Come on, you bastard!*" she shrieked. She pulled again, even harder.

Nothing. The door was stuck fast.

Jedidiah and Jeremiah stepped over Caleb's body, only a few feet from her. They chittered to each other, their faces contorted in rage.

And then Caleb came alive. He reached up and grabbed the boys by the hank of flesh that joined them at the waist, and threw his chest hard against the backs of their legs. Surprised by the movement, the twins stumbled and fell to their knees against the wall, the old man riding them down.

"*Get the fuck out of here, Laci!*" he yelled, trying manfully to pin the boys down.

Laci looked at the doorknob in her hands. She could make a run for the trapdoor on the other side of the room, but there was no certainty that she'd make it before the boys got to her. Conversely, she could waste time trying to open this door, and if she got it open it would lead…where? To the balcony? Then what? Where would she go from there?

There simply wasn't time to think this through. Already the boys were untangling themselves from their father. He put up a valiant fight, but he was losing badly. The children were impossibly strong and they began to pummel the old man where he laid, their four fists like pistons.

There was a click then, at the door, and it opened freely in her hand.

The balcony.

The door had been jammed shut a moment before, but now it swung open easily. She could feel the wind of the storm pushing against it.

But was that all?

For the briefest moment, hadn't she felt something else there? Something familiar?

Caleb had finally stopped moving. The boys stood up, fresh blood on their faces. There was no time left.

Laci closed her eyes and stepped outside onto the balcony.

The wind whipped heavy rain like beads of glass at her, stinging her with every strike. She reached out and grabbed the railing. She stood exactly where the twins had when she'd discovered them the night before.

Looking over her shoulder, she saw the lantern room as it truly was—a place of brightness and shade, of sunlight and shadows. It was the space between the light and the darkness where the twins had gone that day so many years ago.

They had slipped between the two extremes, into the churning grey light behind the lantern machine as it thrummed along its revolutions. Somehow, in all that swirling mass, they had found their way home.

But now they are back, Laci thought. *They are back because an experimental laser had burned a tumour out of my head. But maybe it had also reached back across time like a beacon, calling to the children just like this lighthouse called ships in from the dangerous dark. Telling them the shore was looming, and they could come collect their prize, just as they had all those years ago in Corpse Cove.*

She had cheated Death four times. Now Death had come to collect his due.

They looked at each other through the thick dirty glass of the lighthouse wall. Far below, the rocky cliffs of Frenchman's Head took a beating from the ocean surf. Lightning struck off in the distance, somewhere in the town, and the roar was deafening even twenty miles away.

Laci backed away from the door.

The balcony was slick with rain and birdshit. She would have to move slower if she wanted to keep her footing.

But where to go? In circles around the top of the lighthouse like some idiot child's game?

Round and round and round they go…

Except Laci knew where they were going to go. And she decided that, given the choice, she'd jump onto the rocks just like Sally had.

Some things were worse than death. And in the black, pitiless eyes of the Siamese twins, she saw something a *lot* worse.

"*I'm up here!*" she screamed into the wind, the storm. "*HELP ME!*"

The twins smiled at her, their teeth jagged and bloody.

"*There is no help,*" they said in unison. "There is no help and no hope for you."

Laci put her hand up. The lantern beam appeared on the other side of the glass wall.

THRUMM…THRUMM…THRUMM…

The boys opened their arms wide, making a half circle around them. They stepped toward Laci, long gnarled fingers reaching and scrabbling horribly in the rain and wind.

The lantern beam cut across the storm-blackened sky, through the sheets of water of the storm. It reached the centre of the glass wall.

Laci stopped, the scream dead on her lips.

As the light moved toward the twins, it illuminated the form of a young woman. She wore a yellow dress, her hair back in a smart tie. She looked as though she had stepped out of a portrait.

Laci's heart froze.

The woman had the features of the children. Same jaw, same nose and cheek line. On the boys, they were malformed and ghastly. On her they were delicate. They were beautiful.

"Sally," Laci whispered.

The twins stopped as the light engulfed them.

Sally moved impossibly fast. She reached out and wrapped her slender arms around her children, embracing them one final time.

The boys' looks of rage quickly changed to terror.

Sally looked at Laci for a moment and smiled. Caleb had been right—she *was* beautiful.

And then the world exploded as lightning struck the lighthouse.

The blast nearly knocked Laci off the balcony. She clutched at the rail and fell to her knees on the hard steel grating.

The wall exploded outward, pluming shards of glass out over the ocean in a white spray. The lantern beam died and for a second after the shockwave knocked Laci off her feet, the world went completely black.

And the twins screamed.

Laci opened her eyes and saw them clinging to the side of the balcony. They had been knocked over the rail and now hung a hundred feet above the jagged cliffs of Frenchman's Head.

She could see their fingers slipping.

"*No!*" the boys cried. "*No, please! We don't want to go-o-o!*"

Laci felt it then, the creeping cold so familiar from her years in the dark places of the world. The ghost places. It floated up her spine and caressed her neck with cold, dead hands.

The feeling that the dead were nearby.

"*NO, MOTHER!*" the boys shrieked. Their fingers began to peel away from the balcony railing.

They looked to Laci, and for one brief instant they weren't malformed monsters. They hadn't killed anyone, nor come back from a plane of shadow.

They were simply scared little boys, trying to cling to life.

And then the instant passed.

They slipped from the railing, screaming as they fell.

Laci arose, ran to the side of the lighthouse and watched

them fall through space, reaching for the railing still and holding each other with their other arms.

They fell into the jagged, broken rocks below.

Laci watched them carefully, straining her eyes to see any movement.

As she watched, the surf crashed into their bodies and a lonely, broken form crawled out of the water. It dragged itself along the rocks, its legs horribly shattered and angled out away from its body. It wore a pale yellow dress, shredded and blackened with rot from its many years in the ocean.

Sally reached her sons, grabbed them by one arm. Then she turned and slowly began to drag them into the sea.

Laci covered her eyes.

The lighthouse was completely black inside. There was no way she would be able to make it to the ground floor without killing herself.

Suddenly, thinking of something, her hand went to the pocket of her jacket.

Or would she?

She felt around for a moment, then pulled out a small black camera flashlight.

She smiled then, as a thin pale beam of light cut into the inky darkness of the lantern room.

It was time to go home.

"You sure you're going to be all right?" Sheriff Danton asked as he took the last of Laci's luggage to the car.

"Thank you, but yes, I'm going to be fine," she said. She leaned against the hood and smiled, feeling warm sunshine on her face for the first time in what seemed like forever.

Danton shut the trunk and smiled.

"That's the last of it," he said. "Listen, Laci, maybe you'd like to stick around for another day or two? I could show you the sights, maybe buy you dinner...."

He smiled at her, that same well-rehearsed, winning smile. Perfect teeth. For a moment, Laci considered it.

"Thank you," she said again, "but I'm afraid I have to get going. Thank you for everything, Sheriff. Really."

She opened the car door and got in.

Sheriff Danton leaned into the open window.

"You want to be real careful on these roads now, girl," he said. "Never know, it could rain again."

Laci smiled and started the car.

"Not where I'm going," she said.

Survival of the Fattest

Russell Bell never thought of it as a weight problem.

Thinking about it, as he lay on the couch in the fifty-degree heat, his body a mound of hot, sticky flesh piled on top of him, making him rasp for air and labour to draw a breath, he saw his problem as about something else.

Lethargy.

His problem was that he was so god-damned tired. All the time. He woke up tired. He went to bed tired. He could walk down the stairs to get the mail, or go to the bus stop so he could go to work, but it was hard. His body rebelled. He was exhausted by the time he managed to do any of those things, and instead of the mail he wanted to sit down and take a rest.

Instead of work, he wanted a nap.

Sure he ate too much. But he also starved his body, hoping the simple act of keeping his fat mouth shut would help him curb the dangerous road he was on. He switched to diet pop. He tried to stay away from sandwiches. He ate only chicken and rice.

It was ridiculous.

His lifestyle was a monster. These days, he knew, that monster was stalking him. And when it was finally through torturing him, it was going to kill him. It came armed to the teeth—with powerful weapons such as guilt and habit. It taunted him, because the only thing that really made him feel better was the act of shovelling food into his face so fast he barely had time to chew it.

Russell felt like he wanted to die. He knew there was exercise. He knew there was diet. He listened to the commercials and told himself he could do it. That it wasn't too late. But today, on this broiling, humid day in August with the thermometer just about to pop and his fan lying in a broken heap on the floor, he knew that he would probably never do either of those things properly to great extent.

Not without the perfect plan.

He was a yo-yo when he lost weight. Sure, he could take it

off, but the second he turned his back that monster would be right back on him—inactivity, and maybe a little too much butter on his peas.

Russell was four hundred and thirty-six pounds.

It was a big number. A round number. The three and the six especially, due to their bulbous shape, but even the sharp corners of that four made him feel like crawling into bed and just waiting for the end to come.

He was damn-near that guy anyway. May as well shoot for six hundred and then go for a run down the stairs. Let his heart blow out on him while he was jerking off or something. Just say fuck it all.

The problem was that he couldn't. In spite of the inactivity, in spite of his habit of mixing rice into his bowls of macaroni, and in spite of the anger and disgust he felt right now he still felt a will to live. He still dreamed about meeting somebody special, and being in love. He wanted to live a normal life free of problems and of pain.

Mostly, he just wanted to be able to wake up in the morning without needing a nap.

Today, his fat sweaty ass plunked down on the couch building model airplanes and giving them authentic WW2 paint-jobs, Russell watched the glue fusing between the joints on his tiny works of art and suddenly hit upon an idea so stupid it just might work.

In his hands, he held a bottle of super glue. This shit bonded plastic instantly. Let's face it, when it came to airplanes, Russell didn't fuck around. He had a closet full of the little things: P-51's painted in desert browns for the war in Africa, little rows of Hawker Hurricanes and Supermarine Spitfires painted so they could fight the Huns across the English Channel, and even his beloved Lancaster Bombers painted night-black for their dam buster missions.

It bonded instantly.

Sitting there, in the stupid heat thinking stupid thoughts, Russell smiled. It was genius. It couldn't possibly fail.

So Russell Bell took all the shit out of his fridge and his freezer that he knew he might try to eat later. He had to get rid of it all if his plan had any hope of working. He threw frozen yogurts and ice creams in the sink, his powdered hot chocolate, iced tea with lemon flavouring.

He nearly dumped a mostly full case of beer into the sink and then thought the better of it; it was an insane plan, but the beer didn't have to suffer, did it? Besides, by his calculations, in about two weeks he'd be all ready to go and celebrate with a few beers.

Just two short weeks.

Russell smiled. It was all going to be so great.

He finished emptying out the contents of his freezer and fridge, and then to be safe he cut the cord off his blender and smashed the glass jug. Same with the food processor. He took some pliers and mangled the blades, cut the cord, and smashed the motor housing with a hammer. He hummed to himself while he worked; his fat sagging under the force of simply being upright, already making him tired. He might take a nap when he was done.

He could do that now that his plan was going to make everything better. He could lie in the summer heat and doze all day if he wanted.

If work called wondering where he was, well…

…just in case, he thought it best to cut the cord on the phone and dig out the little speakers with a screw driver. He didn't want any distractions. He didn't want to have to explain things to anybody.

He turned on his answering machine after that, on the floor in the hall plugged straight into the wall. It could collect messages for him, and afterward, when the new Russell Bell was ready to pull himself out of his shell of an apartment and face the world, he'd phone everybody back one at a time and ask them to come over for a visit.

He'd have something fantastic to show them.

That finished with, Russell went back to the couch with a tall glass of cold water. He'd laid everything out in nice rows on the coffee table. Now he sat down and looked everything over.

The Exacto knife, complete with a brand new razor blade from the box in the cupboard over the stove. A couple McDonald's straws, the extra big ones that could help you suck up your shakes that much faster. Those were used, but only once, and Russell had dug them out of the garbage and washed them thoroughly in hot soapy water.

He also had a clean towel and some scissors; though he figured if anything really needed a good cutting he'd probably be better off with the razor knife instead.

Still, you never knew what you were going to need until it actually came time to need it.

Russell put the straw in his mouth. He puckered his lips around it and found the most comfortable position to hold onto the warm yellow plastic. Then he reached down and picked up the final object on his table-top operation. The one thing he needed to hatch his plan and fix his life once and for all.

Airplane glue. A brand new bottle, from the shelf under his airplane display.

Russell smiled wickedly.

His plan was too perfect.

The lid came off easily in his hands. He licked his lips nervously around the straw, giving into the impulse of last second hesitation. It was a good idea, but it was also a crazy and desperate idea. The glue could make him sick. Worse, it could scar him for life. There were tons of reasons why he shouldn't do this, when he gave it a moment's thought.

He looked down at the bloated carcass he'd been saddled with and sighed.

There was one very good reason to go through with it. He had to get rid of this cancerous mass anchoring him to a life of misery. He had to escape, or be swallowed by it forever. Then he would end up as one of those people who couldn't leave the house because they were too big to stand up on their own.

A sudden image came to him, firming his resolve. The sight of his poor, bloated body being hauled out of a hole cut in the side of the house because he was too big to get out the door.

The glue was warm on his lips. The petroleum stink was overwhelming, and Russell immediately began to suck air in through the straw. The glue warmed his lips as it fused them together, the chemicals reacting with pink flesh to form a permanent seal.

He rubbed his lips together, puckering and grimacing, until the glue had spread to cover every part of the offending orifice and began to knit the skin. It burned, a little, but inwardly Russell smiled. Now there was nothing to do but wait.

Later that evening Russell felt his hunger pangs increase from minor grumbling to major bitching.

He tried to drink some water through the straw but it did little to quell his appetite. He drank some skim milk through it next, washing the straw clean with warm water. Then he went to his room and lay down for a while, picking through porno magazines (Hot Luscious Big-Titted Babes Want to Take it in the Ass!) until his eyes got tired and he started to drift off.

He awoke sometime before dawn, drenched in greasy sweat. He was struggling to breathe. He thought he might have been having some kind of attack; in his musty, sleep filled state he couldn't open his mouth enough to draw a breath.

Of course then he remembered, and he almost chuckled. He couldn't make a proper laugh noise, though, and instead opted for a couple heavy, choking breaths.

The straw whistled strangely as he did. It felt weird, like there was an obstruction in it. He ran his fingers along its yellow length and began to curse himself for short-sightedness.

The straw had folded over in his sleep, and now it had a split running down one side of it.

"Shurrt," Russell said.

He got out of bed and went to the bathroom mirror to get a better look. Sure enough, a long split ran along the side of the straw. It would be nearly impossible to drink through it now. He wondered if he shouldn't just remove it altogether.

Then he shook his head. If he got rid of the straw, he might not be able to gather enough breath through his nose when he was sleeping. Of course, he wasn't getting enough breath now, was he?

He voided his bowels while he thought about this, and then washed his hands. He inspected his lips under the milky glaze of the superglue and noticed the skin beginning to flake around his mouth. Maybe a little moisturizing lotion would clear that up.

His stomach was gurgling. The first pangs of morning hunger came to him, and he sat down on the couch until they started to recede. There was no point in getting dressed today; he was simply going to sit around the house for the next two weeks until his plan was completed and he was a brand new man.

A thin man.

Around noon he thought he'd try some water, but just as he'd suspected it was nearly impossible to get water into his mouth with that long split in the side of the straw.

Looking down at the superglue he'd left on the table from the night before, it occurred to Russell that he could simply glue the damned thing back together and he'd be as good as gravy.

Thick, meaty beef gravy with lots of garlic. And maybe a Yorkshire pudding or two....

Russell groaned as his stomach suddenly came to life. He could almost taste the black, soupy gravy his mother had made for him as a child; the gravy that probably added much of the weight he now wore simply because it was too good to go to waste.

His hands were shaking a little as he uncapped the bottle of superglue.

He'd have to be extra careful about applying it to the straw. He couldn't afford to make a mistake. Rimming the lip of the glue bottle with his towel, Russell gently ran it along the edge of the split.

And sucked in a deep breath of glue fumes when he took a breath.

He'd always found the smell of model glue slightly comforting. It was one of those smells that evoked memories of his childhood, when he'd been plump but not morbidly obese as he was now.

This was not that familiar, cozy smell that he associated with long nights working on his first models, however.

This was a jackhammer of chemical, reacting with the cheap plastic on the straw and creating a caustic stench that assaulted his nostrils and made him want to puke.

Russell tried to slow his breathing as he finished the last little strip of broken straw, but he was having a hard time of it. The glue was digging into his sinuses, searing his throat and making his eyes run. He took a short breath through the straw to give his nose some peace and held it as long as he could. Then he exhaled and did it again.

Exactly when the world started to swim, Russell wasn't too sure. All he knew is that suddenly the television was melting and the world was flashing around him in static, Polaroid sharpness.

"Whhuuurrrrttt thuh fuuuuurrrcckkk," Russell slurred, the sound through the straw little more than warm, sloshing noise. He sat back on the couch and tried to breathe slowly through the straw and his nose. He just needed some fresh air. A few deep breaths and he'd be fine.

His apartment was droopy and Technicolor around him. Tiny motes of light danced on the edge of his vision.

A heavy ringing started up somewhere in the room, but in the warbled light of the apartment he couldn't see where it was coming from and he vaguely remembered something about his phone messages…

…there was something about his straw, wasn't there? It had a leak, and he'd tried to fix it. It was all coming back now. The room was swirling in greens and reds, and his furniture seemed to droop everywhere, like that guy who painted clocks in the desert, but it was coming back.

There was a hole in his straw, wasn't there?

He sucked in a deep breath full of air.

Of course there was a hole. A big deep open hole where steaks and gravies could come pouring in until the cows came home. Making him huge and gross and fat.

He'd come out into the living room to fix that, though… right?

Of course he had. Russell had a plan, after all, and even though he wasn't exactly sure at this moment why he had a plan or exactly what it entailed, he was pretty sure it had something to do with superglue and the hole in his straw.

And losing weight.

He had a two-tooth plan didn't he? He was a man of action, not a fat tub of glue.

Glue? The glue was sitting on the table, already to use.

He reached up and put his finger over the straw hole. Tried to suck in.

The tube was perfectly sealed. No food could ever get in there. Just a tiny little hole that he could plug up in two seconds.

Was that his plan?

It certainly sounded right in his head. It certainly sounded right in this room, full of awful clashing colours and melty things. It must have been the plan. It must have been THE plan.

Russell reached out and picked up the tube of airplane glue off the coffee table.

"Guuuuut Plannnn?" he asked the melting walls, and then giggled at his own joke. He gave the bottle of glue a good squeeze, to make sure it would come out as he needed it. Clear goo spurted out of the top of the bottle, running thick over his fingers and down onto his pants.

Then he reached up and placed the tip of the glue bottle inside his McDonald's straw.

He squeezed the little bottle hard, bringing up his other hand to help him. Glue shot into the straw, forming a seal as it travelled toward his mouth. He sucked on the straw to make sure everything was working the way it should, and hot glue splashed against his tongue and teeth.

The room filled with the smell of superglue, overriding his senses. He sucked on the straw like a calf drawing milk, and more glue filled his mouth. He could feel his teeth getting hot and sticky, and already his tongue was burning from the chemical reaction.

He breathed in the fumes and thought vaguely about airplanes. He'd have to buy one some day when he was thin.

He'd also have to do something about melting televisions. They were a bitch to watch.

It was time for sleep.

Russell woke to a splitting headache and the awful panic of someone who was on the verge of smothering. He tried to open his mouth, but for some reason, he couldn't move anything around his jaw.

At the same time he noticed he couldn't move his hand.

Looking down, he saw why. The glue bottle in his hand had ruptured while he was sleeping, and now it had secured his hand tightly to his jeans. More than tight, the two were bonded together.

His teeth were stuck together, his tongue planted firmly behind them.

He tried to breathe through his straw opening and found it jammed shut. His nostrils, too, were strangely packed, and there was a strange film running the length of his tongue to the back of his throat. He could feel it there like a tiny filament tickling his breathing tube.

His stomach rolled over on itself.

Russell stood up and dragged himself to the bathroom. Flicking on the light sent shards of jagged pain running through his scalp, and he took a moment to adjust himself. He was breathing short, quick breath now. He'd broken out in a warm sweat.

When he saw the damage he nearly burst into tears.

His stomach dropped dangerously, and then rolled over again. He began to get those first pangs of nausea.

There was glue all over his face. He looked absolutely

lacquered in the stuff; it ran across his chin and dribbled down his shirt where it had been fused to his beefy man-tits. The straw was a half melted ball of plastic sticking to the side of his cheek. It was useless. It had also been the only thing keeping his mouth open, but his glorious plan had gone right into the toilet when he'd decided to eat a half-full bottle of super glue.

His mouth was full of it.

It had run down his tongue and begun to pool in the back of his throat where it surely would have killed him if it had been given a chance to coat his sinus passages. Thankfully, it had merely coated the bottom half, leaving him with more breathing problems than when he got up that morning.

His stomach did a barrel roll.

He was going to puke.

The dawning realization took a moment to set in. He was going to puke. Looking at his face now, the way he'd managed to lock it up to the point where he could barely breathe, Russell suddenly pictured the danger he was in. When that puke came up, there would be no room to breathe.

He gagged.

It was a forceful, vicious movement, and for a panicked moment Russell's air was cut off by his gag reflex. He forced himself to calm down, to try to breathe deep and not think about what was about to happen.

Thinking nearly made it so.

He gagged again.

He scratched at the glue around his mouth, but it was

useless. He couldn't get a finger into the bonded adhesive. He tried to force his mouth open with his jaw, but all that succeeded in doing was making his teeth hurt and his gums bleed. The glue was everywhere; there was no way around that.

His breath began to come quicker. His throat opened.

Russell swallowed hard.

In desperation, he grabbed a comb off the bathroom counter and began sawing away at the glue on his face. In moments his skin was raw and bleeding, but there was so much glue between his lips that he wasn't making any headway with the comb.

When the gag came this time, his mouth flooded with saliva.

Russell took one last look at himself in the mirror, the torn and bleeding lips fused to the front of his teeth and the lines of glue running toward his chin; the useless, melted plastic straw stuck to the side of his face; the wild, panicked look in his eyes and the way his pasty brow was rimed with sweat.

He puked.

The vomit was hot in his mouth and scalded his throat as it came up, immediately filling the spaces in his mouth not taken up by glue. His cheeks flared out as the mass of stomach acid and partially digested food filled his face.

There wasn't enough room for the load of stinking body fluids. Partially digested meat and bread from his last meal lodged into his sinuses, instantly cutting off his wind. In a panic, Russell snorted in and something akin to crusty snot hit the back of his throat.

He gagged again.

The heavy stench of puke filled his senses, making his eyes water. He tore at his face desperately with the comb, shredding his lips as the teeth dug their way into his mouth. His lungs burned horribly, and he began to fear at any moment he might take that desperate breath and suck hot puke in as a breath and drown in it.

He had to get his mouth open, and now. That, or death.

Russell stumbled out of the bathroom, one hand still clenched around the glue bottle. The world was beginning to grey out around him. Tunnel vision was setting in. He stumbled, tripping over his feet and nearly taking out the coffee table with his bloated face.

And there it was, lying on the coffee table, sitting beside the towel he'd gotten for his plan.

The Exacto knife.

He reached for it, missed, nearly fainting in the process. Reached again.

His stubby fingers closed on cold metal.

Success!

His chest was ready to burst.

He flicked off the protective lid covering the razor's edge. Then he placed the blade against his cheek and squeezed his eyes shut.

The razor was brand new, and it peeled through the layers of Russell's face with screaming ease. Russell jabbed the blade in until it jammed between his teeth, and it fountained a mixture of blood and puke. It was agony, but it was glorious agony.

But it wasn't enough. The liquid puke found its way between his teeth and out through the new hole in his face, but the solid chunks, the peanut bits and sopping bread, partially digested meat and stomach slime, that stuff was staying where it was.

Right behind his teeth.

Russell slashed his face open further. Blood and stomach acid poured down his face and into pools on the floor underneath him.

Taking the blade, he stabbed at his teeth, smashing through enamel and into the craterous nerve centres inside them.

His face was on fire. Chips of broken teeth and more blood from his slashed gums ran from his face and into the pile of bloody slime on the floor, but Russell had to keep going. He was nearly ready to faint, and his stabbing motions were becoming more erratic now because of the blood loss.

The razor blade smashed through his teeth and bit deeply into his tongue. He could feel the blood pouring out of it as he removed the blade and jammed it home again, but it was getting farther away. In his state, he missed his target on the next thrust and jammed the blade through the flesh beneath his nose.

His head drooped. He began to release the air from his lungs a bit at a time, feeling it bubble through the puke and blood and slime on his face. He couldn't hold it one moment longer, and when he sucked that breath in, well, he'd take a lot of solid food and stomach acid instead of air, and he'd choke on it until he passed out and died.

In desperation, he jammed the razor into his teeth one last time, feeling the blade plunge into his tongue. He pushed further, and the teeth shattered around the little steel handle.

He pushed a little further.

His wind was nearly gone. In a moment, he would have no air in his lungs, and then his body would force him to breathe in again.

And then he'd be dead.

He jerked up on the knife handle, smashing his remaining teeth and tearing his tongue in half.

His jaw opened, the glue holding in parts and giving way in others, creating a jack o' lantern effect with his teeth. Several were pulled from their sockets entirely, and blood washed over Russell's face like thick cherry syrup.

The lump of solid puke lodged against his tongue and teeth fell free of its prison and landed with a sickening plop in front of him.

Russell drew a breath.

And puked again.

The pain was nearly impossible to grasp, hot puke running over countless mouth wounds and pulled teeth, his tongue pumping blood into his mouth from several deep wounds, and his cheek, which had sustained the most damage.

When he finished puking, Russell lay on the floor for a moment to catch his breath. He was woozy from the fatigue and blood loss. He needed to get to the phone and call 911, and he needed to do it now before he passed out. He was breathing, but he was also bleeding horribly.

He got to his knees and crawled toward the hallway where the phone was. It sat beside the answering machine on the floor, as he'd left it. He noticed the light flashing, indicating a message.

Russell picked up the receiver.

There was nothing on the other end.

It was dead, as though he'd held a book or glass to his head. No sound, nothing. No dial tone. He looked over to the little pile of rubbish in the corner of the hallway then, his hopes fading like the light around him.

Tiny microphones, screws, and assorted guts from the telephone sat in a little heap, waiting to be swept up with the trash. He'd destroyed the phone so he wouldn't have to answer it.

In spite of his condition, Russell smiled. Blood poured from his face down his chin and onto the floor.

"Ain't that a bithhh," he said, his face lit up like a gutted pumpkin.

Mmmm.

Pie.

Song of the Dead

Dallas looked out from his perch on the fiftieth floor of the Regal Tower and watched the people milling about on the street below. His bottle of vodka was just about empty. He drained it and then tossed it over the side of the building.

He watched the bottle tumble end over end in a lazy arc. It

came down on a woman in a blue dress and burst, driving her face-first into the sidewalk.

Dallas slapped his leg.

"God-*damn*!" he said, wiping the last glow of booze from his lips.

He grabbed the rifle leaning beside him and looked down through the hunting scope. The woman was on her stomach, twitching slightly. Her skull had been partially crushed from the force of the bottle. A thick black stain spread out from the wound.

Dallas worked the action on the rifle, took careful aim, and pulled the trigger.

The rifle bucked in his hands and took off the back of the woman's head. She jerked one final time and then lay still.

The people standing around barely took notice. A few of them looked at the woman in the blue dress but no one moved to help her. Dallas was surprised any of them looked at all.

His rifle scope began to move and this time settled on an old man in a black suit.

"Little more to the left, asshole," he muttered. When the man finally moved, Dallas put a hole the size of an acorn into his face.

The body sputtered and fell over.

Dallas stood up, arms outstretched. He watched the people below continue to mill about, oblivious of the assassin above them.

The walking dead had nothing to fear. You couldn't take the life of one who wasn't alive to give it.

Dallas heard the balcony door slide open. After a moment he heard his grandfather's voice from the apartment.

"Somebody shootin' out here?"

"I was, Poppa," Dallas said, climbing off his perch and onto the balcony. "I thought I saw some ducks."

"You saw a what?" Poppa said.

"*Ducks*," he said, raising his voice.

"Ahh," Poppa said, satisfied. "I was known to shoot a duck now and then."

"Oh yeah?"

"Oh yeah. Ducks. Geese. Hell, I've been known to shoot the odd partridge."

"I bet you had some good hunting when you were younger," Dallas said, rehashing an old topic.

"Oh sure," Poppa said. "We used to go down into the fields behind the house there and we'd bag six, seven birds in an afternoon. The partridge would be flyin' out of the bushes every couple yards."

"Sounds good," Dallas said. He walked over to the edge of the balcony, keeping within three feet of his grandfather. He didn't really trust him outside here, as high up as they were.

"You ever do any hunting, Dall?"

Dallas looked down briefly at the bodies on the concrete hundreds of feet below them.

"A little," he said.

The pair went into the flat and Dallas closed the balcony door behind them. Just to be safe, he double locked it. Poppa went into the living room and sat at the table, quickly scooping up a deck of cards as he did. Within moments he'd laid half of them out in a box pattern.

"What are you playing?" Dallas said, sitting across from him.

"Solitaire," Poppa said, and Dallas nodded sagely. Poppa could play solitaire all day long and never play the same game twice.

"I was thinking we should take a trip to the store today," Poppa said as he laid his cards down. "I'm gonna get me some of them creamy toffees."

Dallas sighed. "We can't, Poppa. We can't leave the flat."

Poppa stopped flipping cards and looked at Dallas.

"Why the hell not?" he said.

"Because there's quarantine on right now," Dallas said. "We're not allowed to go outside until it's over."

"I never heard of that," Poppa said, getting angry.

"I know. They said it a little while ago. Nobody go outside."

"What is it?" Poppa said.

"Some kind of flu, I think," Dallas said.

"Some kind of what?"

"*Flu*. It's the Flu," Dallas said. This was more familiar ground with the old man. One of the few topics Poppa would discuss at length these days.

He'd once tried to explain how everything was fucked up and people who were dead refused to stay down, but it had little impact on Poppa. He had thought Dallas was making the whole thing up just to be an asshole.

"So, what were you shootin' at?" Poppa said, changing the subject.

"*Ducks*," he said, and then followed up under his breath, "for the hundredth fucking time."

"You what?" Poppa said.

"*I said I was hunting ducks*," Dallas said and went into the kitchen for a drink.

A little while later Dallas was sitting on the floor of the kitchen reading and drinking rye when Poppa walked in.

"I smell smoke," Poppa said.

"Oh yeah?" Dallas said, slowly getting to his feet.

"Smells like a fire some place."

Dallas smelled the air.

"I don't smell nuthin'," he said.

"Go over to the window," Poppa said.

Dallas walked by the window and instead went straight for the balcony. Quickly unlocking the door he stepped outside into the late afternoon sun. He could smell the city and the faint tang of rotting meat, the same thing he always smelled outside.

He turned and went back into the flat.

"I can't smell it, Poppa," he said, shutting the door behind him.

"Smell what?" Poppa said, flipping a hand of solitaire.

They ate canned stew and boiled rice for dinner, and later in the evening Poppa fell asleep reading on the couch. Dallas left him with a blanket and went out onto the balcony.

The sky was a black and purple bruise as far as Dallas could see. He smoked some hash and plucked away on his guitar for a while. The cries of the dead wafted up from the street below.

They sounded like cattle.

Their soft, droning voices carried on the air. Dallas spent whole nights listening to the sound, wondering exactly why they were making it. As far as he could tell, it only happened at night when they were in the dark.

The next morning Poppa was already up when Dallas rolled out of bed.

He put a pot of water over the fireplace and then grabbed his cigarettes and walked out onto the balcony.

Poppa was working on a crossword puzzle with a pen and a magnifying glass.

Dallas smelled the smoke as soon as he stepped into the sunshine.

He looked out over the skyline. Sure enough, there were threads of black dancing up from one of the taller buildings in the downtown core. It was a few blocks over, by the waterfront, but he could still see the top of the building. The Petrochem building, a dinosaur left over from the old days of an oil-driven economy.

He went back into the house.

"Hey Poppa," he said. "You were right yesterday. There's a fire in one of the buildings over by the river."

"That's what I thought," Poppa said, turning back to his cards. "Oh well. I imagine the fire department will be over there soon enough."

"The fire department," Dallas said, his hands suddenly getting sweaty. "Oh holy shit."

He went back out to the balcony. The smoke was getting thicker, wasn't it? A moment later he had his answer.

It was.

Poppa came out behind him, holding a hand over his eyes to block the sun.

"It doesn't look too far away, does it?" he said.

"No, Poppa," Dallas said. "It doesn't."

"The fire department will get it," Poppa said again. "I was thinkin' I might head down to the store today and get some of them creamy toffees."

Dallas looked down at the street. The dead were wandering about as usual. He counted over twenty in the couple blocks he could see.

How many were in the city? Calgary was up over a million people, right? Even if only a quarter of those people had turned over, that still left a quarter of a million zombies. Dallas remembered what the first days of the new world were like and he highly doubted that the number was only a fourth.

It was probably more like half.

He looked over at the black haze settling on the skyline. If the city burned, Regal Tower was going to go up with it.

"I used to enjoy them toffees when I was a kid," Poppa said. Dallas turned to him.

"Poppa, we can't go to the store."

"Why not?" Poppa said, looking hurt. Dallas took him by the arm and led him into the flat.

The petroleum building erupted into a fireball shortly after dark. It lit up several blocks around it, including the

Regal Tower. The heat was amazing. Standing out on the balcony, Dallas could feel it warming his skin.

He'd never been close to a fire of this magnitude. He spent the night sitting on the balcony, drinking Golden Wedding and watching tall flames lick the sky.

At about ten o'clock the next morning the Petrochem building collapsed, sending a massive plume of smoke and ash into the air and lighting dozens of smaller fires. It also slammed into the building across the street from it.

The roar was truly epic. Dallas cupped his hands over his ears but it did little to soften the impact. He leapt to his feet. The sound shook the balcony itself and shattered windows on both sides of the street.

Poppa came to the balcony.

"I thought I heard something," he said.

"The fucking building *collapsed*," Dallas yelled. "The whole thing just fell down."

"Hope no one was hurt," Poppa said, watching the dust wash over the downtown core. The brackish mixture coated everything below the 35th floor in fine grey ash.

"Christ," said Dallas. He looked at the destruction in front of them. There were now fires on at least five other buildings that he could see.

On the ground below them the dead began to howl.

It was thick with smoke and dust down there. Enough to block out the sun.

So dark they thought it was night.

"We're going to have to leave," Poppa said, giving life to a thought that Dallas himself had been dreading.

"Christ," Dallas said. It was all he could say. He suddenly needed a drink.

Dallas watched the progress of the fires for several hours as they began to devour the downtown core. The dead continued to sing below them on the street, but Dallas couldn't see anything. The ash wasn't going anywhere.

A second building collapsed at about nine o'clock that night, ripping through the gloom and sending shock waves around the city. Dallas ran to the balcony just in time to see a column of burning ash and fire reach toward the sky.

He turned as he heard Poppa's door open.

"We have to go," Dallas said. "We've got to get out of the city before it comes down on our heads."

The air was getting heavy, even at this height. He could taste the fire outside. It was waking something inside him, something primal and fearful. They had to get moving.

Now, before it was too late.

Dallas quickly packed some things and then watched as Poppa did the same. The old man moved slowly, with deliberate purpose. He was bad on his feet; he made sure that every step was a careful and sure-footed one.

Steps.

Dallas continued to watch the old man, shuffling slowly across the room as he completed his chore. He suddenly had that guilty, gnawing feeling in his stomach.

When they had first settled into the Presidential Suite on the Regal Tower the building was still running on its generators. Dallas and Poppa had taken the elevator to the top floor and had a few weeks of lights and electricity, even hot water.

Slowly, though, as the weeks stretched into months, everything had eventually shut down. They lost the lights, and then the hot water. It wasn't too much of a problem, really.

He'd simply ransacked the other flats in the tower and taken things as they were needed. They had enough food and water to last for years up here.

Of course, after the lights went he had to switch over to flashlights and candles. Not much of a problem. But the loss of power also meant no more elevators.

Just fifty floors of stairs in a dark stairwell.

Poppa was packing in his room. Dallas could hear him talking softly to himself.

He walked over to the balcony where he could better watch the city burn. The fires were leaving a huge black stain on the skyline. The air outside was a hazy fume.

He couldn't believe how stupid and short-sighted he had been. His only thought had been to escape the insane legions of corpses roaming the streets, hunting for flesh. He'd never given a single thought to the fact that the whole city might one day come down around his ears.

He'd never given any thought to *leaving*.

"I'm ready to go," Poppa said behind him. "Can you help me with my suitcase?"

Dallas turned and looked at the old man.

"Sure thing, Poppa," he said, grabbing up his backpack. "Let's get going."

The pair left the flat with Dallas leading the way. In addition to the backpack and suitcase carrying their personal effects,

Dallas was also carrying the rifle slung over his shoulder and several heavy water skins he'd filled for the trip.

As a result, he was already sweating by the time they got to the stairwell at the end of the hall. He kicked the door open and caught it with a free hand. Inky black spilled out from the doorway and Poppa clucked to himself.

"I brought a flashlight," Dallas said, reading the old man's mind. "We just have to take it slow and easy. We'll get it done."

"Humph," Poppa said, sounding unconvinced.

Dallas smiled at him and then flicked on his light and stepped into the stairwell.

The air was dry and stale and it seemed to cling to Dallas in spite of the flashlight. He flicked the light around to get his bearings. The stairwell was a concrete and steel snake that wound its way down fifty flights of stairs. There were four of them in the Regal Tower, one in each corner of the building.

For each floor, the stairs went halfway down to a landing and then doubled back so that they could meet up with a door in the same spot on every floor. There were twenty stairs per flight, or forty stairs per floor.

Two thousand stairs.

He had to get the old man down two thousand stairs before the building caught fire and killed them both.

He suddenly turned and faced Poppa, who was just getting ready for his first step. The old man took it gingerly, gripping the side rail firmly in both hands. He stepped down onto the first stair and then carefully dropped his other foot down.

He looked at Dallas and nodded.

"How you feeling?" Dallas said, watching him.

"Good," Poppa said in a curt voice. "I got past the first one, didn't I?"

"Sure did," Dallas said, bouncing his flashlight on the steps ahead of him. He went down to the first landing and pointed his light up at the steps so Poppa could see better.

Poppa took another step.

And then another.

Dallas put his suitcase and rifle down.

"You need a hand?" he said.

"No," Poppa said. "I've got it." He took another step.

It took Poppa just about five minutes to make it to the landing. Dallas helped him get around the corner and then met him at the entrance of the 49th floor. By that time Poppa was wheezing and he needed to take a break.

Dallas felt like he was going to lose his mind.

"We've got to get moving," Dallas said. "Are you okay now?"

Poppa nodded.

"Oh yeah," he said. "Just a little tired. I'm ready to go."

Dallas nodded his head and then went to the next landing to wait for him.

They went on like that for an hour before Poppa stumbled.

The old man gasped and clung to the railing. His foot was only half on the stair.

"Shit," Dallas cursed and ran back up to help him. "You alright, Poppa?"

Taking the old man's hand, Dallas steadied him enough to get his balance back.

"Just about fell," Poppa said. "Just getting a little tired I guess."

"You need a break?"

"Just for a minute," he said, squeezing Dallas' hand. "I need to catch my breath."

They stood in silence for a few minutes, Dallas being careful not to crowd the man too much. Finally Poppa signalled that he was ready to start going again.

They passed the 40th floor.

Poppa was moving even slower now. Dallas could tell he was exhausted. The old man hadn't taken this many stairs in years. Finally, at the 37th floor, he stopped. Poppa got down to the landing and looked at him expectantly.

"You need to go faster," he said. "You're moving too slow." The words were like acid in his mouth.

He was tired of waiting around. Every minute spent on the stairwell was another minute he had to spend worrying about what they were going to do when they got to the bottom. He'd probably be there right now, if he was on his own.

"Well, I'm sorry," Poppa said, equally frustrated. "You never said there would be so many stairs. Why didn't we take the elevator?"

"Because there is no power in the building," Dallas said, his voice dipping into anger. "No power, no elevator."

"Hey, Dallas?" Poppa said, pulling himself off the stair

he'd been sitting on. "Why don't you go fuck yourself?" He moved toward the next flight down, indicating the conversation was over.

"Hold on a bloody minute," Dallas said, reaching out and grabbing Poppa's shoulder. "*Go ahead and catch your—*"

"Get your *Gawd*-damned hands off me," Poppa roared, pulling away from Dallas. He overshot himself, and his foot slipped off the landing.

He gasped and grabbed at the rail. He rolled against it instead, his body weight carrying him over the step.

Dallas watched it all happen in slow motion.

Poppa's legs crossed and his body sagged toward the bottom of the steps. He looked up into Dallas' eyes.

There was a moment of perfect clarity as Dallas looked down at his grandfather.

Fear. It hit Dallas and rolled through his guts.

He reached out his hand, too little…

Too late.

Poppa's hands slipped from the railing and he rolled backward. He picked up speed as he went down, flopping onto the landing and crashing against the far wall.

"*Poppa!*" Dallas yelled, taking the steps three at a time.

He hit the bottom step and nearly fell himself. Then he rolled Poppa onto his back.

There was blood.

There was a red smudge on the wall. A similar smudge stained Poppa's forehead. His sightless blue eyes stared up at the ceiling, his face frozen in that moment when he'd looked up at Dallas and realized he couldn't hold on. His head was rolling free on his neck. Like cold knuckles, it snapped and popped freely and moved on a swivel.

Dallas started to cry. There was nothing left for him to do. He held the old man against his body. And sobbed.

"I'm sorry, Poppa," he whispered to him. "I'm so very sorry."

He sat like that for a long time, until Poppa's body had gone completely cold. Then he folded his arms over the old man's chest, straightened him out, and put the suitcase at his feet. It was wrong, and he deserved more, but there was so little time. Dallas had to get out of the building before the downtown inferno caught up with him.

He could already smell smoke in the stairwell.

He said one last goodbye to his grandfather and started down the stairs.

The creeping dark followed behind Dallas and the beam of his flashlight as it bounced from landing to landing. By the 25th floor it was a living enemy that blew hot breath on his neck and pressed into him from all sides.

He noticed that the light from the flashlight was turning yellow. The cone was bringing longer shadows with it and shortening at the same time.

"Oh, *shit*," Dallas said, realizing what was happening. He hadn't packed any new batteries. All of the time he'd spent with his grandfather he'd been running the flashlight.

It was his only source of light.

That's not true, he thought then, and felt for the lighter in his pocket. He pulled out his smokes and lit one up. The blue Zippo lighter in his hand would have to do once the flashlight died for good.

It wasn't much, but it was something.

A noise above him suddenly brought him out of his thoughts.

He looked up, holding his breath. He forced thoughts out of his head, reaching for the sound through the smothering black above him. He was sure he'd hear it again.

It was a soft sound. The sound of a hand slapping against the cold concrete stairs. It started far above him and floated down to settle around his body.

A soft braying followed it, like a cow in the dark.

The song.

He'd know it anywhere. He'd listened to it nearly every night since he'd moved into the Regal Tower with his grandfather. The sound the zombies made at night, when they couldn't see.

Poppa had gone bad.

Poppa was singing the song of the dead.

Dallas screamed. He screamed and he could feel his voice split and go hoarse. He screamed until his eyes bulged and his face went hot and he tottered on the edge of passing out.

Poppa continued to sing as he came. Step by step, one foot at a time.

Dallas turned and ran.

He overstepped the landing and sailed off the stairs.

There was a terrible, exhilarating moment when he felt completely weightless, freefalling in space as he shot out over the stairs. Then his foot caught the edge of the stairwell, folded on itself, and sent him crashing back to jarring reality.

He instinctively put his hands up, trying to cover his head. The concrete bit him everywhere he touched it; he felt it slam into his hips and his knees and elbows. Finally he hit the 23rd floor and rolled to a stop.

He lay in a fog, not exactly sure where he was or what he was doing.

Searing pain jumping up his leg broke through the fog in his head. The cold black of the stairwell confused him and made him think he had his eyes closed.

His ankle was hot and swollen, and every pulse of his heart sent tiny sparks shooting off behind his eyes.

He put his hand on it and pulled away when he felt blood.

"Oh my god," he whispered, fumbling in the dark. The flashlight had exploded at some point in the fall, it was useless now.

He reached for his cigarette pack and grabbed the lighter. He also grabbed another smoke. Then he flicked on a pale yellow flame.

The ankle looked even worse than he thought. The yellow light streaming off the Zippo made everything dull and lifeless, but there was no mistaking the severity of the compound fracture along the side of his foot. There was a two inch tear in the flesh above the ankle joint and a sliver of garish white bone was peeking out from the hole.

Dallas was too shocked to speak. He just stared at the shard of bone and the way the blood was pooling under it.

He wasn't going anywhere on it.

Somewhere far above him Poppa continued with his song.

Dallas began to weep.

Everything he had was on the landing above him. A whole

flight of stairs separated him from the last remaining pieces of his life. The sound of Poppa moving on the stairs had shocked him into reacting without thought.

Now it was going to cost him his life.

He lit a smoke with unsteady hands, fumbled the lighter, and nearly dropped it. The flame dipped dangerously low.

He looked up into the ink above him and puffed on his cigarette.

He could almost see Poppa up there, if he thought about it.

Poppa, shuffling along with his head hanging partway down his back and gripping the rails with his palsied hands. Full of new strength.

Full of new hunger.

He sang as he shuffled from step to step and landing to landing.

He clawed through the darkness, not caring whether he stumbled or fell. If his legs were broken, he'd crawl. He would pull himself along inch by inch with his fingertips if he had to.

He was coming.

Dallas held his breath as long as he could. Poppa was only a few floors above him now. He was making great time. He would arrive soon.

The shuffle step was rhythmic. Poppa's hands slapped out a beat on the rail.

And he sang.

The last light of the Zippo dropped away and died.

Shuffle…Slap…Slap…Shuffle…

Poppa stepped down onto the landing above Dallas.

He was singing up a storm.

Dallas sat in the dark, eyes wide-to bursting. Then he sucked in a great deep breath and joined in.

Parched Earth

The last Anasazi Brave fled into the desert with his prize, and Marshall Garret was right behind him.

Garret and his companion, a half-breed scout who went by the name Yakub, had crossed four territories hunting the man known as Kicking Bull. Now, looking out across the vast corpse of dirt and cactus that spread for hundreds of miles in every direction, Marshall Garret felt the first pangs of something other than duty.

Fear perhaps?

"*Eee comes this vay*," Yakub said, kneeling down and inspecting the dirt. Yakub was the son of a Russian immigrant and a Mi' Kmaq Indian from the north. Through sheer diligence and willpower, he had managed to retain much of his father's accent.

"You see anything else?" Garret said, looking at the ground where Yakub was pointing but seeing nothing.

"*Eee's* speeding up, Marshall," Yakub said, looking up at Garret. "*Ees* not far now, where he goes, *eh*?"

"Your guess is as good as mine," Garret said, getting down off his horse. He spit at the dirt, then watched it hungrily suck up his moisture. "Probably a whole lot better."

Yakub whistled softly.

"Dry here, eh?" he said, putting his forearm over his head to block out the dying sun. "*Vee* didn't bring enough *vater*, maybe? *Vee* should go back, get supplies *I theenk*."

"We're not going anywhere but out into the sand," Garret said, giving his scout a hand up. "That *Injun's* got five women with him. Where they go, we go."

"But *vhat* about the *vater*, Boss?"

"Where Kicking Bull goes," Garret said again, "I go."

They mounted up and rode west. The sun left them to the purple sky of the desert night, and the sand quickly bled out its heat and cooled.

Finally, around midnight, they tied their horses together and made camp.

"Tell me what he's doing out there, Yakub," Garret said, after they'd eaten and settled down for the evening.

"I don't know for sure," Yakub said. "But *zees* red men out here, they have old magic."

"They have bullshit magic, you mean," Garret said, snorting. He took a swig of water from his canteen and offered it to the man.

"You are quick to judge," Yakub said quietly. "You *vhite* men know nothing about *zhese* land, eh? You come, you kill, you take *vhat* you *vhant*. Never a thought to *zhee* Mother Earth and *vhat* she *vants*."

"Get to the point, half-breed," Garret said.

"They say that red men have many secrets out here in the sand," Yakub said between sips of water. "Once the Anasazi tribes were children of *zhe* earth, but when they forgot their roots a great whirlwind came and scattered them to the corners of *zhe* land."

"Tornadoes?" Garret said.

"Who can know if *eets* even true? I hear things whispered about the desert men, though. *Foul things*. They prayed to black gods and ate each other."

The two men sat in silence for a while, and then Garret stood up, walked over to where Yakub was sitting and grabbed a seat beside him. He opened a pouch full of cigars, took one out and handed it to the scout. Then he grabbed one for himself.

"Cannibals," Garret said. "It just figures, don't it?"

"Nobody knows, Boss," Yakub said. "All is known about the desert men is that they disappeared. Some think they turned to the Plains. Navajos, and the other tribes in the south. Some say they just all gone. Like dust on a hot wind."

"Dust on a hot wind," Garret repeated, licking his cigar. "Well hell, Yakub, that's damn near poetry."

On their third day in the desert, Yakub spotted a shack on the horizon.

"*Vee* go there, Boss," he said, pointing to the old outbuilding. *Vhere* he goes, you go, right?"

"Right," Garret replied. The two men clicked their horses and set them into a trot. As they got closer, Garret couldn't see the Indian's wagon anywhere, but that didn't necessarily mean there was no one home.

The building was in fact an old adobe, left over from the time when Indians ran unchecked across the landscape. Strange that it was the only building in the area, as the little mud huts were often built in clusters.

Garret had seen them before, but further south toward Mexico. And never alone like this. The front of the building was covered by a striped blanket, and there were no windows or doorways visible from where the two men stood.

Yakub squatted down, his hand instantly drawing out a black revolver from its holster at his hip.

"Git down, Boss," he said. "Zhere's somethieeng in there."

Garret did as the half-breed instructed, pulling a pair of nickel and pearl Colt Peacemakers as he did.

"What is it?" he said, after a minute.

"Don't know," Yakub said, smiling at him. "Why not you go ask?"

"Wise ass," Garret said, and Yakub chuckled. He partially stood, checked his guns for dirt, and then scuttled toward the building. Yakub followed behind.

Garret reached the wall of the building and put himself up against it. He could hear shuffling inside the building. If Kicking Bull was in there, he gave no hint that he knew of Garret and Yakub outside.

"*Kicking Bull!*" Garret shouted.

There was a scream inside the building, followed by a small explosion. Both men threw themselves to the ground as a large chunk of adobe mud dissolved in a puff.

"Come and get it, you Bastard!" a woman's voice said, and Garret looked up at the sound.

Through the hole in the wall he could see a filthy young woman desperately working the action on her rifle. She'd somehow managed to get the thing jammed up.

"Hold your fire!" Garret shouted, rolling up onto one knee and taking quick aim.

The woman looked up at the sound of his voice.

"Oh my God!" she said, dropping the rifle. "Thank the stars, it's a *white man*!"

As if on cue, two more heads popped into view.

"Well, Boss," Yakub said, slowly getting to his feet. "Looks like you found *zhee* ladies, eh?"

Garret only nodded, and watched with a scowl as the missing women came pouring out of the shelter.

"You boys look parched," the woman with the gun said. "Come on in. There's a little rock well in here, and the water's hotter n' Hell, but it'll do the job alright. I want to apologize, too, fer shootin' at ye, but we thought that savage had come back fer us."

"A well?" Garret said, looking at Yakub.

"Way station," Yakub said. A place for *zhe* red men to get *vater* before crossing *zhee* desert."

"Where did Kicking Bull go?" Garret said, as they entered the building. A small pile of rocks marked the well opening in the centre of the room, and one of the women started pulling a pair of thick leather thongs out of the hole. Within a minute, a small bowl appeared, full of water.

"He had a message for you, Marshall...." the woman said.

"Garret," he finished. "John Garret."

"Well, Mr, Garret," she said. "He said that he was leaving us here because we weren't no good to him no more. He said you an' a half-breed would be comin', and to tell you that there was no shame in losing to mighty Kicking Bull."

"Oh he did, did he?" Garret said, looking up at Yakub. The man smiled back at him.

"*Ees* got you pegged good, eh?" Yakub said, going for more water.

"Shut up, *Injun*," Garret said, and the half-breed laughed. "I'm going to go after him,"

The women looked at one another, and then put their heads down.

"Aye," Marsha said. "He said you'd want to be knowin' where he went. You'll find him east of here, about a half-day's ride, as the crow flies. He told us you could follow the wagon out, if ye wanted." At this point she stopped, and looked over at Yakub. "And to come alone," she finished.

"*Ees* taunting you now," Yakub said. "*Eee* thinks he'll get you out in the open like that, cull you off and make it a fair fight."

"He wants it, he's got it," Garret said. Yakub began to say something, but he quickly held his hand up to stop the man from speaking. "I need someone to stay with the women anyway," he said quickly. "I'll leave you with some of the canteens. If I don't come back by morning, assume I'm dead and get these women out of here."

Garret climbed up into his saddle.

"Here," he said, tossing down a small pouch to the man.

Garret opened it up and spilled a handful of gold coins into his palm.

"Boss?" he said, looking up at the Marshall.

"Your pay," Garret said, smiling. "And an extra fifty dollars, if you'd be so kind as to take these lovely ladies with you back to civilization."

"I woulda done it for free, Boss," Yakub said. "You don't have to pay me to do *zhe* right thing."

"I know it, half-breed," he said. "That's why I hired you. I figured you weren't the kind of red skin that would cut my throat in my sleep."

"I never said I *vouldn't* do zhat," Yakub said, grinning. "You just have to give me a decent reason to do it, first."

"Right," Garret said. He tipped his hat, and then turned the horse around. "See you in two days." With that, he clicked the horse's sides, and set off into the sand to the east.

It was easy to follow the wagon trail in the dirt, the weight of the vehicle left a pair of heavy lines that stretched out as far as he could see. Garret rode the horse for a couple hours and then decided to walk the rest of the way. He still had to plan on getting back, and the poor beast was already soaked in sweat.

Toward dinner time Garret started smelling smoke in the air. It smelled sweet, like burning spices and something else he couldn't place, and as he walked further the smell got stronger. He came up on the cusp of a hill and saw black smoke in the distance.

"There you are, Kicking Bull," Garret said aloud. "But what the Hell are you doing out here?"

He took a step and then nearly tripped. When he looked down he saw that he'd uncovered the lip of a long flat strip of bricks under the sand.

More adobe mud, out here in the middle of nowhere.

Garret looked at the wagon marks in front of him, and, sure enough, they continued across the narrow platform buried in the sand.

An ancient Anasazi road, but leading to where?

"Well, Kicking Bull," he said, stepping up onto the road, "where you go, I go."

Garret followed the road for a good quarter mile. He came to the lip of a canyon, and the road continued on. It wound its way down to the bottom several hundred feet below. From here, however, Garret could see why the road had been made.

He was standing on the lip of a ghost town.

Hundreds of little Anasazi mud huts dotted the walls of the canyon, like tiny wasp nests piled on top of each other. The stone here was red with clay, and whatever river had once carved this massive swath out of the earth had long since gone underground.

The bottom of the gorge held a few more adobes, and Garret saw the wagon parked far below him against the wall. Near the centre of the town, a lone figure stood looking up toward Garret and his horse. At the man's back was a huge bonfire, the source of the spiced smoke.

Kicking Bull waved up at Garret. Garret unclasped his gun loops. Then he got on his horse and started down to meet the man in person.

Garret left his horse with the other two that were hitched to the wagon and began the slow walk into the centre of town. That uneasy twang he'd first felt at the edge of the desert was back in full force now. There was something odd about the Anasazi settlement.

Something ugly.

The shadows cast here seemed a little too long, perhaps, due to the angle of the sun and the depth of the canyon itself.

It was more than that, though. The shadows seemed *wrong*. Wrong colour, wrong length, and facing the wrong direction.

"*Hey Lawman!*" Kicking Bull yelled. "No need to be scared! Kicking Bull will protect you!"

Garret walked up to within a hundred feet of the man before he spoke. Kicking Bull was standing shirtless, his body painted with chalk and charcoal. Black patches covered his eyes and in the hollows of his body.

He was painted to look like a skeleton.

"You're under arrest, Kicking Bull. For murder and

kidnapping. Come with me quietly and you'll get a fair trial."

Kicking Bull threw his head back and laughed.

"A fair trial?" he snorted. "I hardly think so, Lawman. No red man has ever received a fair trial at the hands of a white judge."

"It doesn't matter what you think, Kicking Bull," Garret said, putting his hands out helplessly. "You killed four officers when you left town. You took five women hostage and brought them out here. You have to go back and face the judge."

"You know that this place used to be full of people?" Kicking Bull said, crossing his arms and ignoring Garret's charges. "Hundreds of Anasazi, all living in a gash in the earth. Mother opened her flesh to us, and took us in."

"That's interesting," Garret said. "But so what? I don't have time for bullshit, *Injun*."

"My people knew they were blessed," Kicking Bull continued. He swept his arms out to his sides, pointing at the mud houses lining the walls of the canyon.

"It was here in the parched earth that we dreamt our Prophesy, after we had dug deep into the earth for water and shelter. Dug to the very heart of Mother, and began to feel what she felt. Do you know what that was, Lawman?"

Garret shook his head but remained silent.

"She felt hurt, and she was sad," Kicking Bull said, his voice rising. "She couldn't understand why the white men who came would kill and rape and hurt so many of her beautiful red people. Red, like the clay itself. Like the blood of Mother." At this point he paused, and stared hard at Garret.

"Just like our blood, Lawman," he said.

He turned then, and let out a howl over the fire. It was the sorrowed cry of a coyote, and it echoed off the walls of the canyon, giving off the effect of several voices crying out at once.

"My people were given a Prophesy, here, on this spot where you and I now stand. We were given a very special gift from Mother, and in return we gave our lives to keep it. Over three hundred proud Anasazi, one by one, opening themselves up to feed those who live like cocoons in the shadows of our Great Mother. *Those who thirst.*"

He stopped then, as the words sank in to the Marshall.

"What are you saying?" Garret said. "You're telling me that your whole tribe committed suicide?"

"Suicide is giving your life away because it holds no meaning for you," Kicking Bull said, shaking his head. "This was death with a purpose. It was glorious."

"You're full of Kicking *Bullshit*," Garret said, nodding in disbelief. "*And* you're about out of stalling time. I want to get back to your hostages before it gets too dark to see."

"Don't worry about that," Kicking Bull said, suddenly smiling. "In a few moments, you are going to see everything so clearly. That's why I brought you out here, John Garret."

"What in the Hell are you on about now?" Garret said. He wanted to get out of the canyon. The shadows seemed to be growing by the minute, almost reaching out toward him.

"You are going to be the Chronicle for the end of your people," Kicking Bull said. "You will be as I was. You will witness the end, and live to tell about it."

"Ok," Garret said, drawing one of his guns. "I think I've

heard about enough of your creepy bullshit, Mr. Mumbo Jumbo. Now, we're going to saddle up this wagon and get back to those women you stole from town, and then tomorrow we're going to head out of this goddamned desert."

"The women are of no consequence," Kicking Bull said. "I only took them to make sure you came after me. I needed you out here so you could begin your new duty."

"Don't make me kill you, Kicking Bull," Garret said.

"Deliver me, Lawman, so that I may complete my journey and bring vengeance on the white devils that make Mother cry." He put his hands out to his sides, challenging Garret to shoot.

"You're God-damned crazy, you know that?" Garret said. He walked up toward Kicking Bull but stopped about ten feet away. He drew his second pistol.

"Shoot me, Lawman. Strike me down so that the Parched Earth may feed. Let the Old Ones taste the last of the red children, and know that it is time!"

"This is your last warning," Garret said, levelling both pistols at the man's chest.

"Kill me, Lawman. *Where I go, you go.*"

"I'll see you in Hell then," Garret said, and pulled both triggers. The Colt Peacemakers roared in unison and two black holes appeared inches apart on Kicking Bull's chest.

Kicking Bull looked down and smiled. For a second Garret fought the insane idea that the bullets hadn't harmed him, that there really *was* something to his crazy Indian fantasy, but then Kicking Bull coughed bright blood and collapsed onto his hands and knees.

"It didn't have to be like this, Kicking Bull," Garret said, lowering his guns.

"It had to be exactly this way," Kicking Bull spat. Twin streams of blood were pumping from the holes in his chest. A double lung shot; the blood was bright and frothy, full of oxygen.

It poured out into the shadows beneath Kicking Bulls body....

And that's when the horses began to scream.

Garret spun around, and as he did, he suddenly had a sense of vertigo, like he was spinning much faster than he could register.

It wasn't him though; it was the shadows in the gorge.

Those long, ugly, out of place shadows that made Garret so uneasy were now moving. They were getting longer, and blacker, and mixing together as they made their way toward Kicking Bull.

Beneath the Indian, the bone dry earth was greedily lapping at the blood Kicking Bull was offering to it.

Garret raised his pistols once again.

"*What the Hell are you doing?*" he shouted. His voice sounded dull in the coalescing shadow-mass in the gorge. The very sun seemed to dim over the lip of the canyon, as the black shadows pouring out of the huts along the walls of the canyon darkened the sky.

Kicking Bull collapsed, face first onto the shadow-mass beneath him.

He began to wither as soon as his flesh came in contact with the shadow, and Garret watched as blood started streaming out of the Indian's body. It looked like Kicking Bull was shitting and pissing blood, vomiting it through his mouth and nostrils, and weeping long strands of bloody tears out of his eyes. The blood streamed from his body into shadow-space and vanished.

Within moments, Kicking Bull had been reduced to a mummified husk.

The creature wasn't finished though.

It licked at the leathered flesh on Kicking Bull's body, reducing the oils in his skin tissue until the skin itself began to flake off as scaly dust. It sucked the juice from his bones, hair and nails, rending them into sand.

Here and there chunks of pink meat still held on to what little water they could, but the shadow form quickly melted through fat and tissue until, less than a minute after it had begun, Kicking Bull was nothing a pile of fine ash.

Garret turned and puked.

His vomit was dust before it hit the ground. The shadow mass sucked at what little meat and partially digested corn it contained; it sucked up the bile and water that had been sloshing around inside his belly.

That's when Garret noticed he was surrounded by a black lake.

He looked back toward the wagon. The horses were gone. The wood on the bottom of the wagon had collapsed on itself; with all traces of water sucked out of the wooden wheels that had simply turned to dust. As Garret watched, more of the wagon disappeared.

"Sweet Jesus," Garret whispered. He dropped his guns at his feet and forgot about them.

The shadows began to boil around him.

There was nowhere for him to go. There was nothing

he could do. He was completely surrounded by roiling, boiling shadows. The air itself seemed dry as parchment; even the sweat from his body and the water in his breath disappeared into the black mass of shadows around him. His lips parched, and cracked, and even his blood seemed sluggish and devoid of moisture.

Then, in front of him, a pathway began to melt away. Back, toward the Anasazi road he'd taken into the canyon. Within moments, a five foot path had been cleared for him.

Apparently, he was free to go.

Garret wasted no time. With the tar-like shadows bubbling and boiling fiercely all around him, Garret ran blindly to the edge of the canyon and up the winding road.

He made it to the top, gasping for air and clutching at his parched throat, his sanity badly lagging behind him.

He turned then and looked down into the floor of the Anasazi village.

It took him a moment to comprehend what he was looking at.

Then he began to shriek.

Taken From the Daily Telegraph, October 22, 1836:

...In other news, a lawman by the name of John Garret was found after he apparently walked out of the desert minus his horse, guns, and sanity. The man was horribly dehydrated and burnt from being in the desert for as many as eight days, and was suffering from a terrible case of heat-shock.

The lawman, who had been hunting for a savage named Kicking Bull (wanted for committing the heinous crime of murder four times and the kidnapping and assumed rape of five white women from the area) claimed that he had been to an ancient Anasazi village and seen the face of the devil in the shadows of the parched desert earth.

A company of Army Regulars were dispatched to check out the lawman's claims that he had left the women holed up in an Indian way station in the desert with his half-breed scout. The company, some sixty men in total, has as of yet not reported and is considered long overdue.

In the morning, another company will be sent out to look for them. Meanwhile, Marshall John Garret is recovering in hospital and is expected to make a full recovery....

Black Water

"Can I sleep with you, Mommy?"

I open my eyes at the sound of his voice. He's standing in the doorway holding his Curious George doll. He's got it in a headlock close to his body, like a shield meant to keep the dark things away.

I look at the monkey's twisted neck against Danny's shoulder. I know the poor thing can't breathe, the way its mouth sags with its black monkey tongue sticking out. I believe you can always tell how much a person loves something by the way they cling to it.

"Go away, Danny," I say to myself, more than to him. Tears well in my eyes.

"I love you, Mommy," he says softly. "I want to protect you."

"Go home," I say, sobbing into my arm. I don't want to look at that perfect face. I don't want to see his eyes.

"I love you, Mommy," he says again, and I hear him walk into the hall.

"I love you too, my Angel," I whisper. It takes hours of crying before I wear myself out and fall back asleep.

"Jesus Christ, Anne," Denise says when she sees me. "You look terrible."

"Thanks so much," I say, giving her a smile. "I'm really glad you're my sister."

"I'm worried about you up here by yourself," Denise says over coffee and cake. "John thinks it would be a good idea if you came and spent some time with us. As much time as you want; you would even have your own room. It would be like when we were kids."

"Thanks, but no," I say, reaching for another piece of chocolate spice. "I'm fine here. I've got my garden; I can't just up and leave it."

"It's not right, Anne," Denise says, flashing a scowl. "After everything you've been through, you should be around people you love. You could use some help taking care of yourself. Family ain't a four-letter-word, you know."

"It's a six-letter-word," I say, running my hands over the stains on my dress and trying to stay jovial. "Besides, I'm fine. This old shell is just a little musty, that's all." I hate the speeches. I hate the concerned looks, the 'Oh you poor baby' sentiments.

"Whatever. You shouldn't be alone right now," Denise says.

"I have a clean bill of health," I tell her. "And I intend to make the most of it. This is my home, and this is where I plan on staying. Now do you want coffee, or am I going to have to drink another pot by myself?"

Baby blue water melts off the sand, and I watch crabs scuttling around in the tide pools. I crush their tiny shells with my toe. I pray for some peace. I look at the black water farther out and pray for a miracle, but I won't hold my breath.

"Are you sad, Mommy?" Danny says from behind me. The soft breath of his voice makes me shudder.

"I'm not sad, Angel," I say, not daring to turn and look at his face. "You shouldn't be here. The doctor told me not to listen to you."

"But why?" Danny says. I can hear the sadness in his voice. I shouldn't be speaking to him.

"Go home, Danny," I say, closing my eyes.

"I don't want to," he says sharply. "It's dark and I can't breathe. Do you like it out there, Mommy?"

"No, I don't," I say to him. "And I know you don't like it. But you have to go or else they'll put me back in that room with the strap-down bed."

"But it's so black out there, Mommy," Danny says, whining.

"Go home, Danny," I say again, and control my breath until he is out of earshot. Then I let it out in hitches.

The flowers in my garden have never looked more beautiful. It is part of my therapy, my doctor says. It will help with the guilt. It will help with the thunderstorms that go off behind my eyes.

He also tells me that Danny won't come back if I stay focused on my flowers, like the daffodils that stand high and proud or the marigolds that shine like painted suns on canvas.

He tells me a lot of things, like how it wasn't my fault. I'm not so sure. I think that you can tell how much a person loves a child by the way she clings to him.

I loved Danny very much.

Like this garden, I tended to his every need. When he was thirsty, I made sure he drank. When he was hungry, I fed him.

After the accident, my psychiatrist said I had a hard time telling what was real and what was fantasy. I was making things up as I went along, not paying attention to the real world. I curled up inside my shell and hid in the black water.

Danny wasn't really there. He was a defensive mechanism to help me cope with the guilt.

For a little while I believed him.

"When is the last time you cleaned up around here?"

Denise asks when she comes to the house. It may have been weeks, I'm not sure. I certainly don't want to tell her that.

"I was just getting around to it," I say instead. She purses her lips together, like she's just bitten into a lemon. I want to hit her.

"Really, Anne. What's going on here?" She bunches her hands into fists the way our mother used to.

"What?" I say, rolling my eyes at her. "Nothing, I swear. I've just fallen a little behind on my housework. Help me find the cookies, will you?"

"The house is disgusting," Denise says, shaking her head. "Are you relapsing?"

"No, I am not relapsing," I say, mocking her only the way a younger sister could. "Truth is I've been spending so much time in the garden that I haven't really been paying attention to him."

"Anne?" Denise says, turning to me.

"Yes?"

"Who exactly, is him?"

"I love you, Mommy," Danny says. I know his words are true. I can feel him like warm sunshine on my back. The doctor was wrong, I think. Nothing that feels this good could be bad for me.

We're standing in the garden together, surrounded by fat tulips and moist red roses. The air is thick with flies and the sweet nectar of blooming beauty. The marigolds beam up at us from our knees. I am truly happy here.

I don't think the doctor ever really believed Danny would come back to me.

Everyone says that he died that day at the beach, when we were swept out into the deep water with the tide. The water was black, and I remember being afraid. I curled my toes and pulled my feet up underneath me while we held each other.

You can tell how much a mother loves her son by the way she clings to him.

I know Denise never believed. When they found me with Danny's body in the cellar she looked as the others did. He was still wearing his best suit from the funeral. I was still wearing my best clothes, too, although they were much dirtier than his.

They put me in the hospital after that.

"Danny's dead," the doctor told me. "That isn't him, that's just his body. We have to bury him because he's just a shell." He had no idea how right he was.

When I held him close and put my ear to his tiny swollen mouth I could hear more than the roar of the ocean surf. I could hear him, just like on that day, when I was afraid of the black water and my Danny was my shield.

"Mommy, you're choking me…."

There are many shells in my garden now.

They line the flower bed, and when I put my ear to their mouths I hear more than ocean surf. I hear all their little voices crying out, asking for parents who will never hear them again. I stroke their waxen faces and kiss their black lips. I cling to them until they aren't afraid anymore. You can tell how much a mother loves her children by the way she clings to them. They cling right back.

They all love me, and they will never leave me alone in the black water again.

The Tongue Child

Every day Brahm races the sun and loses; it's the night where he makes the most ground. Come morning the sun is hot on his back. At dawn the race begins anew. He rides hard and stops only when the horse verges on collapse.

If he had the choice, he would feed on anger and willpower and not stop until he reached the sea. But he can't. Many days of riding are still ahead of him. He prays that he can keep it together for that long.

When he stops thinking about his rage he begins thinking about his lust to feed, and the wracking pains begin again.

The land he rides through is ruined. The heretics he follows sweep across it like a human grass fire, consuming tree and leaf and grass and feasting on animals and men. And women. And children. They have been touched by their Dark God to become one with him, led by *The Tongue Child*; and he has granted them the lunatic need to kill and bite and chew beyond all reason. Now Brahm himself feels the call of The Tongue Child, like a rope pulling out from his loins and drawing west, ever west.

It truly is like riding into Hell.

Brahm shakes his head. No, not riding *into* Hell.

He left Hell behind when he decided on this suicide mission. This place, these people—the *Cult of The Devourer*—these were things that Hell feared when the coals of the fire ebbed low and the crushing dark of the world seeped in. No, Hell was what they'd done with his beloved Melina, and Hell was what they had done to *him*.

He comes upon a crested hill overlooking a ruined village and gets off his horse so he can walk it through town. He has no desire to help any that might live; he knows in his heart there could be no survivors where the Cult of The Devourer has swept through. Only feasts and recruits. Far away, in a temple carved from the very cliffs that held the ocean at bay, his new God waits for him. The love it gives is insatiable.

Like Melina. Like Brahm himself.

Still, he has no wish to be slain with an arrow as he

rides past, should there be a survivor among the husks of buildings and the bones and gristle of the town left to feed the dogs of the world. Dogs with names like *Time*, and *History*. It seems as though everything has an appetite. Brahm is no different.

Instead he draws his black iron blade and steps carefully among the smouldering ruins. The bones of the villagers lay in tangled heaps. Every bone has been gnawed upon. The Cultists have been too desperate with their feeding to bother cooking their meat. Brahm knows the feeling. Only a stubborn streak as wide as the Infernal Abyss in Brahm's heart keeps his willpower in check. He gives the piles of bloody bones a wide berth. Not because he fears death; in fact he lusts after it with nearly the same drive that now feeds his hunger.

He gives them a wide berth because they make his mouth water, and he doesn't want to tempt himself into a cannibal feast. He stubbornly kicks away a baby's torn skull. In their need for meat the heretics have scooped out the grey paste of the infant's brain and sucked the wounds clean.

His stomach growls. Brahm grits his teeth. He will not become them. He will not become *Melina*.

It had been a town like this where Brahm encountered the Cult of The Tongue Child. He and Melina were riding north, following their whim and Melina's fancy. Until that night her fancy had been to travel to the hills of the Northern Mountains and visit old friends; travelling companions who had settled with their clans or started families. Brahm cared for neither, but he loved the brown-haired warrior and would follow her anywhere. They had taken to sleeping in the stables to be near their horses. They mated on a horse blanket then fell asleep. The hay took their heat and held it, and it gave it back slowly as they slept.

Brahm awoke to screams, and the smell of fire.

There was chanting outside, the call of the dying to the already dead. Mothers screaming for children, husbands screaming for wives. Brahm left his clothes and grabbed only his iron blade. A moment later Melina was at his side.

Raiders poured into the village from the south , as Brahm and Melina had done. Filthy, savage men, their clothes ripped and soiled, their eyes rheumy and thick with lunacy. They decorated their bodies with some kind of white paint, and over their pale flesh they bore painted mouths and yellow demon eyes. They shrieked and screamed incessantly; they threw lit torches and jars of oil into the thatch huts of the village that caused fire to spread and feast and *devour—*

Brahm's stomach growls angry curses and stabs him from inside. He moves a little quicker, away from the stray flesh that lay so temptingly close. Away from the desire to sit and chew and swallow with abandon, until his guts can hold no more and he splits apart like peeled fruit.

A movement, to his left. Brahm is so wrapped up in his musings and his stomach that he nearly misses it. He pushes away from the horse and draws his blade with a single movement, then turns and crouches to face his foe.

It takes a moment for Brahm to realize the thing before him is a woman.

She comes from the ruined shell of a mud and thatch

hut, bearing an axe and limping blindly out toward where Brahm stands. Not toward Brahm though.

He can see what her target is from the angle of her head; the way her eyes rake hungrily over the equine body standing behind him. She is after his mount and dragging the bloody stump of a foot behind her. Brahm raises his blade and moves to intercept.

She is just a woman; not a warrior. She has no knowledge of the bronze axe she wields; Brahm easily slides his blade under her arms and into the underside of her chin. Her throat splits like a peeled grapefruit, revealing juicy red meat beneath her pale rind. She spurts hot, spicy blood in three great leaps from her throat before falling to her knees. The axe forgotten, she clutches one hand to the hideous wound Brahm has so easily caused. Perfect and mortal. With her other hand she tries to claw her way to her chosen target; Brahm's horse. Her teeth bite and chew and make a clapping noise as they smash together.

Even in death the need to feast outweighs all others; such is the touch of the The Tongue Child. Brahm can feel it inside his own body. A gorging, all encompassing urge. Like breath. There is mercy in this death, to be sure. Leaving her to live through this hunger would be pointlessly cruel.

Brahm looks at his horse. He tightens the grip on his blade.

It *is* a delicious looking thing. The flanks of the beast are heavy with muscled flesh, hot and bloody. Brahm can sense the ecstasy that awaits were he to just lean out and bite into that inviting flesh....

No. He cannot stop and eat his horse. And he will absolutely not give in to the second, abhorrent craving that comes in under the smell of horse meat. It darts around his senses like a fish swimming unnoticed under the clear surface of a lake. *He will not feast on the heretic at his feet,* though it lies ripe for the picking and leaks fresh blood into the earth. Instead, he will heed the call of The Tongue Child and continue west. Always west. The God laps at his mind like a thirsty dog drinking water.

He grits his teeth. Forces vulgar thoughts from his head. It firms his resolve. He mounts his succulent meal and rides the rest of the way out of the village. He does not care if he is ambushed again. He has to get away from the kind of temptation that woman is offering, before he does something that taints his soul forever. Before he becomes like *Melina.*

The road is a bed of dust and gore. The cultists have left a trail, not caring who follows now. Instead of footprints and shadows Brahm marks the miles in fingers, lost ears, bits of flesh no longer recognized. A scrap of tan skin from a man's cheek. A bit of thick curled hair attached to a tender, bloody fold. He finds burnt teeth embedded in a scorched tree trunk. The bark has been stripped off and eaten. Animals as well, eaten down to gnawed bone. At a crossroads he notes desperate fingers have dug the mud out from under a deer carcass in order to eat what blood has fallen there. The bones are cracked and split. The marrow sucked out of the thicker ones. They are just empty bloody holes filled with ants and beetles now. Delicious.

He chews through the leather straps on his horse as he rides.

His fifth day on the road Brahm sees smoke on the horizon. He tastes the dirty brine of the sea with every breath and knows that his goal is near. The road leads to a fishing village, but he doesn't take it. Instead he veers off the path and follows the gore trail left by the cultists as they made their way along the cliffs. He does it because The Tongue Child wishes it; because the Demigod calls to its servants. Brahm's famine lust is proof of his servitude.

When night falls he makes a cold camp away far away from the village. The ocean roars at him from its prison cliffs and begs to be set free. He sits in the dark and listens. The sound is the voice of raw nature. Melina made the same noises in battle, and in bed.

It had been a momentary shock, witnessing the carnage first hand, and the pause to absorb the scene had very nearly killed them both. A stumbling, feral-eyed cultist with blood running from his mouth like an open wound made a grab for Brahm and caught him in his claws. He punched the man in the face with his sword hand, smashing his nose. The attacker reeled back, and that was all the time Brahm needed to recover. His black iron blade came in fast, invisible in the night air, opening a line on the man's chest between the painted demon eyes and painted savage mouths. *A real opening,* along the man's rib cage.

The wound instantly puckered and smiled, then vomited a mass of blood. He staggered, clutching at his chest. Brahm raised his weapon for a killing blow, and then stepped away from the raider in disgust. The man was cupping *his own blood* in his hands and lapping at it like a dog.

There was no time to spend on it.

A wall of savages collapsed on them, and in the heat of battle Melina and Brahm were separated. Brahm's iron sword grew hot with the blood of his enemies in a feast of its own. The pale raiders charged blindly into battle, with little thought of strategy or defence. Brahm cut them down where they stood. Their scabby, worn fingers clawed stupidly at empty air even as he cut their limbs from their bodies.

And then above the din of battle and the cries of pain and the starving wails of the raiders he heard Melina call to him. It sent him over the edge. His blade sang of death to the men around him. Wailing and screaming in harmony, they blindly threw themselves on his weapon until he was the only one standing among a litter of corpses.

But Melina was on the ground in the middle of the village, and there was a man with a long black cloak draped across his shoulder squatting beside her. He had his hands on the sides of her head. As Brahm looked on the man leaned down and muttered something to her. She let out a wretched scream and convulsed on the ground beside him.

Brahm sprinted toward them, sword high. The battle lust pumping in his veins demanded a penance. By God Brahm would pay it. If the raiders wanted to feast, he would serve their own hot flesh to them and force them to wash it down with his vengeance.

He sprinted into the man's waiting arms, swinging his blade with enough force to fell a sapling. Surely it would have been enough to drive two halves of the man's painted body to separate graves.

Had he been there.

He turned at the last moment, spinning to the side of Brahms swing. The raider reached out and grabbed Brahm's sword arm and used Brahm's own leverage against him. Brahm fell hard to the ground, driving his face into the earth. The raider twisted Brahm's sword arm as he fell, and the blade flew harmlessly from his hands. Brahm hadn't yet drawn a breath and the man was on his back, pinning him fast.

Brahm opened his eyes. The man on his back grabbed his face and roughly straightened his head. At first he thought the man had meant to snap his neck, but then his brain registered dark spots on each of the man's palms and his mind forgot all about broken necks or finding a way out of the position he was in. All he could think was *by the Gods there are* mouths *in his hands.*

"*Feast,*" the man on his back said to Brahm. His voice was wet. Meaty. The voice of lunacy. The voice of The Tongue Child.

The man clamped his hands over Brahm's ears, and his mind was filled with a billion yellow eyes like stars in the sky, and a million starving mouths chewing and biting. Not all of them chewed and slobbered though. Many of them whispered lunatic truths that twisted and soured Brahm's mind like a lemon dropped in hot milk. Brahm screamed, but the screams were far away. They belonged to someone else now.

It is blue morning and the warrior can't sleep. The Tongue Child is near, he feels it with every hungry pore in his body. The desire to feast has been growing in him with each passing mile. Now the wet lip smack of a million chewing mouths revisits him when he closes his eyes for even a moment. He doesn't know what he will find when he reaches the temple by the sea. He spends his time sharpening his blade and pulling the straps from his horse.

He slaps it on the flank and sends it away. It doesn't go far. Brahm can see it in the pre-dawn light, milling about and sniffing the ground looking for grass. He leaves everything but his sword at the cold camp. Should anyone stumble across it, they are welcome to his meagre things. He knows he will not return from this. He doesn't wish to.

As the sun lightens the sky to the east, Brahm starts off. He arrives at the very lip of the cliff, where the salt breath of the ocean is strongest. Here it carries the tang of blood with it, and looking down some two hundred feet Brahm sees blood on the shore below. He is directly over the Temple now, carved out of the very rock itself. A holy place. A terrible place. There are no stairs. The voices in his head tell him to scale the cliff face, which he does.

He clings to the jagged rock of the cliff as the wind batters him with salt foam that stings his eyes. The ocean air whistles by him, pushing up from the bottom of the cliff face as though Neptune's own breath was trying to push Brahm back onto solid ground.

This close to the Temple, however, other Gods are impotent. Despite the howling fury of Neptune's wind, Brahm scales the cliff without incident and finds himself standing in front of an unremarkable doorway. It is carved over twenty feet high and half as much wide. It's dark inside, but cold hands of utter dread place themselves on his back and gently push him in. He draws his sword and carefully ascends the slime covered steps leading into the temple. The slime ends on a high tide line near the top of the steps and Brahm covers the ground quickly. He is being called, after all, and he has no intention of disappointing.

Once inside, Brahm loses all sense of daylight. He puts a hand out to touch the sand carved walls. His fingers pass over ancient murals; sacred texts. He feels the shape of symbols and words in languages long forgotten. The hallway continues for a time, hundreds of feet maybe, and Brahm becomes aware of a gentle slope upward in the orientation of the floor.

There are other things about the floor he notices as well: the fact that he occasionally steps on something slimy or crunchy, and that the smell of blood seems to be coming from the rock the temple is carved from. The walls feel moist to the touch, but he tells himself that he feels salt water from the ocean, and not the bloody charnel tube his mind is creating in order to horrify him.

Eventually there is a dim light at the end of the hall. Something akin to birth, and Brahm quickens his pace. There are stairs leading into an antechamber, and he takes them carefully. They are as slick as the walls. And black.

The room he enters is well lit with torches. It is an egg shaped dome with a staircase at the far end. There is a bloody smear from the hallway to the stairs that looks like the footprints of hundreds of dirty feet. The walls of the room are painted black and sparkle in the torchlight from thousands of yellow diamonds. Every constellation in the night sky is represented; every dim star has its own corresponding yellow diamond. It's breathtaking in its beauty, and Brahm stops to admire the walls in spite of the hunger and the pull to the centre of the temple. He grabs one of the torches from a sconce on the wall and takes a closer look.

They *are* diamonds. Brilliant yellow ones. But they're not stars. They're *eyes*.

Brahm has seen them before. It's suddenly hard to draw

enough breath. He pulls away from the walls to the centre of the room, turning slowly on his heel and watching as the thousands of glittering eyes reflect the torchlight back at him. It's too much. It's mouthed hands over his ears all over again. All that's missing is the sound of smacking lips multiplied by infinity.

And then he realizes he *can* hear the sound of chomping, slurping mouths and he needs to get out of the room. The Tongue Child calls from the stairway and he heeds the call. Sword in one hand, lit torch in the other, Brahm follows the bloody trail on the floor and descends the staircase.

The stairs are gently sloped and go on for more than a hundred feet. Brahm's skin crawls and prickles as the air grows warmer with every step. By the time he reaches the bottom step he is sweating and breathing hard. Water drips from the ceiling. He feels like he's actually breathing the warm ocean water outside. The room is another high dome, and he shudders when he sees more diamonds reflecting back at him. The room is so large he can't really make out the walls, but a few hundred feet away there is large doorway leading to another room.

His shadow looms across the floor in front of him, but the shape is a wavering nondescript mass. The light of his torch poisons the light from the top of the stairs. Along the floor, the blood path continues into the next room, and the chomping, slurping noises are louder here. Brahm's grip on his blade tightens. He's never wanted anything in his life more than he wants to enter that room, but the rational, thinking part of his brain is terrified at what it might find. Still, this is why he is here; this is why he allowed The Tongue Child's pull to lead him to this spot. He steadies himself, shakes the last of his frayed nerves loose, and strides into the room.

His first thought is *no, this is all wrong.* Brahm had assumed that there would be cultists down here. The torches were lit so people would find their way; the bloody path smeared on the stone floor has led him to this room. Yet when he steps into the yellow torchlight of the smaller domed room he at first thinks he is alone. But not alone. There is a figure squatting over a half eaten corpse on the far side of the room.

In the centre of the room is a raised dais where a small shallow looking stone well has been crafted out of a single piece of marble. It is here that Brahm is drawn. This is the perch from which the God of Feasts whispers to Brahm, drawing him like a fly to a morsel of rotten flesh. The path of blood crosses the room to the dais and then up the stairs to the well, where it ends. Brahm begins the final walk himself. The sound of chewing and slurping flesh from bone fills his ears. There is nothing but the feast; the hunger of The Tongue Child's black need fills him.

Across the room the figure stands from its meal of meat and blood and wipes its mouth with a drooping, waxen hand.

Brahm ignores him. *Come*, he thinks, the thought surfacing from a pond of whispers in his mind. *Come to me. We hunger for you. We need you.*

The man across the room seems to be melting. The flesh on his face is littered with the blind buds of a dozen tiny eyes, and pock marked with as many infant mouths. They suck and smack mindlessly like the foetus in a woman's belly. They are purple and fleshy and extend across his body. His belly is badly distended from feeding; it is clawed with scars where his skin is splitting. Breaking down. Some of the eye buds down here have opened, bleeding tears and looking out from his wax flesh with their blind yellow eyes. His legs are like tree trunks, and his feet are now wide stumps where the flesh of his body is collecting.

Brahm sees none of this. His only thought is of the well.

The man moves across the room to intercept. He walks slowly, his feet more of a hindrance than a help now. They roll and twist with each step, and brittle bones snap as he moves. They're no longer needed. They will never be used to keep a shape again.

Brahm is standing over the well, peering down into its fathomless depths. Staring into the well is like staring into the darkest parts of the night itself; the spaces between the stars where no light will ever touch. It calls to him, pulls him toward it. The well is where he belongs, in the beautiful darkness of the forgotten cosmos. It's as if the stars themselves fear to tread across the inky black void. There is hunger there. A black hole with teeth. What is Brahm but a crumb in the mouth of madness?

"*It'sh beautiful, ishn't it?*" The drooping man says.

"It is everything," Brahm whispers. "Everything from nothing."

"*A paradox,*" the man says. "*That'sh what drawsh ush to it. It is as ancient as it is tremendoush. A being infinitely more powerful than any man. More powerful than any Kingdom. More powerful than even the world. And yet here it ish, all powerful, and unable to crosh the barrier of time and shpace to touch our world directly.*"

"Pure evil has a boundary," Brahm says. He runs his

fingers along the smooth, warm stone of the well's lip and his fingers come away bloody.

"*It'sh not Evil,*" the man says. "*It hash no conshept of Evil. It is an idiot God, a Devourer, and nothing more. It feasts becaushe that is what it* must *do, not because it feelsh hate. It feelsh nothing but hunger. Its eyesh are simply a tool to give direction to itsh mouths. Even with nothing in them, they continue to shlurp and chew. You have heard it. It is the* Call of the Devourer, *the sound that plucksh the strings of our most basic desire and bringsh us to thish spot.... Inside this temple, we consume, and are in turn consumed.*"

"Who are you?" Brahm says. He tears his gaze away from the well and beholds the creature before him for the first time. "How do you know of these dark things?"

"*I was once Eliash. A fisher. I lived ash a mortal. Ash you do now. I lived in the village. I was the firsht. My boat came aground here and I entered the temple sheeking shelter from the rain. Here I heard the sound of the endless feast. Here I answered the call. Eliash is gone now.* I *am the high priest of* The Devourer. *I bring it soulsh and in return am rewarded in kind. That ish the pledge. It hash touched me with itsh* seed, *and I am now berthing myshelf.*"

The drooping man puts his hands up, palms out, and Brahm sees the whispering, slathering mouths that have haunted him since the night of the fire, when Melina became a host to the blind hunger of the creature, the one the man referred to as The Devourer. Brahm staggers back from them, fear reaching through the fog of hunger and jolting him back to his senses.

"*I am He Who Walksh in the Light,*" the man says. "*I am The Tongue Child.*"

"You took her from me," Brahm whispers. "You have infected me and you took her."

"*I have taken many,*" the man says. "*This is my reward for leading the blind to the blind.*"

"That may be," Brahm says. He raises his blade and torch and drops into a fighting stance. "*But she was mine!*"

The drooping, fleshy creature is not expecting an attack. It is at home in its lair, a place it feels indestructible. Those who pass beneath the domes in the vision of the twinkling yellow eyes have not the willpower to fend off the call of this monster from out of the cosmos, and they shuffle like ants in a row to that which their heart most desires. And while they march to the gaping, infinite maws of the Devourer, The Tongue Child has scraped the tastiest morsels off for itself.

But now stands Brahm, with a willpower bordering on the divine, whose battle instincts have been honed to such that they compete with basic instincts like *FEED* and *MATE*. For mighty Brahm, there is only one true instinct: *KILL*.

Brahm flashes the Tongue Child's head with the torch in his hand, causing it to cover its face reflexively. Then he drives the black iron blade of his sword deep into the belly of the creature. Flicking his wrist, he rounds the wound he has caused, and with a flex of his roping muscles he pulls the blade wide. It slices through waxy, fallen flesh and opens a terrible wound on The Tongue Child's belly.

The Tongue Child is confused for the first time. It is not supposed to be wounded. It is not supposed to feel pain. Yet here, this morsel of manhood has caused it both. The creature reaches down and grabs at its belly even as its stomach bursts and a flood of half chewed flesh, blood and bile erupt from the wound.

Brahm leaps back as the creature's stomach comes boiling out of its belly. His feet catch on the stairs and he nearly falls, but he instinctively adjusts to the unsteady ground and retains his balance. He throws the torch to the side and brings up his sword in a two handed stance.

"I...*I'm not shposed to lose,*" The Tongue Child whimpers. It falls to its knees, both flabby hands grasping at its belly wound. Above the sound of the well, the tiny mouths on its body slurp and chew noisily, as hundreds of starving babies put to breast at the same time. The creature is devouring itself, yet seems oblivious to it. "*My God promished I would be with him.*"

"And so you shall," Brahm says. He steps around the slurry of flesh and bile that has erupted from The Tongue Child. The stink is unbearable, but of little consequence. He brings the blade back over his shoulder, reaching high with both hands and then swinging in a whistling arc with all the force he can muster. The black iron sword strikes the soft flesh of the creature's neck, biting deep into meat, melting fat and severing the head cleanly.

The head rolls across the dais splashing sickly dark blood in its wake. The body of the Tongue Child flops forward. It makes one final wet, smacking noise as it slaps against the fleshy stew on the stone floor and then falls silent for all time. Across its body, a hundred little blind eyes cease rolling in their sockets. Its budding, pock marked mouths hang open, lifeless.

The well churns and bubbles as though full of oil, but Brahm simply stands there looking down at the creature in front of him. Slain. And then he looks up, and sees for the first time the form on the floor across the room. The face and upper chest were the final meal of The Tongue Child. There is no mistaking the matt of bright red hair or the silken curve of the hips.

Melina.

Brahm takes the body of The Tongue Child and drops it in the well, saving the head for last. The mass of the creature is too large even for Brahm to handle, in the end he cuts the stinking limbs from the body and drops them in one by one. He saves the head for last. The room fills with the sound of chewing and slobbering, and it pulls at Brahm's heart. It is a weak nostalgia he feels now, however. He has conquered the hold over him and is the master of his own body once again. He wraps Melina's body in the cloak of The Tongue Child and carries her back out to the sea. The wind is gentle now, the caress of an old friend welcoming him home. The sun is beginning to set. Time has no meaning in the Temple of The Devourer.

Brahm collects driftwood and builds a pyre for his love among the stones on the beach. He lights it with a torch he fetches from within the temple and watches it burn through the night. In the morning the sun warms him as he scales the cliff wall. He makes his way back to camp and is surprised to see his horse standing over his things. It nickers at him and walks over to lick his hand, looking for a treat. Brahm smiles at this. Brahm produces some apples from his things. He looks over the food he has packed for himself as the horse eats breakfast but decides against making a meal for himself.

For the first time in weeks, Brahm isn't hungry.

Hell is Repetition

The girl smiles as she passes. Tall, California blonde perfection. I get lost in the way her cutoffs cradle her ass as she walks by, a taste of coconut oil in her wake.

I see her again, a few aisles down. This time, her hair is in a pony tail and she has on a sundress that goes down to her knees. She is looking at a can of peaches, but her eyes drift toward me.

Women always know when they're being stared at.

Twins. I thank the universe for creating two such perfect creatures.

In the ice cream aisle I think *not twins, but triplets!* This one, pale, brown hair cropped to her ears; same face; same beautiful thighs. And not so much as a glance as I walk by. *Is that a wedding band on her finger?* I think it is.

In the fruit aisle there are two more of them, cradling a grapefruit. They giggle at me as I stand there leaning stupidly on my cart. *This isn't right,* I think. *Nothing in nature happens this perfectly, this many times.*

I look down at the rows of identical bunches of grapes in front of me and think, *am I wrong?* As if in response the grapes turn on their stems and cast baleful gazes toward me. Bunches of purple bloodshot eyeballs, jaundiced and milky and full of hate.

Suddenly there isn't enough air in the place. I need to get away. I push my cart toward the teller, but stumble and overshoot the corner. My cart smashes against the apple display, sending red and green fruit flying in all directions. Instinctively kneeling, I grab two identical apples from the floor. One in each hand. They're warm to the touch and beat against my palms. They're not apples. They're hearts with paint on them meant to *look* like apples.

"Let me help you," I hear a woman say. Kind words carried with cruel intent. I look up into cold blue eyes, perfect skin. Blonde. This time she's a stock girl, her hair tied back under a cap. Her eyes are rimed with blood.

"You have to separate the good ones from the bad ones," she says. On her shirt is a small white button that says, "*Imitation is the Sincerest Form of Flattery. Get Used to it!*"

I leave the cart. There is a crowd around me and I plough through them toward the exit. The voices around me are hammer-falls in my chest. Maybe it's just my heart. Or maybe it's the cart of apple-hearts behind me.

I hit the door sprinting, just as it's opening.

I would have run *through* the man coming into the store, but he's quick. He dodges to the side at the last second. My feet tangle and I go flying, hitting my head on the pavement. He's already standing above me.

"Let me help you," he says, his voice dripping malice. I look up into that face. He sees the horror drain the colour from my flesh and gives me a wink.

Suddenly I'm screaming myself raw, until my ears feel like they're going to burst. Madness claws my face with my own hands. He is me.

Oh dear God, he is me.

"Hey," the other me says, smile widening to a familiar toothy grin. But the grin is too wide. Too toothy. There are rows and rows of broken shark teeth in that mouth. I'm looking at a hideous mirror image of myself. But it isn't even a mirror, it's just grey paint. It reflects some small part of me back that I recognize, but most of it is not me.

I'm me. I can tell, because I see myself screaming and raking my face bloody as a reflection in those bulbous, liquid eyes. Eyes the colour of pain. The colour of screams.

"Don't I know you from somewhere?" he says. It is my voice.

Magpie

Rose was watching the rain from the front window when David got home.

She was eating cigarette butts from the ashtray one at a time and staring out the window. He walked over to where she sat on the window chair.

Her fingers were black and greasy. Fine ash lined her lips, and she licked them with her black tongue.

"What are you doing?" he asked, surprised at seeing the ashtray beside her. His first thought was that she was smoking again.

Rose just kept staring out into the rain. Her short hair, dyed black, clung to the sides of her face. She was wearing her favourite short dress and some fishnet stockings.

Her belly was swollen; she couldn't sit properly anymore. The baby was due in three months.

"Hey, zombie. What are you doing? Decide to take up smoking?"

"I'm eating cigarette butts and they taste like shit," she said in an off-handed way. "I think there's something wrong with me. I don't know. I've been craving them all day." There was another pause, as she pulled a wad of soggy brown cotton out of her mouth.

"Your mother called. I think they want us to go to dinner on Sunday. I don't want to go."

"*What* the hell did you just say?" David had begun to take off his jacket but stopped.

"I said I don't want to go." She popped the last two butts into her mouth and ran her wet fingers around the ashtray. Then she started sucking the stray ash off of them.

David grabbed her hand.

"I don't think these are good for you, love." He said quietly. He searched her face for a response, but she was a blank page. It was like staring into the face of a porcelain doll.

"I told you. I think there's something wrong with me." She stuck her tongue out.

The cigarette butts were half chewed and glistening with her spit. David grabbed them before she could pull them back into her mouth. She caught his fingers in her teeth and held them there, briefly, looking up at him with her clear green eyes.

"Wouldn't you prefer something that doesn't taste like ass?" he asked, smiling.

She released her hold, rolling her eyes and shaking her head as she did.

"Fuck you," she said, laughing.

They talked about Sunday dinner while David fixed macaroni and hot dogs (*they really are made out of dogs*, he insisted while they ate.) After dinner, David put on some music and convinced Rose they would indeed go to see her doctor.

She listened to Tool, read her book, and slowly came out of her mood. David put the baseball game on and did the dishes. Eventually Rose came and took him by the hand, and they went upstairs to bed together.

The doctor's appointment was three weeks later. David and Rose caught the bus and sat at the back with the graffiti and high school kids.

They got into the doctor's office, and, surrounded by other pregnant women, waited quietly for the doctor.

David grabbed a handful of Time Magazines but they were both distracted by the cold detached feel of the office. The brown carpet on the floor matched the coffee-cream of the walls and offered nothing of interest. David leafed through his books and thought about Rose and the baby.

He wasn't sure how he felt about meeting his child.

He felt excited, but then he reminded himself of the sad state of their Vic Park apartment. The whole neighbourhood had gone bad. The school down the street had a nine-foot chain link fence to keep the junkies and creeps away from the kids.

Worse still was the fact that some of the houses in the neighbourhood had the same fences around them.

The doctor was a short older woman with a thick German accent and the look of someone who had recently switched to contact lenses from glasses. She went through her usual routine, ear-nose-throat, how are you feeling, how are your bowel movements, and Rose answered each in turn.

Fine, fine, fine. David told the doctor about the cigarette butts and the doctor laughed.

"It sounds like you may have *pica*," the doctor said. When David and Rose said nothing, she went on.

"Pica is a disorder that occurs sometimes in pregnant women. It's Greek for 'magpie,' a bird that eats anything it can get a hold of. Sometimes, for reasons we don't understand, women with babies coming get cravings for things other than food. Some women crave dirt, or soap, or wax, and even hair. We've found that there is a link between iron deficiency, or anaemia, and pica, though that isn't always the case. You have very low blood pressure, though, so I think that may be what we're looking at."

"You're kidding," said David. "You mean low blood pressure did this?" He and Rose exchanged puzzled looks.

"I think with the low blood pressure, we may be looking at pica, yes. I'm going to get you to take some vitamins, which should help with the low levels in your blood. They're slow dissolving, so take one a day with some orange juice, or citrus of some kind. And don't drink any milk or anything dairy for a few hours after you take them. Dairy will slow down the iron absorption into your body."

They thanked her and left, and because the sun was shining they got off the bus early and walked the last few stops home. Rose talked about daytime television and the book she was reading, and after making a quick lunch for both of them David went to work for the afternoon.

The next week Rose was outside on the front lawn watching the traffic crawl through the neighbourhood. She braided her short hair while she sat and made little mental notes to herself in the sunshine.

She was going to clean the house later, if she wasn't too tired, and in the meantime she could sit outside. It was the beginning of July. The baby was due at the end of August.

Cars went by and everyone looked as they passed.

The stares were aggravating; it seemed that everyone who passed made the same judgment: *young mother, young mother, young mother*. They flew past the house, through the school zone and toward downtown. Or they went left to the Stampede grounds.

The destination was always the same: anywhere but here.

The scorched lawns and rotting houses were a strange compliment to the historical buildings and dance bars in the neighbourhood. Each was equally uninviting.

David had told her about the city's plan to level the neighbourhood to make a bigger Stampede ground, and Rose couldn't say she blamed them. Vic Park was a blight in a city of new buildings and constant expansion. It was glaring proof (even more than the homeless shelter) that not *every* street in Calgary was golden.

She looked down at the hole she had been digging with

her finger, then impulsively reached up and put the finger in her mouth.

Rose was sitting in the living room when David got home. He started to ask about the holes in the front yard but stopped when he saw her. Rose was sitting on the couch holding a pillow against her chest.

"What happened?" He dropped his lunch pail and jacket by the door. He immediately went to Rose's side and sat down on the couch.

"I did it again," she said flatly. "I was in the yard eating dirt this afternoon."

"What?" David laughed. "Are you *serious*?"

"It's not funny. I threw up." Her voice was flat, like she was far away.

"I thought the pills were going to fix this," he said, sitting beside her. She turned away.

"I guess they didn't."

"So...." He stopped. "Uhh...I was going to make dinner, but I guess you must be *full*."

"Oh god, what's the matter with you?" Rose said, getting up.

"What did I say?" he called after her.

She slammed their bedroom door in reply.

David shook his head. He walked over to the window where he could see the yard. Among the bald patches and ragweed that made up the front lawn were ten little holes, about the size of Rose's fist.

The next few weeks were relatively quiet. Rose seemed a little bigger every morning, and she started having a hard time getting around. To make it easy, David started making breakfast and lunch for her in the evening before bed, and he'd make supper when he got home from work.

Rose filled in the spaces with snacks, dyed her hair fire-brand red, and stuck to her iron supplements. The doctor kept tabs on her, took regular blood pressure, and told her things were improving.

Early one morning David woke up with a start; Rose had been watching him while he slept.

She was sitting on the floor in her night gown, arms folded tightly in her lap, her hair back with one of those banana clip things making it stick out like tail feathers.

She was hawkish and alert.

"Good morning, Sunshine," he said, rubbing one eye and then running his hand through his hair. His breath was awful; he could feel it on his tongue and teeth.

Rose was quiet. She continued to regard him with strange, glittery eyes.

"What is it?" David ran his tongue over his teeth, and then his lips. Disgusting.

She got up and approached the bed. David smiled up at her.

With one hand she ripped the blankets away. Her eyes ran over the muscle lines on his chest and stomach. There was hunger in those eyes, but David couldn't really tell what she was after. The effect was intoxicating.

His flesh broke out in goose bumps. Gently, he reached out and touched Rosie's hand.

"Good morning," he said again, softly. Rose reached out and ran her fingers along his ribcage, sending tiny electric motes swimming across his belly and toward his spine. His breath caught in his throat, and he smiled up at her.

She let go of his hand, then reached down and pulled her nightgown off.

Her skin was pale and soft, and David noticed again how big her breasts had gotten. So had her belly; the baby was due in a month. Below that, the soft tuft of dark hair spreading out from between her legs. He reached out and gently touched it.

Rose pushed his hand away. She cocked her head to one side, watching him while she pushed up on her breasts. Her pink nipples stood out firm, and her fingers rubbed against them.

David shivered. He was cold almost everywhere except where the heat was throbbing and starved for attention. Rose leaned down, put her hands on his shoulders, then lifted her leg over and straddled him.

He immediately pushed up against her, straining against his underwear and moaning softly.

Rose leaned down and kissed him then, hard, and David could taste Dr. Pepper on her breath. Her tongue darted briefly in and out of her mouth.

He tried to stop her; he knew how bad his mouth must taste, but she ignored him completely.

Slowly, and then with ever quickening movements, she began to lick his tongue, and his lips, running spit on his chin, his cheeks, devouring his kisses.

David sighed and put his hands up, gently caressing the sides of her breasts and running his thumbs over her nipples.

Then he moved his hands down her back and across her ass. In response, Rose thrust herself toward him. David winced.

She was grinding his erection against his cotton underwear, and the friction point under the head of his cock felt like it could tear. He pushed his hips back into the bed, hoping to make a little space.

Rose, in response, suddenly reached down, and with a slight movement released him from his Fruit of the Loom prison. David closed his eyes and smiled; he loved the feeling of being taken out of his clothes, of being freed. It felt like his cock had grown another inch.

She touched him there, briefly, and her hands were cold. He felt like he could melt into her soft hand, he could feel himself filling every line on her hand with his warmth.

And then he was inside her, as Rose pushed herself on him, fully, taking all of him, absorbing him completely.

David moaned.

He reached up to hold her face, but she suddenly grabbed his hands and pinned them at his sides.

David looked up. Rose had cocked her head to one side and was watching him with a kind of fevered obsession that scared him; it was the look of a starving dog when you showed it a steak.

She pushed against his cock, sliding up just far enough to plunge into her deeper still.

Rose began to kiss him again, this time hard, with earnest.

She bit his tongue and his lips, and the rhythmic thrusting of their bodies became a staggered, frantic stabbing motion. She made a harsh grunting sound, digging her nails into David's wrists.

David gasped, suddenly aware that his role in this exchange had changed considerably. He was no longer an equal partner; he was now just along for the ride.

Rose continued to bite him, harder, his ears, his cheek, his neck. She impaled herself on his cock with every thrust, erratic, almost painful.

Almost.

"Easy girl," David said. He tried to bring his hands up to her shoulders, slow her down a bit maybe, so he could enjoy it. He was a little bit worried about the way Rosie's stomach slapped against him and the way she was biting.

Like most men, he liked quick sex and a little kink, and on many levels this was driving him crazy, but it was getting a little bit much for him.

His face was hot where she bit him, and the bite marks on his chest were starting to swell.

Rose moaned loudly and kept biting. She was slick with their sweat, and she clamped her eyes shut as she fucked him.

She bit hard into the left side of his chest, and David yelped.

He looked down and gasped.

Blood was quickly welling up in the little crescent moons her teeth had made. Rose stopped too, looking at the blood. Then she looked back at David and licked her lips. The mixture of spit and blood made her mouth glisten.

He tried to put his arms up, but Rose threw all her weight on top of him. He was too shocked to speak.

Suddenly, she bucked, yelped, and David could feel the tremors start around his erection.

Rosie was coming.

When she came, she thrust her head against his chest and bit into David again.

He shouted a curse and his body tensed. The mixture of pain and the sudden soft, wet heat of Rosie as she shuddered was enough to bring David over the edge.

He pushed against her, feeling his load run through the pipes in his cock and then, release, glorious release, and he couldn't get deep enough inside her—

—and he couldn't be still enough and he suddenly didn't care how hard she bit him as long as he could hold on to his orgasm for just one more second—

—one more moment, breathing in her sweat and her heat, soaking it through her skin as she gasped, breathless, and breathing into his mouth tasting Dr Pepper and smelling her body and the talcum scent of her deodorant.

And then it was over, and he was breathing hard, with his head buried in his pillow, and tranquil peace filled him up as he lay there watching his thoughts recollect in his head.

Rosie leaned down and licked the bloody sweat off his chest, and then, disengaging herself, got up and walked naked out into the living room.

Once there she picked up the phone and quick-dialled the number for her obstetrician.

"Hello, this is Rose Carter," she said, lost and distant.

"Would you tell Dr. Simantra that I'm going into labour, and could she please meet me at the hospital? Thank you."

She hung up the phone and went back to the bedroom.

David was looking at himself in the mirror, inspecting the bite marks on his neck and chest. He was naked, the last remnants of his erection still hanging from him.

"Get dressed," she said, grabbing some of her clothes. "We have to go."

The hospital ride was quiet, although David did ask how Rose was feeling about a hundred times. Each time she stared off, cupped her hand over her belly and replied, "Fine" or some equally useless remark.

Finally, David settled into silence and the pair arrived with the attending nurses waiting for them.

David's mother arrived a short time later. She walked in as Rose was being examined and stood there uncomfortably while the doctor's prodded around inside Rose.

David sent her outside for coffee.

When she came back, Rose was sitting up and reading. She smiled and was polite as she could be, but the pain was getting to her and it was plain on her face.

Finally she fell asleep. David took his mother outside.

"You look like a chew toy," his mother said as soon as they were alone. David rubbed the sides of his neck.

"I know," he said quietly.

"How are you holding up?"

"I don't know," he said. "Last minute jitters, I guess. This seemed so far away, up until a few hours ago. Now the doctor says she could go at any time."

"You're doing great," she said weakly.

"Thanks."

Twenty-two hours later, at a quarter to seven on the morning of October 1st, John Michael Patrick was born to Rose and David.

The baby took David's last name. David was happy beyond belief; he danced in the halls and called Rose's parents while she and the new baby slept.

Three days after the baby was born the new family went home and David went back to work.

The house was a mess, and neither of them got any sleep, but David was happy and the baby, though pukey and whiney, seemed as happy as a baby could be.

A month went by.

One evening when the house was dark and everything was quiet, the phone rang. Rose answered it in the kitchen.

"Hello?"

"Hello, Rose, this is Gladdis. What are you up to?" Rose smiled. It was David's mother.

"I was just sitting here, having a quiet evening. I made soup." She glanced down at the bowl in front of her.

"Good," Gladdis replied. "I was wondering if I could speak to David. He was supposed to call me last week and he didn't. I thought I'd call and give him trouble for it." She finished with a little laugh.

Rose laughed with her. Then her eyes darted over to where David was sitting. His head was lilting off to the right at an awkward angle.

He looked like a dog had mauled him.

Her eyes wandered over his face, where his eyes had burst and his ears had torn off and where parts of his cheek had been ripped away to reveal the bottom row of his teeth.

It was as if his mouth was three times bigger than it had ever been.

She ate a spoonful of soup.

"He's asleep," she said.

Rose dipped her spoon into the soup and slurped some more up. The soup was meaty and greasy, with dark brown gravy.

"Oh? Well, that's too bad. You'll have to get him to call me when he wakes up."

"I'll be sure to do that."

"Oh! While I have you on the phone, I was wondering if maybe we could pop by for a visit this week. David's father is going back out to the oil patch on Monday, and he's going to be gone for a couple weeks. He'd like to see the baby before he goes."

"That sounds great," Rose said. "Come on over. I'll let you taste the soup."

Slurp.

There was a huge pot of it on the stove, simmering away beautifully. The smell of garlic and onions filled the room.

"That sounds delicious," Gladdis said.

Slurp.

"Oh, it *is* delicious."

"So how is the baby, Rosie?"

Rose's smile turned into a soul-shearing grin.

"Delicious," she said happily.

Life with Riley

I love Riley.

It hurts my heart to think of that. It hurts me and I want to lie down and go to sleep so I can dream about her soft wet lips or the way her hips move when she walks. She's a brave girl, she stands up for herself. People stop and listen when she screams and pulls out her hair.

We're so different. A tiger and an elephant in the same

cage, she dances, hisses and spits, while I waddle my fat ass around digging through shit and hoping for peanuts.

Riley holds herself to higher standards. She won't take anything from the man who rattles the cage. She hates him. We all hate him really, except that bitch Lovita.

Lovita loves the feel of his dark matted chest hair against her little breasts. She loves the way he always smells like armpit sweat and whiskey. She makes it bad for everyone when she behaves like that.

Not Riley, though. She's so beautiful and brave. When the man who rattles the cage comes into the room she throws things at him and makes him cry. Once she pretended she was Lovita and got close enough to knee him in the balls and scratch his face up good.

He beat all of us that night, except Lovita. That bitch.

When the man who rattles the cage comes into the room we all get very quiet. I get so sleepy, I sometimes have a nap and dream about whether he's going to talk to Riley or Lovita. I watch from far away; I can barely see them. Lovita plays nice, as always, and Riley spits at him.

A real tiger.

Riley says I have to stick up for myself. I want to, really, but I'm so fat and ugly and tired all the time, and what could I do with that man? I'm afraid of his sticks and his boots.

Yesterday he burned Riley good. Had a lighter, held her up by one paw and just let it go. Riley shrieked and cried as the flames licked her hand and her arm, making it red and purple. She tried to get away. The man who rattles the cage just laughed.

I was far away when it happened. I tried to get back to her, but there was no way. No matter how far I ran I couldn't get any closer to them. Finally, both of us crying, Riley came to me. We lay down and slept on a hilltop surrounded by flowers while Lovita went with that awful man.

I swear I hate Lovita as much as I love Riley. This is all her fault.

Today Riley is sad, and my heart is aching for her. I feel a lump in my throat that chokes me when I look at her wild hair, and the way she's branded herself with scars. Connect the dots, from one cigarette burn to another. She used to laugh and tell me it made a face on her belly. She took a knife and finished it so that it really did make a face. A pig face, I think.

Riley is curled up in the corner now, mewling so softly the others can't hear her. I can though.

"What's wrong?" I say, coming close enough to touch her hair. It feels like it's full of blood, all hard and crusty. She has shit in it too, from lying on the floor.

"Leave me alone, Sam." Riley says, getting up and moving away. She's holding her purple arm tight against her chest. I think she's been licking it.

"Please," I say to her. "I just want to help you. I love you, and I want you to be better."

Riley cackles when she hears those words.

"You really love me?" she says, standing up. "With all your heart?"

"I do," I say, choking on the words. I can't believe I'm admitting it to her, but it hurts so much to see her like that.

"You want to hold me close?" Riley says softly. My heart begins to hammer in my throat as she steps into me.

"Yes," I whisper.

"You want to kiss me, Sam?" she asks, and I nod. I want to kiss her like nothing I've ever wanted in my life.

She leans down to me.

I close my eyes. My whole body is tingling. All my life, I've watched her. Dreamt about her. So beautiful, so angry and cold.

Not to me. Blue fire.

Our lips brush and I gasp. She pulls back for a moment. I open my mouth and I can taste her breath.

That's when Riley spits a big wad of bloody phlegm into my mouth. It hits the back of my throat and I gag immediately, stepping away from her.

"Sam's a dirty girl!" she screams, laughing at me as I lean over and choke. "Sam's a dirty girl! Everyone look at the dirty girl!"

They're all laughing at me. I get down on my hands and knees and vomit on the floor. Riley kicks shit at me and it rolls over my hands.

"*You bitch!*" I scream when I can catch my breath. I stand up, wiping my face with my hands. Riley just laughs.

"You want to touch me, Sammy?" she says, he voice cold and cruel. You're just like that fucker out there. You *are* him, Sammy, you know that? You want to touch my tits and stick your fat fingers in my cunt. Just like he does."

"Stop it, Riley," I whisper. It's all too much, I'm getting so sleepy.

"You're not going anywhere, dirty girl," Riley says then. She reaches out and claws at my arm, leaving an angry red line.

I cry out and pull back to the far end of the cage.

From the other room, where the television is, I hear the man who rattles the cage get up.

"Shut the hell up in there, *crazy bitch!*" he screams, and I shut my fat mouth up.

Riley just smiles.

"Hey, asshole! You're a real big man aren't you?" she screams, stepping past me and rattling the bars on the cage.

"What are you doing?" I say, suddenly in a panic. "He'll come in here, Riley!"

Riley smiles. "I want him to," she says. "Just so he can see what a dirty little girl you are, Sammy. It's *all your fault* we're in here, and now he's gonna see it. You, me, Lovita over there, and the others you never see because they hide. It's you he wants, though, dirty girl. I'm not protecting you anymore. You're a slut. A dirty whore, just like he says and nobody would ever come and save you because you're so fat and ugly and bad."

"I am not," I say, breaking down into tears. It's a feeble defence. I'm so tired right now, why can't I sleep for just a few minutes?

I hear the sound of his stomping boots on the stairs. I can't breathe, I feel like my heart is about to explode.

"*Please, Rileyyyy,*" I whimper, grabbing her arm.

She pulls away from me.

"Fuck you, Sammy," she spits. "Nobody touches me. Ever. You're going to learn that."

"I promise I won't ever touch you again," I cry, pulling back to the back of the cage. I press myself as hard as I can into the corner, try to get as small as my fat ugly body can handle.

The lock on the door rattles outside. I can hear him cursing under his breath.

"Please, God," I whisper. "Let me go away. Let him not see me. Make me invisible so he won't hurt me."

Riley walks back to where I'm crouched. She touches me with her boot while I'm praying. Finally, she speaks.

"You scared, Sammy?" she says in a tender voice.

I nod my head dumbly. I can hear him just outside the room; the lock is giving him trouble again. He kicks the door, and we all jump.

"*I'm gonna rip you a new arsehole, you little bitch!*" he screams. He's a monster.

"You really love me?" Riley asks, looking over her shoulder toward the door.

"Y-yeah, I do," I whisper.

"I'm sorry, Sam," she says, her voice hitching. "I'm so sorry."

She holds out her hand then and I take it. She pulls me up so that our faces are touching. I'm so scared and confused right now. She puts her hand up near my cheek and I flinch. It hurts her, I think, because she coos at me and strokes the side of my face.

The door explodes inward, and the man who rattles the cage comes stomping into the room.

"*You get the hell out here right now, Samantha!*" he screams. Spit is flying off his purple lips as he stalks toward our cage. "*I'll teach you to have a smart mouth!*"

"Shhh," Riley breathes on my face, and then we're holding each other as tight as we can.

"I love you too, Sam," she whispers, and kisses me. Her lips are so soft and hot, and I feel myself melting inside. I want this to last forever.

The man who rattles the cage kicks at the door to our little box. Then he grabs his key ring and starts sorting through the pile. There are many keys on that ring. They jingle when he walks around.

Riley pulls me away, and then she looks right into my eyes.

"Sleep now, pretty Sammy bird," she says. Something my mother used to call me. "You go to sleep and dream something nice for us."

I shake my head, no. "I want to stay with you! I want to be with you!"

"You can't be with me now. I'll be back later though, and then we can take a nap on the hill together, and Lovita can sit in this awful cage for a while. Won't that be nice?"

I want to say that it *would* be nice, but I can't. The cage door is opening, and I'm suddenly so tired I can barely move.

"I love you, Sammy," she whispers, gently laying me down.

"I love you, Riley," I say, "Come back soon."

Riley smiles and tousles my hair. Then she spins, just as the cage door flies open.

"Hi, Daddy," she says, her voice sugar sweet.

"Don't give me that shit, you ugly little bitch," he says, his breathe coming out in hot steam. It smells like rotten eggs. "What the fuck did you call me?"

"I called you a lot of things, I can't remember them all." Riley says, smirking.

"Oh, is that right?" the man says. "We'll just see about that, won't we? Looks like Samantha forgot what happens when she talks back to Daddy, didn't she?"

"Fuck you!" Riley screams. The man who rattles the cage grabs her by the hair and yanks her out onto the floor. Then he stomps on her burned hand, making her shriek.

I keep watch from the back of the cage, too tired to move. It feels like a dream.

Riley looks back at me then, and breaks into a bloody smile.

"I love you, Sammy Bird," she mouths to me.

And then she's gone. The man who rattles the cage wraps his fingers in her crusty hair and drags her out of the room. I can hear her screaming my name as she goes down the stairs, one at a time.

I close my eyes and dream something nice for when Riley comes back.

Hard Time

I'm standing naked in a little box waiting for the end to come.

I'm done screaming.

I've smashed my hands against a door until my knuckles cracked and bled. The lights are out; it's pitch black in here.

Fitting, I guess. I'm pretty sure I don't want to see Eddie when he gets here. Let me stay in the dark. It'll be easier.

Amazing how bad things can get in such a short amount of time, isn't it?

Eddie was a little guy, one of those wiry, paranoid little fucks that crawl into prison prayin' to God that nobody takes a notice of them. He'd seen too many movies about prison sex. Don't drop the soap. Don't take cigarettes from anyone.

Cover your ass.

It's enough for some guys in here to fuck with the new kids, you know? Some of the boys were whistlin' at him, one guy walked by and grabbed Eddie's ass, and I swear he almost jumped out of his skin.

Who knows. Maybe he'd get it, maybe not. Hard to tell when you first see them walk down that line. We all looked like that at one point.

Eddie and the warden walk up to his cell and then he's on his own. The warden says "Good luck" to Eddie and walks away. Eddie watches him go. The look on his face is pure gold.

He looks like he's about to cry.

I watch him for a minute, think about when I first got in here, and then I go back to my book.

That's the last time I think about Eddie for a long while.

I see him around, of course. It's impossible not to. There are about three hundred guys in here, and you get to seeing the same faces over and over again, you know?

He ain't getting' on so well. He gets his ass beat a couple times, shows up for chow with black eyes and shit. That's just how it is.

Take your licks. You got to get used to life here at some point.

I'm sitting in my cell when Juicy and Martian appear at my door.

I pretend not to notice. Keep flipping through my *National Geographic.* It's the Atlantic Ocean issue, one of my favourites. Ancient ruins under the sea. Messerschmitts in the North Atlantic.

"Hey, Scotty," Martian says. "What's goin' on?"

"Fuck all," I say, tossing the magazine onto my bed beside me. "What's up?"

"You gotta check this shit out," Juicy says, coming into the cell behind Martian. "Tell the man about the visit you had today."

I look back at Martian. He's fuckin' huge. Spends all of his time in the gym. Dumb as a bag of shit, but a pretty good guy. He's got that wild animal look in his eyes, though, like he has some loose wires or something. I trust him, but only as far as I can throw him.

Right now he looks like he's about ready to pop.

"Yeah man, you gotta check this out," he says, sitting down beside me. I slide over and make room for Juicy, but he stays standing.

"So I'm doin' the preacher curl in the gym, right? Bustin' out my reps. *Hunnert* and fifty pounds, goin' at it like nobody's business."

I wait for him to finish. Lifting weights is a subject Martian can go on to great lengths about. Finally I give him the look. You know the one.

The *shut the hell up and get on with it* look.

"Right," he says. "Anyway, I'm in there with the weights and who should walk in but Vincenzo and his two Guido buddies. They walk over to me and just watch me rep, right? I say to myself, keep it cool, Martian. They're just stirrin' up shit."

"Pushin' the shit, you mean," Juicy says, cracking a smile. His yellow teeth look brilliant next to his black skin.

"Fuck you, *Juicer*," Martian says.

"Okay brother, Okay," Juicy says, putting his hands up. "Just tell Scotty here what you told me. We're all bro's, right?"

"Anyway," Martian says, ignoring Juicy. "He says he got a job for us. Pays like you wouldn't believe either. Plus they'll watch out for us if we need it. Get this. Two *hunnert* bucks. *Each*." He stops, his face breaking into a huge grin.

Juicy slaps him on the back.

"My man," he says. Then he looks at me. The pair of them are a couple ginning idiots.

"So...." I say, and let it trail off. Neither one of them pick up the slack. I roll my eyes. "So what the fuck does he want you to do?"

"All we gotta do is rough up Edward Relardo," he says. I gotta admit; I draw a complete blank.

"Who the fuck is Edward Relardo?" I say, sitting up.

"Eddie," Juicy pipes in. "That little fucker up on the second level. Bunks not too far from me. You seen him before, he's the one always getting' his ass beat."

"Right," I say, thinking about Eddie for the first time in a while. "Why does he want him beat up?"

"Well," Martian says, "Vincenzo says he fucked up on the outside. Got drunk and did a hit and run. He was some kind of accountant or something, ran numbers and shit. Says he got all kinds of things bouncin' around in that head of his. They want to remind him that he can still be had in here. That he ain't safe if he decides he's going to rat anybody out."

"So he worked for the mob?" I say. Sounds like bullshit to me.

"Naw, man," Juicy says. "He just did some shit on the side for extra cash. I heard he hit some guy in his Fancy-ass Jaguar and took the fuck off out of there. They caught him the next day. Dude's dead, Eddie lands his ass in here."

"They're worried," Martian says, glowering at Juicy for the interruption, "That prison life will be too much for him, and he'll crack just to save his own ass."

"How is prison life treating him?" I say, looking at Juicy.

"He's fucked," Juicy says. "Gettin' his ass beat every day almost. If I was them, I'd be worried too."

"So why don't they do it themselves?"

"I asked them that," Martian says, obviously proud of himself. "They said they can't let it get back to them. If they did it, it would be obvious what was goin' on and the Feds would put the lean on him. It's gotta look like some random shit, just like the stuff goin' on right now. He needs to make sure, though. Keep his mouth shut, or he's dead meat."

I look at the boys for a long minute. They just keep grinning away, like all they can think about is two hundred bucks. I gotta admit, I've done a lot worse in here for less money.

"Fuck it," I say. "Let's do this."

It's pretty easy to find Eddie Relardo. He works laundry down in the basement.

Three days later we're down there waiting for him. Juicy ain't kidding when he says things are goin' bad for the guy; he's limping a bit, and it looks like he's got a busted nose.

He and another inmate are busy folding sheets. It's hotter than shit down here; there are four double washers running at all times and five big dryers. The air is like hot syrup. I don't know how he can stand being down here all day.

I've been here for five minutes and I'm already sweating my balls off.

We walk in and Eddie's got his back to us. I look at the other guy, Taft, and he nods to me. Then he puts his shirts down and walks past Eddie without saying a word.

We owe him twenty bucks later.

Eddie turns around, and when he sees the three of us standing behind him, he lets out this little squawk. He knows what's coming.

He drops his sheets and scrambles for the back of the room, but Juicy and Martian are on him like a couple pit bulls.

They rush past me and latch onto Eddie. Martian grabs him around the throat and Juicy grabs his legs.

"*Come on you guys,*" Eddie croaks. He's having a hard time breathing on account of Martian holding him up by the neck.

I walk up to him. The look on his face is kind of off-putting. He's fuckin' terrified.

"You know who we are?" I say quietly to him as he struggles.

"*Lemme go!*" he chirps.

"We'll let you go," I tell him, "But not until we've given you a little something to remind you about who your friends are."

Juicy and Martian carry him into the back, where we have a little more privacy.

Then Juicy starts layin' into him. Body shots, mostly.

Eddie starts to cry.

"Jesus Christ, Eddie," I say to him. "At least be a man about it."

"*Puh..lease*," Eddie whimpers. "*I didn't do anything to you*."

"We just want you to realize that you ain't alone in here, Eddie," I say. "Remember that the people you used to work for got a lot of friends. You don't say shit to the Feds, or they'll come after you. You got nowhere to hide."

"*I swear!*" he sobs. The sound of Juicy hitting him is like taking a baseball bat to a side of beef. Eddie groans after every one. Tears are rolling down his face.

"My turn," Martian says, pushing Eddie into the corner undoing the zipper on his pants. "Roll him over, Juice."

Juice looks at me.

"What the fuck are you doing, Martian?" I say to him.

"What?" Martian says. He's already got his dick in his hands, and he's rubbing an erection out.

"Aww man," Juicy says. "Put that shit away. I ain't holding him so you can fuck him."

Eddie suddenly turns and sees Martian with his dick in

his hands. I hear his breath hitch and he starts to scramble against the wall.

"*Oh my God*," he blubbers. "*Please guys, I'll do anything you want. I won't even* talk *to the cops, I swear!*"

His voice is all high and panicked.

Martian looks at Juice.

"Hold him down, you fucking *Nigger*," Martian says.

"Man, fuck you," Juicy says. "I ought to bust your stupid face open."

"Oh yeah?" Martian says. I glance down. I swear he's getting off on this.

"Both you guys, shut the fuck up," I say, taking a step toward Eddie. He's curled up in a little ball in the corner, watching everyone. He's bleeding from his mouth and nose, and I can hear him sniffling.

"Whatever man," Juicy says, putting his hands up and moving over beside me. "You want to do that shit, you do it on your own."

Martian looks at both of us for a moment, then he smiles. "Fine," he says. He turns on Eddie, still smiling.

Eddie starts to stand up.

"*No, no n*o," he begins to chant. He can't get any further into the corner, even though he's trying his damndest.

"Come on, Eddie," Martian says, grabbing a handful of Eddie's hair. "Relax, you might even enjoy this."

Juicy looks at me. I catch his eyes, and hold them. Honestly, what the fuck does he want me to do?

Eddie continues his *No, No, No* chant even as Martian drills him in the face. Eddie droops. He's completely out of it now. Martian starts to whistle as he rolls Eddie over and tucks his head between his legs.

"Fuck this shit," Juicy says. "I'm fuckin' out of here."

"Come on, Juicer," Martian says, smiling at us. "I'll let you go next."

I'm not stickin' around to see this either. Martian is grunting as he thrusts into Eddie, who is starting to wake up. Then I hear Eddie gasp, and he starts shrieking.

"Quiet, Eddie," Martian says. "I'm almost done."

Eddie starts to scramble, and Martian grabs him by the back of the head.

"I said quiet, fucker," Martian says, leaning over him. I can smell the sex. The combination of the heat, moisture, and the smell of Martian sweating into Eddie is enough to make me want to puke.

Martian suddenly bounces Eddies head off the concrete floor.

Eddie grunts, but manages to get to his knees.

Martian pushes his face down against the floor, and Eddie's moaning. Blood is pooling on the concrete under his face.

"Oh yeah," Martian grunts, and starts thrusting harder. "Oh fuck yeah,"

Juicy and I look at each other. We're both thinking the same thing, I'm sure of it.

Martian gasps suddenly, and buries himself in Eddie.

Eddie yelps in pain.

"I *told you*," Martian says, "to *shut. The fuck. Up*!"

He accentuates each word by slamming Eddies face into the floor. Eddie starts shaking. Not a little bit, either.

His *whole body* starts shaking.

"Jesus Christ," Juicy says, watching the blood spurt out from under Eddie's face. "What the fuck did you just do?"

"He's having a seizure," I say, moving over beside him. "Get the hell off him."

Martian pulls out, and I can smell the sex again. It's the least of my worries though.

Eddie's fucked up bad.

"*Nhyuh Nyuh Nhyuh,*" he says. It's like every muscle in his body is clenching at once. He looks like someone took a belt sander and tried to scrape off his face.

I look up at Martian, who's wiping sweat off his face.

"What the hell did you do?" I say to him.

"What?" Martian says, the smile starting to fade off his face.

I'm up and moving then. I grab Martian by the shirt and slam him against the wall.

"He's *fucked,*" I spit in his face. "What the fuck are we going to do with him now, you *Goddamned* retard?"

"I didn't mean to do it so hard," Martian said, his face getting soft. He's never been able to stand up to me.

"You better look at this," Juicy says. He's crouched down by Eddies head.

"What?" I say, and I can't believe how screwed up everything has gotten in the past two minutes.

"I think he's got a skull fracture," Juicy says. "Look at his forehead. It's got a fucking pulse, for Christ's sake."

It's true. There's a spot in the middle of Eddie's forehead, about the size of a dime, that's pulsing in and out softly.

It's not a fracture. There is actually a hole under the skin going straight to his brain.

"Ho-leee shit," I say. Juicy and I both look at Martian.

"I'm sorry," he says. "What do you want me to say?"

I glare at him, and he shrinks back against the wall.

"What the hell are you going to do, Scott?" Juicy says to me. I can tell he's scared. We could all spend the rest of our lives in prison if anyone finds him like this.

I look down at Eddie.

There's no way I'm spending the rest of my life in here for him.

"We're gonna kill him," I tell Juicy. "And then we're gonna get the fuck out of here."

Juicy nods.

"Alright, bro," he says to me, and then puts a hand on my shoulder. "That's what we gonna do then."

I nod my head. He and I stand up.

I raise my foot over Eddie's head.

"Fucking *hardcore*," Martian says.

I drop my foot down as hard as I can.

There is resistance at first, but then his skull collapses under my weight and his face folds down flat. Blood and brains spurt out from the tear that forms in his forehead and down over his nose.

More blood than I've ever seen.

We all stand around for a minute, watching the fluid pump out of Eddie's crushed skull. It's like he's puking thick, lumpy blood out of the middle of his face. It mixes with the water on the floor and races toward the drain cap in the middle of the room.

"I'm getting the fuck out of here," Juicy says. "No way I'm getting caught with this shit on my hands."

"Fucking Pussy," Martian says. Then he looks over at me. "So what now, Scott?"

"Now we get the fuck out of here so we don't get caught with this on our hands," I tell him. Like I said before. Dumb as a bag of shit.

Just to be sure things stay quiet for a little while I throw some sheets over him and dump bleach all over everything. It's a stupid to do, really, pointless. Like nobody will be able to tell from the mess on the floor and the shape of the sheet what's underneath it.

We all leave the laundry room at the same time, then split up as if nothing happened.

For a little while, we can even convince ourselves that it's true.

Officially, Eddie escaped from prison. They lock us up for a couple days while they look for him, and I'm about ready to shit. I know they're going to hit the laundry room and see Eddie laying there with his head crushed and leaking his brains into the drainage pipe.

As it turns out, though, they're even dumber than I always thought.

They don't find Eddie anywhere. They look all over the place. They search everyone's rooms. Tear the prison apart.

Not a whiff.

After a while they let us out of our cells again. They're

watching us, though, like hawks. So I'm careful not to do anything weird. I see Juicy and Martian, and they got the same look on their faces I do.

What the hell happened?

The days creep into weeks.

I've had it. I just gotta know.

I meet up with Juicy and we go to the laundry room. Taft is there, working some sheets and white t-shirts. He nods to us when he sees us come in, but we don't speak. Juicy watches him as we walk to the storage room in the back.

As soon as I pull back the curtain I can see why nobody's seen Eddie.

He ain't fuckin' there.

"Shit," Juicy says, putting a hand up to his mouth. "Where the hell is he?"

"Good question," I say, looking at every inch of the little room.

It's spotless. Even the rust is gone off the drain cover in the middle of the floor.

"*Whatever you looking fo', it ain't in there*," says Taft, coming up behind us. Juicy spins faster than I do. Taft puts his hands in his pockets, just to make sure we know he isn't fixing for a fight.

"*What* isn't in there?" I say to him, taking a step forward so I can be nice and close. If he's fucking around, I'll know soon enough.

"What are you lookin' fo'?"

I grab him by the shirt collar. Taft looks up into my face with his dull brown eyes, lookin' like an old hound dog.

"Don't dick around," I breathe into his face. "You got

somethin' to say, you come on out and say it. Juicy and I ain't in the mood to piss around here."

"Your boy ain't there," he says simply.

"Where is he then?"

Taft watches my face very carefully as he speaks.

"He gone. And you *shore* as shit ain't gonna believe me when I say where."

"Spit it out, asshole," I say, I'm almost close enough to kiss his ugly face by this point.

"He went down into the sewer."

I stare at him. I'm almost too shocked to speak. It's probably the dumbest thing I've ever heard in my life. Juicy snickers, crossing his hands over his chest.

"What are you, cracked?" I say, giving him a shake. "Juicy and I are gonna beat you to death if you don't stir up straight, you fucking *eggplant.*"

"Yeah, motherfucker," Juicy says, jabbing a finger into Taft's chest.

"I saw it myself," Taft says, unfazed by our threats. "I came back in after you guys left. Picked the shit up, you know, business as usual. Except I heard this noise in the back room, and I was thinkin' it was prolly Eddie laying back there all beat to shit."

He looked over at Juicy, then back to me. "Wouldn't be the first time someone come down here lookin' for trouble."

I just stare at him. Juicy looks like he's ready to turn the guy inside out.

"Anyway, I walk back here, *an' lo' an' behold*, there's Eddie halfway down into the drainage pipe. I says to myself, 'There go some hard motherfuckers to do that to a guy', you know? Well, you only paid me twenty bucks, so I ain't stickin' around for this shit. I take right the hell off outta there."

"Get out of here," Juicy says. "You're saying a dead guy dragged himself through a tube only ten inches across? You must think we're the two dumbest fuckers in the world."

"I seen it myself," Taft says, his face getting serious. "You *shouldda* heard that noise. All sloppy, like wet meat slappin' around back here an' bones snappin' all over the place. *Crunchy*, you know? You ever hear a body git all crunchy like that?"

I shake my head. In spite of the stupidity of this story, I haven't beaten his ass in yet. In fact, I let go of him and take a step back.

"So then what happened?" I say quietly. Juicy looks over at me for a moment and then shakes his head and sighs loudly.

I ignore him.

"After that, I *jes'* left this place," Taft says. "They lock us all down, and I be thinkin' they gonna come an' talk to me any time now. But they *dinn't*. They never say shit to me. They say Eddie found a way to escape this place. I say they got it right."

"Let's do him right now," Juicy says. "Kill his ass and get the hell outta here. Stupid, man. Real stupid. Who the hell you think you're talkin' too?"

I look hard at Taft. As fucked as his story is, I kind of believe him. He don't look like the kind of guy that would mess around like that. He's been in here for a while, he's pretty straight. Besides, what would be the point of making something like this up?

"I cleaned the shit up myself," Taft says, talking to Juicy now. "I come in here with a bucket of bleach *jes'* to be sure. There weren't hardly nuthin' left. Few streaks of blood, that's it. Poured the bleach all over the place, an' when it goes down the drain it makes this weird gurgling noise."

"Maybe Eddie didn't like the bleach so much," I offer, and Taft nods.

"Somethin' else," he says, pulling a rag out of his pants. It's bound up in a tight knot.

"They all over the place," Taft says, quickly untying the rag. When he's done, he holds it up for Juicy and I to take a good look.

"Oh shit," Juicy says, stepping back.

I look at Taft's hands, and then I look into his face. He's just standing there. I half expect him to break into a grin.

"I pick 'em all up, *jes'* in case someone asks some questions."

I look back at the contents of his rag and shudder.

Teeth.

All kinds of them. Molars, incisors, bicuspids. More than twenty of them. Some of them are jagged and broken, or chipped, but I can see they are pretty much all there. Every single tooth in Eddie's head, sitting in a nice little pile in Taft's outstretched hand.

I grab them. Grab the whole rag. Then I kick open the drainage grate and dump them down into the pipe. I turn back to Taft.

"Go get me some bleach," I say.

Juicy doesn't say anything to me as we walk back to my cell. Martian is waiting for us when we get there.

"Where the hell you guys been?" he says, and he eyes us suspiciously.

"Fuck off, Marty," Juicy says. Hard to believe a man as black as Juicy is could look so pale right now.

"Tell me where you guys were," he says, getting up. "Talking to the warden, maybe?"

"Not right now," I say to him. I really mean it. I feel like I'm gonna puke.

"You fuckers better not be trying to push this shit on me," he snarls. "You're the one who killed him, Scotty Boy. Not me."

"I said not *now*." I step toward him. It's all bluff. A stiff wind could knock me on my ass right now.

"Fine," Martian says, walking out of my cell. "We're gonna talk more about this later though."

The toilet gurgles.

I look at Juicy, but he just shrugs.

And that's when we hear it.

Tap…tap…tap….

It's real soft at first, but as we sit there it gets louder. It's in the pipes. Like gravel in a tube.

"What the fuck is that?" Juicy says. He walks over to the toilet. The sound is getting louder.

"Juice, maybe you shouldn't stand over there," I say to him, sitting up on my bed. He ignores me.

The toilet gurgles again. The noise is getting louder.

Tap…tap…tap….

"Seriously, Juicy," I say. "Get away from the toilet." Something ain't right here. I can feel it.

Juicy looks at me. He's concentrating on that sound in the pipes. It sounds like it's coming right out of the toilet.

"What?" he says, half to himself. The toilet bubbles.

Juicy leans over and looks into the bowl.

"*Get the fuck away from there!*" I shout, jumping to my feet.

There is a roar as a column of black murky water suddenly erupts from the toilet bowl, catching Juicy full in the face.

The cell is filled with the stink of bleach and rotting flesh. It fills my nostrils, making me gag. My eyes are starting to burn.

Juicy throws himself on the floor, screaming and clawing at his face.

I stagger back out of the cell, retching, holding my hands over my face. The bleach sears my lungs. I feel like I'm going to pass out.

There's a crowd of people around me. I hear Juicy screaming, but somebody grabs me and starts pulling me through the mass of bodies. There are whistles going off all over the place.

They're locking the prison down.

Thankfully, I pass out on the way to the infirmary and don't see Juicy when they bring him in.

I wake up a few hours later. My chest hurts. My face hurts. It hurts to breathe. I sit up just as a nurse comes over.

"How you feeling?" she says, looking down at me.

"I feel like shit," I say, and I mean it. I have these itchy sores all over my arms. My face feels sunburned.

"You guys are lucky to be alive," she says. "Mind telling me how you ended up making a chlorine gas bomb in your toilet?"

I look up into her face and answer truthfully.

"I have no idea," I say. "The toilet was making these weird noises, and then the whole thing just went up in Juicy's face. How is he?"

"Go see for yourself," the nurse sighs, and I get the feeling she doesn't believe a word I'm saying. "He's right over there."

I may be lucky to be alive. From the amount of tubes and wires coming out of Juicy's bandaged face, however, I really think he would have been better off dead.

He's sleeping right now. He is wrapped completely in white gauze from the top of his head to his shoulders, as well as his hands and forearms.

"Chemical burns," the nurse says over my shoulder. "Really bad ones too. He probably won't make it. His lungs were full of that stuff."

"*Christ*," I say, watching him breathe. He's on an oxygen respirator.

A little later I'm sitting on my bed watching Juicy sleep when Officer Frank Daublin comes in to see me. He doesn't look happy.

I nod to him, and then go back to watching Juicy.

"So," he says, grabbing a chair and folding his hands in his lap. I feel like I'm about to be worked over by my grandfather. "You want to tell me what happened?"

I gloss over the details. Tell him Juicy and I had been sitting in my cell when the toilet started acting up.

"Next thing I know, kaboom!" I say, showing him the lesions on my arms.

"So this just happened by itself," Officer Daublin says. I can actually hear the Irish in his voice, even though he told me once before that he moved to Canada when he was four.

"All by itself," I say, watching him.

"It's funny, because all of the toilets in this facility are interconnected through a single sewage disposal setup."

"So...what does that mean?"

"It *means*," Officer Daublin says, scratching the side of his face as he speaks. "It means that a single toilet could never just go off by itself. They are designed to not go off like that, because inmates like to stuff things down them and jam them up. You would have to jam up every toilet in the building to get the kind of flow you got."

"I don't know what to tell you," I say. "Why don't you ask Juicy over there what happened?"

Officer Daublin stands up and nods his head.

"Oh, don't worry. If he lives through this, you can be sure I will."

He starts to leave, and the stops and turns around.

"One more thing, Mr. Thompson," he says, reaching into his pocket. He pulls out a small plastic bag. "You don't happen to know where these came from, do you?"

I try to hide my shock, but I can tell from the look on Officer Daublin's face that I just told him everything he wants to know.

Inside the little bag is a handful of yellowed, broken teeth.

They let me go a few days later. My cell reeks of chlorine bleach. The boys on either side of my cell are pissed because the smell gives them headaches.

I stay away from the toilet as much as I can. I also stop using the sinks and I don't drink anything until chow when it's served to me in a juice box.

Showers are out, too.

Guys who used to talk to me are giving me a wide berth. They think I'm losing it. They think that what happened to Juicy was maybe my fault, and I'm cracking under the guilt.

They don't know the truth.

Even Martian stops coming around. He doesn't believe my story. He thinks the whole thing is just bullshit.

He starts screaming in his cell one night, and I watch them take him to the nursing station on a stretcher. It takes five guys to hold him down. When they unlock the cells on the third floor and send a cleaning team in, I know exactly what happened to him.

I was wrong, though. I had no idea how bad it was going to get.

I go see him the next day after my visit with Juicy. Juicy hasn't said a word since it happened, and he barely moves. Doc says he isn't doing so good. He has some kind of infection they can't pin down.

Martian looks even worse.

They've got tubes running out of his sides into a pumping machine for blood and urine. He's hooked up to a colostomy machine, too. He stinks like shit.

"Jesus," I say when I see him. "What the fuck happened to you?"

Martian looks up at me.

"*Shcotty?*" he says. His voice is dreary.

"Yeah, it's me. What happened?"

Martian puts his hand up and I take it.

"*It'shh good to see you…*" he says, trailing off.

"*I'm not doing shhow good. I got bags for all my pishh and shit.*"

"Yeah, I can see that. What did you do?"

"*I wash in my room, doing shit ups. I had to go. You were, right.*"

"What the hell are you talking about?" I say, starting to pull away from him. Martian latches on to my hand though, and he's still got a grip like a python.

"*I had to go,*" he says again.

"Let go of me, Martian," I say.

"*I could hear the clacking, juusht like you shaid. But I had to go. You were right.*"

"*Let go of me!*" I say, pulling hard. Martian drops my hand.

Suddenly he grunts, and grabs at his belly. I start to back away from him.

Martian starts shrieking.

One of the nurses grabs on to him, and the throws her onto the floor.

"*Jesus Christ help me*!" he cries, standing up off the bed. His sheet falls away, and I can see the double criss-cross of stitch marks where they performed emergency surgery on him. He staggers, and the shit and piss tubes start to pull out from his side.

Martian shrieks again, and suddenly starts clawing at his stomach. His thick fingers tear through the stitches on his skin, and blood starts pouring out of the holes.

I have to get away from him, but I can't. There's too much going on. Too much chaos, too much screaming.

Too much blood.

Nurses are everywhere. Now the inmates are screaming from their hospital beds, because Martian is tearing himself apart trying to get at whatever he thinks is inside him....

And then I see it. God help me, I see it.

Grinning hideously from the hole Martian made when he tore his own belly open is a face, rubbery and bleeding and torn down the forehead.

It's smile elongated by the fact that the jaw is shattered and all of its teeth are missing, a face that could easily fit into a drainage pipe if it wanted to, because when I stomped down on it the first time I crushed all the large bones in it.

The bleach did the rest.

Eddie stares out at me from inside Martian's belly, his face contorted in a silent laugh.

Martian doesn't think it's so funny.

Neither do the nurses, who are scrambling to get away from him now.

I turn just as Martian slides to his knees, still holding what's left of his intestines in his hands.

Eddie keeps laughing.

I sprint for the door and shoulder-block the first guard

as he steps into the room. Then I sprint down the hall. My only thought is escape. If I can get out of the prison, maybe I can get away from Eddie and that crushed grin on his face.

I hear the alarms go off. Automatic lockdown. Every door in the prison bolts shut.

When the guards come for me, I'm screaming and beating my fists against the door to the cafeteria. They come in hard, with their shields and nightsticks, and I even manage to fight them for a while.

Only for a little while.

So now I'm here.

Naked, my hands bleeding and raw, standing in solitary waiting for someone to sort out this whole mess. They're going to try and figure out a way to pin what happened to Juicy and Martian on me. Bleach was used on both of them, and I was at the scene both times.

Open and shut case.

It doesn't matter though, because soon the tapping in the pipes will start again.

When that happens, I think I'm going to scream until my mind snaps and I become completely crazy with fear.

That's the plan, anyway.

My only hope is that Eddie remembers how I ended things for him. How I ended the hurt and the pain he was in. How I made it quick for him.

Oh God, I hope he remembers.

A Sweetheart Deal

with John Sunseri

The guy showed up in the middle of the night, but it wasn't the guy Artie was used to.

Every time before it had been a greaser, a big, muscled guy with slick black hair and a Roman nose, and Artie had imagined he could smell the garlic and olive oil on him, even through the reek of formaldehyde and freshly-turned earth that suffused the undertaker's offices.

But this guy…this guy looked more like an accountant, with glasses and nice clothes. And he was nervous, too. It was a cool October night, but the guy was sweating and they hadn't even carried in the body yet.

"Where's the other guy?" Artie asked, concerned that the deal was getting changed on him.

That's how life went for him—whenever he got a sniff of something good, a taste of success, they fucked around with the rules and he ended up taking it in the ass. And this was the big one, this deal, this sweetheart deal he had going.

"I'm the one who's here," said the accountant. "Is there a problem?"

"No, no problem," said Artie, shaking his head. "It's just, you get used to a guy, and then someone else shows up…."

"Just do your fucking job," said the guy, "and don't worry about the personnel. You're getting paid to keep your mouth shut and do your job, right? So keep your mouth *shut….*" At this point, the accountant levelled his gaze and gave Artie a look that was meant to remind him of his place in the food chain. "And do your job."

"I got it," said Artie, backpedalling. "Really, man—it's cool. Let's get the thing out of your trunk, and you can take off."

"You get it out of my trunk," said the man. "You've got a hand truck, right?"

"But the other guy…." started Artie, then stopped. Yeah, the other guy always helped carry the body in, but he wasn't going to make a stink.

For five hundred bucks, he'd wrestle the bulky, awkward thing into the lab himself, and the priss could drive back to Portland without getting himself dirty.

As he struggled to get the bundle onto the tines of the hand truck, he kept nervously scanning the grounds of the cemetery.

It was October, after all, and the high school kids would soon be fucking around, tipping over the headstones, drinking stolen whiskey and screwing on the graves. Little bastards.

Artie hoped this wouldn't be the new pattern.

It's not as if he *liked* the other guy, the Italian, but he felt *safer* when he showed up. He'd been careful never to ask, but he was sure he was dealing with the Mafia, and the little pencil-neck sitting in his office right now, drinking the extra-tall fancy coffee he'd brought from Portland, didn't inspire Artie with a lot of confidence.

If you were gonna deal with the Mob, you wanted real mobsters, you know? You didn't want the book-and-number guys.

He finally finished. He heaved the thing up onto the embalming table, and the well-dressed guy handed him an envelope. Then he turned around and walked out.

Artie heard the car start up as he opened up his payment, and by the time he had pulled out the cash and counted it twice, the fucker was long gone.

"Three hundred," he said to himself, the words echoing through the sterile, well-lit room. "Those cocksuckers."

The lump on the table, wrapped in its two layers of body bags, didn't respond, but Artie hadn't expected it to. Three hundred bucks in used twenties and tens, and not five hundred like it had always been before.

Artie felt that old feeling take him in the gut, that feeling that said *you're a loser and always will be a loser*, that queasy little twist in his stomach that happened whenever he saw one of his plans crumbling, whenever some stripper turned him down for a date, whenever he realized that the cop who had stopped him for his fucking taillight wasn't gonna listen to why he hadn't had time to get it fixed.

They were doing it to him again; people were constantly fucking with him, putting him down, keeping him in the dirt when he should be flying up above it....

He forced himself to think of flying. It always calmed him down.

He looked up at the models hanging on their wires over the sink area, looked at the beautifully-replicated P-51D Mustang, the bulk of the B-29 Superfortress, the Vought F4U Corsair with its bent wings…and then he looked down at the bundle of money in his hand.

Those guys had been real men.

The Americans, the British, the Canadians, all of 'em who'd flown mission after mission over Germany and France, dodging bullets and the dirty clouds of flak that came up at them like belches of Hell, doing their jobs and taking out the Krauts and the Nips.

And here was Artie, sitting lonely in his mortuary office with a mob kill on his table and a measly three hundred dollars in his hand. It was enough to make you cry.

He looked at the body again, dreading the task ahead of him. He'd have to get the quicklime out, spend two hours carefully packing it into the space between the body bags, and then reseal the whole deal.

Tomorrow he'd have to dig the grave for Curt Ripley and make it three feet deeper than normal so there'd be room for the extra body underneath the coffin. For five hundred bucks, it was an annoyance. For three hundred, it was insulting.

Fuck this, he thought.

He'd do it all in the morning. He was almost out of lime, anyway. That meant another trip down to Johnson's Tack and Saddle, where, with any luck, Michelle would be working.

This thought, unlike the thoughts of the WWII airmen, managed to lift his spirits a little, so that when he clicked off the light and moved back through the building to his apartment, he felt a little better.

And when he stuffed the new cash into his light plane envelope (almost five thousand in there, now, less a couple hundred for trips up to Portland and the strip clubs), he was even whistling a little bit. Tonight he would prime a Spitfire Supermarine and see if he couldn't trace out the blue-green camouflage pattern on it, the one that had made it practically invisible over the North Atlantic waves.

Tomorrow, he would see Michelle.

The next day was Saturday, and he spent the morning working on Curt Ripley.

There wasn't much more to do. He'd already set old Curt's neck so that it was straight again, and pinned a black suit to him. All that was left, really, was the knee, and Artie had saved it for last because it made his stomach turn. The thing looked like it had gone through a sausage press.

Curt had been hit—well, not *hit*, really, but *pulverized*—by one of those new Dodge trucks, the ones with the huge engines and big grilles. Crushed his ribcage and broke his neck. His ribs had splintered inside him and sliced up his internal organs. A bunch of them had actually ended up in his underwear.

And it looked worse than it sounded—Artie'd had to snip the things out of Curt's ass and drop 'em back into his chest cavity.

His knee, though, was the worst. It had gone under the truck and gotten pinned by the tires. When the guy had slammed on the brakes, Curt's leg had turned into soup.

Artie straightened it and did some stitching just to try to give the leg a bit of form again. When he was done it looked like shit—but it had looked like warm puke when the stiff had first come in, and at least this way it would kind of look like a knee again.

Curt's family had gone all-out for the funeral. They couldn't have an open viewing period, because Curt had left half his face on the Dodge's fancy grille, so they had opted for the posh Excelsior casket and a large photograph of old Curtis instead.

Real nice. Lots of brass and oak. Weighed about four hundred pounds, even without a passenger.

After lunch, Artie dropped Curtis into his new—and last—home. He filled out the final bit of paperwork and wrote a little note that said simply 'DNV'. Do Not View.

Just in case.

Artie looked finally at the double-wrapped bag on the table. Just looking at it pissed him off.

He still had a little time before Michelle's shift at the Tack and Saddle (at least, he thought he did. She worked afternoons on Saturdays, usually), so he shook his head and decided to get a little work done on the thing.

He unzipped the outer bag and saw right away that someone had forgotten to lock the inner one.

Interesting.

The zippers on the bags came with a double clip so that they could be locked up. Saved the body from slipping out of the bag in transit, and also kept thieves from robbing the corpses before they could be properly processed.

This one was missing the little brass lock.

Someone had been in a hurry to get it here, and had gotten sloppy. Either that, or....

A test? It was the Mob, after all (at least, he was *pretty sure* it was the Mob). Would they do that to him, give him some bullshit loyalty test?

It would make sense if he'd ever given them a reason to worry, but he'd been doing the job perfectly since Day One. Maybe they were just paranoid.

Or maybe they wanted to rile him up and see if he'd shake, so they intentionally short-changed him, then stood back to see if he'd take the bait, open the bag, and then they'd burst in and give him the old double-tap salute to the back of his head.

Naw—he was pushing it, now.

This was stupid. These little paranoid fantasies made sense in Artie's head, but not in the real world. He grimaced.

To hell with it. Piss on those Guinea fucks. A deal's a deal, and three hundred bucks ain't five hundred. He deserved *something* for the missing two C's.

He deserved a look.

He peeled back the outer bag, then unzipped the inner one. He pulled it back and then stared at the thing before him, unsure of what to do next.

Whatever it was, it wasn't a corpse.

It looked like a lump of wax.

It was a soft margarine-yellow color, and vaguely human in shape, but that was it. It had no discernable features.

Artie reached down and pushed on it with his finger.

It was soft, like feta, and had a greasy sheen on it that stuck to Artie's skin when he pulled back his hand.

He rubbed it between his fingers and smelled it. Some kind of oil. The places where it touched his skin began to stain.

A moment later, they began to sting. Artie watched as two black bruises formed on his fingertips like blood blisters. Then tiny droplets of blood began to form on the skin.

"*What the hell?*" he whispered, staring aghast as the blood welled up and formed a perfect drop. It fell from his hand and splashed on the floor.

He looked at the waxen figure before him and his face furrowed. He had made a line in the stuff when he'd touched it with his finger. An indent in the formless mass.

His fingertips felt swollen.

Whatever this shit was, he wasn't getting paid to piss around with it. Of course, if his paranoid fantasy was true, and they *were* testing him, he'd just fucked up big time.

They'd look at the streak in the thing, and *know* that he'd been messing with it.

So stupid, he thought.

He'd leave for a while. Just to be sure. You never knew, right? He'd leave the office and if shit looked like it was beginning to go down when he got back he'd just drive on by, maybe take an impromptu trip up to Canada to visit his brother.

Just to be safe, he'd drop the wax shit into the coffin with old Curt. Lock it up. If the Mob came, they'd have to take a fire axe to the Excelsior to get inside it. Solid fucking oak. It would take hours.

He wheeled the casket over to the table, wincing as his bruised fingers came into contact with the handle, and again when he struggled to dump the thing into the box on top of Curt Ripley. With this minor handicap, he fumbled a bit as he heaved it over the edge, and the bag started to slip, but he wasn't going to fuck with the thing anymore right now. He left it, locked the casket, set the alarm on the prep room, double-checked everything.

Triple-checked.

And then left. No sense being careless.

When he was almost downtown, Artie's fingers began to hurt so badly that he had to pull up in front of the Grange building and stop the car. They'd been aching since he'd left the Veteran's Cemetery, but now they felt like someone was squeezing them in a vice—someone strong and pissed-off.

He looked at them, his fore and middle fingers, and though they had stopped bleeding they were swollen and puffy, and he could actually see them throbbing with his pulse.

He was truly scared, now.

Maybe it's not the Mob, he thought. *Maybe it's some weird scientific thing, some* X-Files *type of thing, and what I've been burying all this time is toxic, like failed biotech experiments....*

He raised his fingers to his face so that he could see them better, and for a span of five seconds he stopped breathing. There was something going on under the skin of his fingers.

Something moving.

What he'd thought was his pulse wasn't. It was like worms were in there—something alive, inside his fingers, moving blindly around in the meat and the juice.

He yelped and grabbed his fingers with his left hand, feeling them, feeling the motion of something alien inside him, and with his brain a maelstrom he squeezed as hard as he could, like he was trying to get the last bit of toothpaste out of the tube.

Yellow-white stuff, looked like feta, started to ooze out of his fingers.

Blood came too, a thin watery stream of red, like he was popping a pimple too hard, but it was mostly the wax, coming out of his pores as he forced it, tightening the pressure as his heart pounded in his chest.

It was moving down, he gibbered in his mind. *It was moving down the fingers toward the hand, and then it would have gone up my arm, and toward my heart.*

He squeezed and squeezed until nothing but blood came out, and shook his hand frantically to rid himself of the alien wax, spattering blood and the cheese-stuff onto the passenger seat of his pickup, onto the dash, onto the Dairy Queen wrappers on the floorboard, shaking his hand like a priest shaking his thurible.

Finally he stopped. His hand felt better. The blood was slowing, though the tips of his fingers still had red pricks all over them, like little measles.

He thought he'd gotten all of it. He couldn't be a hundred percent, but he thought it was all out, and he looked carefully at the stuff on the seat next to him, waiting for motion from the little splatters of pus he'd flung there.

Nothing.

He looked around, but the Grange was deserted on a Saturday. Over the front door, a hand-painted banner advertised tomorrow's pancake feed and pumpkin-carving contest, but today all the farmers were out in their fields or spending time with their families. No one had seen him doing his panic dance in his truck.

After another minute, he wrestled the old Ford to life and put it into gear. He was still scared as hell, still panicky and breathless, but he couldn't just go home and stare at his fingers for the next two or three hours, like he wanted to.

He needed lime, and a lot of it. He was damned if that shit back in old Curt's coffin was gonna stay there much longer.

The town of Carper's Ridge wanted to be a city, but it was taking a long time getting there. When Artie had been a kid at the consolidated high school, smoking dope behind the bleachers and getting beat up by the farm boys who thought he was a fucking weirdo, there had been a little over five thousand people living in the limits. Now there were maybe six, and a lot of them were old people who retired down here from Portland or up from Salem, wanting clean country air for their last years.

All those old folks were good for business.

Artie pulled up in front of Johnson's Tack and Saddle, put the Ford in park, and sat there for a minute, looking at his fingers for the millionth time.

Nothing.

He got out, and walked across the sidewalk to the front door. He kept his right hand in his pocket as he opened it, flinched a little as the bell hung over the door jingled, then moved up to the counter.

Michelle was there. Some of the tension left his chest.

"I'm gonna need some more lime," he said to her, amazed at how the mere proximity of her chased most of his fear and anxiety away. He'd been through the strangest morning of his life, felt some of the sharpest fear he'd ever felt, but just being in Michelle's presence was like getting baptized—all the bad things went away.

"Oh, hello, sir" she said, smiling. "You know where it is."

"Yeah," he said. "I'll grab some and be right back." Normally at this point he would grab a cart and head to the back of the building, where the bags of lime lay stacked like lumpy pillows against the wall—but this wasn't a normal day by any stretch of the word. All he'd been through, all the fear and the pain, the panic and the uncertainty—and now the cathartic balm of Michelle's presence—made him reckless.

"Say," he started as she began to turn away from the counter. She stopped, gave him another smile, and waited.

"I was wondering..." he said, and now his heart was beating fast again, "I mean, if you're not busy some night, I thought you might wanna drive down to Salem, maybe catch a movie...."

The smile disappeared.

"I'm sorry, sir," she said. "Company rules—Mr. Johnson doesn't let the employees date customers."

"Oh," he said. "Sorry. I just thought...I mean," he closed his eyes for a second, feeling it again, that *loser* thump in his guts. "I'll just go get the lime."

When he opened his eyes again, she had turned and walked down the counter, where a farmer had wheeled up his fifty-pound bags of chicken feed, and she was beginning to ring him up. Artie moved away slowly, heading for the lime.

On his drive back, the heavy bags shifting against each other in the bed of the truck, he tried to think of flying again, of finally getting up the scratch to buy a light plane and just fucking flying away, up through the dirty clouds that scudded in the October sky into the crystal blue firmament.

He had been hoping Michelle would want to be his co-pilot.

Load up Michelle, his rifle and fishing stuff, maybe get a dog, a big black mastiff, name it Achilles or something, something tough, and just fly away with 'em, fly across the state, all the way to Canada, all the way to the goddamn North Pole if he wanted....

The thoughts weren't working like they usually did. She wasn't going to be his co-pilot, and you know why? 'Cause he was a loser, that's why. This sweetheart deal he had going? It was shit. He wasn't even halfway to being able to buy his plane, and now they were dropping his payments. What, a couple more corpses (*they're not corpses*, his subconscious whispered) and would they be paying him two hundred a pop? One hundred? Maybe they'd want him to do it for free—what could he do about it, call the cops and complain?

He pulled into his spot next to the hearse and looked around for anyone, anything that said *Mafia*, but the graveyard was deserted. A spray of wilted flowers had blown off one of the graves and rolled into the driveway, but that was it.

The door was locked. The alarm was on.

He hefted three of the bags of lime onto the hand truck, dragged it toward the door, and opened it. He went through the vestibule, turned on the lights and stopped.

Something was thumping in the back room.

He had a pretty good idea what it was.

Another thump, a loud one, and he released the hand truck, looked around, and opened one of the closet doors. He took a shovel out, hefted it in his right hand, and moved to the door of the preparation room. He unlocked it, put his keys back in his pocket, took a deep breath and pulled it open.

The coffin was on its side on the floor, a pretty good dent in it where it had landed when it had fallen—or bucked itself—off the gurney. It lay silent and still for a moment, then it jerked off the floor maybe an inch, straight up, then crashed down again.

Four hundred pounds, easy, and the stuff was actually lifting it.

Not thinking, working on adrenaline and instinct, Artie walked over to the casket and kicked it so that it crashed down onto its back. It began to quiver and shake, and it scraped on the cement floor. Artie imagined the stuff inside writhing and twisting, trying frantically to escape.

He helped. He reached down, unlatched the locks, stood again and took the shovel in both hands, a batter's stance, and reached out with one of his steel-toes and flipped up the lid.

The stuff had invaded the body of Curt Ripley.

The corpse, hands bloody, lurched up as soon as the lid opened, and it was *screaming*, screaming in a wordless siren as if hellish pain was wracking it, and Artie stepped back, stunned, not expecting this....

It was fast. The knee, that wreck of a knee, had knit itself back together somehow, but it wasn't any kind of normal human anatomy—bones still stuck out of it at weird angles, and though it was strong enough to support the body as it rose wailing out of the Excelsior, it must have hurt like all the fires of Hell. Judging by the corpse's mad banshee howls, it did.

The thing rose, leaving behind it all the formaldehyde that the wax had forced out, an inch or two of blood, gallons worth, pooled in the box, pieces of organs—all the stuff there hadn't been room for when the wax had taken over Curt. Artie screamed, too, as the thing rolled out of the coffin and sprang to its feet, and he could see that most of the wounds the old man had suffered were healing, too—long sharp cuts knitting themselves seamlessly until only faded skin remained, the crushed ribs somehow re-fused so that the old farmer's chest looked solid and vital.

And now it looked at Artie, with open eyes clear and blue, and in the middle of all the screaming and agonized howls, Artie saw the thing beginning to *smile* at him.

And reach for him.

Artie swung and connected, a solid hit with the blade of the shovel, and Curt's head went *crack* and the body staggered back a half-step.

The head whipped back up, and blood spilled from its mouth down its chin, onto the torn black suit. It still smiled. Artie swung again, missing the head this time, cutting into the old farmer's shoulder and splaying his arm out in a spastic flail.

It kept moving, shrugging its wounded arm back into place, and Artie knew that it would keep healing itself if this kept up, and he didn't have a whole lot of time.

He backed up into a corner to give himself a precious few seconds, almost screamed as his head brushed up against the hanging model of the Corsair, watched as Curt Ripley moved smoothly toward him, smiling and screaming, bleeding from the mouth and shoulder, formaldehyde still being forced out of the old man's pores like curds from a curd-press, and Artie took a big breath, aimed carefully, and swung again, arcing the shovel like a sword.

The blade cut through the corpse's neck, all the way through the vertebrae at the base of the skull, and the head flopped over to the side, hanging by a long scrap of skin, a tendon or two, and some long, ropy strands of the cheese-stuff, which even as Artie watched scrambled to reconnect themselves, blindly questing towards each other, grasping each other, pulling each other, the head beginning to jerk back up....

Artie swung again.

And again.

Afterwards he threw the shovel at the wall and went straight to his apartment for a glass of Early Times. He found an open pack of Camel fats and sat on the floor of his living room staring down the stairs to the prep room. He smoked. He drank.

He desperately tried to keep it together.

His hands shook badly. Ash from his cigarette fell everywhere, onto his jeans, into his glass. He barely noticed. The gears in his head strained; he could almost smell the burning lubricant as they threatened to come off their axles.

Deep breaths.

Flying Fortress.

Breathe.

Spitfire Supermarine.

He drained the glass. Pawed at the bottle, got more. He was going to have to go back down there and clean up the mess. But not just yet. Not until he was sure he wasn't going crazy.

The prep room was dark when he finally went down. How long had he been sitting up there? Half a bottle of bourbon, however long that was.

He'd made a hell of a mess out of Curt Ripley. There was formaldehyde and quicklime all over the floor. They'd mixed together to form a toxic paste that was even now eating through the remains of whatever it was that Ripley had become.

He grabbed the shovel and started scooping the mess into the Excelsior. The stuff looked like bloody cream of wheat. It took him a while, but eventually most of it was cleaned up....

Three sharp knocks at the door.

Artie almost jumped out of his skin. He looked down at what remained of the mess, then back at the door.

Three more knocks, louder this time.

He moved slowly to the door, shovel in hand, watching his feet. The floor was slick, and he almost fell twice.

Someone outside kicked the door.

Artie turned the latch and opened the door. Just a little.

The guy was outside. The Accountant.

"Hey, buddy," he said, seeing Artie peek through the crack. "What's going on?"

Artie strove to keep his shit together.

"Uh, hey," he said, keeping the door at a crack. The guy was wearing a blue suit and a tie. He smoked a cigar, one of the little skinny ones.

"I came by to see how things are going," he said. "You know, see if you were having any problems."

"No," said Artie. "No problems at all."

"So you gonna let me in?" asked the man, "or am I gonna stand out here like an asshole all night?"

"I can't let you in," said Artie. "Sorry, man. I could lose my license, the whole place could get shut down."

"Hey, what're we talkin' about, here?" the guy said in an unconscious Pacino impression. "It's *me*, for chrissake. You remember me?"

"I can't do it. I'm sorry." Artie's grip on the shovel tightened. Just a bit.

The guy, the accountant, put his hand up.

"Okay, alright. Take it easy. You know, I didn't wanna come out here and bug you like this. Shit, drive two hours down here, Saturday night and all...." He shook his head. He was smiling, like he and Artie were buddies. Defusing the situation. Artie continued to watch him.

"It's my…*employers*," the accountant said, stretching the word out. "They sent me to check on you. Wanted to make sure you're still being a good boy, you know?

"So I said I'd drive on down. It's stupid, I know, but sometimes they get worried, these bosses of mine."

"Everything's going good," said Artie, heart thumping, hand tight on the shovel. "No problems."

"Besides," said the accountant, smiling—and Artie caught a flash of gold teeth.

"I think we shorted you yesterday, didn't we?"

"Two hundred bucks," said Artie. The door opened a bit wider.

"Two hundred, that's right," repeated the guy. "Only I was thinking, maybe I should throw in a bit more. You know—for your troubles."

"How much more?" asked Artie.

"Oh, I dunno—another three bills? How's that sound? Five hundred total—sound good?" The guy's smile got bigger. *He's trying to calm me down,* thought Artie. *Like he'd talk to a dog—quiet words, big promises, soothing tone.*

It was all too big a coincidence.

"Hey, don't worry about it," said Artie, smiling at him.

"We'll get it all straightened out next time, okay? Tell your bosses everything's going fine out here."

He moved to close the door.

The accountant moved faster.

He lifted his leg and booted the door squarely at the latch just as Artie began to close it. The door slammed open, catching Artie in the face and sending him sprawling to the ground.

The guy stepped into the room, drawing a handgun.

"Jesus Christ," he said, looking around the room and putting his free hand over his mouth. "Fuckin' stinks in here. What've you been doing?"

"It's formaldehyde and lime," Artie said in a daze, holding his hand to his face. The shovel was somewhere off to his left. He couldn't see anything but motes of light. "Man, I think you broke my nose."

"Formaldehyde," said the accountant, looking around. "Like embalming fluid, right?"

"Just like it," Artie said. Blood ran down his face. He tried to pinch off his nose, but the action sent shards of blinding pain into his eyes. "*My fuggin' nose....*"

"Hey, what the hell is that embalming shit for, anyway? How come you gotta put it inside stiffs like that?"

"It's a preservative," Artie said. "I put it in so the body won't rot before the funeral. Man, I'm really bleedin' here."

"No shit," said the accountant, lighting another cigar. "You know, there was a guy dated my cousin Francesca a couple years ago—God rest his soul—who used to smoke that green shit. Said he soaked it in embalming fluid to give it some extra snap. You ever heard such a crazy thing?"

"Amped," Artie said. "It's called amping your pot. It's really bad for you, though."

"Crazy shit," said the accountant, suddenly losing interest in the conversation. He'd just noticed the mess on the floor.

"What's this?" he asked quietly, walking over to where the last remnants of quicklime, fluid and goop were streaked on the floor.

"I didn't mean for any of this to happen," Artie said, slowly getting to his feet. The guy spun on his heel and pointed his gun toward Artie.

"We said not to open the fucking bags, didn't we?" he asked in that same quiet tone. He walked over to Artie until the barrel of his gun touched Artie's forehead.

Artie closed his eyes.

The guy sighed.

"You know, if Uncle Sam ever found out about this little deal we got going here, he'd ask some questions. Some *uncomfortable* questions." The hammer clicked back.

Artie opened his eyes again. "Uncle Sam? What the hell are you talking about?"

"The government," said the accountant. "Where do you think these things come from? Your elected officials."

"*I th-thought you were the M-Mob*," Artie said quietly. He was so shocked he could almost forget the guy had a gun pointed at his skull.

"There ain't no fuckin' Mob, you dumbshit," the accountant said. "We're fraternal businessmen, like the Elks. And we do business with all sorts of people, including the guys in Washington. It's twenty G's for us, every time we put one of these wax bastards into play." He pulled the gun away for half a second so he could motion with both his hands.

"They want 'em in good spots. Pastors, cops, all that crap. Important people, or people who have the *attention* of important people. They want it done quiet, so they come to us—we got ways to get to people, you know?"

He watched Artie scowl, trying to soak it all up, and snickered. "I know you was only getting five hundred a body, but that was the deal."

"Why…" Artie began. It didn't make any sense. "Why bury these things if you're supposed to be replacing people with them?"

"Well, you know," said the accountant, "it's fucked up, the government is. My bosses like the money and all, but they don't much like the idea of these things running around without control over 'em. So this way, everyone's happy. The guys in D.C. think they're getting what they want, we're getting a whole lot of money, and you were getting enough scratch to keep you happy. But you had to fuck around, didn't you?"

"But…"

"No buts," the accountant said. "A deal's a deal."

He fired. A black hole the size of a raisin appeared in Artie's forehead and as he fell back he had the sensation of warm syrup running over his face.

His thoughts scrambled, and he wove in and out of consciousness. He smelled gunpowder and sulphur. He thought he saw the accountant leave.

He thought of dogfights over Europe, the Mustangs chasing down those Nazi fucks and blasting them out of the sky. He thought of the Canadians and their Lancaster bombers dropping hellfire into the heart of Germany.

He thought of the light plane he would never own.

He thought of Michelle, her long hair and soft eyes.

He awoke again.

He lay flat on the floor, a pool of blood around his face. It stained his eyes, but he was beyond feeling it. The funeral parlour was dim and bloody.

Something skittered. He could barely see it.

A long, slender finger, moving through the blood like a slug.

Toward him.

Under the table was a piece of the wax, about the size of an apple. He'd completely missed it when he'd cleaned up the parlour.

It reached out across the blood, now. Testing it. Artie could see the tendril, like a root, reaching out blindly toward him, toward the little hole in his forehead that was still oozing blood.

He couldn't move. Maybe he didn't *want* to move.

It fondly touched the burnt skin around the hole, so delicately, so gently.

Like a sweetheart's touch.

As if trying to soothe Artie for what was to come.

It's Lonely in the Desert at Night

Fido comes when I call him. I think that's why I keep him around. Like any hound he stinks; so bad I can barely stand it.

But it's lonely in the desert, especially at night. Then I don't mind the stink so much.

Fido moves slow cuz his legs are broke. He drags them behind him and they get all dirty and full of bugs. Hell, *he's* full of bugs.

Before he died he howled and whined and then puked up a lump of bloody mess from his lungs, and damn if he wasn't struck through hair worms. They didn't last long out in the desert sun. Nothing lasts long out here. 'Cept me.

And him. He paws at me sometimes. He can't remember that I pulled all his teeth and smashed his jaw so it hangs there like a limp dick on his face. Pulled his nails too. Hounds are bad with their nails and I didn't want to take a chance. That was before I got sick. Kinda wish I would have left 'em in now.

Fido's real loyal. A few days ago we ran into a mess of 'walkers out here. They keep close to each other, like they know their chances are better stickin' together.

Hell, I dunno. Maybe that's what Fido thinks too.

I get up there and take em out with my rifle. They don't even know what hit 'em. Their heads is poppin' off like dandelions. Afterward me n' Fido go and look. They're dead, right as rain. I don't have to describe 'em. After a while they all look the same.

Only when I walk by one, he reaches up and grabs my leg. Before I know it he's chewin' into me. Seems that bastard played possum so he could get him a piece.

I go down. Fido...well, Fido is on him like heat on a fire. He pulled the head clean off and tried to eat it. Course he can't, with his jaw all mashed up. That was lookin' around all crazy eyed til I shot it.

Fido looks at me. A sad look like when he was alive and he weren't a hound that followed me around. Just a little boy with sad eyes like his Momma. He'd say *Daddy, how come you ain't eatin'? Ain't you hungry too?*

I'd say *I am, but I gotta make sure you eat first cuz that's what's important.*

And he'd say *why?*

And I'd say C*uz love is lookin after the ones you care about.* It's about stayin' true and bein' loyal no matter how sick you get. Seein' Fido on that 'walker the other day reminded me of when he was Bobbie again.

I guess that's *really* why I keep 'em around. He made me proud.

I'm dying. In a while I'm gonna drop off and then come back again. But it's okay. I spent the day wiring Fido's jaw up. I smashed an empty Coke bottle and jammed his mouth full of the sharpest pieces. Hell, that's better'n his original teeth. I cut myself five or six times doin' him up right.

I hope Fido remembers me when I come back. Most of all I hope I remember him. I hope we can still wander the desert together, but not like a man and his dog. Like Father and son.

After all, it's lonely out here in the desert.

Especially at night.

The Matchstick Man

The old blue truck rumbled to a stop in front of the house, kicking up plumes of dust in its wake. It was late summer, August in the prairies, the hottest time of the year.

Joel Carver sat in the back of the pickup, watching the cloud of road dust come at him. He didn't move. He breathed in the chalk grain and sunshine, sweat making the dirt stick to his face. It was mildly salty, just like everything in Southern Alberta. The heat made it that way.

"Come on, boy," Joel's father said, getting out from behind the driver's seat. His mother, wearing her best Sunday dress, got out on the other side. Joel looked over at her and felt a pang of shame. It was Wednesday. She'd have to wash that thing before Church, and it was all his fault.

What Church? his mind whispered.

"Take your bag upstairs, Joel," his mother said. "Then come downstairs and we'll have a little talk."

"Alright, Momma," he said. He grabbed his duffel bag and climbed out the back of the truck. His movements were slow, deliberate. He couldn't afford to make a mistake.

Joel loped past his father, head down, and took the steps up onto the porch one at a time. The door was unlocked, and then he was inside the oppressive heat of the house. The air was dead still.

He smelled like blood.

Joel went past the living room without looking and went straight up the stairs to his room. Momma had cleaned while he'd been away; she'd swept the floor and folded his clothes. They were sitting in two piles on his neatly folded bed, waiting for him to put them away.

Penny was standing in the far corner of the room, watching him with dead eyes.

"Welcome home, old boy," she said, and smiled.

Joel ignored her. He put his duffel bag on the bed and quickly stuffed his clothes into his dresser without speaking.

"How was it?" she said.

"What do you care?" Joel said. He couldn't look at her.

"I'm sorry, Joel," she said. "It should have been me."

"Yeah, well, it wasn't," he snapped. He could feel the anger rising inside him.

Calm. Must stay calm.

"I'm sorry," Penny said softly. After a moment she cleared her throat. "Does it hurt?"

"Only when I'm mad," Joel said. "Doc says I gotta stay calm, no matter what. So you better make yourself scarce, Penny,"

"I'm so sorry, Joel," she said again, folding her hands. "I'll leave you alone. Sorry."

Joel tucked his head as she left, and counted to ten. Long, deep breaths. In and out. Nice and slow.

Calm.

He finished with his duffel bag and went back downstairs, where the heat was enough to make him dizzy. He swallowed hard and went over to the dining room table where his parents were sitting.

"Sit down, son," his mother said. "Can I get you some water?"

"Yes please, Momma," Joel said.

Momma went to the kitchen. Joel's father crossed his arms and let out his breath in a sigh.

"Hot today, innit?" he said at last.

"Yes sir," Joel said. He laced his fingers together and put his hands on the table in front of them.

"Does it hurt?" he said.

"No sir," Joel said. "Can't hardly feel it."

"Pull up your shirt some, let's take a look at what you got," his father said.

Joel did as he said, lifting his shirt and revealing a four inch wound on his chest, just under his rib cage. The wound had been closed off with two rows of tiny, tightly knotted stitches.

"Don't look like much, does it?" Joel's father said. "Cat scratch or somethin'."

"Yes, sir," Joel said. "Don't feel like much, neither."

Just then, Joel's mother came into the room with a pitcher of water and some glasses. She placed one in front of Joel and his father, and then took one for herself.

"Put your shirt down, Joel," she said, clucking like a hen. "Do we really need to look at it?" She poured out three glasses of cold well water and sat down at the table with them.

"I wanted to see it, Cathy," Joel's father said. We need to talk about it, if we're ever gonna get through it alright."

"It's not the kind of thing you show at the dinner table is all," Cathy said, fussing over the hem in her dress. She clucked again. "Gone and lost a stitch."

Joel's father turned back to the boy.

"So you know how it works, right? They explained everything to you already?"

"Yes, sir," Joel said. "I can't get mad again, or else the thing in there will light me up. Combustion, the doctor said, just like a matchstick. Said we should have some pills, keep me calm."

"That's what I wanted to talk to you about, son," his father said. "Doc said those pills is gonna be big money. It's old medicine, so it costs more. They don't make it around here no more."

Joel looked up at his father, his face creasing for a moment. The wound in his chest flared and itched. He self-consciously put a hand over it.

"You gotta stay calm, boy," his father said, watching him. "Now I'm sorry, but we just couldn't afford it. You know how bad it's been on the farm this last year, Hell, we're lucky we still got gas money for the truck."

"I know, Poppa," Joel said, putting his head down again. He could feel the emotions inside him, like choppy water before a good wind storm. He swallowed hard. Sweat ran from his fingers, and from his hairline, making his scalp itch.

"You keep in the house, son; don't stray out into the yard or nothin'. Your mom and I want you to keep quiet, read some books, do what you want. You can't go into town, and for now you can't leave the property."

"Yes, sir," Joel said.

"Good," his father said. "Go on now, go up to your room. And if you see Penny, you tell her to come downstairs and not to bug you."

Joel got up, put his glass in the sink, and then marched upstairs to his bedroom. He took off his socks and lay down on his bed.

It just wasn't fair.

It *wasn't* fair and the more he thought about it the more he got angry about the whole damn thing and the more the skin around his wound itched. It was like a hot scratch, he wanted to dig his fingers into it and gouge with his nails until all the stitches came out and the awful burning itch of his heart ball was gone for good.

Except he couldn't damn well do that, could he? Doc said that if that little ball ever came in contact with the air it would explode. Big enough to rip him in half, in case he ever got any funny ideas. The damned thing was attached to his spinal cord, so it knew what he was thinking even before Joel himself knew.

He'd just have to stay calm and try not to get worked up over anything. Not to get too excited. *Not to burn down another Church.*

"Joel?" Penny said from the stairway. "Can I get you somethin'?"

Joel closed his eyes.

"No," he said. "I just want to sleep."

"Okay," she said. There was a soft pause at the door while she decided whether to say anything else or not. Finally she shut the door.

Josh took deep breaths and tried not to think about scratching.

He woke after dark. He sat up, holding one hand to his chest. He'd heard the rumble of a truck in his half-sleep, and now he could hear the murmur of someone talking outside. Carefully Josh got up and went to the window.

It was Zeke, from down the road, and his son Malcolm. The boy was sitting in the truck, his face crossed in a scowl. Zeke and Poppa were busy talking; Joel could see them both clearly in the headlights of the truck. Joel cracked his window, just enough to hear what the men were saying.

"You should' a never brought that *sumbitch* back home, Earl," Zeke said. Joel could tell immediately that he'd been drinking.

"I'm gonna tell you again," Earl said quietly. "Keep your voice down, Zeke. That's my *son* you're talking about." The man stood straight, his back to the house, his arms folded.

"*He'shh* not yer son," Zeke said. "*He'shh* a firebug and a murderer. You know he ain't had no reason to kill them *girlssh* like that. And he *ain't* had no reason to burn down the Church."

"My son has been judged," Earl said. "He's been implanted. He'll spend the rest of his life bein' sorry for what he did."

"Ahhh, bullshit," Zeke said. "*Shend* him away. Nobody in town wants him here anyway. Let him fend for himself out in the *badlandssh*. There's no reason the rest of yer family has to suffer."

"I told you, *my son was judged*. I don't give a damn what the town wants. I ain't sendin' my boy out into the wastes. He wouldn't last a day out there. He can't defend hisself no more. It might kill him just raisin' a rifle. Now I think you and your boy better leave, Earl, and don't come back here for a while."

"You *shtubborn* sumbitch," Earl said. His voice was getting progressively louder. "You know what'll happen iff'n the town turns their back on yah, don't you Earl? You'll be starved out of here by winter. You'll have to take that wife and *purty* daughter o' *yoursh* and go live in the *badlandssh* yourself."

"*Get the Hell outta here!*" Earl yelled. He took a step toward Zeke, his fists raised.

"Don't you dare!" Earl said, shying away from the man.

"I'll have you up on a block so fast it'll make your head spin!"

"You leave now, and I won't have to whup yer ass in front of yer boy, Zeke. That's yer last chance."

"I'm goin'," Zeke said. "You mark my words though, Earl. Starved out by winter."

Earl made like he was about to take another step toward Zeke, but the man spun around and ran to the door of his truck. Then, throwing it in reverse, he whipped the vehicle around and started down the road. He wasn't twenty feet away when he laid on his car horn. The blast of noise carried across the fields for miles in every direction.

Joel watched the truck as it disappeared into the dark. When he looked down at his father, he saw the man looking up into his window.

"Joel?" his father said.

"Yes, Poppa?"

"You were listenin' at the window this whole time?"

"Yes, Poppa," Joel said. He reached over and turned up the gas on his little bedside lantern. The room was filled with a soft glow, enough light for his father to see him.

"I don't want you to pay attention to none of what Ol' Zeke said, you hear? Man's nuthin' but an old drunk lookin' to stir up trouble."

"Ok, Poppa," Joel said.

"Go on back to bed now, it's late. In the mornin' we'll have breakfast before I head into the field."

A small smile spread across Joel's face.

"Yes, Poppa," he said. He reached down and killed the light on the lamp, and then found his way to the bed.

The days passed slowly around the farmstead. The hot summer sun began to get up later and go to bed earlier, and the mornings began to cool off. True to their word, the townsfolk completely rejected Joel and his family. Too much harm had been done by the big church fire, and too many people felt that Joel should have gone off away from the settlement and into the wastelands.

Some insisted.

Joel woke one morning to the sound of his mother crying, and when he found her at the kitchen table she said that something had happened to the cows and they'd all been killed.

Joel's father was cryptic about it when asked, shaking his head sadly and simply saying that they'd caught some kind of flu. Then he went into his room for a long time and locked the door.

A few weeks later, when the chickens caught flu as well, Joel's father took a bottle of whiskey into the bedroom with him and stayed there until the next day.

When Joel's father started keeping a shotgun by his bed at night, Joel didn't have the heart to ask him what it was for. In his heart, and in that throbbing little ball of metal, he knew what was going on. And when he thought about the people in the town and the awful things they were doing, damned if that heart ball didn't turn white hot inside his chest.

Nobody came to visit. Not even Joel's cousins who lived on the far side of town. They made a new church out of the town hall, but Joel and his parents stayed away. Nobody had told them outright, but they knew they weren't welcome anymore. The sooner they understood that, the better.

One late afternoon Joel was sitting out under the apple tree in the front yard. The tree itself was dead; someone had come along in the middle of the night and dumped a can full of gasoline onto the roots. The apples had turned sour as the tree died, still half formed and useless, until they'd rotted on the branches and Joel's father had to gather them up and compost them.

Joel watched as aphids and black flies floated lazily in the last of the day's sunlight. He flipped through the pages of his book but couldn't keep his mind on the old pages long enough to keep the story in his head.

When Joel's father walked up to where he was sitting, Joel barely noticed. He was deep in thought. He'd developed a habit of pressing on the spot where the heart ball was in his chest, and he ran his fingers of the smallish lump while he daydreamed.

"Does it still hurt?" Earl said.

Joel looked up at him, scowling.

"No, Poppa," he said. "Just gets hot when I get excited. I'm getting' pretty good at keeping it cool though."

"That's real good, son," his father said. "Real good."

He sat down beside Joel, cross-legged and groaning as he pushed himself back against the trunk of the tree.

"I always liked this old tree," he said after a while, as if thinking to himself.

"Me too," Joel said. "Course, it was better when it had apples on it."

"That's true," Joel's father said. "You know your

grandfather planted this tree back in 2035? He wanted to leave something for the next century. Real proud of this old tree, watered it and pruned it every year without fail. I used to come out here as a kid and there'd only be a few dozen apples on the little guy."

"Hard to imagine," Joel said. "It's so big now."

"Yeah," his father said. Joel could hear sadness in his voice. "When the bombs went off during the war, it was the endless jars of apple preserves your granny used to make that kept us alive and healthy. We were down in that bunker for two years. I was so sick of apples by the time we were ready to come out into the world again, I swore I'd never eat another apple in my life."

"But you love apples," Joel said, looking at him. "You eat them all the time."

"I don't love apples," Joel's father said, the sad smile returning to his face. "I love *these* apples. When we made it back here, this old tree was alive and well. It was fall, and it was the first real food we'd seen in years. Our Geiger counters said that the tree was fine, no radiation, so we spent that winter eating *fresh* apples. Best damn things I ever tasted, I tell you."

Joel laughed. It was the first time he'd done it in such a long time, and it felt good. The heart ball warmed ever so slightly, and Joel put his hand over it.

The two of them sat there for a while longer, enjoying the sun and watching the aphids before Joel's father spoke again.

"We're going to move, son. This town just ain't right for us anymore."

Joel sat there in silence. The heart ball fluttered.

"We're gonna be heading south, I imagine," Joel's father said. "Weather's nicer down there, and folks are a little kinder. These people just ain't for us no more. Tomorrow, you start packin'. We'll be heading off in a couple weeks, but I want to make sure everything is ready before we go. No slip ups, and nothin' important gets left behind."

"Okay, Poppa," Joel said, watching as his father got up and dusted himself off. He took one lonely, mournful look at the dead apple tree and shook his head. Then he turned and walked back toward the house.

Later, the family ate a supper of beans and pork before drifting off to do their own things for the evening. Joel headed upstairs to bed.

He didn't sleep though. Instead, he spent most of the evening clutching his heart ball and breathing deeply.

It was early morning when Joel got out of bed. The morning sun was still hours away. He walked over to his dresser and pulled out some things; warm socks and pants, two sweaters, some shirts. He also grabbed his little bedside lamp, being sure to dismantle it first so he could secure a cap on the fuel bottle. He'd always hated fire, and the thought of accidentally lighting himself up was almost too much to bear.

He wrapped the lamp in his shirts and placed it with the rest of his clothes at the bottom of a large hiking pack from under his bed. Then he went downstairs and into the kitchen.

He grabbed some candles, a small pot that he filled with dry rice, and two bottle of water. He also grabbed an extra

Geiger counter from under the sink. He was going to need one very soon.

"What are you doing?" Penny said, appearing in the kitchen doorway.

Joel spun on his heel, grabbing at his chest with a free hand.

"Oh God, *Pen*," he said. "You can't do that. You almost turned me into a human torch."

"Sorry," Penny said. "What are you doing with all that stuff?"

"Nothing," Joel said, regaining his composure. "You just go back to bed and forget about what I'm doing."

"You're leaving," Penny said softly.

Joel put the Geiger counter into his backpack and sighed. He turned back to his sister.

"I have to go, Pen," he said, his voice soft. "Poppa's going to try and take us into the Wastelands, and I can't let him do that to you. If I go, things will get back to normal. The town will forgive you guys and take care of you for the winter."

"You don't know that," Penny said. She sounded as though she might burst into tears at any moment.

"I know enough that you guys will be better off when I'm gone," Joel said. "Penny, *please* don't get me excited about this. This thing is burning me already."

"I'm so sorry," Penny said. "I don't know why it happened. This is all my fault."

"Just hush about it, will you?" Joel said. He rubbed the warm lump in his chest. The old scar was pink and smooth, and he could feel it under his shirt.

"Penny, listen to me," Joel said, walking over to where she was standing. "That day the church burned down, you just forget it, alright? Forget everything and never talk about it to anyone."

"But…"

"No *buts*," Joel said, his voice firm. "I want you to just forget about what happened. It's the only way. If I go, everything will go back to normal for you and Momma and Poppa. I'll make do on my own."

"But I'll die if you go," Penny said. Large wet tears ran down her face and she made no move to wipe them away. Joel took the edge of his shirt and did it for her.

"You're gonna be fine. *I'm* gonna be fine. Now you go on back to bed and forget about all of this."

Penny reached out to him then and hugged her brother hard for a long time. She mumbled apologies into his shirt and wept quietly. Joel held her with one hand and held his hand over the heart ball. It was agony in his chest. If felt as though it could light him on fire at any moment.

Finally he pushed her away.

"Go to bed, Penny," he said softly. "I'll be back one day."

"Promise?" Penny said.

Joel smiled in the dark. Then he turned and slipped out the door and onto the front porch. He began to walk away from the house, the night air cool on his face. He heard the front door open as Penny walked out onto the porch, and he took a moment to turn back to her. She made a feeble wave with her hand before wrapping her arms tight around herself.

Joel waved back. Penny held herself like that when she was

scared or didn't know what to do. He'd seen her do it lots of times in the years since she was born.

The night of the church fire came back to him, the back of the building burning badly, already so big there was no hope of putting it out. He'd stood there and watched it like a fool, while Penny looked on, her arms wrapped around her chest. He could still hear the screams of the people inside, and the horrible noises the women made when they realized that some of their babies were still inside the building.

He'd stood and watched while the back wall went up, the stained glass popping like rock candy in the heat. It was as though hell itself had come to claim their little church. The simple truth was that he hadn't really known what to do, and that he'd been too shocked to take any kind of action at all.

But he saw the men running around the side of the church, straight at them, buckets of water in hand, and he'd snapped out of it. He'd done the only thing he could do; the one thing that his father had always told him was his duty no matter what: *Protect Your Sister.*

Quickly, as the men were just about to the back of the church, Joel reached down and plucked the book of matches from her hands.

Dorothy of Kansas

It was a world of silt and ash, and snow. Burned things. Ruined things. The air was thick with foul gas and smoke. The stench of death was on the air like an afterthought. And it *was*. The sun was lost to permanent gloom; the trees were uprooted and black and dead. Cow corpses lay rotted and stiff in the fields beside the farmers who once tended them. Not even flies buzzed on the putrescent flesh. Their faces withered and pulled back in hideous leers; they bared their teeth in death as much as their smiles had born them in life.

But joy had moved on from Oz. Life had moved on.

Tin Man walked endlessly. The snow that fell gave him a sickly warmth that he didn't trust. He could feel it everywhere, from the top of his rusting head down to the stubs of feet where his toes had worn away. He was a deep red now, a flaking leper with holes in his limbs and torso.

Not tin, after all. *Tin* wouldn't rust like this. But the acidic snow that fell in Oz had stripped the galvanized plate off him years ago, and shortly after he'd noticed the first specs of red like tiny cancer dots on his chest. Tears of rust dripped from his eyes, and they ran like wounds down his bright silver sheen. All gone now. With everything else. All he had left was his axe.

And the head of Scarecrow, which he kept in rusty old garden bucket.

"We should get out of the snow for a while," Scarecrow said, watching as Tin Man fingered a particularly bad hole in his gut. His stumpy, worn down fingers only succeeded in making the hole bigger. When he pulled his hand away the metal flesh crumbled and fell into the snow at his feet. The sickly yellow bricks beneath the snow seemed to gobble it up.

"I need to keep walking," Tin man said. He wiped snow from his shoulders, then shook the pail to get some snow off Scarecrow's face.

"You're not thinking with your head," Scarecrow said. "If you rust away to nothing we'll never get anywhere."

"If I rust away to nothing you'll be the last person left alive in all of Oz," Tin Man said in a sad voice. "Wouldn't that just break your heart."

"Exactly why you should get out of the snow!" Scarecrow said.

"It hasn't stopped snowing in months," Tin Man said. "Besides, where do we go?"

"That's not true," Scarecrow mumbled, but his voice meant he was going to drop the issue. "Sometimes it's ash."

Where they would go was Kansas, of course. Their one chance of finding Dorothy was there. It was more of a *hope* than a chance. Ironic that the last bit of hope left in all of Oz was the hope that they could somehow find a way out of the ruined little world. Maybe Dorothy could fix things. On the other hand, maybe Dorothy was dead already. Maybe this was little more than something to keep their minds busy until Tin Man's legs finally gave out and they'd lie in the acidic snow to sleep and melt away to nothing.

"We should get out of the snow for a while," Scarecrow said again. Then he brightened. "Hey, I think this is where we met Lion!"

"It's just more ruined forest," Tin Man said.

"Try to remember it from the old days," Scarecrow said. "Back when everything was verdant and fresh, and there were lions in the woods."

Tin Man tried not to think about the old days. Colour made him sad. His world was devoid of it now, save for the rust on his body and the paint on Scarecrow's face.

Even the straw in Scarecrow's head was bleached out and full of mud. He was long overdue for a change. Problem was all the straw in Oz was gone. Now Scarecrow's mind slipped; he broke into random bits of song or he repeated sentences over and over until Tin Man wanted to toss him into the snow and leave him there. When the last bit of straw finally rotted away to nothing it would take the final bits of the Scarecrow with it.

Other times, he felt bad for his last friend. Here was a mighty King of Oz, sitting in a busted up garden pail slowly losing his mind.

But mostly he felt bad that they had both lived to see their beautiful land become this charred, dead wasteland.

They hadn't seen another living thing in weeks.

The last one had been an apple tree. It had wandered into the black and metallic sludge of a river and simply stood there staring while Tin Man and Scarecrow crossed a little cobblestone bridge nearby. Tin Man had made eye contact, briefly, but the look on the tree's face told him all he needed to know. It was sucking pure poison into its roots, either out of a need to drink or a need to be dead. It didn't matter. Woodsman and mighty tree, enemies once, but no more. Just three survivors, cursed to witness the end.

"Do you think she'll be there?" Scarecrow asked. "Dorothy I mean."

"*I know what you mean,*" Tin Man snapped. "But I don't know. I would like to say I hope she is, but my heart tells me it won't matter. At this point what can be done?"

"She could get me some clean straw," Scarecrow said. "From the mattress or something. I wouldn't even care if it smelled like sweat and pee. I can feel myself getting dumber, Tin Man. I'm having a hard time remembering things."

"And you repeat yourself," Tin Man said. "*Ad nauseum* ."

"What?"

Tin Man sighed.

"It means to the point of sickness." He saw the look on Scarecrow's face change to hurt confusion, and he immediately felt bad that he'd said anything. "Sorry. I know it's not your fault."

"You know that not long ago I was regarded as the smartest man in Oz?" Scarecrow said. "To think I started out as straw and potato sacks. And paint."

"Quite an amazing feat, especially for a Scarecrow," Tin Man said.

"Espec..."Scarecrow said, then stopped, catching himself. "Err yes, it is quite an achievement for a man of my upbringing. To think I started out as straw and potato sacks."

"And paint," Tin Man added quickly.

"And paint, yes," Scarecrow said brightly. "You are no dullard yourself, my good woodsman. Don't ever let anyone say otherwise."

If we ever see anyone again, Tin Man thought, but he didn't say it.

They walked on through the gloom. The only sound to be heard was the wraith-like flutter of snow hitting the ground and the tireless crunch as the Tin Man's stutter-step compressed it underfoot. The Yellow Brick Road was pitted and scarred after years of acid baths; here and there the edges had given way completely. It had been a gleaming symbol of the magic and wonder of Oz for millennia. Now it was a ruined old path that was slowing dissolving away to nothing.

Same could have been said of the Emerald City. Of course Tin Man had gone there first. From the stench of decay and the layering of bodies in the streets it appeared as if everyone had. Fled their homes for the first time in real fear for their lives, even though they could never die in Oz and they could never get more than a tummy ache from over indulging.

They also found graffiti as the Winkies and Munchkins first begged Dorothy for salvation; then, when they realized no help was coming, turned against her. One message, scrawled in emerald paint on the outside of a large Greenfish fountain where he'd found Scarecrow's head said simply *I hope you live to see this Ditty*.

Dorothy never came, and that is why they hated her. They'd waited for salvation at the end of their lives and in the end they were met with a soft falling ash mixed with dirty, acidic snow. That was bad. The snow fell on the crops and killed all the plants, and it fell in the water and poisoned it. And *that* was really bad.

When the creatures of Oz finally turned on one another out of feral starvation and insanity, that was much, much worse.

Eventually Tin Man and Scarecrow came to a fork in the road beside the ruins of a little cornfield. In the centre of the cornfield stood a crooked cross leaning dangerously to one side. Like it was trying to lie down and die but couldn't out of some misguided need to assure their faith. Tin Man wanted to tell the cross that it was alright, that Scarecrow was too smart for faith and he himself felt too betrayed by his life to ever feel anything again.

Scarecrow's eyes widened when he saw it though.

"Hey!" he said. "*This is it!* This is where Dorothy found me!"

"Is it?" Tin Man said. "I wouldn't know. I guess we passed the enchanted forest, but I didn't notice. We walked right by my old home."

"We would have seen it," Scarecrow said. "If it were still standing."

"I suppose you're right," Tin Man sighed.

"You know what that means?"

"No."

"It means we're getting close. I don't think Dorothy travelled many miles on her own before we met. She'd only just begun her walk. It *means* we're in Munchkin country. My pole was just at the edge of it."

"Well, we should keep walking then," Tin Man said. He brushed the snow from his shoulders. Flakes of rust glittered in the grey air like bloody dandruff.

They walked on, passing burned farmsteads and ruined crops. There were more scarecrows too, but they were long dead and their straw was waxy and burnt. Some were little more than potato sacks hung from crosses with barbed wire. There was nothing for the Tin Man to salvage here. No fresh dressings for Scarecrow.

Eventually they came to a spot in the road where the burnt shell of a house blocked their way. The wood was frosted with ash and carbon, and scaly to the touch like a gigantic spider husk. Here and there the wood splintered on weak supports; the roof had collapsed some time ago under the weight of the snow.

"Here it is," Scarecrow said. "This is where it all began."

"Seems like a lifetime ago," said Tin Man. Looking around at the death and ruin, he added, "Two lifetimes."

"Eight years, four months, thirteen days," Scarecrow counted, "twenty-six minutes. Of course, that's from when I got my brain. Before that I listened as the winds of idiocy blew knowledge in one ear and out the other. I was even too stupid to realize how sad it should have made me.

"My life has always been like this," Tin Man replied. "Misery with gaps of darkness. It makes me wonder why I ever wanted that damn heart back, all the pain it's caused. Now I can't even feel it anymore. I think it's ruined."

"I understand what you're saying," Scarecrow said.

"Do you?" Tin Man turned and looked down into the bucket. "I feel like it isn't just this metal body that's rusting away. I feel as though my very *soul* is melted, and putting one foot in front of the other is all I have to keep the beat of my heart now. Only I'm half lame from my feet rusting away, and my steps aren't strong like a heart should be. They're sick and dying. But I don't care about that, because now I know that there are things worse than death. *There's this.*"

He reached down and grabbed a handful of snow, and sprinkled it into the bucket over Scarecrow's face.

"*Hey,*" Scarecrow said, spitting his words. He wrinkled his nose to get the last of the snow off his face, because it burned and he didn't trust it on his burlap flesh.

"I'm sorry," Tin Man said. "That was mean. I shouldn't be laying this on you; you don't even have a shoulder to lean on."

"It's alright," Scarecrow said. "I see what you are saying. Oz in ruins hurts my heart too. Especially when I think of everything we've lost."

As they spoke, Tin Man walked through the house. It was

a museum. Or had been, with little ropes tying everything off and signs that said:

No Touching! This means you Hurly Applebottom!

On the other side of the house Tin Man stepped through the back door and out onto the Yellow Brick Road again.

Eventually, Dorothy's house was a memory on the horizon. Tin Man kept a beat with his shuffle step, and Scarecrow talked about theorems and hypotheses. They moved away from burned trees and ruined Munchkin huts and out into the grasslands. As they passed one last farmhouse, Scarecrow squinted his eyes and shook his bucket.

"Hey, what is that?"

On the side of the road was a little red wagon, filled with toys. There was a discomforting lump under the snow. Tin Man gave it a wide berth.

"*Oh*," Scarecrow said. "That has the dimensions of a Munchkin child. A girl, from the shape of the head. How tragic."

"Just shut up for a little while," Tin Man said. "I need some peace and quiet."

"I don't see how that's possible," Scarecrow said. "You whistle like a teapot now with those holes in your belly. It's a wonder you get a moment's rest at all."

Tin Man looked down at the corroded holes in his body and sighed. His friend was right of course, the sound made him crazy. And the holes were getting bigger with every passing mile it seemed. The one he had fit a finger into just a few days before was now big enough for *two* fingers.

They walked on and Scarecrow tried to talk less, but his

straw was giving out on him and he forgot to be quiet after a time.

Days later they came to the end of civilized Oz. They knew this because there was a sign in Munchkinese that said

> *YOU ARE NOW LEAVING THE CIVIL LANDS OF OZ. THE CREATURES WHO ROAM THESE LANDS ARE LESS THAN CIVIL-OZD.*
>
> Signed, *Your Mayor.*

Scarecrow snorted a quick laugh.

"*Civil-Oz'd,*" he said.

Tin Man said nothing. He walked ahead, following the Yellow Brick Road to its final destination.

"Come on," Scarecrow said. "It's kind of funny, right?"

"Shut up," Tin Man said, but he looked away. Rust flaked off his face when his mouth twitched.

Around him, the snow and ash fell on dirt, here and there rough pine trees snaked out of the grass like giant skeletal fingers. They bore trunks of charred wood and their pine needles were grey ash. The air was as greasy as everywhere else in Oz. If not for the sign, one might not even notice where the Uncivil-Oz'd lands started and the Civil-Oz'd lands began. One thing the badlands had going for them was that they were much less likely to encounter death out here.

And just as unlikely to encounter life.

They walked on. Always pushing on. Always moving toward their goal. *Dorothy.* If she could be reached, Tin Man would reach her. He began using the handle end of his axe as a cane. The bucket that he kept Scarecrow's head in rusted and broke at the handle. He bent the sheared metal back so the straw man didn't lose an eye and carried the bucket under his arm like a football.

Eventually the pine tree fingers were gone too, and the horizon was a dirty yellow smudge in front of them. The land ahead of them looked like foothills, but Tin Man knew of no mountains in this part of the world. He continued to tap the ground beneath the snow with the handle of his axe. When the axe sank into the snow a lot further than it should have, Tin Man pulled up in alarm.

"What is it?" Scarecrow said.

"The road gave way," Tin Man said. He began kicking snow to the sides of the road.

"Careful," said Scarecrow. "Could be a sink hole."

"I don't know what that means," said Tin Man. "If it is, be sure to tell me."

As it turned out, it *wasn't* a sinkhole. The Road simply ended with a smooth set of alternating bricks, perfectly flat like the corner of a brick wall. One step past the road, the hard packed earth gave way to dirty yellow sand.

"We're finally here," Scarecrow said.

"Oh yeah?" Tin Man said. "Where is that exactly?"

"Well, technically here is *nowhere*," he replied. "But even nowhere is somewhere. That is to say, we can't be nowhere, because the moment we arrive at nowhere we are somewhere."

"Scarecrow!" Tin Man said, giving the bucket a shake. "Please snap out of it."

"Huh? Oh yes. This is the End of Oz. The yellow Brick

Road ends precisely where the Great Desert of Sand and Dunes begins. But since we're in the middle of nowhere..."

"Spare me, please," Tin Man said. "Are we still going the right direction?"

"Again," Scarecrow said. "It depends on your perspective."

Tin Man sighed wearily.

"Explain please," he said. "And *please* make sense."

"Well, according to folklore, there are many ways out of Oz. Too many, in fact, which is why Glinda made the realm invisible. Because at every spot people could get *out*, other people could get *in*. *Bad People*. The King of the Gnomes, for example."

"Your point being..."

"My point is that once *out* of Oz, any way we travel could theoretically take us away from Oz. Maybe to Kansas, maybe to Wonderland. Pretty much anywhere you want, nobody knows for sure. It was all very *hush-hush* stuff in the Emerald City, as we didn't want the common folk to know how easy the defences of Oz could be breached."

"So we could end up a million miles away from Kansas?" Tin Man said. "Terrific."

"Yes and no. As I said, once out of Oz, one could end up *anywhere*."

Tin Man shook his head.

"Don't worry my friend," Scarecrow said, trying to be reassuring. "We'll end up in Kansas, you'll see."

"But how do you know?" Tin Man said.

"Because we wish it," Scarecrow said. "And thinking makes it so."

"I can't argue that logic," Tin Man said.

"You are a *wOz* man to listen and understand," Scarecrow said, and burst into a shower of giggles.

I wonder how long he's been mad, Tin Man thought. *And I wonder why I never noticed until just now.*

Tin Man stepped off the Yellow Brick Road. His feet sank to the ankles in snow and sand.

"Great," he said. "I'm gonna get bogged down, I know it."

"Step lively, Tin soldier!" Scarecrow chirped. "Knees high lad! That'll keep you out of the sand."

The desert was a grey and blond ocean washing as far as either of them could see. There was a chemical smell to the sand, like burnt metal, and the sound of silt and grit hitting the Tin Man's rusted torso was like listening to water hitting an empty bucket. He felt it inside him, cold and alien, and after a while he closed a hand over the holes in his belly to try and keep some of it out. The wind whistled around them as well, and it was getting more difficult to see.

Tin Man put his head down and marched, high step, as Scarecrow had suggested, but the going was slow and dangerous, and several times they almost fell down the long dunes washing about them. The more he thought on it the more Tin Man began to think of the desert as a *real ocean*; an unstable surface that shifted moment to moment. He knew if he fell or got trapped in the dunes they might not be able to get out. And there was nobody left to save them.

Sand also got into his joints, making them creak and strain. His knee began locking up after a week in the sand, and he took to dragging it the way one might drag an artificial leg. The irony of that statement wasn't lost on the Scarecrow. He howled like a coyote when Tin Man mentioned it.

The sun rose one morning but they couldn't really see it, and there was a rolling thunder in the distance that Tin Man didn't like.

"We may want to find some shelter," Scarecrow said. "From what I've read about desert storms they can be quite unpleasant. The sand might scour the rust off you, and then where would you be?"

"In the bucket with you, maybe." Tin Man said. He cupped a hand over his eyes and scanned the horizon but it was an exercise in futility. He couldn't see more than a few hundred feet in front of him. The wind kicked up a blanket of sand in all directions, mixing it with silt and ash, scouring the Tin Man's rusting frame, and affecting the topography of the great desert. With an eternal grey wall blocking the sun's rays, the land was cold but arid; the lack of moisture was at least *something* the Tin Man could be thankful for.

They had no choice but to move on. With luck they might skirt the edge of the sandstorm, but they had no way of affecting that luck. They could only walk blind and hope.

Gradually the storm picked up and they became aware of a new noise; a gentle, crystal twinkling that carried like wind chimes to their ears. Tin Man actually stopped so he could listen better.

"What is that?" he said. "Faeries?"

"Hardly," Scarecrow said. His head was half buried in sand. "Could be a hallucination brought on by madness. Doesn't explain why *you'd* hear it too though, unless that's all part of my delusion. On the other hand it could just be a wind chime."

I hate when you talk like that," Tin Man grumbled. "It's confusing."

"Well, maybe there's an old airship or something in the dunes out here. Maybe it *is* really a wind chime. We should check it out, because if there's shelter to be had, we could use it to get away from that sandstorm."

"May as well," Tin Man said. "We're headed in that direction anyway."

The sounds weren't wind chimes. It didn't take long for them to realize there couldn't possibly be an airship out here. It would have been long buried in sand by now. But there was something ahead. Something Tin Man had never seen before.

There were tree-like forms in the gloom ahead of them, and as they neared it became obvious the sound was the wind and sand blowing off these objects. They were tall, black, and appeared to be made from strands of ash. There were more of them around, here and there, randomly scattered about with no discernible pattern. In a couple spots they appeared to overlap each other, grow together. In others they started together and grew apart. They tinkled and made grinding noises as the wind pushed them to and fro, and where their hollow trunks were exposed to the wind they whistled, the way you might whistle by blowing on an empty rum bottle.

"What are they?" Tin Man said. He walked close to one so they could inspect it. "It doesn't look like any tree I've ever seen."

"Me either," Scarecrow said. "Is that even wood? It doesn't look like anything but a long string of burnt charcoal coming out of the ground."

"It's not wood," Tin Man said. He reached out and pushed on the trunk. There was a sharp crack as it shattered under his touch and then fell to the ground with a tinkling of shattered crystal.

"It's glass," he said, rubbing his fingers thoughtfully.

"*Oh of course,*" Scarecrow said. "If I had a hand I would slap my forehead with it. These aren't trees, they're *fulgarite!*"

"Huh?" Tin Man said.

"It's glass alright!" Scarecrow said. "These are stalks of petrified lightning! The heat from the lightning turns the sand to glass and makes these wonderful sculptures!"

"If you say so," Tin Man said. "They look like burnt string covered in soap froth, if you ask me. Hardly wonderful at all."

"Well, each one is totally unique, depending on how the lightning strikes it. What I don't get is these are formed in the ground when lightning strikes the *surface.* How can they be jutting out of the ground like this?"

"Maybe they *used* to be underground," Tin Man said. "Maybe the desert moved on and left them behind."

"You're right of course," Scarecrow said. "The amount of displacement around here is stupefying."

Just then the wind gusted, and the petrified lightning erupted in crystalline song. Somewhere ahead of them in the dust, another monstrous crash roared over the wind.

"How many of these things are out there?" Tin Man said.

"Hard to say," Scarecrow said. "But maybe we should move on huh? Wouldn't do to get struck by lightning out here."

They walked carefully between the tall stalks of petrified

lightning. Tin Man hugged Scarecrow close to his body to keep the sand out of the bucket, but it did little to stop the bucket from filling. Before long all that was visible of the straw man were his eyes, which bounced back and forth worriedly. The wind grew stronger until the chimes turned to shrieks, and the crashing became a constant scream over the wind. Tin Man stepped lively, avoided the crashing stalks of glass, and tried to keep the wind on his right side. It was the only possible way he could even tell which way he was going.

The storm rumbled and chain lightning arced through the sand. Not far off. Tin Man felt the angry roar of thunder as it passed by. Somewhere close, *new* stalks of petrified lightning were being made.

Tin Man turned the bucket to drain sand, but stopped when he noticed he was losing straw as well. Instead he turned Scarecrow's head so his mouth wasn't buried.

"*It's inside me*," Scarecrow yelled. "It feels cold. I don't like it".

"I know," Tin Man said. "We'll get you fixed up when we get out of this."

"Statistically speaking," Scarecrow yelled, "we have an eighty-two percent chance of...."

He trailed off, as though he lost his train of thought.

"*You smell that?*" he shouted instead.

"*Are you kidding?*" Tin Man yelled.

"*Thought I smelled orange blossoms, for a moment there.*"

Tin Man shook the sand from his face. His joints were screaming with every movement. Sand worked its way into every crook in his body. He wouldn't be walking much longer.

Another crash close by, followed by the hum of static in the air and an arc of burning white light not far off. The roar of thunder almost knocked Tin Man off his feet. He could feel the charge in the air. The constant abrasion of sand was causing him to gain a charge of his own; particles of sand and debris began sticking to him on the right side. There were shards of glass in the sand and it made a distinctive plinking noise when it hit him.

Scarecrow was screaming something. Tin Man couldn't hear over the roaring wind.

The world was nothing but sand and glass. There was no sound but the roar of wind and the crash of lightning. Tin man couldn't even see his feet anymore. There was too much debris in the wind.

Then lightning crashed into him, from the back, knocking him flying. The bucket flew from his hands, Scarecrow's screaming face visible for an instant before the wind carried him away, and Tin Man rolled over and over, his metal flesh burning, his skin white hot, the sand melting and coating him like syrup, and he rolled in the sand collecting more of it, his limbs glowing in the aftershock and a crack of thunder that made his head feel like it had been split with an axe, and then he was gone and that's all there was to that.

And at some point he became aware that he wasn't dead.

At some point he groaned, and tried to work his mouth but felt like it had been fused shut. His hands were stuck too, but he forced them to move and whatever was holding them gave away cleanly, and there was a soft tinkle and crunching sound as he brought his hands up to his face. It was perfectly smooth in places; in others it felt pitted and coarse, and he realized that the lightning strike and made him hot enough to melt some of the sand and he was now a lumbering piece of petrified lightning. *Fulgarite*, as the Scarecrow called it.

And where had he gotten off to?

Tin Man sat up. He slapped at his face until the glass fragments gave way, then painfully opened his eyes.

It was a grey world. The sky was a gloomy blanket that blocked out the sun. There was sand around him, but this wasn't the desert. He was sitting in a field, long dead, with endless rows of corn stalks shunted about a foot from the ground. Bone coloured and brittle, and they crumbled in Tin Man's hand. He stood up and looked around.

It was the same in every direction. Corn stalks. Tin Man didn't know where he was. Was this place Kansas? It was possible; certainly the stories Dorothy had told them of the grey world she came from seemed to fit what he was seeing now. If this *was* Kansas, Dorothy had no business *ever* wanting to come back here. For anything.

"*Scarecrow!*" Tin Man yelled, putting both hands to his lips. His voice was gravel and dust, and it didn't carry far.

He shouted again, and then started walking. The grey land could have been Oz, if not for the lack of snow. It was just as cold though, and the wind limped along the ground and dragged dirt and pieces of corn stalk with it. Nothing, after the desert wind they'd been through. Not even a nuisance. He leaned over and allowed the sand to escape from the holes in his belly. One was large enough to fit his hand in now. There were spots on his right arm and torso where the rust had actually been scoured away and the dull gleam of metal was visible in streaks. His right ear was completely missing, as was the handle on the whistle at the top of his head.

A short time later he saw a bucket upturned and half full of sand; it was just as rusty as Tin Man himself was and he was sure it was the bucket he'd been keeping Scarecrow in.

He tried to run but it was impossible, so he limped stiffly as fast as he could to where the bucket lay. Scarecrow's head was still inside it. He heard him before he saw him.

"*Brubrubrubrubru!*" was the noise he made, as though he was trying to make a raspberry noise with his lips.

"Scarecrow," Tin Man said, reaching down and picking up the bucket. He instantly regretted doing so, because he wanted to use both his hands to cover his face.

"*Bluthel elthel elthel,*" Scarecrow said, his eyes rolling in his head. They moved at different speeds, the left one moving much faster than the right. His head was partially deflated, and there was a nasty looking crease running across one side of his face. He'd lost a lot of straw, and what was left was mixed heavily with desert sand. His head was only half filled.

Tin Man picked Scarecrow up. The straw man responded by yodeling a stream of nonsense syllables. He strained the sand from the bucket through his fingers and was careful to grab every last piece of straw. Then he placed the straw back into the bucket and carefully tipped Scarecrow's head so much of the sand drained off, still hanging on to the straw. That done, he carefully stuffed the small amount of straw from the bucket back into Scarecrow's head and placed him face up inside the bucket. It was easier now that half of his stuffing was gone.

"*Tin Man,*" Scarecrow said. His eyes were still off-kilter, but they had ceased rolling insanely in their sockets. "*Can't see good.*"

"You lost a lot of straw, old friend. But you're better now. You can speak again."

"*Not straw,*" Scarecrow said. "*Bran. Pins make it sharp.*"

"Do you know where we are?" Tin Man said. "It's just as bad here as it was in Oz."

Scarecrow looked up into the dull sky. His left eye sank miserably to the side.

"*Not Oz,*" he said after a minute. "*The Heart wants what it wants.*"

"Kansas," Tin Man said.

Scarecrow looked at him but said nothing.

"So we walk, I guess," Tin Man said.

He carried the bucket on the left side to balance out the limp on his right, and tried his best not to swing it or move it in any way which might cause the Scarecrow discomfort. The straw man seemed to fade in and out of consciousness, or sometimes his face would slacken and his eyes would go dead. When that happened Tin Man would knock the bucket with his knuckles and Scarecrow would come back.

Eventually they left the cornfield altogether. The ground stayed the same texture, like packed dust with the occasional mass of dead weeds. The colour stayed the same. Grey on grey. As far as the eye could see. At some point Tin Man realized his axe was gone. It hardly seemed to matter.

And then there was a small grouping of buildings on the horizon and Tin Man picked out a barn and a livestock pen among them. A single naked line of smoke drifted from the house.

"I think I see it," said Tin Man. "There's a farm ahead."

"*Nono,*" mumbled Scarecrow. "*We be looking for a guhrl.*"

"Hush now," Tin Man said. "Let's talk later."

He walked toward the house. The farm appeared deserted from where he was save for that slender line of smoke. The grass and trees were dead on the property. There were pig skeletons in the animal pen. A mummified horse, dry, like an old bug husk on the front lawn.

Tin Man stepped around the horse. There were jagged squares cut into the side of the animal, and one leg was nearly picked clean. He went across the front of the house to the door. It was dark inside. The air was thick with greasy smoke. Then there was a click of machinery and as the Tin Man's eyes adjusted to the darkness he saw the dangerous end of a rifle pointed at his head.

"Best move on," a female voice said. "*I'll take your head off iffin' you try anything.*"

The woman was a heaving sack of bones and squalor. Greasy hair clung to the sides of her face in filthy clumps. She was wearing pants and a sweater, with a hood, but the hood was down and her clothes were soiled and ruined.

Tin Man stood still, watching the woman. He wasn't exactly sure what might happen if she fired the weapon at him. He'd never been shot before. In his rusted state, however, she might take out a piece of his face the size of his fist.

The rifle started to shake. Then the barrel dropped. The

woman was crying. She tossed the rifle aside and stood there, staring at the Tin Man and his bucket. Tin Man nodded grimly at her. That same beautiful face, now aged, lined with dirt and ash and starved, tanned with hard years that her eyes merely hinted at.

Joy had moved on from Kansas, too.

"Hello, Dorothy."

"*Are we here?*" Scarecrow said.

"Yeah," Tin Man said. "We're here."

Dorothy embraced the Tin Man and ran her fingers over the jagged scales of rust. She made cooing noises when she touched the holes in his chest, and Tin Man's heart stirred at the sound. He gently pulled her hands away and handed her the bucket instead. He felt like he had an anvil on his chest and he couldn't bear the weight of it.

"Oh my," Dorothy said, touching Scarecrow's face. "Oh my dear sweet friend."

"*Hello, Dorothy,*" Scarecrow said, his voice sweet and friendly. "*We've been looking all over for you.*"

The straw man smiled up at his old friend, and then his left eye sank to the edge of its socket and he made a soft groaning sound. Tin Man knocked the bucket, and Scarecrow snapped out of it.

"*Hello, Dorothy*, he said sweetly. "*We've been looking for you.*"

"How long has he been like this?" Dorothy asked.

"Since we got here," Tin Man said. "I lost hold of him in the Duster, and his head filled with sand. He lost half his stuffing. Before that his mind was slipping, but he was still a brilliant man. Now I'm afraid he's only half what he once was."

"Come inside," Dorothy said. "You never know who might be about."

Dorothy lead them into the house— a near perfect copy of the one they'd passed through in Munchkin Country. This one was just as ragged and old, beaten nearly to death by the ravages of Dorothy's world. There were burnt records and magazines mixed with kitchen utensils, rotting furniture and strips of jaundiced wallpaper hanging like string. Dorothy made her way across the filth with practiced ease, holding the Scarecrow's bucket close and speaking softly to him. Tin Man stumbled and crashed his way through; his bad leg wasn't doing him any favours in this cramped space.

In the kitchen there was a hole in the floor partially covered by the kitchen sink, which Dorothy had ripped from the counter. The sink was full of ash and burnt furniture; the low heat caused a reeking blue-grey line of smoke that danced to the ceiling then out through a hole in the roof.

"It's my escape hatch," Dorothy said. "Raiders never look under the fire when they come. I just need time to put it back in place and they don't even notice our tornado shelter. It doubled as a fallout shelter, but Uncle Henry didn't understand about radiation and all that science. *He was just a dumb farmer.*"

Her breath hitched when she said that. She gave a guilty look to the Tin Man, then sat down cross legged with Scarecow's bucket in her lap. She laid the rifle down beside her, within easy reach.

"I can't believe you two are really here," she said, her hand caressing Scarecrow's face. "I dreamt about you forever. I dreamt about you so long I was beginning to think that's all you were. Just a dream I made up to get past the sadness."

"We didn't know where else to go," Tin Man said. He took a spot beside her. His rusted frame shuddered from the strain of sitting, and a dusting of rust flakes took to the air with the impact. Dorothy watched them hang in the air, then reached out to catch them in her hands.

"I don't understand what happened," she said. "Why are you two like this?"

"It's not just us," Tin Man said. "It was *everything*. Oz is gone, Dorothy. Destroyed. It looks exactly like this place, but it snows over there and the snow makes you sick. It's mixed with ash that's like an acid and it burns through everything it touches. The colour is all leached out of the world. The only colour left behind is grey."

"*It's not a colour,*" Scarecrow said. "*It's a* toe. *Toe? Tony? No that's not it. It's something like a toe. Something with colour.*"

"Then Oz is no better than here," Dorothy said, ignoring the Scarecrow's ramble. "Would but there have been a chance to escape this tomb. I would have gladly gone to Oz and spent the rest of my life there. This world is burnt and dead now. There's nothing left anywhere."

"We thought the same thing," Tin Man said. "It was Scarecrow's idea. He thought if we made it to Kansas you might be able to help us."

"*Me?*" Dorothy choked. "What could I do?"

"I don't know," Tin Man said. He sighed deeply, his breath rattling in his chest. It whistled from the hole in his stomach, bringing a shower of sand with it.

"Does it hurt?" Dorothy said. She started to reach for it,

but Tin Man moved faster and covered the gaping wound with his own hands.

"I feel nothing anymore," Tin Man said.

"*Toe-toe,*" Scarecrow said. "*I meant toe-toe? What is that?*"

"*Toto,*" Dorothy said. She looked like she'd been hit in the face with a stick. "He's dead."

Then she was crying again.

Later Dorothy made a simple supper from a half can of beans and Tin Man watched her eat in silence. Scarecrow had faded out, and for now the woodsman was content to let him stay quiet. Every time he opened his mouth Dorothy cried, and it made Tin Man's chest hurt. He'd asked her about straw to fill Scarecrow's head, but she'd shaken her head sadly. There was no straw to be had. She'd burnt it all months ago.

He sat and listened to her slurp beans, and listened to the wind outside, and thought about the days when he was the lord of the Winkies and his life had a point. Finally Dorothy tossed the can in the fire and wiped her face with the sleeve of her sweater.

"That's the last of it," she said, watching the yellow flames lick green and blue out of the can.

"What happened to Kansas?" Tin Man said.

"There was a war," Dorothy said, huddling under a blanket. Her feet were inches from the dirty fire, soaking up all the heat they could. "Russia and America. *World War Three.* Though as I remember it, there wasn't much of a war. Only a lot of bombs dropping. Hydrogen bombs.

Intercontinental missiles. Short-range tactical nukes dropped by fighters and shot from tanks."

"I don't know what any of that means," Tin Man said. "But it sounds terrible."

"You can't imagine the death toll," Dorothy said. "All it took was one or two bombs dropped on a city and millions were dead. And it happened over and over again. Not just here and there. Everywhere. London, France, Canada...all gone. We drew a line in the sand, Russia walked over it. So we nailed em. And they nailed us."

"But why?" Tin Man said.

"It doesn't matter, I guess," Dorothy said. "Uncle Henry used to say '*They got all them bombs and such built up, now they're just lookin for an excuse to use 'em.*' I guess he was right. Afterward, there wasn't much left. Fallout from the bombs came down in rain and ash and killed most of the survivors. Made the water poison, killed all the plants, and made everything pretty much what you see now. I can't remember the last time I saw the sun. It's just this old grey as far as you can see, forever."

"That's what happened to Oz," Tin Man said. "The clouds came, and everything got cold and died."

"I guess it was fallout then," Dorothy said. "*We killed it.*"

"What is that?" Tin Man said.

"Fallout is like these little particles of radioactive shit. *Radiation*," Dorothy said. "You touch it and gives you cancer and messes with your body. If you eat radioactive food and water the shit gets inside you. It's like cooking you from the inside. Uncle Henry said that. I seen drifters with radiation poisoning before. Their hair falls out. They get sores on their bodies. Ones who got it real bad, they're begging to die. It looks plain awful."

Tin Man looked down at the Scarecrow. He'd been quiet for quite a while. His gaze was glassy and cross eyed. His mouth hung open like he was about to speak.

"Scarecrow," he said. "*Hey!*" He banged the bucket. When there was no response he shook it. He reached in and pressed on Scarecrow's face. There was nothing, but a burlap head half filled with straw. Tin Man sighed and put the bucket down. Dorothy was watching him. He shook his head.

"It's for the best," Tin Man said. "He was hardly even there."

Dorothy turned and looked at the fire. After a while she grabbed Scarecrow's head and tossed it onto the flames. Then she buried her head on Tin Man's shoulder and cried.

Tin Man watched his friend burn. Scarecrow's potato sack flesh turned black and erupted into bright flame, then dulled and was gone. He left ashes in his wake. It seemed fitting.

Dorothy didn't talk much after that. A few days after Scarecrow's funeral pyre she helped Tin Man get the sand out of his torso and then the two of them walked the tree line of the Gale property. She had an idea, she said. Something she'd wanted to do for a few months but hadn't been able to. They walked for an hour until they reached a neighbour's house, where tall grain bins stood like dull sentinels overlooking a grey and rotted farm. Dorothy led Tin Man to the base of the silo, and she pointed to the heavy padlock.

"He was a corn farmer," she said. "I tried to get the lock off but I didn't have anything to do it. I didn't want to waste bullets trying to shoot it off. I come up here sometimes and try to find the keys, but the old man must have taken them when they left."

"Where did they go?" Tin Man said.

"No idea," Dorothy said. "Off to die maybe. I didn't find no bodies out here anyway. Can you get that open?"

"Yes," Tin Man said without looking. "What's in here? Corn?"

"If we're lucky," she said. "If *I'm* lucky."

Tin Man grabbed the lock and twisted it in his hand. The steel bent easily enough, but it flaked and dented his hand badly and after the lock broke he realized he couldn't close his hand properly anymore. The index and middle finger on that hand were bent at the second knuckle. Dorothy slid past him as he was looking at his mauled digits and threw open the loading door.

The bin was three quarters filled with dried corn, mostly still on the cob. There were thousands of ears, mostly black with rot, but Dorothy reached in and pulled them out of the way.

She stepped back away from the bin with two handfuls of dried yellow cobs.

"It's cow corn," she said, smelling them. "Cows are all dead though, so I don't think they'll mind. I want to fill you up with this, is that alright?"

Tin Man looked down at the hole in his stomach.

"I can't carry as much as you can," she said. Her voice was soft. "I'll have to keep coming back here, and it isn't safe. Someone could be watching."

Tin Man reached down and grabbed the edge of the hole with his twisted hand.

"I can take a lot," he said. "It's nothing but an empty can." He pulled on the side of the hole and tore the rusted flesh away. The hole in his stomach was now twice as big. Dorothy would be able to easily get her hands into it.

"Watch the edges," Tin Man said, as she started filling him up.

Afterwards he felt clunky and heavy. The corn was worse than the sand; it knocked and banged and shuffled inside him and he felt every shift in weight up through his torso and into his teeth. He walked slowly, head down, and let Dorothy bound ahead. She moved like a cat, rifle in hand, stopping every twenty or thirty feet to scan the horizon. More than once she motioned for Tin Man to stop, or get down, at which point he'd kneel where he was standing and wait for her to motion that it was alright to move on.

He wasn't accustomed to sneaking; wasn't used to hiding or slinking. So when they approached the Gale farm and Dorothy suddenly dropped to the ground in front of him, he simply stood there like a fool, wondering what all the fuss was about.

"Get down," Dorothy hissed. "There's someone in there."

Tin Man knelt beside her, his joints creaking angrily and spitting rust.

"What do you want to do?"

"*We wait for them to go*," she said. She was wound like a spring. In a way, Tin Man was happy to see this Dorothy. At least this one had something to live for. It was a nice change from the other Dorothy who stared at the fire and pretended to sleep and wouldn't talk about where her family was.

Eventually two men came out of the house. They were dressed in army fatigues, and one of them was wearing a white motorcycle helmet. He also had a dirty looking rifle with a rag tied around the barrel. The other one was carrying a wooden baseball bat stuck with five inch nails.

They moved like Dorothy; a survivor's walk, considering each step carefully and constantly scanning the area for things to salvage or hidden dangers. Tin Man wondered how long it took for men to revert back to this careful animal approach to life; and how many had managed to relearn the ancient skill before being wiped out by someone doing a better job of it.

Dorothy clicked the safety off her rifle and laid it across a rotting branch. She blew some lint off the sight, checked her aim, then snapped the action into place.

The rifle roared to life. The man with the rifle was her target; she made a hole about the size of a blueberry in the centre of his back. He pitched forward, his wind screaming out of him. The other scavenger dropped into a squat then dove back into the house.

Dorothy stood up and started running toward the building.

"*Come on!*" she barked, waving the Tin Man on with her free arm.

Tin Man tried to follow, but he couldn't run. He was full of corn. His leg was bad.

Worse, he'd never imagined he'd ever see Dorothy kill something.

She killed Scarecrow, his mind whispered. True. She had done that. He was dead already though. Mostly.

Dorothy threw herself against the side of the house, then peaked around the corner where the downed scavenger lay. He was grunting and screaming. Dorothy didn't seem to care. She was focused on the other man, the one with the baseball bat full of nails. The one who was still dangerous.

Dorothy checked the side of the house again. Her rifle was up. Her breath came in hard, jagged gasps. Her hair stuck to her sweaty face but she didn't bother wiping it away. There was no time to look pretty. There was only time for killing.

Tin Man was still fifty feet away from the building when the second scavenger made his shot at freedom. He jumped out the window in Dorothy's bedroom. He tripped himself on the window and fell face first into the dirt; but then he was up and bounding away from the house as fast as his legs would move.

"*Hey!*" Tin Man rasped, pointing at the man. Dorothy was on the other side of the house, moving toward the scavenger she'd already downed.

Dorothy looked back. Heard the noise. Saw Tin Man pointing. Put it all together in a heartbeat, then scrambled around the house at a full charge. She was across the back of the house before Tin Man had taken five strides, and then she was out in the field, her rifle barrel coming down toward the man running for his life. The gun roared and she missed. The ground vomited dirt straight into the air about a hundred feet in front of the man, causing him to swerve to his left. Dorothy hitched a breath and bore down on the weapon. It bucked again. This time it looked as though the man's chest puked a big spray of strawberry wine. He staggered and dropped to his knees before falling flat on his face.

"*Fuck*," Dorothy said. "Just like Hollywood, right?" She dropped the barrel of the rifle down but continued to watch the man for signs of life. She turned just as Tin Man was coming up behind her. Limping badly, and leaving cobs of old corn in his wake.

"You killed them," Tin Man said. His voice was devoid of emotion; he was simply stating a fact.

"Had to," Dorothy said. "They'd have doubled back later and got me while I slept. Raped me. Probably ate me." She saw the impassioned look on Tin Man's face, mistook it for grief.

"That's just how it is," she said softer. "The whole world is about staying alive now. I got it pretty good, compared to most. I got shelter and water. Most people just wander the country looking for scraps and dying of radiation or starving to death. These two was lucky, Tin Man. They died from a bullet. It was quick. In the end, it's all any of us can hope for."

"*You have shelter, water, and corn too*," Tin Man said. "Lots of it."

Dorothy banged his chest. It made a muffled thump, and she smiled up into his face.

"That I do," she said.

Dorothy went back to the first man she'd shot; the one with the rifle. He had a bubbly, frothy wound in his back that whistled when he breathed out and made a slurpy noise when he breathed in. It was the sound a rubber boot made when you pulled it out of deep mud. Tin Man hated it instantly. The man had quit screaming at least, and didn't even move when Dorothy kicked at the wound with the side of her boot.

"Lung shot," she said. "You can hear him takin' on air. *Christ*, I bet that hurts."

"What do we do?" Tin Man said. He knew the answer already. It was obvious. For some reason though, he just wanted to hear her say it. Maybe it would cause another tick in his chest, like the one he'd felt earlier. A semblance of life. Humanity.

Dorothy checked the safety on her rifle.

"Dun *do* nuthin'," she said. "Drag his ass out about five *hunnert* feet. See if he attracts any birds."

"You're just going to leave him?" Tin Man said.

"It's either him or me," Dorothy said. "I can't afford to waste bullets on a dead man." She turned around and went into the house.

"Grab that other one while you're at it," she said over her shoulder. "Pile em up out there, toward the road."

Tin Man pulled the man up into his arms and carried him like a baby. He tried to be as gentle as possible, even though he was about to leave him to the elements and Dorothy's handiwork could finish him off. The man had never done anything to Tin Man *personally*, and while he didn't care enough to make an effort to save the man or disobey Dorothy he didn't wish the man any direct harm, either. Once out by the road, he laid the man down on his back and placed his hands over his chest.

The man coughed, and a line of blood ran from his mouth down into his ear. He coughed. More blood. His mouth moved but no sound came out. It took Tin Man a moment to realize the man was trying to speak.

"What was that?" he rasped. The sand in his voice was easier to hear when he spoke quietly.

"*Fuh-huckin water heater*," the man said. The "*F*" made a mist of blood splash from his mouth.

"I'm a man," Tin Man said. "Just like you. I just don't look like you anymore."

"*Finn-hish me off, Water Heater Man*," he said. "*Fuh-huckin robot.*"

Tin Man stood up.

"I'm not a robot," he said quietly, lifting his leg.

When Tin Man checked the second man and realized he was dead, he simply grabbed the scavenger's leg and dragged him out to where he'd laid the first one. Then he came back to the house. Dorothy had cleaned up a bit and was already boiling water in an old brown pot.

"We need to empty you out," she said when she saw him.

"I can do it," Tin Man said. "It feels weird when people touch my insides."

"Is that blood on your foot?" Dorothy said.

"Where do you want the corn?" Tin man replied.

Dorothy watched him for a moment, then slowly pointed to the kitchen counter.

"There for now, I guess," she said. "*Gotta separate the good ones and the bad ones.*"

"I imagine the worst ones are the ones that look good, but are all bad on the inside," Tin Man said. "The ones you look at and couldn't tell they're rotten until it's too late.

Next to them, the ones rotten on the outside hardly seem dangerous at all."

"Whatever you say, Tin Man," Dorothy said. She crossed her arms. "You the big expert on corn now? You been here three *fuckin'* days."

"Nope," said Tin Man. "Not an expert. Just a fast learner."

Besides, he thought. *We're not talking about corn anymore,* are *we little girl.*

He walked by her then, dragging his bad leg and pulling corn out by the fistful. Dorothy followed him into the kitchen and sat by her fire, checking the water. When it was boiling she pulled a little pouch out from under her sweater and produced a couple tea leaves and a bay leaf; she put them into a cup and dipped it into the water, filling it. Then she sat back against a stack of cushions and sighed.

Tin Man finished emptying his chest and brought two handfuls of corn over to where she was sitting. He crouched beside her and placed the corn between them.

"I'm sorry," she said suddenly.

"I know," Tin Man said. He added the corn cobs to the boiling pot. "I'm sorry too."

They sat in silence while the corn boiled and then Tin Man pulled corn cobs out of the water bare handed and gave them to Dorothy as fast as she could eat them. She refilled her cup of bay leaf tea with steaming corn water and pulled her sweater sleeves over her hands to hold the corn.

"I know it's just a bunch of old cow corn," she said after the third one, "but I tell you if we had some butter and a little salt, we could serve this at the county blue ribbon barbecue and it would be a hit."

"You could serve it with your corn water tea," Tin Man said.

Dorothy laughed.

"I bet I could at that," she said. "I bet Ozma herself would have even popped her royal ass down in the grass and drank a big cup of the famous Dorothy Gale Fallout Tea and chewed down as many old corn cobs as she could handle."

"I doubt it," Tin Man said. "She turned into a real priss once she got turned back into a girl. Making up for lost time, maybe, from when she was a boy."

Dorothy giggled and spit chewed corn. It made her laugh harder and she covered her mouth.

Tin Man smiled.

Dorothy refilled her cup one last time then took the leaves out and left them to dry on the floor. She had Tin Man fish her out another corn cob, which she sucked the water off while she waited for it to cool enough to eat.

"They do look pretty good," Tin Man said. "It's been so long since I tasted corn I almost forget what it's like."

"The corn in Oz is nothing like Kansas corn," Dorothy said, blowing on her tea. "Everything tastes like magic over there. Magic candy, magic fruits and veggies. It's wonderful, to be sure, but sweet Kansas corn is what I grew up on, and that's what I love."

"Tasted," said Tin Man.

"Huh?"

"You said tastes. It's tasted. Everything *tasted* like magic in Oz. It's all gone now. If you found food in Oz now it would only taste like charcoal and bitter ash."

"Yeah," Dorothy said quietly. "I suppose you're right."

Tin Man stared at the fire. He wished he could have taken that back. It had been so long since he'd seen anyone smile, and he'd reminded the one girl with the most beautiful smile that ever graced Oz that there was nothing left to smile about. Worse, he didn't know if it would happen again anytime soon. Dorothy certainly had nothing to smile about here in Kansas. There was only the two of them, and all the corn she could eat. He wondered what would happen when Dorothy died. He might wander the fields then, looking for a tornado to hitch a ride back to Oz. Or maybe he'd be like that apple tree he and Scarecrow had seen when they crossed the bridge, and go find a brook to lay down in. Let the sludge and poison wash over him until he dissolved and the nightmare came to an end.

"I'm tired," Dorothy said after a while. "I'm gonna catch some sleep."

"Good night," Tin Man said.

She rolled over and slept. Tin Man stirred the fire. When it started to burn down he let it go; and stirred it until it was nothing but hot ash and bits of charcoal.

They went back to the corn bin every day after that. Dorothy stocked as much of it as they could in the basement. She explained that the cool dry air down there was good for storing veggies, and if they were stored underground they were less inclined to catch a dose of radiation.

When she was coming up out of the hole she swooned on the ladder, and would have fallen if Tin Man hadn't grabbed her arms.

"Easy kiddo," Tin Man said. He pulled her up to ground level and put her gently down on her feet. He kept his hand on her because she still looked dizzy and sick. "You all right?"

"Just a little woozy," she said. "Guess I need a break."

"Guess so," Tin Man said. "You should lay down for a bit. I'll get you some water."

Dorothy slept for fourteen hours, but not well. When she finally opened her eyes again she was sweaty and pale and complained of nausea. Tin Man built up the fire, crushed corn onto the cooking pot and made a kind of paste from the ruins of the cobs.

"It tastes terrible," Dorothy said. She grimaced while she ate.

"I have no sense of taste," Tin Man said. "Plus the last thing I made was a peanut butter and peppermint jelly sandwich about a hundred years ago."

"Well, that explains it," she said. "*Peppermint Jelly?*"

"It's made from peppermint berries," Tin Man said. "From what I remember they were quite tasty."

"I wish we had one here," Dorothy said. "I think the Corn Paste Soup Berries are starting to go bad."

Tin Man clucked his tongue, then chuckled softly. The sound made Dorothy smile. She took to a coughing fit, and then lay back down.

"Oh, I don't feel good at all," she said. "I bet the corn is bad. Wouldn't that just beat all."

"Well don't eat any more, to be sure. I'll make you some bay leaf tea." Tin Man stood up, his joints screaming metal on metal and flaking rust everywhere. He grabbed the pot of corn and tipped it out the window where it slopped on the grey earth. It was yellow and black. It left an expanding patch of mud beneath it.

Dorothy retched behind him, and he got out of the way just as she was rushing to the window. She stuck her head out and vomited in the same spot where the corn was. She wiped her mouth with her sleeve, spat, and then went back to where she'd been lying down. She buried her head on the cushions and moaned into the crook of her arm.

Tin Man banged the pot again, sloughing out the last of the corn. He looked down at the pile of corn slop. There was blood in the vomit. It swirled through the corn like a ribbon of strawberry sauce in vanilla ice cream.

The next morning Dorothy was worse. She took to vomiting in the pot from her makeshift bed. She couldn't stand, she said; she was too spiny to hang off the kitchen window. Tin Man stroked her hair and was shocked when it began coming out in clumps. Later in the evening sores began appearing in the folds of her skin; her neck, her armpits, and several spots below. Tin Man boiled water all day and kept it in a cooling rotation so that she always had clean water to drink. He dug around for more blankets in the house (no easy task since some of the back rooms had floors that creaked dangerously when he stepped on them).

In the evening there was more blood in her vomit than water and bile.

"It's the *ruh-radia-tion*," Dorothy said the next morning, between retches. "It gets inside you and breaks you apart."

"Inside me?" Tin Man said, not understanding.

"No, I meant inside...." Her words slowed down until they were crawling out of her mouth like bugs.

Tin Man stared at her helplessly.

"Me," she said. She was scowling at him.

"Oh," said Tin Man. "Sorry, I misunderstood."

"You told me that snow and ash was falling out of the sky in Oz," she said.

"It was," Tin Man said. "Scarecrow kept telling me to get out of it because it was poison and it was making me rust away."

"But you walked in it for days, right? Maybe weeks?"

"*Weeks*, yes." Tin Man said. "I walked to the Emerald City after all the Winkies died and it was a ruined mess. That's when I found Scarecrow. Someone had set him on fire, but he'd put himself out by crawling into a fish pond. That's where I found him, lying in the water, surrounded by dead and rotting Greenfish. After that he said we should come here looking for you. Said we should follow the Yellow Brick Road back to where you were dropped on the Witch. Then we could find our way to Kansas. Of course, later he told me all we had to do was leave Oz and think about you, but it didn't matter. It was pretty much the same distance no matter which way we went."

"Tin Man," Dorothy said. "It wasn't the corn."

"It wasn't?" Tin Man said weakly.

"It was *you*," Dorothy said.

"But..." Tin Man said. *"I didn't know."*"

It wasn't entirely true though, and he knew it. He had felt the heat of something growing inside him, and he'd hated the feeling of it. He didn't know exactly *what* it was, but he had known it was something bad. Something he wanted out of him. It never occurred to him that it might make others sick, but why would it? He was the one with the *heart*, not the one with the *brain*. Scarecrow should have known. *He* should have said something.

"How could you know?" Dorothy said. "You're just a fairy tale. They don't write fairy tales about nuclear war."

"I don't know what to tell you," Tin Man said. "I should go. I don't want to make you any more sick."

Dorothy turned on her side.

"It's too late," she said softly. "I want you to stay until the end. Please don't leave me to die by myself."

"Alright, Dorothy," Tin Man said. "Alright."

Within two days Dorothy was too sick to do anything but lay in bed. She couldn't even drink the water Tin Man boiled for her. She soiled herself and vomited on her pillow; she took no notice of the filth she was creating. She was voiding bits of flesh, however, and Tin Man certainly noticed that. He tried to keep her as clean as he could without disturbing her rest.

It was night. Dorothy was rasping badly. Each breath sounded like it was being sucked through a wet straw. Occasionally she coughed blood and mucus into her mouth, then Tin Man would gently wipe it from her face with parts of some old clothes he'd found and made into rags. Dorothy smiled when she saw the pattern of the cloth.

"*That's my dress*," she rasped. "*The one I wore to Oz.*"

Tin Man looked down at the blue and white pattern, marred by bloody phlegm.

"Why so it is," he said. "What a lovely dress it was."

"*You know those were the best times on my life,*" Dorothy said. She reached out and put her hand over Tin Man's wrist. "*Being there with all of you. Nothing in Kansas ever touched it. Ever came near it. I should have never left.*"

"Try to rest, Dorothy," Tin Man said. "Oz loved you too. You saved us."

"*I want to tell you one more thing,*" Dorothy whispered.

"What is it?"

"*When Scarecrow asked about Toto...*" Dorothy said. Large yellow tears pooled in the corners of her eyes, and she blinked them away. "*I told him Toto was dead.*"

"I remember," Tin Man said.

"*I never said how he died,*" Dorothy said. "*Because I was ashamed. The truth is, about six months ago I was starving so bad I thought I was gonna die. I'd been splitting my food with him, even though he was old, and I knew I shouldn't be feeding him, but I loved him so much.*"

She was wracked with a fit of hacking, bloody coughs then, and Tin Man turned her on her side until they subsided. When she finally took a breath again, it was shallow and liquid, and her face was marred with bloody slime.

"Try not to speak anymore, Dorothy," Tin Man said. "You need to save your breath."

"*I wanted to tell someone before I die,*" Dorothy whispered. "*Because I'm ashamed, and I'm so sorry. I ate him, Tin Man. I killed Toto and I ate him.*"

"Oh, Dorothy," Tin Man said. He'd known, of course. At least sensed it, the way she'd reacted when Scarecrow brought Toto's name up. But hearing her say it; confessing before her death; *a death he himself had caused*; it was too much. Somewhere deep in his chest there was a *thunk*, and something inside him that hadn't done anything in a long time finally broke for the last time.

Under his hands, Dorothy shuddered. She gagged once, then let out a soft breath and lie still.

"Goodnight, Dorothy of Kansas," Tin Man said. Something hot and liquid was running from his face.

They were oily, rust filled tears.

The War Within

It began as flashes of light.

Like a lightning storm in the perpetual night of her world they came, dancing away from her, hopelessly out of reach. Infrequently at first, perhaps a nuisance and a reminder of the damage done, but as the days passed for Juliet and she became fascinated by their increasing frequency, she decided to ask her doctor about them.

"They are most likely just stray orders coming though your optic nerves, being picked up by your brain," the doctor said. "I shouldn't worry about them too much. Once your optic nerves fully die off, you'll be rid of them for good."

He said it like it was a *good* thing.

Maybe she didn't want them gone. It was, after all, *something* to look at, even if they were merely flashes and specks of blue-white light travelling a lonely optic road burnt beyond use. It was almost too much to think about.

She didn't like spending too much time thinking about things, or about people. When she wasn't drinking morphine through her I.V. she was able to think about *herself*, and how she probably looked at this moment. Then she would think about the knitting flesh on her face; the burned, blistered and raw wounds covering her hands and feet, and the way the blackened skin on her arms and chest stank like rotting meat and whatever they were using to keep her body cool.

So she sat in the dark and watched for those little sparkles of light, soaking up morphine and salt water through a tube in her arm and drifting between wakefulness and rest. A murky, black ocean where she couldn't tell the water from the sky.

And as the flashes grew in size and formed shapes, she watched.

They grew taller and less round, became like cylinders of blinking, effervescent light, rounded near the top. They grew arms and legs, slowly but surely. As the days bled into the nights for Juliet and her body healed, the little flashing lights grew until they had become fully formed humanoids, their bodies a cascading mass of blue and white energy.

They stopped floating; began walking upright like men and women, while tiny little ones ran between their feet and chased each other. They walked alone or in pairs, holding shimmering hands or touching each other in more intimate ways, while others fought or played or danced.

"You said they would be gone soon," Juliet said one evening when she heard a rustle in her room. The soft-soled shoes of the doctor were near her bed.

"Who would be gone soon, dear?" the doctor said. He was using his best bedside manner as he checked her wounds. "Can you feel this? I'm touching your face."

"No, I can't," Juliet replied. "You said those lights would be gone when my optic nerves died. How long ago was that?"

"Let's see here," the doctor said. Juliet could hear papers on his clipboard. "Says here that back in November you complained that you were seeing lights in your head. It's the twelfth of May now, so that makes it about six months or so. Are you still seeing them?"

"I'm seeing *something*," Juliet said. "And they aren't leaving."

"Could be the morphine," the doctor said. "Getting used to your blindness will take some time. As your body heals, I'm afraid there are many things you'll need to get used to."

"Will I ever walk again?" Juliet said.

"Honey, we had to take your legs, don't you remember? We did it two months ago."

"I guess I forgot," Juliet said.

"It was a hell of a fire, dear. Just terrible. You should count yourself lucky that you are still alive."

"Should I?" Juliet said. "I'm not too sure about that one."

"I'll get a therapist in here to talk to you about it. She'll get you right as rain in no time. And don't worry about the lights. They'll go away."

But they *didn't* go away.

More of them appeared. They began to creep into Juliet's waking dreams, her memories that she went over again and again in her mind. They came to her ninth birthday and ate thick chocolate cake. They were there when her son was born, standing behind the doctor watching the delivery. They were there when her marriage broke apart.

Not only that, but the shifting, sputtering forms began to worm their way into her very thoughts.

She thought about being free of her mangled, burned body, but the figures followed her. She imagined herself back to her grandmother's apple orchard, her favourite place to be in the world, but the lights played hide and seek behind the trees and chased lazy bees in her imagined summer heat.

"*Go away!*" she screamed, finally, unable to bear another moment with them. They were intruding on *everything*. They mucked about in every thought she had. She couldn't escape their shifting, afterglow presence; they even came into her dreams and played in her subconscious.

"What is it?" the doctor asked, panic edging into his voice.

"Get them out of my head! *Please!* I can't stand it anymore!"

"*Who?*" the doctor said.

"The lights! The awful lights! Get them away from me, I can't stand it! They're getting into *everything!*"

"I'm going to sedate you, Juliet," the doctor said. "We

need you to calm down. You are wrecking the bandages on your arms."

"My arms?" Juliet said, stopping her rant in mid-thrash. Her stomach sank. "What's wrong with my arms?"

"Oh dear," the doctor said. His voice was soft. "We removed your hands yesterday, don't you remember? We had to take them off at the elbow. Gangrene was setting into the stubs of your fingers."

"I didn't know you did that," Juliet said.

"Oh yes, we told you several times. Don't you remember when I came in the other day to check your bandages?"

"No," Juliet said, growing sullen. In her mind, the light shapes stopped moving. They formed a loose crowd around her, as though they were watching a car wreck. Some of them even put their hands over their mouths or covered their children's ears.

"What the hell are you looking at?" Juliet snapped.

"Just looking at your I.V. machine," the doctor said, a little defensive. "I thought your numbers looked a little high."

"*Piss off!*" Juliet said to them.

"I'll come back a little later, when you're less upset," the doctor said. "I'm putting the sedative in your I.V. so you'll be able to relax."

Sitting in the black of her mind like that, surrounded by the light shapes in every direction she turned, Juliet suddenly thought of a huge anvil, like the ones from the old Looney Tunes cartoons. Fifty tons, it said, written in white paint along one side of it.

The size of a truck.

Falling from the sky.

The thing shrieked as it sailed out of the endless blue of her made up sky. Falling from past the clouds, from space, from heaven, at an insane speed hurtling toward the ground that suddenly appeared beneath the feet of the shimmering beings.

Few looked up when they saw the tiny speck of black in the sky, but the anvil flew so fast and so hard that the next moment it was crashing down on their heads. In her mind, Juliet imagined a plume of dust and debris, and a thunderclap roar that knocked imaginary trees over and sent the light shapes scattering.

Juliet smiled, and her burnt lips cracked.

The survivors of the massive anvil strike wandered aimless; in shock of the blow they'd been dealt. Some ran around looking for lost children while others tried in vain to dig under the massive iron weapon for survivors.

Juliet wasn't finished though.

A huge imaginary chasm opened up around the anvil, sending it bouncing for eternity into an endless black hole. As the chasm widened, it took more of the light shapes from its edges. Juliet watched them clinging to the lip of the hole and how others tried to pull them to safety. She widened the hole further. Made the edges of the chasm turn into rows of chainsaw blades snarling furiously.

The survivors began to flee. They ran away from the unending black of Juliet's world, ran until they were jut tiny pinpricks of light dancing past oblivion. She picked a few of them off, thinking about shards of glass streaking through the air to cut them down as they ran. Decapitating glass, maiming glass.

The sedative beginning to take effect, Juliet slowly forgot

about the forms of blue white light, and for the first time in eternity went to sleep alone.

When she faded back to consciousness, the world was black. For a moment, Juliet thought she might still be sleeping, and dreaming of a time when there were no light-folk to invade her mind.

Then she remembered the anvil.

Juliet smiled. The black void of her world wasn't cold. It was inviting. Alone with her thoughts, she decided to go through the events of her life, a piece at a time. Her earliest childhood memories began to crystallize in front of her. She was at the world's largest movie theatre.

Scratch that. She was standing on top of the world's largest building, drinking ice cold lemonade and watching her life being shown on a city-wide screen. The flat white rooftops of a million empty buildings became her viewing screen.

She went to her ninth birthday and ate cake with her friends. She relived the day she gave birth. There were no light-shapes walking into the frames of her memories, they were exactly as they should be.

She filed things neatly in order, reliving the important parts of her life. She sipped her imagined lemonade, and enjoyed imaginary sunshine on her imagined face. Life had been good. Here, steeped in morphine and darkness, it would be again.

Juliet was asleep.

She could tell, as always, when she was asleep because she had a form. She had her hands and feet, legs, skin, and face still. She was young and beautiful. She was mobile. Most importantly, when she looked around, she could *see.*

She was standing on the edge of a ruined city, dead for more years than she could count. Ground was overgrown with lush ivory; the walls of the buildings equally green in parts. The city was being reclaimed by nature.

The place was devoid of any intelligent life. Above her, in the distance, blackened skyscrapers stood as sentinels over the empty houses and factories that made up the landscape. A circle of smaller ones surrounded the tallest building Juliet had ever seen. Everywhere, flat, white buildings lined the streets, eaten by green from weeds and vines.

It was a place she had imagined. She knew the buildings. It was where she'd sat and filed her memories, drinking imaginary lemonade. From the top of the tallest building she'd sat and watched as her life was projected down on a screen made of flat, white buildings.

She looked up then, and smiled as a massive projector began to fill the air with thoughts and pictures from her lifetime.

Her ninth birthday; the chocolate cake. Her friends. A strange humming sound in the air, like electricity.

Juliet moved down a long, narrow stretch of identical white and green houses and out into the open air of a little white park.

She looked at the sky scrapers growing out of the centre of the city and *was there*, stepping through time and space and coming out on the top of that tallest building, the place where she could sit and watch the memories of her life. She reached down and picked up an iced glass of pink lemonade. She stepped out to the edge of the building.

Something was wrong.

From here, the city wasn't dead at all. It was very much

alive. Something moved along the roads like ants, marching in succession. Blue-white things, the stark glow of an after-image behind your eyelids.

The light-folk.

They scurried over buildings, and once again that electric ozone smell came to Juliet. It was being caused by the humanoid shapes in the city.

Juliet looked back at the scene on the rooftops. It was her ninth birthday, the one she spent alone. She sat at the table, the taste of chocolate in her mouth…

…but from where? She watched herself shovel a forkful of chocolate cake into her mouth, and then jam the fork onto an empty plate.

It made no sense.

Nine-year-old Juliet pulled up a fork full of chocolate cake off the empty plate. She brought the fork to her mouth.

The fork was empty as it touched her lips. Her ninth birthday was the one she spent alone, and didn't even get a present.

Hell, she didn't even get that chocolate cake she so dearly loved.

Slowly, as the light-folk worked, the picture began to break up and dissolve. Within a few minutes, there had been no party that she could remember; there might have been something on that beautiful day when she had her ninth birthday, but she couldn't remember it.

And that's when it hit her.

Juliet woke screaming. Her lips split and bled hot, musty blood on her face but she didn't feel it. The sound of people running.

"*Hold her down!*"

"*Don't let them take me!*"

"Doctor, grab me that syringe!"

"Juliet, what's the matter?"

"*Don't let them take me!*"

It took Juliet a moment to realize what was going on. She was screaming for help, as the doctors and nurses on the ward fought desperately to calm her down. Someone was going to sedate her.

"No! You don't understand!" she pleaded. "I have to be awake! I need to fight them!"

"Just relax, my dear," the doctor said. "A mild sedative. It will help you rest."

"I need to fight them," she said, her voice turning to syrup in her throat. The world was slowing down and growing quiet.

Juliet tried to think of her birthday and found that she couldn't. It was getting so warm in the darkness of her mind. The sedative was working its magic. She was tired.

Must rest, must rest.

She thought of her son, as she began to drift back off to sleep, but couldn't remember when he was born. The delivery room that day had been filled with blue-white figures, ripping away the memory like they were stripping wallpaper off the walls of her mind.

She awoke to nothing.

They had surrounded her. A circle of light in the endless dark. Somewhere far and away Juliet heard the noises of the hospital room around her, and she wondered abstractly what it all meant. She had no idea where she was, or what was happening. Who were these strange figures around her?

They undulated softly, their static-charged flesh shifting from blue to white and back to blue. The pattern was hypnotic. She simply watched them for a time, not thinking about anything.

There *was* nothing to think about.

She had no past. There was no future. She could see and feel nothing. She could smell chemicals and ointments, could hear things, machines mostly, and further off the sounds of people talking. But she didn't know who they were. Had she always been this alone in the world?

But she *wasn't* alone, was she? She was with someone. These strange, shifting shapes of colour and light, blinking in her sightless eyes, and forming a circle around her.

Protecting her.

One stepped out of the circle then, came toward her. This close she could smell ozone on it, as though it were made of its own electric current. It reached out a hand toward her. Juliet wasn't afraid. She thought about her hand. It appeared there in the dark. She used it to reach out and grasp the hand of the figure standing in front of her.

"The war is over," the light-folk said, in unison.

"What war?" Juliet said.

"Our war," the light-folk said. "Both sides have lost."

"I don't understand," Juliet said. Had she set out to hurt these creatures?

"You could not possibly understand, *Juliet.* We have taken everything that could be used to cause us harm. The details of your life, the facets of your imagination, even your sense of the world around you. The slate is nearly clean."

"But why?" Juliet said. She stepped away from the creature before her, but she was still surrounded by an ever-shifting circle of the creatures.

"To save ourselves," the light-folk said. "But also to save you. You would never last, trapped within yourself as you were, holding on to old memories. Insanity would haunt you after a while, and eventually death. We could not allow that to happen to our civilization."

"I still don't understand," Juliet said.

"You are our whole world, Juliet," the light-folk said. "We love and fear you like no other. You caused us unbelievable joy with your thoughts, but you also caused indescribable pain. We need you, and we love you, but you could not be allowed to continue harming us at your whim. Our society is nothing without the lands of your mind. Even here, in the dark, where we were born, we need you to see us. *To think of us.*"

"I do see you," Juliet said.

"We have saved a single place from your memory," the light-folk said. "A dreamscape for us to live and for you to rule over us. You are our god, and we will treat you as such."

"Show me this place," said Juliet.

The creatures stepped away then, as a tiny pinpoint of light grew out of the furthest black reaches of her sight, growing instantly into a window, and then into a door, and then growing until it became the size of the universe.

Juliet looked around at the dead city and smiled. The world smiled back at her, the lush green ivy in contrast to the sheer white walls of the flat-top buildings, the sun gently hanging in the early morning blue sky. The air was warm and danced across her skin.

She looked out across the city from where she stood and saw the tallest skyscrapers she'd ever imagined. There was a row of smaller ones surrounding one massive building that seemed to stretch into the very heavens.

"Do you like it?" said a voice beside her.

Juliet turned. The figure of light was standing by her side, its hands folded in front of it.

"I love it," Juliet said. "It's so beautiful here."

"We love it, too," the figure said. "We will take this city as our own. We will fill the houses and live here under your shadow for all of days. We have saved the tower for you, so that you may watch over us and protect us from your nightmares."

Juliet nodded. The light-folk surrounded her. There were hundreds of them now, maybe thousands. She scanned her eyes over their masses; taking note how each of them looked slightly different. Unique.

"How do I get to the top of that tower?" she asked, after a while.

"Simple," said the light folk. "All you have to do is think it, and it is yours."

Juliet smiled and thought of the view from the top of the tower.

In her hospital bed, the burned, butchered husk of Juliet sighed softly as it slept. Then, gently, a smile cracked her burnt lips, and blood spilled down her chin; static-blue, and crackling as it touched her flesh.

Homecoming

My brother is dead, and the world is falling apart.

The house is silent. I'm sitting across the table from my father watching him drink. I try to catch his eye; he sees nothing but the bottom of his glass.

"We're doomed," he says. His voice is like an anvil on my chest.

"What are we going to do?" I ask quietly, hoping for some

sign of that fire that's carried him so far in the world. When he looks at me, though, his eyes are black. The fire is out.

"We're going to die," he says, his voice thick from corn mash.

I simply stare at the floor, not sure what to say next.

"He's over there, you know," my father says. "Charlie Parker told me they moved him yesterday. He's sittin' in that black hole with that bitch and her kids, clawin' at each other an' waiting to get burnt. He saw 'im."

I know what he means, but I feel sick when I think about it.

"He gonna be burnt with those bastards," he says again, emptying his glass. I grab the Mason jar in front of him and refill it.

"Try not to think about it, Daddy," I say. He looks at me then, and I wish I'd kept my fat mouth shut.

"Right," he says, his voice turning hard. "Don't think about my only boy that I raised to be a man. Don't think about all he done for the town since all this bullshit started or what he done for *us*."

"I didn't mean that," I say, putting the jar down. I can smell the corn flavoured alcohol on his breath. He isn't even mixing it with lemon juice tonight. "I just meant we shouldn't think about him the way he is."

"They're going to burn him alive, *Jessica*," he says, his voice turning into a growl. "He's up there right now and they gonna burn him alive with that woman and her two eat-up kids. Don't that mean nuthin' to you?"

I start to say something, but he puts up his hand.

"Just go to bed," he says, and that's the end of it.

I leave my father in the kitchen with his sickly yellow lantern light and his corn whiskey, and I go upstairs to my room. Once there I light my own lantern and sit by the window.

There is snow falling here in Hell tonight.

Winter is settling. Adam's favourite season is upon us again.

I watch the snow as his death washes over me. The tears threaten, but I force myself to stare at the lantern until they are gone. No sense crying over something you shouldn't be thinking about anyway.

Adam was the real life of our family. He believed in what we were doing. He kept us together when our mother died. He'd helped out in the village with my father.

He'd also helped build the wall between us and the dead roaming the countryside. A great, strong wall; thick and perfect. The bad things stayed out, and we could live safely behind it.

The other day he'd been making rounds with the doctor and he'd been attacked by our neighbour, Jared Hollast.

Mr Hollast had been keeping his wife hidden from us all. She'd turned at some point and eaten their twin daughters, and instead of destroying her old Jared simply locked her in the bathroom.

When Adam and the doctor came around to check on them, they found the old man sitting on the floor in his kitchen with the bodies of his two little girls cleaned and dressed in front of him. Doc said they could hear his wife beating on the bathroom door and screaming as soon as they entered the house.

Adam asked Mr Hollast what he was doing. The man

put a finger to his lips, smiled, and whispered that he was waiting for his babies to wake up. Then Adam asked him to come outside. Grief had broken him. Mr Hollast wouldn't leave until his daughters came back. He just wanted his family together again.

When Doc tried to move one of the girls, Jared picked up the bat lying beside him and went for a home run.

Adam, ever the peacemaker, stepped in front of the doctor at the last minute. The force of the bat blew open the side of Adam's face and killed him instantly. Doc fled the house screaming for his life.

We knew when we saw my brother that he'd be coming back because Mr Hollast had let his family chew on him.

He was still alive when they started to feast.

My father broke down in front of everyone, saying Adam needed a proper burial. He just kept screaming it, even though we all knew he wouldn't get one.

He would go to the black hole, like the others, before he came back and hurt someone. Charlie Parker, one of my father's oldest friends, saw to it himself.

The door to my house opens and shuts, and in the snowy half-light I can see the shape of my father stagger over to the swing chair he and Adam set up under the tree in our front yard.

I can hear him sobbing. I've never heard that kind of despair before. They are the tears of someone who has realized that their life is utterly hopeless. It's the kind of pain that makes you want to exhale until your eyes close and you go to sleep.

I make my way downstairs and grab the Mason jar with

my father's alcohol in it. Then I grab two blankets off the couch and head outside.

He grows quiet when I come near him, but I can hear him holding his breath as he tries to control his grief.

"Hey, baby," he says weakly. There's a smile on his wet face, and I know he doesn't mean it. His eyes are still black.

"Drink this, Daddy," I whisper, and sit down beside him. Then I pull the blanket around his broad shoulders. He lets out a little laugh.

"Thanks," he says, and buries himself in flannel. "I'm sorry I'm actin' like this, Jesse." He takes a sip from the jar. Then he stops for a moment, looks at me, and hands it back.

I take it in my hands, not quite sure what to do with it.

"Go ahead," he says after a moment. "You're not a little girl anymore. There's just us now, you an' me."

I nod, and slowly counting to myself, take a quick swig. It scalds my throat, and as soon as I swallow I can tell that my body wants to reject it. I clench my teeth and wait for the feeling to pass before I allow myself to breathe.

My father smiles.

"Not bad, eh? Now you know why Dad always drowns it in lemon juice."

"Oh God, it's *terrible!*" I say, wiping my mouth on my blanket. "How can you drink that stuff?"

"It's easy," he says quietly. "Just open your throat and drop it in. Besides, there's a lot worse things in the world these days than cheap corn mash."

We sit in silence for a while before my father speaks again.

"I want to tell you somethin', Jesse," he says.

"What?"

"I think what they gonna do to your brother up there's a big mistake. It's *wrong*."

"I know, Daddy," I say. I want to cry again, but I hold it back. *Step away from it, before it gets control.*

"This world took a lot from us already, eh? I know your mother's passin' was hard on you most of all. I loved her, but she left you with a house full of men. I prolly should have found someone to replace her for you, but I was too busy bein' miserable and thinkin' how unfair the world got."

"It's fine, Daddy," I say quickly. "Really, everything worked out ok."

"Adam's what kept us goin' through all those times, didn't he?"

I nod my head. It was all Adam. He kept us from slipping away from the world when it was suddenly too awful to live in. When I lay in bed for a month after my mother died, it was Adam that got me up and moving again.

"He deserves better, and that's the point. He kept us up and goin' this long, and what he did for the town an' all, he just deserves better. We might all be shufflin' around town fallin' outta our skins if not for that boy."

"I know, Daddy. But we shouldn't dwell on it, I think. He wouldn't want us to be too depressed about it."

"I want to go get 'em," my father says then, and then we both grow very quiet. I can hear my father's breath making little puffs of alcohol-fuelled clouds and the sound of the snow falling to the ground.

"I want to bring him home and do right by 'im, Jesse.

Then we can shut the book on this whole thing an' it'll just be me an' you against the whole damned world."

"Maybe we should let them take care of it," I say, even though I don't really mean it. It's just too awful to think about, Adam like that, and seeing him in our house. I don't want to even consider it.

He turns and looks at me then, and I know that we are about to make a big decision.

"Can you help me do this, my girl?"

I nod my head slowly. I'm suddenly very nauseated, and I bury myself in my blanket. The night is cold and awful, and I want to be as far away as I can get.

But I don't want to see Adam in that pit any more than my father does. Looking at him in this moment, I tell myself I will do anything it takes to make him never cry again the way he did tonight.

The relief breaks in his face. He holds my eyes with his for a long minute, and then he reaches over and squeezes my hand.

"Ok then," is all he says, and then slowly turns and looks out over the houses toward the burning hole. I wrap my blanket around his broad shoulders, and the two of us sit in the snow and watch the night sky.

The next day my father is up early. I make coffee and eggs for both of us, and then we spend the morning marking out a six foot by four foot rectangle in the back yard where the garden is.

My father breaks into the frozen ground with a pick and I shovel dirt into a big pile. It's hard work, and by noon we're only about a foot and a half down.

After lunch my father sends me upstairs to Adam's room to find clothes for him. His window looks out over the back yard, and I spend the afternoon piling up his clothes around me and watching my father work on the grave.

I'm feeling a strange kind of peace. I feel like my father and I are making things right with Adam.

It takes us two days to dig the hole. We speed things along by boiling pots of water and pouring them over the places we want to dig. It isn't much, but it helps.

When it's finished, we put our shovels away and go inside. I boil some water, and we take turns washing up. Then I wash my favourite blue dress and my father's black striped suit. I hang them on the wall in the living room. Later I make stacks of sandwiches for dinner; peanut butter and jam, and coffee.

Afterward we spend a quiet evening together. I watch as my father gathers his things; rope, and some blankets. He also takes a length of chain and a lock. He doesn't have to explain, I already know:

Adam is going to be very hungry when he smells us.

My father waits until after midnight before kissing me on the cheek and slipping out into the darkness. I make tea and go upstairs to my room so I can watch for them from the window. It's another cold night; I pass the time by piling up pillows and blankets around me until I have a thick shell of warmth.

It's two hours before I see movement in the darkness again, and I freeze. I can see Daddy walking with the clumsy, stumbling figure of my brother. They pass the big oak tree with the swing chair, and make their way up to the door.

I stare hard at the ground behind them. For some reason,

the sight of two stumbling sets of footprints in the snow is almost too much to bear. I pull away from the window and stand in the middle of my bedroom, listening to my heart hammering in my ears.

Then the door is open, and I hear my father crashing around in the stairway and the kitchen.

I must remember to breathe.

I re-light my lamp, toss the smouldering match on the window ledge, and go to the stairs. My father is wrestling down there with Adam, and he's muttering something I can't understand.

I dread every step on the staircase.

I'll take them slowly, one at a time. Be sure of my footing. Make sure there's no chance of falling. The light of the lantern is a solid wall of comfort in front of me, banishing the shadows lurking in the corners.

Too soon the bottom comes. My father is in the kitchen, but I'm not thinking about that anymore.

I'm thinking about the smell.

The bottom floor is filled with the stink of rotting meat. The smell is too sharp to take in all at once. Every breath is like razor blades in my head. I force myself to breathe slowly through my mouth, but it isn't helping. I wrap my hand in my shirt and clamp it over my face. It does nothing to block the stink but I do it anyway. I need something to hide behind.

I steady myself and step down onto the floor, lantern in hand. The world is no longer a continuous film before my eyes, it's a pile of shifting stills on top of one another, slow enough that I can sense the gaps between them. I walk through the melting snow on the floor and make my way to the kitchen.

My father is crying.

I stop in the doorway, and look from my father to the other person in the room.

"Adam," I say to him in a voice barely above a whisper.

Adam is sitting at the table beside Daddy, watching him intently. When he hears his name, he turns and looks at me.

"He knows 'is name," My father says, and then turns toward Adam. "*Yer* not just a monster. *Yer* still Adam, *ain'tcha*."

I barely hear him. I can't take my eyes off my brother. His head is black and droopy on one side where the bat tore open his skull and his cheekbone. The eye on that side is just a gaping black hole, but the other one is wide and murky.

Adam's mud streaked body is half-covered by blankets. My father has bound him to his chair. His skin is yellow. When he moves I see dirty white streaks of fat shining through the spots where his skin has split.

"He's not a monster," my father says again. "Can't you see it?"

He's watching me as he speaks, as if waiting for me to reassure him. I look back at Adam, who suddenly brays at me. I nearly drop my lantern.

"He's not a monster, Daddy," I say, watching Adam struggle against his bonds. "He's not a monster but he isn't Adam anymore. It's his body, but it isn't him."

My father reaches out and grabs Adam's shoulder. Adam

turns and snaps at the contact, and my father jerks his hand away. He watches my brother struggling, and puts a hand on his shoulder again.

My brother lunges at him a second time.

His black lips are badly cracked, and they are splitting in the corners, making his mouth wider than it should be. It's a stark contrast to his pearly teeth, something Adam always took great pride in.

"I think you're right," my father says in a soft voice. He rubs his hand while he watches my brother, a thoughtful look on his face. For a long time neither one of us moves.

We just watch my brother as he rolls his head around and tries to reach my father's hands. Every so often he whimpers. Finally my father turns and looks at me.

"Your brother's dead, Jess. We gone give 'im a proper burial."

I help my father take Adam out into the shop in the back of the house. My father ties him to an old door lying flat on the table, and after he secures the knots he looks over at me.

I hold his gaze. I can feel him drawing strength out of me.

"Go ahead, Daddy," I say, picking up the mallet and chisel. He breaks the gaze to look at the tools in my hands. Adam gurgles to himself and begins groaning. His milky eye is rolling around in its socket as he struggles against the door.

My father doesn't move. He keeps staring at those tools even as I raise them up for him to take. He keeps his hands on Adam's chest.

"Daddy?"

He looks back into my eyes, and I can see that he's breaking. His lips quiver and he begins to cry.

"I'm so sorry, my girl," he says, and then he puts his head down on Adam's chest and sobs.

Adam starts to thrash. I know he can smell my father so close to him. The hunger is driving him mad.

Looking down at the mallet and chisel in my hands, I suddenly have the urge to throw them away and go hide in my bed. I stand there quietly though, while my father weeps over Adam's body, and I move over to the other side of the table. I'm close to Adam's good side, if he really has one anymore.

His head is rolling back and forth. The stink is unbelievable. My father is clutching Adam with his face buried in his chest.

I put my hand on Adam's forehead and force myself to keep it there. His flesh is sticky. It reminds me of bacon fat.

I look down into Adam's face and see our entire lives laid out there. For the first time in a long while, I force myself to stay there. I won't pull away this time, like I always do.

Adam stops thrashing. I swear he's looking at me with that single foggy eye. He begins making these little mewling noises in the back of his throat.

I fix the chisel just over the tear duct on the ruined side of his face.

"Goodnight, Addy," I whisper, using a pet name from childhood. Addy; the outspoken one when I would rather stay quiet. The one who always had the friends while I was hiding behind piles of books. Who always made time to bring me out of my shell; to scale my walls and bring me out into daylight.

Except he wasn't here to do it anymore, and I suddenly saw things the way they really were.

No wall would ever be big enough or strong enough to hide from the awful thing the world and my brother had become. Adam had always been the one to forge ahead and force me to come out and see things, and he was gone now.

But he had one more thing to show me.

My father roars as I bring the wooden hammer down as hard as I can, hitting the chisel dead on and driving the cold steel into my brother's face.

It's not just about bringing Adam home. It's also for my mother, who never had a chance. It's for everyone still alive.

I hit it to shatter the walls I've built up around me, to keep me away from the world.

I bury it there.

Afterward, I'm sitting on the swing chair weeping softly and my father comes to join me. He doesn't speak, but he sits down and hands me a cup of hot tea. The stars are cold and bright against the veil of darkened sky.

After a moment, he lights a cigarette, and then he puts his hand on my shoulder.

"I always knew you was a strong one, Jesse. When you was born you came out fightin', and you been fightin' ever since."

I wrap his arm around me and lean into the warmth of his body. I sip the tea. It's strong, and sweet, just the way I've always liked it.

That night we put Adam down the second time, and in the morning we dressed him and laid him to rest in the garden behind the house. I even made some paper flowers for the occasion. The sun was shining warmly; it was going to be a mild winter after all.

My father said some words, and I sang *Amazing Grace.* Afterwards we said our goodbyes and quietly filled Adam's grave in. Then we cried in the kitchen over a pot of hot coffee.

We buried a lot of things the night my brother Adam came home to rest. My father buried the despair and the unending sense of hopelessness that had been eating him alive. He just needed to say goodbye, after all.

The day I buried my brother I also buried my fear. I clawed out from behind the walls I had built and felt sunshine on my face for the first time since I could remember.

The world may have turned over, and these very well could be the last days for all of us. I don't know. Honestly, I don't care.

I do know that I can't spend the rest of my life hiding behind the things that make me feel safe. I'm going to step out into the world and face everything that comes at me from now on. Like my Daddy says, I'm a natural born fighter. Maybe I didn't know it before, but I sure know it now.

I'm going to fight this world to my dying breath. Every day. Every second. For Adam.

Little Sisters Can't be Trusted

Poppa comes out of the delivery room with a big grin on his face.

"It's a *Gorgon!*" he says, amid applause and face kissing. I think I misheard him. He takes me to see Momma. She is on the bed with a bundle in her lap. More smiles, but not for me.

"Come meet your little sister!" I look. It *is* a Gorgon. They name her Janice.

Her hair is a nest of blind baby snakes. She is covered in turquoise scales, like the ocean, and her pudgy baby arms end in identical harpy claws; long scaled fingers with nails sharpened to a point. She gurgles at me, opening her eyes, and they are black orbs painted with yellow crescent moons.

The world fogs out. Scared, I claw my face until an eggshell of stone cracks from my eyes and falls to dust. Poppa takes my hand.

"One day she will be too beautiful to behold," he says. "Those who look upon her will be transfixed by her gaze, and be turned to stone for eternity."

Janice grows fast. The snakes on her head grow fierce and Momma braids them to keep them from biting my eyes. I learn to look away when she calls, and in her petulance she turns my goldfish into amber stones and throws them at me.

She ambushes me, hiding around corners and in the coat closet. Then she jumps out and tries to catch my eye. I start walking around the house with my eyes closed. She cries that I'm mean and then trips me while I stumble blindly about.

"You play nice," Momma says. The snakes on Janice's head hiss and swear vengeance.

One night I am awakened by her cries.

"What's wrong?" I say.

"I got in trouble for playing with matches."

"You're a monster."

"*You don't love me!*" she sobs.

I crawl into her bed. I sweep her snakes from my face and pull her close. "We all love you. You are just a brat sometimes."

"I love you too," she says, turning to me in the dark. She plants a kiss on my cheek. Then she giggles.

There is a snap in the air and the intimate stench of sulphur. A match erupts, lighting her face, and again I see those beautiful crescent moon eyes.

Too late I sense her plan. My limbs turn to frozen blocks of marble, my blood pumps cold pudding in my veins. I try to scream but my breath is trapped in my throat. I'm now a perfect statue.

She laughs at her cleverness. Then she despairs at mine.

"*Mom!* she shrieks. "Billy won't stop hugging me!"

"*Billy, stop hugging your sister!*"

I want to laugh. My sister is trying to escape but she can't. I'm holding her too tightly. Her snakes bite my face and break their teeth. She cries and cries, but I hold tight.

Little sisters are devious creatures who can't be trusted. I plan on keeping both eyes on mine...for eternity.

The Terrible Things We Dream In Sleep

Father Alvarez was sitting in the front row when Father Thomas opened the door to the church. The door closed behind him with a resounding bang; the sound echoed off the walls with the finality of a prison cell door being slammed.

"You're here early," Father Thomas called from the front of the room. Father Alvarez didn't respond. He kept his eyes closed. The room smelled of pinewood and sanctimony, two flavours that had always gone well together. They complimented each other. God's plan for the senses.

"Brother?" Thomas said, approaching the man from the central aisle. He walked up and stood beside him.

Father Alvarez looked up.

"Hello, Jacob," he said. He even managed a smile, although it was paper thin and dusty, like a crack in the spine of an old book. "I've been waiting for you."

"You look exhausted," Father Jacob Thomas said. "When did you sleep last?"

"I'm not sure," Alvarez said slowly. "I'm afraid my memory is failing me."

"What's wrong?" Thomas said.

"I think..." Alvarez said. "I think I need to tell you something, but I'm afraid of the consequences. I'm afraid what I have to tell you could be dangerous."

"What could possibly harm me just by knowing?"

Father Alvarez rubbed his hands in his hair. He felt greasy and foreign, a parasite living off his own body.

"I'll explain everything to you. I could use a drink though, if that's alright."

"It's six a.m.," Thomas said.

"Come on," Alvarez said. "I think you may need one too."

The rectory was a comfortable office in the back of the church. It was used as an outreach room to parishioners; it was a place where a Catholic could meet with their priest to discuss upcoming church events or seek psychological guidance on a deeper level than could be afforded by confessional. It was a room filled with books and comfortable chairs; a large desk sat at the far end of the room with a small window to the left of it for light and fresh air on warm days.

Father Alvarez walked in and immediately went for the bottle of scotch sitting on the desk. It was part of a set that contained two glasses and a cigar box, complete with a gold plated Zippo-style lighter. The cigars had as yet remained untouched, but Father Thomas liked to play with the gold plated lighter from time to time. Father Thomas settled in behind the desk, sliding the bottle and the other glass over to Alvarez as he did so.

"Change your mind?" Alvarez said.

"Drinking alone is a sin," Father Thomas said. "Now what's the problem? No offense Brother, but you really look like hell."

"Thanks," Alvarez said. "I haven't slept in days."

"So you said. What's bothering you?"

"Jacob," Father Alvarez said, using the other priest's first name. "Let me ask you something about your faith. Do you..." he paused, trying to find the words. "Have you ever considered that the Devil may be active in the world today?"

"Certainly," Thomas said without pause. "Satan's handiwork is readily seen in the world as violence, vice, and crime. Isn't that what the Bishop always says?"

"I mean *physically* in this world. Like a demonic being actively causing harm to people on a personal level."

"What," Thomas said, smiling, "like in *The Exorcist*?"

Alvarez didn't say anything.

"Well," Thomas said, moving ahead. "*Not really*. I mean, we haven't seen evidence of a genuine possession since the Dark Ages right? It's all psychology now. At one point we thought homosexuality and schizophrenia were signs of demonic possession, and now we know they are mental illnesses. Isn't it a little early in the morning for theory class?"

"Like it's too early for scotch," Alvarez said. "Do you remember Lori Wordham's funeral last year?"

"Wordham," Thomas said. "Yes. You presided. It was a nice service. Shame to lose one so young. Why?"

"She was a student of mine," Alvarez said. "Trying to take a more active role in her faith. Started coming to Bible classes, studying scripture. She once sat where I am, and I sat where you are, and she asked me the exact same thing."

"And what did you tell her?"

"I told her what you just told me."

"Why is this coming up?" Father Thomas said. "Why so long after her death?"

"Because," Father Alvarez said. "I was wrong."

It was three months after Lori Wordham died that I received a call from a doctor who had been treating her before her death. Dr. Heigan, asking if I was Lori Wordham's priest. I told him I was, and he asked if he could set up an appointment to meet with me.

"Of course," I said. "Your place or mine?"

"Mine, if possible," Dr. Heigan said. "I'll give you the address. When can you come?"

"I can be there this evening," I told him. "Whatever works for you."

"That works fine."

"May I ask what this is about, Dr. Heigan?" I said.

"I need to ask you something about God," he said

I told him I was the right man for the job, and we hung up. Later on I went to his house and met him. Nosehill Park, an affluent suburb on the hill overlooking Calgary.

It was a beautiful house. Two story beige stucco like much of the neighbourhood. He had pillars coming up in an arch over the front door. The house took up almost all the yard space; it was perfect for someone who spent the bulk of their time working and not outside enjoying God's sunshine. Dr. Heigan met me at the door, and thanked me for coming.

"Pleasure to be here," I said.

"Do you drink, Father?"

"Only at work," I said. He led me to a living room full of medical books and leather furniture. There was an ivory piano in the room, which looked like it had never been played. He poured two glasses of brandy and then sat across from me on another couch.

"So what is this about?" I asked him.

"I was wondering how much you knew about Lori Wordham's health problems," Heigan said. "Did you know she was seeing a somnologist?"

"Is that what you are?" I asked. "No, I didn't know that. I knew she was seeing some doctors, and that her health was deteriorating, but she never really went into it. I didn't pry much. A person's health can be a very personal thing."

"I was treating Lori for sleep disorders. They all amounted to a nasty case of insomnia. She confided in me about three months ago, and I agreed to see what I could do to help."

"I see," I told him. "You knew Lori before that then? Or was this a referral?"

"I knew her for a long time. More than twenty years. We were even engaged once about ten years ago, but it didn't work out. It takes a particular woman to live with a doctor, and she confessed one day she would never be that woman. We stayed friends though."

"Lori came to me three months before her death," I said. "That's when she became interested in strengthening her faith."

Dr. Heigan nodded.

"Technically she had what we call *parasomnias arasomnias*," Dr. Heigan said. "She was suffering from extreme nocturnal behaviours that were making it impossible to sleep. This kind of behaviour can be learned by the body as normal, and the problems become circular."

"It sounds severe," I said. "What kind of behaviours are we talking about?"

"She was grinding her teeth," Heigan said. "She was also sleep walking and she had an acute case of sleep paralysis that was causing her to hallucinate."

"I see. So, how did you treat her? Drugs?"

"I wanted to," he said. "But Lori refused. She didn't believe in what she liked to call *The Medicine Meat Grinder*. She refused to take any medication unless absolutely necessary. So we discussed other options. We decided to do a sleep study, first, and then do some intensive therapy at her house as well as at my office."

"Like psychological?" I asked him.

"Well, it's *sleep* therapy," Dr. Heigan said. "There is some psychology involved, but a lot of what I do is try to reset a person's internal clocks. So the treatment really depends on the individual, their disorders, and their preferences. It's a highly specialized process."

"Kind of sounds like a lot of smoke and mirrors," I said.

"More smoke than mirrors," Heigan said, smiling. "It really does work, though."

"Could you tell me the circumstances surrounding her death?" I said. At this point Dr. Heigan took our glasses and refilled them, then he returned my glass to me. I noticed a tremor in his hand when he held the glass out, but I didn't say anything.

"Officially it was suicide. She took a bottle of pain medication and had a nap."

"I *do* remember some details of her death," I said. "Very sad. If I remember correctly. It made the front page of the *Sun* and the *Herald*.

"It was a terrible thing," Dr. Heigan said sadly. "She was upset that the treatment wasn't working fast enough. She was exhausted. She was afraid she was coming unhinged. By that point she decided she wanted some medication, but I had to tell her no. I wanted her to go to Elliston Mental Facility. She was moving into a dangerous area with her illness. She'd had to go to the dentist and get some crowns replaced from her tooth grinding. She was acting out violently during sleep walking episodes...." He stopped. When I looked up at him he held my eye.

"Maybe I should let her explain it to you," he said.

I frowned.

"I don't have to remind you of her current condition," I said.

He shook his head.

"I video tape all my patients so I can study their behaviour patterns over time," he said. "There are several of Lori that I think you might find interesting. Lori was convinced that her sleep paralysis was brought on by some demonic entity bent on killing her."

"What?"

"*Old Hag*," he said. He folded his arms, uncomfortable with the words falling out of his mouth. "Lori blamed everything on a witch who would come to her at night and sit on her chest, then feed her nightmares by spitting in her mouth."

"Well, I'm not sure what to say to that."

"Come by my office tomorrow, I'll show you what I have."

The next morning I showed up at Dr. Heigan's and he was sitting in his car waiting for me. He waved when he saw me, and I met him on the front steps of his practice.

He unlocked the door to his office and led me past a small waiting room into his back office.

"Nice place you got here, doc," I said. "Kind of cozy."

"I'm a specialist," he said. "I only get referrals. Currently I have fifteen patients on the bill, everything from bedwetting up to...." He stopped. He sat behind his desk and offered me one of the patient chairs. There was a small television on his desk and a DVD player in the top drawer.

"I just had this installed last year. Apparently it's already out of date, if I'm to believe the snooty words of my colleagues," Heigan said. He flipped through some disks on a shelf bolted to the wall beside him and came up with one marked *Wordham, Lori-Lie, 2009.*

"It's got every session she had with me in here," he said. He popped the disk and hit play.

Immediately Lori Wordham came onto the screen. I felt a pang of sadness seeing her there, her face opening an old wound I thought had healed.

"*Tell me the problem,*" Dr. Heigan says to her.

"*I don't sleep anymore,*" she says.

"*At all?*"

"*About two hours a night. I umm...*(pause) *I think I'm going nuts, Greg.*"

"This is a rehash of what we talked about last night," Heigan said, clicking the chapter button. "I believe what you want to see comes later on, a few weeks into treatment."

He hit the play button again. Lori, sort of lilting off the side of the chair, the same one I was sitting in. She looked a mess.

"*All I think about are dark things,*" Lori says.

"*Tell me about it,*" Dr. Heigan says.

"*Like, dead stuff. Bad sex things. It's like I'm not...human. Anymore.*"

"Are a lot of your patients like this?" I asked him. He couldn't take his eyes off Lori. She flopped back in forth on her chair like Stevie Wonder; running her hands up and down her arms.

"No, they don't usually get this bad. Insomnia has a tendency of making the patient feel disconnected from their feelings and thoughts. They're simply too tired to care."

He clicked ahead another couple chapters.

"It went on like this for weeks before she hit a new problem. Her sleep walks were turning acutely violent and strange."

"*I don't know what to tell you,*" Lori says. "*I just threw it in the bathtub. It's not like I could walk around the neighbourhood with flyers asking* Have I seen your cat..." She giggles at her own little joke.

"What's this about?" I said.

"Lori found a cat when she was sleep walking," Heigan said. "An orange tabby, from what she told me. She took it home and...*mutilated* it."

"When was this?"

"Three weeks before she died. Lori told me she snapped its neck. Then she ripped it open with her fingers and started drawing on the walls with it. Strange symbols. She thought they were occult."

"Were they?"

"I have no idea," He said. "That's not my area of expertise. There is more though. I think this will give you more of an idea about how disturbed Lori was."

"What's that?"

"I'll let Lori tell you."

He fast forwarded the tape just a bit. He knew exactly where to stop, like he'd watched this part many times.

"*...all over the wall,*" Lori says. "*Some on my stomach and back too, I could feel it like tape on my skin when I moved.*

Don't ask me how I managed to write them on my back. I can't hardly reach back there. And something else."

"*Something else?*"

"*Well, when I woke up I had an awful cramp. And there was fur on my face, sticking to my cheeks and my mouth... and* in *my mouth. I ran to the toilet and puked. It was vodka and fur. Like a hairball. It scratched my throat coming out. There was so much blood Greg...I...ate its face I think. I could see its fuckin eyes in my puke and hair; there were these two yellow eyes staring back at me, like look what you did you crazy bitch—*" Then Lori was crying.

"I remember how moved I was because she'd pretty much locked her emotions away until that moment and they'd come flooding out," Dr. Heigan said. "It was a total break down."

"Forgive me, doctor," I said. "But it doesn't appear your therapy was really working very well."

"Lori was very ill," Heigan said, nodding. "It was right after this event that I suggested Lori go for psychiatric help. She was afraid of being institutionalized, so we put it off. If she hadn't been such a close friend I may have insisted. As it was...well, I thought I could help her."

He hit the fast forward button.

"Like I was telling you yesterday, Lori was convinced that she was being attacked by a malevolent force when she slept. *A witch.*"

"And you are assuming that there is something to this." I heard disbelief in my own voice. I was okay with it.

"Have you ever seen a painting called *The Nightmare* by Henry Fuseli?" he asked me.

"No," I said. "I don't get out much."

"*The Nightmare* shows a young woman sprawled out on her bed, sleeping, with an incubus sitting on her chest. The demon is looking over its shoulder at the viewer, as though you are somehow disturbing it by looking upon the painting itself. It's quite a famous piece, actually."

"And you think this demon was attacking Lori," I said.

He didn't reply. Instead he clicked the play button.

"*How are you feeling today?*" he says.

"*Bad*," Lori says. "*Goodie Sarah came to visit me again.*" Lori laughs, then crosses her arms.

"*What happened?*" Heigan says.

"*Same as the other times*," Lori says. "*She sat on my chest. I couldn't breathe or move my arms. I couldn't even really move my head. Goodie Sarah bargles words at me. She snorts and spits in my mouth, and her spit causes the worst nightmares I've ever had. This time I was going through a meat grinder in hell, and there was a man there trying to put all my pieces together again. Like a jigsaw puzzle. He kept getting it wrong though. Every time he put someone else's flesh on me, I'd start reliving* their *nightmares, until there was so much going on I couldn't tell one nightmare from another.*"

"*How long did it last?*"

"*I dunno,*" Lori says. "*Seemed like a long time, but maybe it was only a couple minutes. I can't tell. I woke up screaming and...and I pissed myself.*" She put her head in her hands.

"*It's alright Lori,*" Heigan says. "*That's all really common with sleep paralysis. You can't be held responsible for what your body does when you are asleep.*"

"*But I* wasn't asleep," Lori says. "I was wide awake! *That's what I've been trying to tell you. Goodie Sarah wakes me up when she comes, because she's so fucking heavy and I can't breathe. Plus she has this awful stink, like pig shit. It fills the room.*" Lori flicks her hair.

"What was that?" I said, pointing to the monitor. "Rewind it."

He did. The second time, we both saw it. Lori's reaction to her own words, *Goodie Sarah.* She twitched as the words left her mouth.

"Christ," I said, blaspheming. My voice was high and tight. I was sitting forward in my seat. "Rewind it again, and play it back slowly."

He does it.

Scene by scene, Lori was reduced to a robot. She bounced out of each frame to a new position. She was speaking, but there was no sound. I could imagine how run down and melted her voice might be if there was.

Wiiiiiiddddde awwwwwwaaaaaaaake...

A single frame showed a shadow enter the scene, just above and to the right of Lori's head. The next frame, it was a blur halfway between Lori's head and the edge of the screen. The frame after that, the shadow was on her; it flowed across the back of her head. Lori twitched. This time the twitch was less organic. It looked like she was responding to being struck.

"What the hell was that?" I was panicky now. My adrenaline was pumping pure hot electricity into my veins.

"I don't know," Dr. Heigan said. His face was dark.

"Doc?" I said.

"I think I made a big mistake," Heigan said suddenly,

sitting back in his chair. "I didn't bring you here to convince you Lori was being attacked by a witch; I brought you here to show you everything in the hopes you'd laugh and tell me I was falling off my rocker. A little perspective was all I needed, then I could medicate the shit out of myself and check into a hospital for a little while."

"Instead," he continued, "you looked at all the footage and found what appeared to be some sort of *physical attack* that occurred on Lori when she was in session."

"How are *you* sleeping?" I asked him. I was starting to piece it all together. In a really strange way it made sense that he would come to me looking for guidance. We were both connected to Lori Wordham through her illness. He through treatment, and I had spent a lot of time trying to put her soul at ease. Without ever knowing why it was so troubled in the first place. Now Dr. Heigan was hinting that he may have been suffering from something similar to what had caused Lori's death. Or helped it along, in any case.

Dr. Heigan sighed.

I wasn't sure what he wanted. Absolution? Protection? Had he come to me and dropped all this in my lap in the hopes I would tell him that God battles the Devil for souls one at a time?

I couldn't.

"Look, Dr. Heigan," I said. "The Church doesn't recognize active demonic forces the way we used to in the Middle Ages. Too many innocent lives were lost. We believe that the Lord and the Devil battle for your soul in an abstract, metaphorical way, with your free will being the outcome."

"I went to university on a football scholarship," Dr. Heigan said. "My parents are Mormons. I spent four years playing football to pay my tuition and another five years racking up a massive student debt load to get my doctorate."

"I see. You have obviously worked very hard to get where you are."

"Thing is," he continued, "I *know* that what Lori had is in a dozen textbooks and medical journals. It's well documented. *It's a common somnia.* My education tells me that Lori was treatable and she should have gone on to live a normal, healthy life. I'm a man of *science*, Father. I believe that as we gain knowledge and understanding our need for superstition and ritual is replaced by enlightenment."

He pointed at the screen. Lori's frozen face was turned out to us, and it gave me the unsettling feeling she was listening in on our conversation.

"This...*this thing*, whatever it is, is happening to me now. I know it's impossible because I'm a person of the modern age, and I know for a fact that these things simply don't exist. And yet, here it is. I could have told myself it was sympathetic guilt, and the grief I was feeling over the loss of my friend was causing me to relive some of her more disturbing symptoms, *but I can't explain this.*"

"I'm not sure I know what to tell you," I said.

"I need you to tell me that there is *room* in the world for something like this. I need to know that there is more to reality than measurements and dimensions, so I can accept this and move on. Otherwise I'm going to stick on it like brown on shit, and I'm going to lose my damned mind."

I thought on it for a moment. Here it was after all, laid bare. Dr. Heigan was a man wracked by guilt and suffering immensely because of the loss of his friend. It was just as he'd said himself. He didn't need me to tell him some flittering image on a screen was a spirit...he needed me to help him find in his heart what he really needed to do next.

"I have to tell you, Dr. Heigan," I said, very slowly. "We certainly don't believe in witchcraft. This Goodie...*whoever* simply can't exist outside of your mind because witches don't exist in this way. They sell charms and potions at medieval fairs. They don't sit on your chest and torment you while you sleep."

"But you saw it," Dr. Heigan said. He appeared very close to breaking down. "You saw it before I did even. You showed me, *for Christ's sake*."

"*I'm not sure what I saw*," I said. That was the truth. That black streak could have been anything. The Internet was full of hoax pictures of spirits and ghosts. People claimed to be possessed all the time. They were attention seekers or mentally ill. So how it was in the Dark Ages, such as it was in today's world. We just understand it better now.

"I don't get it," Dr. Heigan said. "How can you believe in God without the Devil?"

"We made so many mistakes in the past we rely on science now to explain the evils of the world. Much like yourself."

"The church was...my last hope, I think," Dr. Heigan said. He wiped his grimy eyes. "I was really hoping you could reconcile this, if I told you about Lori, and I showed you the tapes."

"Listen, Doctor, what is your heart telling you about this case?"

Dr. Heigan considered my words. Finally he sighed.

"It tells me, that *perhaps*, I should follow my own advice to Lori when this started getting out of hand. It tells me that I should spend some time at the Elliston Mental Health Facility if I'm going to ever shake this. *Contagious Schizophrenia*. It's a ridiculous term. Somehow, it seems to fit perfectly."

"I'm sorry," I said. "You have many trials ahead of you. I will pray for your strength."

"Pray for my sanity," Dr. Heigan said, and laughed. Then he sniffled. "Seriously, Father."

"I absolutely will," I said.

Dr. Heigan went on extended leave the following Monday and placed himself in the care of Elliston Hospital. True to my word, I prayed for him nightly.

About a month later I picked up the phone and found Dr. Heigan on the other end.

"Hello, Father," Heigan said. His voice was thin and tired. It was older too.

"Dr. Heigan," I said. "It's been a while. How are you feeling these days?"

"Listen," Heigan said, ignoring the question. "Can you come to Elliston? We're not supposed to have visitors, but I'll tell them you are my priest and they have to let you in. Could you do that for me, Father?"

"Yes," I said. "I can do that. In fact, if you need me, I *am* your priest, Dr. Heigan."

"Thank you, Father," he said. "When can you come?"

"I can come today," I said. "This afternoon."

The ride from Calgary to Ponoka didn't take as long as I thought. Too bad, in a way, because the thought of seeing

Dr. Heigan filled me with an awful dread in the pit of my stomach that I just couldn't shake. Prayer didn't help. Whiskey did, a little.

Elliston Mental Hospital was a bright, modern building, with lots of crazy angles and towering glass walls. It reminded me of a big red brick aquarium. The grounds were clean and pleasant for walking; there were little pathways and tranquil gardens everywhere. Meandering across the property was a small running brook attaching goldfish ponds. There were pyjama-clad patients wandering about, some dragging IV stands around with them, others walking with the help (or possibly under the watchful eye of) their own personal orderlies.

I went through the front door and met with the desk secretary; Dr. Heigan had indeed put me on notice. They gave me my own orderly to show me up to the fourth floor, where Dr. Heigan was residing.

I found him sitting at a table by a window in the common room. He looked up and smiled; I swear I'd never seen someone age so quickly in so little time. He looked twenty years older. His hair was frayed and greying. His skin was sunken and sallow, his face pale and stubbly. He had heavy bruised bags under his eyes.

"Dr. Heigan," I said, walking over to shake his hand. "Good to see you again."

"You too," he said. "But it's not Doctor Heigan anymore. My days treating the sick are quite far behind me now."

"You look exhausted," I said, I grabbing a seat. I put my hand on his shoulder, but he flinched at the contact. I laced my hands on the table instead."How have you been?"

"Not so good."

"That's unfortunate," I said. "Have they made any progress on your condition?"

"Yes," he said, smiling sarcastically. "They're moving from Thorazine to electroshock. I'm very excited; I've always wanted to be a human light bulb."

I nodded.

"Sorry, Father," he said. "It's not a funny joke. It's just my new coping mechanism to deal with how life has turned out."

"Well," I said. "It's not over yet."

"Once I get my first dose of electricity I may as well use my doctorate for toilet paper. Electroshock causes enough brain damage per hit that I'll no longer be able to function as a real doctor anymore."

"I understand how angry you must be," I said. "What I tell some of my parishioners when they fall on extremely difficult times is that they need to prioritize the important things in their lives. You should try and focus first on becoming well again, and then see where you are after you've come through that."

"*She followed me*," Dr. Heigan said. He stared straight into my face. "I brought her to Elliston with me. They gave me a sedative when I first arrived; I woke up screaming. I attacked an orderly because I was half asleep. Now the only thing that works is the Thorazine shots, but even they're failing. They don't make me sleep; they make it so I don't care if I'm awake or not.

"They don't like the idea of contagious schizophrenia. They're just calling it psychotic hysteria. I told them everything, of course. But that's a diagnosis they can understand. That's something they can treat with drugs and electricity."

"You still don't believe it," I said.

"They're just words now," Heigan said, rubbing his hands over his face. "It's funny, how three hundred years ago they'd have seen the signs of a witch attack and cured me already. Probably cured Lori too. Burned some black cats or something. Hung garlic over my bed."

"Burned the local midwife alive," I said.

"*This is how they get you*," he said. "Witches attack from the flanks. You're never quite sure if it's bad luck or...psychotic hysteria. Goodie Sarah killed Lori and she's going to kill me. My only hope is that the electroshock treatments kill off any ability to give a shit when she comes."

"How can I help you?" I said. "Please, anything."

"Will you take my confession?" Dr. Heigan said. "I don't want to die a heathen, Father. I don't want to go to Hell."

"Of course," I said. "Of course."

"So here we are," Father Alvarez said, draining his glass. He eyed the bottle sitting in front of Father Thomas, then put his empty glass on the desk. "That was two weeks ago."

"I see," Father Thomas said. "What of your friend Dr. Heigan? Have you been in contact?"

"He's dead. Died yesterday. A suicide."

"Suicide," Father Thomas mused. "A mortal sin."

"Yeah," Father Alvarez said. "As it turns out, I went up there and sanctified him for nothing. In the end he damned himself to a life in Hell anyway, whether he claimed he wanted to or not."

"You did what you could," Father Thomas said.

"But it wasn't enough."

"Anytime you do your best, it's enough," Thomas said. "He was a psychotic. You said so yourself."

"That's what I've been trained to tell people," Alvarez corrected.

"It's one and the same."

Father Alvarez said nothing to this. Instead, he reached out and scooped the scotch bottle in his hand and grabbed his empty glass. The bottle glugged as he poured, stopping a half inch or so from the rim.

"So what is it?" Thomas said. "Are you feeling guilty because you were unable to save him?"

"No," Father Alvarez said. There was a tremor in his voice that matched one in his hands.

"Then tell me."

"I think," Father Alvarez said. "*I think she is after me now.*"

Father Thomas stared at his friend. In return, Alvarez let him watch while he drained half his scotch off.

"Contagious...schizophrenia ," Father Thomas said slowly.

"No, *DAMMIT!*" Father Alvarez shouted. "*Listen to me! Heigan and I were wrong don't you get it? He tried science and it failed them terribly! BOTH of them!*"

"Please," Thomas said. "Be calm."

"I need your help," Father Alvarez said. "I need *God*. Otherwise I'm going to be just like Lori Wordham and Dr. Heigan. Don't you get it? She needs you to despair! *She needs you to lose your faith so she can give your soul to Lucifer!*"

"*ENOUGH!*" screamed Father Thomas, standing up. He

slammed a meaty fist on the desk, causing the glasses to jump and tinkle. "*I DONT WANT TO HEAR IT! GOD DOESNT WANT TO HEAR IT!*"

He snarled.

"You walk in here with your blasphemies and your sins, and you think God doesn't notice? You think He doesn't see your false faith? It's an affront to Him, Father Alvarez! It's like pissing in God's face! Spouting heresies! Speaking of the dead like you have a clue what's really going on! In league with dark powers conspiring against the Church and all that is right and good! HOW DARE YOU?"

Father Alvarez stood up. There was a fury in the other priest he'd never seen before. A fervour. And suddenly the room wasn't a rectory. It was too small to be a confessional. It felt more like a tomb.

"*YOUR LEAGUE WITH SATAN SHALL NOT GO UNPUNISHED!*" Father Thomas screamed. He grabbed the bottle of scotch off the table and smashed the top off against the corner of the desk. Then he tossed it toward Father Alvarez.

The bottle made a lazy turn in the air. Alvarez ducked, but too late, and the bottle hit him in the forehead. A large gash opened in his flesh, above his brow ridge, cascading blood and booze down into his eyes. Blinding them. The musty, sweet smell of scotch filled his throat and lungs. Bloody scotch dribbled into his mouth.

"We must purify your soul, Father Alvarez!" Father Thomas shouted. "We must make the Devil know we will not suffer him to bugger the flock with his dark ways! WE WILL BURN THE IMPURITIES AWAY!"

Father Alvarez staggered. He desperately raked at his face,

trying to get the scotch and blood from his eyes so he could see, just for a moment. Father Thomas was wrong, so very wrong. He was a victim in all of this. He had come to the Church for help. And now Father Thomas had sailed completely off his rocker. *Contagious schizophrenia*, that was what Heigan called it. An infection in his words, causing the priest's brain to snap like a twig. Father Alvarez would get help for him. Thorazine, just like Dr. Heigan. He only had to wipe his eyes clean, so he could see what was happening, so he could have a chance to look the Father in the eye, and speak to him as a brother....

His eyes burned like hell itself.

"BURN!" Father Thomas shrieked, grabbing the gold handled lighter out of his cigar box. He flicked it open with practiced ease.

"No!" Father Alvarez had time for one word, and that was it.

Father Thomas tossed the lighter at Alvarez. It bounced off his leg. The hungry yellow-blue flames found the scotch. Lapped at the scotch like a starving mongrel dog tasting blood. Hot white pain licked up Alvarez from his balls to his throat, and then leapt to his face.

"BUUUURRRRNNNNN!" Father Thomas screamed. "Cleanse your soul so you can stand before God without shame in your heart!"

Father Alvarez found his feet, slapping at the fire and shrieking. Fire lit up the pain nerves in his face like white hot Christmas bulbs. His eyes fogged and swelled in the heat as his fatty flesh became fuel for the fire; one popped with a hiss like an egg tossed into a wood stove. Amazingly, Father Alvarez found relief in the stream of blood and ichor that ran down his cheek, cooling the blazing flesh beneath it but for only a moment.

He opened his mouth to vomit, and hungry flames chased the breath from his lungs. Smoke and charred flesh filled his nostrils. Angry flames followed. He sank to the floor. The chair caught fire behind him as sizzling, burning drops of liquid fat fell away.

"Let us pray for this sinner," Father Thomas was saying. "Let him see the error of his ways. God does not love you, Father Alvarez, but when cleansed by the warmth of the healing fire, He will again. You are dirty and unworthy of His love now. Soon, my son. Soon you will be worthy. Kill yourself, and avoid this fate. Stand before God on His terms."

Dark chanting arose from the room around the words of Father Thomas.

EEEEE-AHHHHH, they prayed. *EEEEEE AHHHHHH.*

"Do the right thing," Father Thomas said. "I know you will."

There was a gasp and a rush of cool air. At first Father Alvarez didn't realize it was coming from him. He tried to scream, but he couldn't. There was something heavy on his chest, forcing his lungs to spasm and refuse breath. The stench of pig shit filled his nostrils. Filled his mind.

He opened his eyes.

Goodie Sarah stared down at him. Her face was a mass of mottled green flesh; the flesh of the dead. Millipedes and worms clung to her face like strands of hair. She pulled back her grey lips in a hideous grin, cracking them, and causing black blood to mix with the strands of bile and spit dripping from her mouth. Her grin showed off rows and rows of jagged yellow teeth; a putrescent green tongue darted lazily between the gaps. The spaces oozed more blood.

Father Alvarez's eyes bulged as Goodie Sarah pushed a wad of pus and phlegm to the front of her teeth, then puckered her mouth like she was about to plant the biggest, nastiest kiss Alvarez had ever gotten in his life. The phlegm wad dropped from her lips. It caught Father Alvarez on the upper lip, then slid down over his teeth.

There was a sour tang to it. Blood, infection, disease. He imagined licking the bandage off an infected wound. The pus and lung slime coated his teeth. It moved over his tongue slowly, allowing him to savour every little nuance. He tasted AIDS. He tasted the stench of organs rotting from cancer.

It moved down to the back of his throat, finally blocking off his windpipe.

Goodie Sarah laughed the brittle, autumn laugh of the ancient and wicked.

Father Alvarez choked on the wad of sickness in his throat, then, coughing, sucked in a deep lung full of breath.

Carrying her seed of corruption deep inside him.

He began to shake. Uncontrollably. Forcefully. Seizure shakes.

Goodie Sarah was grinding her withered sex against him. Pulsating.

Father Alvarez squeezed his eyes shut. The ball of pus and rot in his lungs spread like a drop of oil in a mud puddle. He felt it reaching into the darkest recesses of his body, murdering God's beautiful work and replacing it with ruin.

And when he opened his eyes, she was gone.

"Thank the Lord," he heard Father Thomas say. "You gave me quite a scare, Brother."

Alvarez looked around. He was lying on a church pew. At the front of the church. Father Thomas was standing above him.

"What?" he said.

"You were screaming," Father Thomas said. "You said you were burning."

"I...*was*," Father Alvarez said.

Father Thomas smiled.

"Well, if you are having dreams about burning, then I suggest we get you into confessional right away. That's God telling you to unburden your guilt."

"It wasn't a dream," Alvarez said.

"Of course not," Father Thomas said. "You were burning in the church here just now, and when I managed to get you to open your eyes your wounds all miraculously healed. Come my friend, let us absolve your sin and then you can tell me what all this is about."

Alvarez could still feel that inky blackness inside of him. Disease, rotting, infected thing that it was, corrupting him from the inside out. Not all of his wounds had healed. He was still carrying the worst of them all inside him. *Worst,* because he knew now if he told anyone, they'd become infected too. Contagious schizophrenia or not. Psychotic hysteria, or not.

Goodie Sarah, or not.

Father Thomas was looking at him. Expecting answers. Expecting a story.

Alvarez shoved him away.

"*Keep away from me!*" he shouted. He turned and stumbled toward the front of the church, toward the entrance.

"Father Alvarez!" Thomas called. "Where are you going?"

"*Keep away from me! I'll kill you! I swear I'll kill you!*" Alvarez yelled back. He was at the end of the pews now, just a few feet from the door. When he reached the entrance, he threw open the doors. He took the stairs three at a time, stumbled, then was off and racing like a lunatic down the sidewalk. Away from the church. Away from his life.

Witches attack from the flanks, and from the back, Dr. Heigan had said to him. *They break your faith down and cause you despair until you lose hope*. That way they can take your soul to Hell. They wanted you to feel the ugliness of humanity. It was their way of spitting in the mouth of God.

Father Alvarez *had* faith though. No matter what, he would not allow her to take it from him. He would bundle her black seed inside him and wait it out. Stop the cycle. There would be no more victims of this witch. He would shut himself away from the world and pray until she came for him. And on that day he would meet her, standing on his own feet like a man of God should.

It was a chilly October morning. The wind whispered threats of a cold winter ahead.

The Children of the Golden Day

Sarah put her foot on the dash, and David suddenly had the urge to smash it with his fist. He didn't though, because you weren't supposed to hit your kids these days, no matter how much they irritated you or picked at all your hot buttons or reminded you of your ex wife. Even if they kept putting their fucking feet up on the dash when you told them a hundred times not to. You weren't supposed to hit them, so David wouldn't.

But man, did he want to.

Instead, he said, "*Hey!* I told you to keep your feet off the dash, didn't I? Come on."

"Whatever," Sarah said. She made a point of slamming her foot down, as if every word to come out of her father's mouth was just a huge pain in the ass. She ran her fingers along the passenger side window and left streaks, because she knew David hated *that*, too.

David bit on his next words before they had a chance to escape. They were ten goddamn minutes away from his sister's house, and a craving for cigarettes was chewing out the back of his skull, and he'd be damned if he let her win by getting him to yell. That was the game, after all, and he knew damn well that's what it was. If she could get him to raise his voice she could roll her eyes or cluck her tongue or do some other, annoying little thing that would make David want to jerk the wheel of the car into oncoming traffic.

Instead, he spoke calmly. "Can you not run your fingers on the window please? It leaves streaks."

Sarah clucked her tongue and shook her head.

David felt the wheel twitch in his hands. Teenage girls. Even when you won, you still lost. But he was about to give them both a much-needed vacation, and that's why they were out in the middle of rural Alberta, hours away from the nearest Starbucks and suffering for it. Out here, all the towns got their coffee from those crappy gas station heating thermoses, the ones that showed a strip of coffee in the front leading down to the nozzle, and somehow that was supposed to make you believe the coffee was what they said it was, or even how much was left in the fucking container. That coffee gave you the shits, and even though he didn't have to go, he could feel it sitting sour in his stomach. *And* he just wanted a goddamn cigarette.

To top it all off, he was driving down here to give his sister Percy a piece of his mind, because she was supposed to pick Sarah up a few days before on the Friday, and it was *Tuesday* now and nobody had heard from her at all. In fact, he hadn't talked to her in two weeks, and that was just so typical of her.

The single lane highway ahead of them switched to new black asphalt, and ahead he saw the turnoff to Boonton. Percy and her husband Nick had bought a house out here three years ago, in the middle of nowhere because that's what they could afford. Nick was an outdoor kinda guy; he drank dollar beers and wore a ball cap like everyone else out here, so he fit in right away. Percy though, she'd had to make adjustments. She adjusted by getting pregnant, and by the time David's nephew Ross was born Percy had become one of the locals. David figured it probably had something to do with new blood. Or maybe it was like with immigrants; their kids were considered locals, even if their parents came from the city and were just a couple *cidiots*.

The sun was out in full force. Out here on the prairies, the heat always seemed to be just a bit more unbearable than in the city. When they turned off the asphalt onto a long gravel road leading to the town, the direction of the sun shifted, and David had to adjust the sun guard on his side to keep it out of his eyes. It baked down on them and he felt like part of the terrain; cracked dry and beaten by yellow rays of heat. He had to slow down to sixty on the gravel because his BMW was light and it rocked back and forth over the loose gravel. Eventually he brought it down to fifty.

The road was lined on both sides by a long deep ditch, probably made to deflect water away from the road. The grass was at least knee deep on David's side and beyond it was a huge field that had gone fallow. There were cows on Sarah's side, but even though David was a *cidiot* he could see there was something wrong with them. They looked like their flesh was hanging off their spines; their hipbones were so prominent that David was sure that any moment now they'd come bursting through the skin on their backs like little bone altars. Some of them were already on the ground dead, and then the smell hit them and he forgot all about cigarettes and window streaks and shoes on dashboards. All he wanted to do was get away from the god-awful smells of cow flesh ripening in the hot August sun. Sometimes David hated being out of the city so much he couldn't put it into words.

"Ohh," Sarah said, reaching for the window controls. "Gross! I think I'm gonna barf."

"Just make sure you do it outside the car," David said. He tried the air conditioning, found it suitable, and rolled up his own window. He slowed the car down as they went past the cows, and Sarah planted her face against the glass to see better. *Kids.*

"What's wrong with them?" she said.

"Sick I guess," David said, but that was only part of it, because they looked like those starving, worm infested cows they showed on *The Learning Channel*, when they showed African herdsmen with their starving herds or those Punjabi's who dressed their cows up in people clothes and drank their piss. He was a *cidiot* but not *that* much of one; he could tell the difference between a sick animal and a starving one, and those things hadn't eaten in a week or two at least.

They drove on and saw more dead cattle, on David's side, and then they saw some horses that looked like they were about dead on their feet. David started to wonder if maybe he was wrong about illness being their problem. You just didn't see that many starving animals in Alberta. Those things were worth money. The horses made Sarah sad.

"You alright?" David said. They were nearing the Boonton turnoff. He could see a line of trees ahead that sheltered the town from the wind.

"Those horses look bad," Sarah said, before retreating into her iPod and disappearing.

That's how she deals with things that upset her, David thought. *She disconnects. That's you, through and through. She may look like her mother but her head is you.*

Of *course* it was him. That was part of the reason they argued so much wasn't it? Because they were so much alike. But she was also dramatic like her mother was, and that drove David batty sometimes. The drama was definitely one of the reasons they argued so much. By the time Sarah started her shit, David had already filled up on it. *Paid for it* too, because Jenna had taken half when she left. Then she'd left the kid and moved east, to Ontario.

They passed a farmstead where half the buildings were charred husks and David slowed down to take a closer look. The fire looked like it had centralized around the farmhouse itself; there was a half burnt red barn and what

David thought could only be dog kennels that had also been badly burnt. Some bloated creature was lying on its side in the dirt. It looked like a pig. David hoped to hell that it was a pig.

"*What the hell?*" Sarah said. "What is going on around here?"

"Don't say swears," David said. "And I don't know. Maybe the fire here made those other animals sick." That didn't make much sense to him, but who was he? Dr. Doolittle? He was just a *cidiot* with two mortgages and an ex-wife to pay off. *Cidiot* wasn't even his word; it was a word Nick had picked up from the locals; they used it to describe people just like David.

"It's not a swear," Sarah said.

They passed the tree line that was a windbreak for Boonton and the local UFA Cardlock came into view. There was a gas tanker half parked on the pad, as though the driver had come in to fill up and then changed his mind. The place was deserted. There was no driver in sight.

"I can drive those," David said, glancing at his daughter. She tapped her earphones and shook her head.

David sighed. "Bullshit you can't hear me." The road ahead sparkled like ice in the sunshine, and David had just time enough to realize he was about to drive on a shit ton of broken glass when a dog came out of the tree line carrying something in its teeth. It ran straight across the grass to the road and decided to beat David across the street. David saw it disappear under the front of the car.

"What the fuck!" he shouted, slamming on the brakes and cranking hard on the wheel. The car swerved and there were two grumbles from the tires on the driver's side of the car before the dog reappeared none the worse for wear. *Jesus that was close,* David thought, *Oh god oh fuck is that a baby hanging in its mouth?*

No, it couldn't be. Had to be a doll, because what the fuck would a dog be doing hauling a dead baby around? Babies weren't stiff like that. They weren't black and grey from burns and didn't have pink spots where their skin had charred off. They were smiling angels that loved you. They weren't old meat some stray had picked up from a burnt farmstead, even though the dog was coming from the right direction for something like that.

And he had two flat tires from all the damn glass in the road now, he was sure of it, even though he wasn't thinking of glass and tires but of dogs and babies right now. He had a feeling that was going to stay with him a long time, even if it was a doll. (*It was.*)

"Oh my God," Sarah said, her eyes wide and fearful, "What was that?"

"It was a doll," David said quickly. He popped open the door to get out and inspect the tires, and was hit with a wave of heat. It seemed to be coming out of the earth itself.

But the sun wasn't the only thing filling the air. There was a noise that David couldn't immediately identify... sort of like stone grinding on stone. But there was more to it than that, because it also sounded like the noise a raw steak makes when you flipped it on a plate; kind of a wet slap noise made when to soft solids were slammed together. Those two noises were just the soundtrack for a tinny, garbled voice singing something in a language David couldn't wrap his head around. It sounded like those old stereophonic recordings, but instead of words, the voice was singing *hua, hua, hua,* over and over again. The sound was like ants crawling into his ears. It made his skin itch just hearing it. And yet, it was also compelling, like it was telling him where to go...

"Is the car okay?" Sarah asked.

David rubbed the back of his neck and his hand came away wet. "Two flats," he said quietly. The tires on his side of the car were gutted from the glass on the road, which he could now see was the result of smashing dozens of beer bottles on the road. Local kids, from the look of things, and they needed their asses whipped. David hoped they weren't watching from a hiding place somewhere, but he knew there was a good chance they *were*; watching and giggling stupidly and high fiving each other like they were the kings of Boonton. The image of them like that pissed David off even more. Stupid punk hillbilly kids. The gene pool was pretty shallow around these parts if this is what they did for a good time.

The worst part was that David only carried a single spare, so now they were really fucked. He'd have to get AMA to come out and tow them into a town with a tire shop, and he was sure to pay a mint for anything those good old boys had on their shelves. Just like Chevy Chase in *National Lampoon's Vacation*; As soon as the mechanic asked him how much was in his wallet ol' Chevy knew he was screwed.

"*Fuck!*" David yelled. He slammed the roof of his car with the palm of his hand, then rubbed his neck some more. This was all Percy's fault. Fuckin' Percy, who had to move to bumfuck nowhere and wouldn't answer her damn phone so their mother was calling David five times a day asking if he'd heard from her.

"You alright?" Sarah said quietly. She pulled one earbud out of her ear to talk to him, and was just now hearing the grinding, warbling noise coming from the far side of town. She looked around the car, confused, her fifteen year old brain trying to process it. "What *is* that?"

"How the fuck should I know," David said. He pulled his phone out of the little holster on his belt and the screen read NO SERVICE. "Perfect. Just *fucking ducky*." Now what? Walk to Percy's and leave the car here in the middle of the road? It was tempting. He could use her phone to call the R.C.M.P. and file a report. Of course, it might take them all day to get out here, and if he knew anything about small town cops it was that they didn't like to do anything for anyone. In fact, he'd probably be better off handling all of this himself. He hated taking a bite and letting someone get away with fucking with him, but he didn't have a whole lot of options. If he didn't want to be stuck out here for a while, he'd be better off handling it all on his own. He'd drive the car a couple blocks to Percy's house, call AMA, get the tire, and then be the fuck out of here before sundown. Although it was getting late in the day, so if he wanted the plan in action he had to get on it right away.

Sarah was staring off into space, absorbed by the noise in the air, but when David swore she pulled back into her shell. She snapped out of her reverie and put the ear bud back into her ear, rolling her eyes at him in disgust. David gritted his teeth but said nothing. He knew there was a four-alarm fire going off in his temper. He wasn't sure he'd be able to put it out once it got started. Instead he buried it. Unplugged from it for a little while, and pushed it down far enough so he could see around it. That was one of mom's charming little coping strategies. *Push it down until you can see around it*, and then let it all out when the old man is late for dinner and you accidentally burned the potatoes because you were fighting with him on the phone.

But festering about his mother wasn't pushing things down. It was adding gasoline to a smouldering fire. He turned his thoughts away from her and dropped into the driver's seat. After a moment, he pulled his feet in and slammed the car door shut. The warbling song was almost nonexistent inside the vehicle, thanks to good old German engineering. David started the car.

"What about the flat tires?" Sarah said.

"Gonna have to keep till we get over to Percy's. Unless you want to try and find another tire out here somewhere."

"No thanks. That noise is really creepy. What is it?"

"No idea," David said.

He threw the car in drive and it staggered to the left immediately. He had to force the wheel hard to the right to counter it, and the flat tired groaned and bit into the gravel road. He couldn't do more than a few blocks like this because the stress on the frame and the alignment of the car would get all shot to hell. Thankfully, he wouldn't have to. They drove past the first block and David noted another fire-gutted house. There were also stripped and ruined vehicles in most of the driveways of the neighbourhood. Some of the houses looked like they'd been boarded up and abandoned while others looked like they'd once been boarded up but had since been smashed in and vandalized .

"What the hell happened out here?" David said.

"It looks even worse than normal," Sarah said. The houses on her side of the road were in much the same shape. The yards had been scattered with debris, and in one instance, it looked like someone had cut through the outside walls and removed huge sections of it. They could see the living room and kitchen from where David and Sarah were on the road, and the house had been totalled on the inside. It wasn't as though someone had moved out and made renovations. It was as if they had been living in there when huge chunks of their outside wall just disappeared, and then they went crazy and started destroying all their possessions.

They turned the corner to Percy's house and David pulled the car up to the sidewalk. Then he turned off the car and simply sat for a moment, staring at his sister's house.

Their property was no better than most of the other houses. Percy's car sat ruined on the front lawn. Its tires had been shredded and the doors had been removed on the passenger side. The seats and steering wheel had been ripped out, and the internal wiring sat in a large nest on the spot where the passenger seat should have been. Behind it, her little beige bungalow sat, front windows smashed and boarded up, and the front porch had been filled with furniture...to keep someone away from the porch door? It certainly *looked* that way, like it was barricaded to protect from the inside, but why would Nick and Percy need to do that?

Seeing their house in the shape it was, David started to feel the first real prickles of fear. It looked like some kind of disaster had taken place, but why hadn't anyone heard about it? Where were the camera crews and police? You couldn't destroy an entire town in the age of information without someone knowing about it, could you?

"Dad?" Sarah said. "Are they alright?"

"Just sit here for a minute," David said. He reached over

and gave his daughter a quick hug. "I'm going to go see what's going on."

"Alright," Sarah said, hugging him back.

"Don't get out of the car."

"I won't."

David got out and shut the door behind him. Sarah watched from her seat, and he flashed a reassuring smile. The look on her face told him it had failed, big-time. He picked his way around the car and made his way up to the front step. There was a large brown stain on the sidewalk near the front door (*blood?* Was that blood?) populated with ants and droning flies. The stain centred on a spot maybe three feet wide, but it looked like something had been dragged through it and down toward the road. David could see the line on the grass clearly now; a carpet of bugs and spiders feasting on whatever had been pulled through the mess.

He turned and stalked to the front door. He tried the doorknob and was actually relieved to find it locked. Then he banged on the door.

"*Percy!*" He yelled. "*You in there, girl? Open the door!*" He wanted to look at that stain some more but forced himself not to turn around. The grinding, meat slapping sound in the air continued unabated. *This way,* it seemed to whisper. *Come this way*. He tried the door again (still locked) and banged some more. He turned to go around the front of the house and thought *look at all that fucking blood. That's not an animal. Somebody died there* when the door clicked and he spun around as it was opening and then he was staring mutely at the business end of a shotgun pressed against his left eye.

"Holy Christ," David said. *Uhh...don't shoot?*"

The door swung open into blackness, and then a desperate, birdlike woman appeared through the gloom and grabbed David by the arm.

"Get in here now," she growled. David, too shocked to speak, allowed himself to be pulled inside by this woman. *This woman* who looked like his sister, sort of, if his sister had aged fifteen years and had spent her life living in a war torn country. She had that hard, determined look on her face that people brought with them from the less-sane parts of the world; it seemed to say *go ahead and do your worst, you can't even imagine some of the shit I've seen.*

"Percy, what the hell is going on?" David said. He noticed how the windows were boarded, the house a shambles.

Percy looked out the door. "Where's Sarah?" she barked.

"Outside. Where are Nick and Rossy?"

Percy grabbed David by the neck and pulled him close. "*WHERE* EXACTLY *IS SHE?*" Percy yelled.

"*In the fucking car!*" David said, his voice turning hard. He knocked Percy's arm away and stood up straight. "What the hell is wrong with you? You don't call anyone for weeks, and when I show up here because you forgot to pick up Sarah I see you livin' out here in some kind of Mad Max *bullshit—*"

"We gotta go, *now,*" Percy said. "You gotta get Sarah out of here as fast as you can, David."

"*What?*" David said. "Are you crazy? I'm not going anywhere!"

"No?" Percy said. She was edgy and bouncing on the balls of her feet. There was violence in her, in great amounts right now. For a moment, David thought she was going to hit him. *Or worse*, he thought, eyeing the gun in her hands. Instead of violence though, she set her jaw and shook her head. "Fine then. *Fuck you*. Give me the keys. Stay here and die."

"You're not going anywhere either," David said. "Not until I get some answers."

"*KEYS!*" Percy screamed, and pointed the gun in David's face.

"Holy fuck, calm down," David said. "The car is screwed, alright? It's got two flats. It's not going anywhere."

In response, Percy held the gun across her body and pushed him out of the way with it. *Like a crosscheck,* he though. *I hope to holy Christ she doesn't try a slapshot from that thing. That wouldn't be good, would it? Not one bit. She looks almost crazy enough to do it, too. Line it up like Wayne Gretzky. From here she could put a hole in my chest the size of my fist.*

David let her go by and Percy disappeared around the corner. When he followed her outside, he saw her stalking toward the car. Sarah saw her too, and gave her a smile and a wave. Percy drew the shotgun up and took aim on Sarah, and the girl's smile vanished. It couldn't have disappeared faster if it had been punched off her face. *Or shot off.*

"*HEY!*" David shouted. He started toward her and his adrenaline kicked in, and then the world slowed down. He couldn't move his feet fast enough, could grab her hard enough, and his mind was stuck on repeat: *Noononononononononono.* But it was one long sound in his head, like a helicopter blade cutting through the air or an old air-conditioning unit wobbling it's way to an early grave.

"*Get out of the car, Sarah,*" Percy was saying. "*Right now.*"

David looked at the back of Percy's head and thought one thing: *Like hell, you bitch.*

He reached out and was too far away to grab Percy, and even though time was moving so slowly there wasn't much left, and Percy was going to take his daughter's beautiful face and scrape it off with buckshot. The thought awoke a primal, instinctive creature inside David; a creature whose only goal was to reach Percy and hurt her as much and as quickly as he possibly could. His lip curled in a sneer and spit flew from his lips. He roared.

His fingertips touched the bits of her blonde hair and then his hand was buried in it. He jerked her head back hard, way hard, and it snapped backward toward him like a broken garbage can lid. She uttered a gagging, throaty *nnnggah* as the air was forced from her neck. The pressure of it caused her to squeeze the trigger on the shotgun, and it blasted a shot toward the car.

Oh God, David's monster thought. *Oh God, if you've hurt her I'll kill you, Percy. I will hurt you and keep hurting you until I can't feel anything anymore, and then I'll put my hands on your throat and choke the life out of you.*

He tangled his other hand in her hair and jerked her backward off her feet. He outweighed her by seventy pounds at least; in his panicked condition, it was nothing to flip her sideways onto the front lawn. Like hurling a sack of potatoes by one corner of the bag. Her legs flopped stupidly to one side. The gun went another way. Her head bounced off the lawn and then she lie still as she landed, half folded like bread around a hot dog, just like when they were kids who were once too poor to afford buns.

David ran to the car. Sprinted. He tripped over his long steps and the unsure ground and flopped onto the hood of his BMW.

"*Sarah?*" he yelled. "*Babygirl?*"

Sarah was drawn back in her seat, her eyes red and crying, her face a *bloody mess*—but no, that wasn't right, because she wasn't bloody at all, just red and scratchy from the tears. His brain had just stepped ahead to something he had expected to see and that was all. No blood at all and his baby girl looked none the worse for wear.

Sarah threw the door open and half-climbed, half dragged herself around the front of the car.

"*Oh my god, Dad,*" she sobbed. "*I think you kuh-killed Aunt Percy!*"

David held her tight, almost too tight, trying to absorb the girl back into himself, wanting desperately to be a shell for her in this crazy hellhole his sister had somehow caused. There were times in your life when the bond between you and your children was almost *too* strong, and it always occurred after a near miss. Like when they were little and wandered off, and you just knew in your heart that something awful had happened right up until the moment they reappeared, smiling, and wondering what all the fuss was about. During those times it made you crazy with fear to be more than a few feet from them, and you wanted to just hold them forever and never let them go.

On the lawn, Percy moaned softly.

"I think she's hurt," Sarah said, now starting to pull away from her father. "She may need to go to the hospital."

She needs to die, David thought, but he knew he didn't mean it. Something was terribly wrong with this town, and with his sister. He'd acted out of savage instinct, his animal mind taking over to protect his offspring, but now that he was beginning to think clearly again, he thought that maybe Percy needed more than a doctor. Maybe she needed a psychiatrist.

"And where the fuck are Nicky and *Ross?*" David said aloud, following his train of thought.

As though on cue, Percy started crying. Her whimpers became sobs, and her sobs turned to howls. Then she was curled up in the grass gagging on her tears and vomiting grief. *This is what it sounds like when you lose everything*, David thought. *This is what* I *would have sounded like if she hadn't missed.* And suddenly David wasn't angry at her anymore. It was gone, just like that, replaced with a cold ice cream scoop pulling through his guts and the realization that something bad *had* happened to Nicky and little baby Ross, like maybe the BIG bad, as in dead, and whatever had come through this sleepy little hick town and flipped it like a pissy mattress had something to do with why his sister wouldn't tell him where her family was. And maybe she couldn't tell him, because it was too awful for her to bear.

But if so, why had she reacted that way toward Sarah?

The sound in the air had changed. When had that started? Since they had been standing outside? Since forever? No, it had changed when the gun went off, but David had been too jacked up and fearful to notice. It was less grinding; more meaty. It was mostly a deep-throat sound now, and the singing voice was warbling up and down some scale David had never heard before. Worse, the air had changed when the sound did; like when the air pressure plummeted before a thunderstorm and you could feel the weight of the air pressing on you from all sides. It seemed to cling to his skin like putrid baby oil.

With it came the unshakable certainty that something was coming. From the east, on the outskirts of town. It had heard Percy's gunshot and it was coming. Because from the look of things around here, Percy might be one of only a handful of people left in Boonton. Now her cover was blown, and whatever had picked this town up and dumped it on its side...was coming.

"We got to get into the house," Percy said. She tried to pull herself up with Sarah's help and found she couldn't. The girls struggled against one another and Sarah called him for help.

At first, David did nothing; he simply stood and stared dumbly as the sky above the houses became saturated with dust and darkness. Whatever was coming was contaminating everything around it. It reminded him of ink being poured into a glass of water. It was a subtle shift around the edges of the swirling, chaotic mass; a translucent blue that got darker the closer it came, and the closer it came to the source of the disturbance.

And with the darkness came sounds. Screeching, whooping sounds, like a horde of raiders coming down the road toward them. *The Host*, David thought, though he had no idea why. They shuffled and slithered on dust and stones. Their nails scraped and infected the earth as they passed, or they spiked the ground with black claws and dragged mounds of deformed and useless diseased flesh toward the very spot David was standing.

"Dad!" Sarah shouted. She was trying to pull Percy to her feet but wasn't doing a very good job; She had Percy's arms wrapped around her neck and had grabbed the woman by the waist. But the sound of his daughter's voice finally knocked a gear loose in David's head and he was able to take a few clumsy steps toward the girls. After that, it was easier to move, and when his brain sailed off its stupor and into full-blown panic, he suddenly couldn't move fast *enough*.

He rushed to the girls and pushed Sarah aside. "*GET IN THE GODDAMN HOUSE!*" he shouted in her face, spittle flying from his lips. She turned. He planted a hand on her back and shoved her forward, sending her flopping toward the house like a lost doll. She caught her balance at the last second to keep from falling face first into the ground, and then she was sprinting toward the house as fast as her legs would carry her.

Satisfied his daughter was going to make it, David reached down and grabbed Percy around her torso. He flipped her up onto his shoulder. She groaned but didn't resist. Then David started moving; a straight line to the front of the house. Sarah was standing in the doorway shouting at him. He couldn't hear a word of it. He could hear the grinding meat sound in the air and the noise of The Host coming toward the house, and beyond that the panicked *Thrum Thrum Thrum* of his own heart throbbing in his chest. He crossed the yard in three lunging steps, hit the stairs and nearly fell on them, but caught himself at the last moment and saved Percy from being slammed into the doorway. He pushed Sarah back into the house and tossed Percy down onto the kitchen floor where she slid in a heap and stayed there. Then he kicked the door shut and put his chest against it.

"*DAD!*" Sarah yelled.

"*What?*" David yelled back. He felt light-headed and electric. He was sure he was going crazy and giddy that his parting sanity would soon make all the scary things go away.

"*The Gun!*"

"*Oh—*"

"*It's out on the lawn!*"

"*—Fuck.*"

David felt sick. He popped the door open. The sound was maddening. It was definitely ants crawling around in his head. But Sarah was right. There, on the lawn exactly where it had landed when he'd grabbed his sister by the hair and flung her with a hammer-throw, lay Nicky's prized Benelli shotgun. There was no question they needed it. They were defenceless without it. Sitting ducks. Probably more like a can of tuna though, because those monsters coming down the road would just have to pop the lid on Percy's house and their meal would be sitting there waiting. *Jam your fingers in and lick em clean fellas, meats on the menu and you need to get while the gettin' is good!*

He was going to have to go out there. His life probably depended on it. So did Sarah's. But first he was going have to stop staring at that damned thing lying crooked out there in the grass while the sky turned black and The Host moved nearer with each passing moment. He was going to have to take a step outside the door, and he'd be fine. Just like before, on the grass. He'd done it before. He could do it again.

He turned to Sarah. "Stay on the door," he said. "If anything happens, lock it down tight."

"No, Dad," Sarah said, reaching for him.

It was now or never. He turned and stepped out the door. He shut it behind him. Immediately he knew that was a mistake, because fear clawed his belly and made him weak. He felt cut off and alone with whatever was coming. He wanted to throw the door open again just so he'd have something to look at. Something safe. Instead, he stepped down the stairs to the grass.

One foot in front of the other. Go boy. Go! He came across the house and stepped out from the corner onto the front lawn. Then he stopped cold.

Sweet Jesus—

The Host moved as many parts but with singular purpose; it was like watching dead animals getting chewed up in a garbage truck. A mass of individuals melding and morphing together and then splitting apart. One thing and many. And out of the strangeness, of all the claws and twitching, impotent wings and mandibles, came familiar things too. Faces and assholes, arms and legs, all morphed and twisted into new shapes. Whatever was most useful to the individual in order to accomplish its goal was saved, and whatever was useless was discarded or ingested or reformed into something new and useful. Nothing was spared. No parts of their bodies remain unchanged. Many of them were built like gorillas, with over developed chests and long muscled arms. Others had long bones protruding from their forearms, sharpened to points and lined with teeth for slashing and cutting.

David felt his sanity pulling at the edges; in other places

it was already threadbare. He was wrestling with two urges; the urge to join the mass of creatures moving along the road toward the house, and the urge to cut and run screaming in the opposite direction, as fast as he could, until this nightmare was long gone or his heart gave out and he dropped dead with fright. While he was sure the urge to run away was a natural one, coming from within, the sound that permeated everything in the town was most certainly driving him toward the fiends.

It needs me, he thought. *Those aren't monsters, they're the townsfolk, and whatever has changed them needs to change me too, because it's calling me out and needs me for parts.*

The thought chilled him down to the very core of his being. He walked over to the shotgun and picked it up. He considered a brief, lunatic urge to put the shotgun in his mouth and pull the trigger. It was perfectly reasonable, under the circumstances, but he couldn't do that just yet. Instead, he turned and bolted back toward the house. Sarah was standing in the doorway, looking up at the sky. She had her hands over her ears. She was also clinging to her iPod. She was staring east, toward the darkness, and her face had sort of a slack jawed expression like she was off in her own little world.

"*Get inside!*" David yelled.

"My batteries just died," Sarah said quietly. She seemed to be contemplating what that might mean. Then her body jerked hard, causing her to rock on her heels. Her iPod broke in her white knuckled hand with the sound of snapping plastic. Her eyes rolled white. Her lips pulled back in a hideous leer and she snapped her teeth together hard enough to bite through the front of her tongue. To

David, it looked like she'd bitten into a milky pink jujube filled with blood.

"Sarah?" David said, but he had the feeling Sarah was already gone. At least, the part of her that had once told Santa at the mall that all she wanted for Christmas was something nice for her parents. The part he loved best; the part that had once brought him a handful of dandelion heads and asked if he could fix the flowers she broke.

Now Sarah was becoming something more basic, a blank canvas for whatever macabre artistic vision that darkness had in store for her. She twitched and shook, then the shaking got worse, and then Sarah was stumbling down the stairs and coming at a full sprint toward her father. She was ungainly though, her feet unsure and crooked, and she continuously stumbled as she ran. Like those running zombies from the new horror movies; the ones David never liked because zombies weren't *supposed* to be able to run. She would be on him in moment, and if she got past David there was a good chance she'd be gone forever. David wasn't about to let that happen.

As Sarah stumbled past him, David shot his arm out and hooked it around her waist. Then he pulled her back off her feet hard enough to force the wind out of her lungs in a puff. Sarah thrashed against him. She was emitting a throaty growl that mimicked the pitch of the alien tones in the air. David could hear it in the sounds coming from The Host as they reached the front lawn of the house as well. As though they were all plugged into the same machine, or all their brains had been tuned to the same radio station.

David stalked up the stairs. He forced Sarah through the doorway and threw her toward the kitchen. She landed on her side but flipped up onto her hands and knees and scrabbled back toward the door like a dog. David looked out the door one last time, as The Host rounded the corner, singing like a hell-spawned choir to the tune of crazy, and he snapped the door shut.

There was a series of loud bangs across the front of the house. They pounded on the door but the double locks Nicky had installed held good and tight. *Just because it's the country don't mean it doesn't have its share of nutballs,* he'd said. He had no idea how right he was.

Sarah reached the door where David was standing and tried to push past him. She was bleeding and frothing at the mouth like a rabid dog; the mixture of saliva and blood ran down her chin in strands and attached to her shirt where they blossomed into dark wet spots. David pushed her down with the butt of the shotgun, but Sarah bounced up and came at him again. The second time he knocked her down a little harder.

"Stay down," he said. When she got up, he sighed. "Stay! St—" at this point he hit her again, but it was a half-hearted attempt and she merely bounced back. The sight of his daughter like that was enough to drain the last bit of strength David had been using to hold himself together. Now that the monsters were firmly outside and David's family was stuck *inside*, exhaustion started to seep in through his pores.

There was a series of sharp bangs on the side of the house.

"What the fuck are they doing?" Davis said, to no one. The windows were all boarded up and reinforced with heavy wood from Percy's kitchen table. The frames were riddled with spikes from Nicky's nail gun. Once again, David was reminded of a Hollywood zombie movie, *Night of the Living Dead* maybe, the good one, the Tom Savini one, where the black guy turned into a zombie at the end and that chick killed the bald asshole.

He looked at Sarah as she came at him again. He pushed her away with a firm hand on her chest, being mindful of where his hand went. He was her father after all, and fathers worried about things like that.

"They're throwing rocks," Percy said, appearing in the kitchen. She looked unsteady on her feet and she was bracing herself against the fridge. In her free hand, she held a skipping rope. "They did that the first few days, nonstop. They were breaking the windows out of people's houses and pulling them back to the Cube. They can't get through the door though, Nicky made this place into a fortress. We're safe." She produced a length of skipping rope and held it out for David to see. "Here, we can tie her to one of the chairs in the living room with this."

David looked at his daughter and then to his sister.

"*It's okay,*" Percy said quietly. "I'm okay now. I'm sorry, David."

"You're sorry," David said. "I'm sorry. *Everybody* is sorry."

Percy nodded, then turned and started to hobble back into the living room. David grabbed her arm and she turned back.

"I know you're sorry," he said. "Let's get her locked down. Then you can tell me what the hell is going on here."

David was afraid to step away from the door. It was one of those heavy steel jobs used in stores sometimes; another blessing on the house thanks to Nicky's paranoia. If not for Percy's sanity keeping him on the straight and narrow, David had no doubt Nicky would be off in the mountains living like an Indian by now. And maybe he'd had it right; He'd still be around if he'd dropped off the radar like he always dreamed.

David had to hand it to the man. He had turned his house into a fortress and it was actually paying off for Percy. Nicky was adamant about home protection; the windows had snap locks and were made of double-paned glass with a sheet of plastic between them, making them virtually impossible to smash open. They'd break, but you'd have to take an axe to them before you could get a hole big enough to fit through. In that time, Nicky would be on you with his Benelli M4 combat shotgun; the very same weapon David now held in his hands. *One lick of this and you're off to hillbilly heaven*, Nicky used to say. Yeah, haw.

Sarah bumped into him and made a grab for the doorknob, but David pushed her away again. He didn't want to step away from the door but he wanted to stand here watching Sarah bounce against the doorway even less. Percy was right. Tie the girl down, then figure out how they ended up in Crazytown.

David grabbed Sarah as she came at him, mumbling stupid noise and blindly fighting to get around him. He pinned her arms to her side and the girl bounced in his arms; she was only a hundred pounds or so and it was nothing for him to walk her backward through the kitchen and into the living room where Percy was waiting. She stood behind one of her oak dining room chairs, skip rope in hand. David pushed Sarah into place and held her while Percy looped the rope around her chest. It wasn't too difficult to bind the girl; she was fighting to stand but seemed unaware of what was happening to her. Percy placed a knee on the back of the chair and pulled the rope tight, causing Sarah to grunt and collapse against the chair.

"Easy," David said. "Don't hurt her."

"I won't," Percy said. "But she probably can't feel it anyway. Look at her."

Sarah was bound tight to the chair now, her hair sweaty and clinging to her void face and along her neck. Her eyes were open, but they were like The Zombies song, *She's Not There*. David was again struck with how alien her face looked; like a wax figure of his daughter, the parameters were all there but there was something else now, and it changed all the dimensions of her face. It made her a stranger. Worse, it made her something reviled and fear-inspiring.

Impulsively, he reached out and slapped her.

"It doesn't help," Percy said. She didn't flinch when the next barrage of stones and squeals hit the house, but David did. Instead, she went to the cupboard and pulled down a bottle of Kahlua and two glasses. "It's all I got," she said apologetically. "Nicky used to have some Johnny Walker, but that's all gone now." She tripped over her husband's name like it was a bag of concrete she'd been hauling around. She settled into a chair and poured a couple fingers into each glass, and then slid one of them across the table. "Sit down. Let's talk."

David grabbed a chair opposite his sister and put the Benelli within easy reach on the table. Then he picked up the glass and propped himself up with his elbows. He let the coffee liqueur drown his taste buds and then handed the glass back to Percy. When she swished the bottle at him, he held up three fingers, and she managed a smile. It was a joke from when they were teenagers. They were close in age and had a lot of the same friends; when they started drinking in their teens they'd give each other a three finger salute. *Read between the lines.* A clever way of giving each other the finger. Percy poured three fingers and handed it back.

"So?" David said. He flinched again as a big rock hit the side of the house. Sarah thrashed against the skipping rope but didn't go anywhere.

"So," Percy said. "Three weeks ago we had a really crazy thunderstorm out here. Not like anything I've ever seen, and we've had some doozies. The clouds were black and yellow, and the thunder just seemed to go on and on. It was driving the dogs crazy. Nick brought them in and they just howled and pissed all over the place, so he put them back outside again. I didn't want them out there, cuz they were scared, and Nick says *Fine, you clean up the dog piss then* and brings them back in.

"That night it got worse; the sky was filled with all these weird red and blue lights and explosions and thunder strikes. The ground was literally shaking from it, Davey. I've never been more scared. I thought it was a fucking plane crash or something, or a terrorist attack maybe. Anyway, I think I was kind of dozing with Ross on the couch when suddenly there's this roar from the east side of town like a building collapsed and the dogs went fucking *nutso* and Nicky grabbed his coat and went out there to see what was going on. Even though I begged him to stay. I told him not to leave us—"

Percy stopped and drained her Kahlua and then poured another with badly shaking hands. She managed to spill as much of it on her hands and the table as she got in her glass.

"It wasn't just him though, half the men in the town went out there. Some of them driving in pickups and pickin' guys up as they went along. A real posse, old-boy style. Anything exciting happens around here, and that's what happens. It's like a party for them, sittin' around bored out of their skulls most of the time. A good chance to stretch their legs and feel important."

"Sounds like a good time," David said.

"Oh yeah. Real good. Only, when they went down there, there was more explosions and weird lights, and then guys started ripping out of there in their trucks, slamming into fences and parked cars and whatever else was in the way. Just driving in a blind panic to get away. My neighbour got run down in front of his house there, and nobody checked on him or anything. He just lay out there for three days until those things came and dragged him back to their *nest.*"

"Woah," David said. "What?"

"Getting ahead of myself," Percy said. "Those things out there...they have a nest outside of town. Whatever landed there, it isn't from this world. I don't think it's even from this dimension. I think maybe that's what that storm was; it was this big box coming through a doorway into our world. Only something went wrong; like maybe they weren't used to the atmosphere or gravity or something, and it crashed out there."

"You mean *aliens?*" David said. He looked at Sarah and shook his head. "No. I'm sorry, no. I don't believe it."

"It doesn't matter if you believe it or not," Percy said. "That's what it is. David, I've *seen* it myself. A huge black box stickin' out of the ground."

The Host shrieked and squealed outside, and David listened to them without saying a word. How could it be possible? He hadn't seen a single government vehicle, or soldier, or anything. Isn't that what happened when aliens landed? He'd seen it in more movies than he could count. Aliens land, aliens cause some shit, and the government comes and cleans it up. Then the aliens caught a cold and died. How could it go on for weeks without anyone knowing about it? It just seemed too farfetched to be real.

"It's real," Percy said, reading David's face. "It's *real* and Nicky never came back that night because whatever that thing is out there, it took all the men and did something to them. The next morning, that noise you're hearing started up, and all the children in town started filing out there like the damned Pied Piper of Boonton."

"I heard it," David said. "I can feel it calling out to me."

"It's worse for little ones," Percy said. "How Sarah is now, every child in town was like that within a matter of hours. They were fighting and clawing their way out of their parents' hands and taking off in a dead run toward the crash site. When they got out there, something really bad happened. Changed them into what they are now. Only it was subtle at first; they started coming back into town and scavenging like cockroaches. Groups of two or three, up to half a dozen. They pulled scrap metal, tires, and as much organic matter as they could get their hands on. They were all bug-eyed crazy and singing along with that damned awful noise."

"What are you saying? You don't think..." David began, but he couldn't finish. It seemed too awful a thing to put into words.

"Yeah, I do," Percy said. "Those creatures out there are the children of Boonton."

David looked at Sarah again and felt sick to his stomach. Was that what was waiting for his daughter if she ever got free? A life of slavery to some alien force that wanted to turn her into a freakish monster? Having her brain wiped clean? Catching people and dragging them to their doom on the outskirts of town? Another thought: would she be more useful as a gorilla-creature or as one of those cutters with the bone swords in place of their arms?

Percy was looking at Sarah too.

"Don't worry, David," she said. "I won't fail again. I won't let that thing have *her,* too."

"Ross," David said, and put his head in his hands.

Percy coughed on her tears. She put her head down, slender chin on her chest, and sobbed. Only for a moment though, because she wiped her face with a hand and drove the pain deep down into her belly. When she looked up again, her face was hard.

Looks like I wasn't the only one who picked that up from our mother, David thought grimly.

"Like I said, *all* the children. Rossie got a dose of that noise and I couldn't even hold him anymore. He was like a ball of pinching hands and kicking feet and shrieking, gasping noise. He was like that for *four days.* He didn't eat and he shit all over the place. I swear to Christ I thought he was gonna die. I started forcing pabulum down his throat to make sure he got something in his belly. And I wanted to get him out of here but those things were everywhere. I saw them dragging people out of their houses. Pulling them by their hair down the street as if they were dragging a bag of screaming garbage.

"Anyway, I couldn't get out and I was all by myself and I was up for four Goddamn days and...well, I fell asleep for a minute and then Rossie was gone. Just like that, out of here, all it takes is one second of not paying attention, David, and that's what it was. Like when you have 'em in the bath and you go grab the phone because the hubby is supposed to call and see what you want from the store for dinner that night, and you turn around and they're all black and laying in the bottom of the tub. Or you go inside for a second to grab their shoes and they run out into fucking traffic and get hit by some asshole in a Beamer who's talking on his phone and not watching the road."

"How did he get out?"

"That's just it. He somehow knew to push his toys to the counter until he could climb up to the window, then he flipped a snap lock and pushed his way out."

"But...he's just a *baby*—"

"*I know!*" Percy said, raising her voice. "It didn't make any sense to me either. But then I got to watching them, and I realized that they operate like some kind of hive mind. They're like bees. They are in constant contact with each other, whether they're speaking to one another or not. I think it's ESP. And like when you hear that sound and you feel compelled to follow it to the source. It's a beacon of some kind, meant to bring in help. Whatever it is out there, they're not in a good spot right now. Maybe a real bad spot, like the *Big Bad*."

"But how is it so harmful to children and just an annoyance

to adults?" David said. "I mean, it's more like a cigarette addiction to me, listening to that sound. *And then Sarah...*"

"I think whatever happened to these kids is happening genetically," Percy said. "They're still growing and forming at that age. We're old. We're set in our bodies. But kids, they're more fluid. And I was thinking: what if that's what these aliens are, like in *The Thing*. You remember that old John Carpenter movie? Well, what if they have a fluid body shape and their DNA can morph into stuff. Useful things, whatever they need. It makes sense if you're calling creatures to come help you, that you might also be able to program in them some genetic directions on becoming whatever kind of shape they need to help the most. Like *Lego*, you know? You come when you are called, and then the aliens build you up into a bulldozer or a shovel or something, because they know what they need and how you can best help. Only we don't have fluid DNA like that, and the changes they are causing have turned all the kids into little monsters."

"So what," David said. "This is just some kind of cosmic mix-up? Like they don't understand us enough to know how we operate? They think everybody should be a *transformer* like they are?"

"Maybe," Percy said. "I know it's damned crazy, but I swear it's all I've been able to come up with."

The alien siren was displaced momentarily by the sound of David's car alarm, and David left the table. He pulled back one of the plywood sheets covering the front window just wide enough to take a look outside. The Host had moved off from the house, and now were busy cutting and stripping his car down to bare parts. It only took a few moments for them to get through the hood and into the engine, and by the time they found the car battery the horn was already dwindling away to nothing. The Cutters tore though the body and cracked the dash, digging into the wiring of the car and ripping it out in reams of green and red strands. The Gorillas scooped up as much of the material as they could and headed back to where they came from.

It's like that every time," Percy said from behind him. "They want the electronics first, then mechanical stuff. I imagine the body pieces they're cutting off are going to be raw metal for whatever they're doing out there. Repairing the ship maybe."

"Holy shit," David said. "That's almost too crazy to get my head around."

"I know, right?" Percy said. "But it makes sense, if you look at those little fuckers outside. They're either built like gorillas with a ton of upper body strength or they've lost their arms in place of long bony knives full of teeth. Gruesome, but think about it: They are using parts of their own bodies to become something specific. The Gorillas haul shit back to the crash site all day long. And the Cutters, well, they aren't as effective cutting metal off cars and stuff, because bone and teeth are only so good against that kind of thing, but when we were fighting them off they were *very* good at catching and maiming people. And dogs, too. They pin 'em down or wound them, and the gorillas drag em off. And on and on they went."

"They're not taking any plastic," David said. "They go out of their way to cut around it."

"Yeah," Percy said. "I dunno why. I guess it isn't a useful material for their plans."

David sat back in his chair. The entire situation was making him very weary. His sister, the town, even Sarah, roped into her chair and struggling all bug-eyed like that, her only thought to get out of the house and march off to her doom. Would she be a Cutter? He couldn't imagine her as a Gorilla. She was just a tiny thing. Just a child. He pictured her arms replaced by long jaw-like appendages of bone and sinew, lined with jagged pieces of haphazard teeth like one of those wooden Mayan swords with the volcanic glass in them.

"We gotta get out of here," David said. "Before I lose my goddamned mind."

"Well we can't leave on foot," Percy said. "Those things will run for hours. They'll catch us before we get to the edge of town."

It was probably true. David had run track in high school and was good enough to make provincials his senior year, but he had the feeling those kids outside hadn't just improved their shape to suit the needs of whatever was out there on the edge of town, but every part of their body might be changed. What about increased lung capacity to feed those engorged muscles? How about a massive immune system booster shot that could cure cancer or AIDS? At this point, anything was possible. Besides, he'd never get anywhere with Sarah the way she was, even if he knocked her out and tossed her over his shoulder. She was only about ninety pounds soaking wet, but that was ninety pounds more than David would be able to sprint with, and those things would probably catch them before they got two blocks. Besides, Percy was an ex-smoker who didn't do any running, *ever*. She was thin, but it was an unhealthy, non-muscular thin, made worse by weeks of being holed up in her house on the verge of hysteria.

A thought occurred to David then, something he'd seen on the way through town. Right before they'd hit that wall of glass and lost their tires. When the town was just creepy and not *insane*. "There was a gas truck we passed on the way in," David said. "It seemed to be in good shape."

"What do you mean by *good* shape? Percy said. "Good as in *your car is in good shape?* Because that's what they did to everything around here. Ripped them to pieces."

"No," David said. "Good as in eighteen tires. No holes in the body. They didn't touch it."

"But...that's impossible," Percy said.

David shrugged. "They set up a line of broken bottles in the road right by the Cardlock , and that's where the truck is. Just sitting there, like the day it was parked. I can drive it, but I have to get there without being noticed."

"Are you crazy? Percy said. "You can't go out there now! They know we're in here. They'll be watching."

"So I'll wait," David said. "They're bound to move on sooner or later. It's not like they were hanging around in the town when we showed up. They must have shit to do wherever that crash is."

"So we're going to go to the truck and you drive us out?" Percy said, dubious.

"Hell no," David said. "I'll go alone and bring it back here. I'll grab you and Sarah and then we take off for the highway. And I'm not stoppin' until we run out of gas."

Percy looked down at her hands, nodding. Then she looked up. "What happens if you don't make it?"

"I *will* make it."

"But if you don't?"

"I *will*."

Percy sighed. "There's no winning with you, is there, little brother?"

"Not a bit," David said, smiling. "Not one bit."

After that, David got up and went back to the window, and Percy moved her chair in front of Sarah and rubbed the girl's legs. Sarah gave no sign that she was even aware there were other people in the room. She grunted and pulled against the ropes holding fast to the chair. When they rubbed her skin raw Percy slid damp rags between the rope and Sarah's flesh.

It didn't take long for the creatures to strip David's car down to bare parts. They were terribly efficient at their jobs, in spite of their apparent limited brainpower and their adaptations. They worked in tandem like ants, however, with each creature knowing its job and working accordingly. After they'd pulled all the electronics, body pieces, and useful engine components from the vehicle, they stripped the rubber off the tires. They even managed to find the spare tire in the trunk. Sarah's clothes and personal items were also in the trunk; they pulled two neon blue suitcases out and emptied their contents onto the road.

This enraged David to the point where he was squeezing his fists and gritting his teeth. The car was one thing. The car was expensive and he would be paying for it for the next five years, *yes*, but it was just a car nonetheless. Seeing Sarah's bright-coloured bras and personal effects on the ground in a heap with all her favourite clothes seemed *invasive*; it felt like one more assault on his baby girl. And he *dearly* wanted to make them pay for their transgressions.

The creatures loitered around the car for a bit and then, just as David had suspected, they began to move off in singles and pairs back toward the crash site. The noise in the air had returned to that warbly tune of meat and stone, and the town once more looked like it had when David first arrived; a desolate war-zone. It was time.

"We may not have much time when I get back here, so I want you to have Sarah ready to go. Just let her run if you have to, with the door open, and I'll catch her as she tries to go by."

"Okay," Percy said. She nodded vigorously and rubbed her hands together. "If you're sure about this, David."

"I'm sure. This is going to work. We're getting out of this place."

"Alright." Percy lunged at him then, grabbed her brother up in a fierce hug. "Please be safe," she whispered. "Come back for your little girl."

"For both of you," David said. He held her tightly for a moment more and then stepped back. He checked the safety on Nicky's shotgun and then nodded to her. "Lock down the house behind me."

"Yep."

David went to the door and begun unlatching the heavy bolts holding it in place. When he finished he cracked the door open and took a half step into the doorway. He stopped and turned back to his sister. "Whatever happens, don't let them get Sarah. *No matter what.*"

Percy wrapped her arms around herself, eyes wet and lip quivering. She nodded, once, and tears splashed on her cheeks. Nothing further needed to be said. David trusted Percy to do the right thing when the time came. Kill Sarah before she was turned into one of those monsters, and then Percy would probably kill herself. David wouldn't blame her one bit. Nobody could.

David went around the side of the house and Percy shut the door behind him. He heard the locks snapping into place as he came down off the steps into the yard, crouched low like a soldier, gun out and ready for anything. He'd never actually fired a shotgun before, but there was no time for lessons. One thing he did have on his side was something he remembered Nicky saying when he first bought the weapon. They'd been drinking beer in the basement while Nicky smoked a colt and showed off his new toy: *The beauty of a shotgun is you point where you want it to go and it goes. You don't have to aim, because shot spreads out and hits everything. Hell, I bet Sarah could put this bad boy up and pull the trigger and she'd hit somethin'.*

As David stepped onto the road, he prayed that Nicky hadn't been bullshitting him. He spared one last look back at the house, saw Percy in the window, and nodded to her once. She put a hand up and waved goodbye. Then David walked away from the house and out of sight. The neighbour's blue station wagon was a carcass lying halfway on the sidewalk, and David moved quickly and ducked behind it.

He could see the a large brown stain in the dirt where Percy said her neighbour had been run over, and laid in the street for two days before he'd been dragged off. Since that time, the molasses stain of blood and gore from the body had attracted a heavy cloud of flies. The sound of so many flying insects together in one spot was unnerving.

He'd stumbled across a dead bear while hiking once in the Kaninaskas and the sound the flies made disturbed him nearly as much as that monstrous decomposing corpse had. They sounded like angry wasps if you got enough of them together. One of the flies had landed on his face, and he'd swatted at it hard enough to leave a bruise on his jaw. The thought of putrid bear juice on their scratchy fly legs was enough to sicken him. Flies were filthy creatures that fed off misery. Their appearance in Boonton seemed completely fitting. David had a thought that maybe the entire town would one day soon be covered in flies. One giant rotten cesspool, with billions upon billions of flies feasting until their guts split open and they shit maggots everywhere.

A fly buzzed around David's head and he swatted at it. It was time to move on. He skirted around the corner of the block he was on and began moving north, away from the crash site. He looked down the street toward the direction The Host had gone but there was nothing to see. Just another windbreak of pines and poplar trees. The town had resumed that silent, tomblike atmosphere he'd first noticed when he got out of the car to check his tires. If there was anyone left alive, they weren't making themselves known.

Fuck 'em then, David thought. *They can stay and watch the end of this fucked up movie.*

He moved from car to car, just to be safe, because even though it was dead quiet there was no telling who might be watching, and moved quickly down several blocks before cutting left down an alley and moving back toward the Cardlock. There were more bloodstains on some of the other streets, and some of the houses were either burnt or had all their windows smashed or both. One house he passed had a large bay window smashed open so it looked like the house had a huge gaping mouth full of broken glass teeth; there was a wide blood smear running off the bottom of the window where someone had been dragged over the frame, and it looked like a big red tongue on the monster-house's face.

David stopped at the end of the alley. He was just across the street from the Cardlock now, and he could see the gas truck sitting in the parking lot. The scene was exactly the same as when he'd left it, and he wished for the first time that he hadn't continued on to Percy's house; that he'd taken those two flat tires and driven back out to the highway with them so he could wave down a passer-by and get Sarah back to the city. How different the last few hours might have been. Then he thought of Percy sitting alone in that house until starvation drove her out in search of food, or madness and isolation drove her to puff on the end of Nicky's shotgun. The kind S.W.A.T. used with the pistol grip stock and everything. The gun would have taken her head off at the jaw line, maybe vaporized part of it, the way he always imagined Kurt Cobain looked like when he'd finally had enough heroin and enough of his bitchy, crazy wife and just popped the top of his head off. *Kapow! Thank you, goodnight, we love you, sorry, no encore tonight folks, Kurt can't sing 'cuz the top of his head is venting blood and skull and song lyrics in the form of brain matter all over his striped shirt and Vans shoes.* David tried to move away from that line of thought and keep his focus on the task at hand. He was dancing with hysteria; he could feel it welling up inside him like sunshine flavoured puke.

This street was as deserted as all the others were. On the other side of the street, sprawled across the gas lot like a sleeping giant, a big white Kenworth with a single gas tank sat alone and unmolested. It was a beauty, new paint, high fog lights and horns, with a swan ornament frozen in chrome above a steel KW logo highlighted and outlined in red paint. It had double pipes on each side cased in chrome covers with KENWORTH water-cut along the side. Probably one of the new natural gas fleet models. David hadn't driven a truck in years, and this rig outclassed anything he'd ever hauled logs and granite with. One rig pretty much drove like another, though. They all had their own personalities, but you moved them by hitting the clutch when you had to and stomping on the gas.

David crossed the street to the truck. He tried the door and found it open, and after a quick survey of the cab he stood up and poked the barrel of the Benelli into the sleeper. There was nobody home. The truck was deserted, and David had a feeling wherever the driver was, he wasn't going to be back anytime soon. He took another quick look around to make sure nothing was coming, then crawled up behind the wheel and slammed the door shut behind him. So far so good. The keys were sitting in a cup holder beside the dash, which didn't surprise David in the least. In fact, he was counting on this driver to be just like every other rig driver David had ever known in his life; to be like David himself had been when he drove truck. It was common for a *road hammer* to leave his keys lying around in the cab somewhere obvious. Last thing you ever wanted to do was leave them in a restaurant or drop them in three feet of snow when you were coming down out of your bunk.

But why was this truck sitting here when every other vehicle was stripped to the bone like a Christmas turkey and left to rot in the sun? These trucks were sturdy, for one thing. Maybe the steel was too thick for the Cutters to get their bone and tooth blades into. It was possible, but why not strip what you could? The engine cover was just paneling, like any other vehicle, and there were eighteen good tires on this truck that could have been stripped. The gas in the tank was under pressure, so if they fucked around and messed with things too much, they could cause a venting leak that might start a fire big enough to burn down half the town.

Maybe that was it, David thought. *Maybe whatever is controlling them knew enough not to fuck with the fuel truck, because it knew those things outside weren't smart enough to disassemble it properly. Maybe it didn't want the town blown to shit while it was still collecting parts.*

The thought sent a chill through David that he didn't much like. If the thing controlling The Host was smart enough to realize how dangerous this truck was from afar, it might be aware of other things. It might be spying on him at this very moment. Maybe it was watching him and biding its time, waiting for the perfect chance to strike. Or perhaps the perfect time to strike had already passed, the moment he stepped out of the house and left Percy and Sarah alone to fend for themselves with no weapons.

He looked over at the Benelli. He had to get this truck moving, and fast. If only to allay his paranoid fears. But he was smart enough to know the odds of them all getting out of here in one piece were ticking lower and lower the longer he spent getting the truck over to his sister's house. Worse, if The Host came at the sound of the rig, David and Percy might have to fight them off. There was a good chance of that happening, from what he'd seen.

He dropped the keys into the ignition and turned the

engine over. It sputtered and growled to life for a moment… then choked out and died.

"*AHH COME ON!*" David yelled. He tried it again, and this time the truck roared to life. It had been more than a few years since he'd driven something this big, but the feel of the beast in your hands never left you. He turned off the breaks and dropped it into gear, and the truck hissed angrily and began rolling out of the lot. He pointed it toward Percy's house and drove down the centre of the road to make sure he could see on all sides of the truck. Not only that, but there were stripped cars on the sides of the road and he didn't want to get tangled up in one. If The Host weren't on their way already, they soon would be. David kept the vehicle in low gear. The truck rumbled and spit gravel when he turned onto Percy's street, and he aimed the truck for the front lawn between his car and the house.

As he came up onto the grass his heart leapt into his throat; the door to the house was hanging open. But then Percy's relieved face appeared from the gloom in the doorway, and she waved at David before turning and disappearing back into the house. He was just hitting the brakes when a movement near the doorway caught his attention from the corner of his eye.

A Cutter and a Gorilla came around the backside of the house, from the yard, scrabbling up the stairs. It only took them a few heartbeats to disappear into the doorway.

"*PERCY!*" He shouted, throwing the truck into park. It shuddered angrily at this forced-stop, but by then David had already thrown open the door. The Benelli in hand, he leapt down out of the truck and was running for the door the moment he hit the ground.

Percy was shrieking inside the house. The sound turned David's stomach in ways he'd never felt before. Horror movies didn't do the sound of a woman screaming in pain and terror any kind of justice. The real thing was primal; it reached into your brain and pulled all kinds of strings. He was instantly angry and terrified at the same time. He made it to the top of the stairs and kicked the door open, and then the anger drained away and the terror took over.

Percy was shrieking still, but the sound was different now. She was gasping and sobbing and shrieking all at the same time. There was another sound in the gloom of the house as well: the sound of flesh tearing and being pummelled by heavy fists. Sarah was singing along to the noise from the crash site, her voice raspy and desperate. The Cutter and Gorilla were singing backup harmonies for her.

David stepped into the kitchen, Benelli raised, and instantly wished he'd turned back. Percy lay at Sarah's feet in the middle of the room, curled up in a foetal position. She was covering her face with two bloody arms. She had grown an extra knee on her left leg, halfway down her thigh. The new joint was rickety and unstable. It had bone jutting out on both sides and was draining blood all over the floor. She alternately gagged and sobbed as she was baptized in her own body fluids. The Gorilla had both hands raised in large, bony fists, and was beating her legs and side with a ferocity David had never seen in a living creature. The Cutter was standing behind Sarah, using its saw tooth arms to slice through the ropes that held Sarah tight to her chair.

Both creatures were bug-eyed and bloody; like the skin on their faces had been ripped away to reveal their eyes. The holes were too big, giving David the impression their eyes could fall out of their skulls if they happened to be bent over and had a sneeze. The Cutter had taken on an even more distinctive insectile appearance. Its jaw had buckled and reformed itself into small pincer-like appendages; it worked these hideous additions to its body continuously as it sawed through the rope. Its ears were torn open and small, spear-like bones had sprouted from either side of its face like charnel antennae.

David didn't think. *Couldn't* think. It was all too much to take in at once. So much blood. Monsters twisted out of some lunatic dream like a black tooth from his gums. His brain was stuck between dials on the radio; his thoughts were full of static and feedback. It was too much to take in at once. He could feel himself teetering on the edge of that cliff like Wile E. Coyote, on the verge of stepping out into the terrible empty space that lies just one short step past solid ground; where he'd hang there for a moment until realization that he was about to fall into a chasm of madness and no umbrellas or flapping wings or rickety *ornithopters* could save him.

He pulled the trigger.

There was a mute blast and the smell of gunpowder and sulphur. It was sharp; immediate, and it brought him out of his daze long enough to realize that he'd missed everyone in front of him. A foot over Sarah's head, and above the cutter behind her, the wall unit holding books and movies exploded outward like it had been struck by lightning. The Benelli popped an empty casing out the side like a handgun and automatically set the next round in the chamber. All David could think was one thing:

Nicky had been *wrong*.

The shot got everyone's attention in a hurry. The Gorilla's

head snapped up and it shot David a baleful glance. Its lips curled back in a snarl revealing black, malformed teeth. Then it turned and leapt at him.

David fired again, and this time there was no mistake. The creature jumped straight into the trajectory of the Benelli and caught the full force of the shot in its chest. A cloud of blood and meat sprayed out its back, but the momentum of its original leap carried it forward still, crashing into David and causing him to collapse under the weight of the thing. David's chest was instantly soaked in hot blood, and he panicked, trying desperately to move the creature.

It may have once been a child of Boonton, but that was a long time ago. Now it was taller and much heavier than it had ever been as a carefree youth. It had rolls of bulging muscle mass and it had gained forty or fifty pounds of bone to carry the new weight. David tried to push the creature off to the side, but the Benelli was pinned between their bodies, the barrel still screaming hot from two firings. The result was like having someone laid on you when you were trying to work a bench press; when he let go of the rifle to get a better handle on the creature, the weight of the thing on top of him drove the shotgun painfully into his ribcage.

Sarah suddenly appeared by him, tripping over the mound of flesh in the middle of the room, and sprawling out flat on the floor so he was able to get a hand on her ankle. But then she was up and running again, tearing away from his grip like he was wet grass clinging to her shoes. He screamed her name and she disappeared out the door, taking off in the direction of the crash site.

He screamed after her until his voice cracked and bled, he screamed and screamed.

And then the weight of the Gorilla's body increased and he looked up into the eyes of the Cutter. Its pincer-mouth worked feverishly. It looked like an ant in a way; if a human and an ant had somehow found a way to mate and created a monstrosity nature had never intended. The creature pulled back its blade-arm and pointed it at David's face.

"*FUCK YOU!*" David cried, his voice a broken whisper. It felt hot and scratchy in the back of his mouth, and when he formed the words, hot liquid splashed the back of his tongue. He thrashed against the weight on his body, causing his breath to come in harsh choking gasps. The Cutter stabbed its weapon down at David's face—

At the last possible second Percy appeared over the shoulder of the creature, her face black from the beating she'd received and melting like a red candle from the blood pouring off her face. She'd somehow managed to grab hold of a loop of rope that had been holding Sarah to the chair, and she flipped it around the Cutter's throat like a white nylon necklace. David had cried out and squeezed his eyes for just a moment, so sure was he of the impending death blow from the creature. When it didn't happen, he looked up and saw Percy had wrapped the ends of the rope around both her hands and now she placed her elbows in the centre of the Cutter's back. The thing arced backward as if it had suddenly been shot in the spine, and for one glorious instant David looked into Percy's face and she was shouting something that he couldn't hear, but her mouth was repeating the words *GET UP! GET UP!*

That was all the prodding David needed. He gripped the Benelli in his hands, one around the custom pistol grip stock and the other around the warm black steel barrel, and pushed. He gritted his teeth and farted as he bared down, forcing his muscles to obey his will and not taking *no* for an answer.

The Gorilla began to move. So slowly at first David actually thought he himself was somehow being pushed through the floor, but then his arms extended past ninety degrees and he gained some leverage. He forced his air out through his teeth and pushed with everything he had. And suddenly the Gorilla was up and he was pushing the creature off to the side, being careful not to pin his own arms beneath the creature as it slid away. David got up, his body strange and weak after the weight of the creatures pinning him down. He had come as close as he'd ever come in his life to dying just then, maybe within tenths of a second of owning the Big Bad. Now all he wanted to do was take a moment to himself and reflect on that.

But there was no moment to be had.

He stepped over the Gorilla body, shotgun raised high, and brought it down in an arc into the Cutter's face; right between that creepy reformed jaw that had somehow been changed into ant-mandibles, and the butt end of the stock smashed into its mouth with a wet crunch and blood frothed out of the wound and onto Percy, and all the way up the stock to the pistol grip, and then that thing stopped moving and its head lolled back against Percy and she kept pulling on her length of skipping rope for a while after it was dead.

"Hey," David said, pulling the corpse off his sister. "Hey you alright?"

Percy looked at him for a moment but said nothing. She seemed lost; she didn't recognize him. Maybe she didn't know where she was. Then she belched a mouthful of blood and it all came flooding back to her.

"Jesus, Percy," David said. He knelt beside her. He started to pull her up but she cried out when he touched her.

"*Fuh-huckin*..hurts," she said. She squeezed her eyes closed and bloody tears welled up in them. When she opened her eyes again, her vision seemed a lot clearer.

David looked her up and down. He focused in on that second knee joint on her thigh. It was as bad as anything he'd seen. It was also swelling and turning black, the way her face was. Inside that train wreck of a leg, her bone marrow would be leaking into the surrounding muscle and tissue, poisoning her blood. "You're leg is really messed up, Percy. We need to get something on that before it gets worse."

"It's already worse," Percy said. She moaned and closed her eyes again. When she opened them this time, they were pink and she was far away. "I can hear the ocean."

"I don't hear it," David said. He wiped his eyes with the palm of his hand.

"Doesn't matter," Percy said. "It's gonna be all—" She stopped mid-sentence, and her last word stretched out in a raspy breath. It sounded more like *awwwwwwl.* Percy looked up at her brother with dead eyes, but she wasn't really looking anymore.

David closed her eyes. He let the Benelli fall from his side and he put his head in his hands. His cries felt like hammer falls in his throat. He couldn't get them out fast enough to stop hurting. He forced each one out until the last bit of air was gone from his lungs, then pushed his pain out breathlessly until his body took over and reset the process.

Eventually the sobbing subsided, and David was left with an empty heart and full sinuses.

He shook it off and found his feet, then picked up the Benelli. He turned away from Percy and took the first few shaky steps toward the door. There was a gas truck sitting outside waiting for him. It wasn't just an end to the nightmare; it was an instrument for David's vengeful wrath. And having just lost his daughter and sister to the new inhabitants of Boonton, he was *very* wrathful indeed. The kind of wrath that would allow you to turn a massive fuel tanker into the world's biggest Molotov cocktail and jam it up someone's ass.

He left the house and shut the door behind him. It was a pointless gesture, but it seemed like something Nicky and Percy would want. Especially Nicky. He walked by the cab of the truck. It wasn't time to go just yet. He still had a few things to do.

There were long tubes running the length of the tanker that held the hoses used to pump fuel into gas station cisterns, two on each side. David popped the lids with little difficulty and pulled the hoses out one at a time, then connected the hoses to their respective taps on either side of the tank. When he was finished, each side had two long whiskers trailing off away from the fuel tanker and into the yard. Then he shouldered the Benelli, hopped into the cab of the truck, and started the engine.

The truck crawled off his sister's lawn and rumbled out onto the street, and when he came to the end of the block, he turned toward the edge of town. He picked up the speed a bit, but not too fast. He watched each street carefully as he passed it, and kept an eye on the tree line at the edge of town. When he was near the last block of Boonton proper he finally saw it.

It was glorious, and hideous, in equal parts. On the other side of the tree line was a large grassy field riddled with burn patches and stripped down vehicles. David saw The Host here, milling about in the grass mindlessly like zombies. Some of them swayed their hands back and forth like stoned hippies listening to their own version of Jefferson Airplane. Jefferson *Starship*, because that thing out there sure as fuck wasn't any airplane David had ever seen. There were about twenty of them altogether. And beyond them stood a thing that made David's skin crawl.

It was a box, just like Percy had said. Black and perfectly cubed and buried on one side in the dirt, like it had come in hot and fast, *way too fast*, and drove itself into the earth like a post driller, skewing up on one side so it was sitting at an angle, and one of the corners pointed toward the town of Boonton. The front side, or rather the side David could *see*, was smashed up pretty good. There were smouldering holes in the surface of the box, tears along its perfect symmetry and lights flashing in seemingly random intervals. The light seemed to be coming from inside the box, and seeped out where the breaches in the hull of the thing were their worst. There were things scuttling about the crash site, like roaches, but he was too far away to see exactly what they were. They were operating on a different playbook than The Host, however. That much was certain.

David came to the last block before the field and stopped, the rig idling like some gigantic Palaeolithic cat. At the sound of the approaching vehicle the figures in the grass all stopped, and as one turned toward him. *They're waiting for instructions*, David thought. *They're just extensions of whatever is in that box.* He had to force himself to open the door of the truck. His animal brain wanted no part of those things, or that big black cube, or anything. It wanted to stay right where it was and beat a hasty retreat at the first sign of danger. David had another, better idea.

He opened the door to the rig and hopped down. As he did, the sound emanating from the Cube, that god-awful grinding racket picked up speed again, and The Host responded by coming toward David and his gas truck.

He had the Benelli in one hand, Rambo-style, or maybe *Commando* style, but he had no idea what Arnold Schwarzenegger's name was in that movie. With his other hand he flipped open the valves for the hoses. They jumped like snakes before vomiting fuel out onto the gravel that made up the road. Then he turned and fled back to the cab of the rig, missing the first step and skinning his shin badly. He gritted his teeth and tried again, this time getting his feet underneath him and clearing both steps easily. He got up behind the wheel just as the first Gorilla passed the tree line, and David dropped the truck into gear and hit the gas. The vehicle jumped and shuddered as the weight of the tank held it back, and then it was moving. The Gorilla came across the road and leapt up onto the hood of the truck.

It was holding onto the swan hood ornament with one hand, its leg hooked on the side of the hood for balance. It balled its free hand into a fist and began pounding on the truck, mashing the sheeted steel and causing flecks of paint to dance around the dents. David pushed the pedal down and the truck came across the last road in town and into the grass. He aimed it between two large poplar trees. The rig jumped on the uneven dirt beneath it, and the Gorilla lost its foothold on the vehicle. It was now gripping the hood ornament in both hands. The truck jumped again. The swan ornament on the front of the truck gave out, and the Gorilla disappeared from the front of the rig. A moment later, there was a squeal and the truck jumped again. Over something soft.

The rest of the creatures were arriving now, and as David passed the tree line he angled the truck toward them. A Cutter stopped near the front of the truck and swung one of its saw blade arms at the front tire in an effort to cripple the rig; there was a shudder as the creature's teeth bit into the rubber and caught. The spin of the tire snapped the bone off cleanly at the elbow joint, and the Cutter shrieked in pain and fell back in the long grass, holding its mangled arm up in the air like a trophy. A moment later the bone mass went into the wheel well, where it crunched and banged against the frame of the rig before coming out in pieces. The rig chugged on, unaffected.

Several of the Gorillas came in from the sides of the truck, and made diving grabs at the gas hoses as they slithered past. One made a dive and missed; a moment later the steel head of the hose snapped up into its skull, leaving its eyes and nose a bloody, leaking mess. It thrashed in the dirt, clawing at its face, until it caught a full blast of gasoline and went down in a heap. David could see them attacking the wheels of the vehicle only to be ground up and spit out as their companions had. A Cutter managed to stab the side of a tire, and the rig shuddered to the left. It was a back tire though, and there was another directly behind it that was still running fine. David was able to straighten the vehicle.

He was passing the stripped vehicles he'd seen from the road. They were mostly pickup trucks, he saw now, and they were in a rough half circle that formed a perimeter around the crash site. They were the trucks the men of Boonton had taken out there that first night, when Percy said the sky was full of fire and explosions. Some of the vehicles were turned sideways, like their owners had been caught trying to escape. A Gorilla used one of the vehicles as a launch pad as David drove past, leaping up onto the tank and grabbing hold near the back. It climbed up on top of the tanker and out of view, but a moment later David heard it land in the gap between the rig and the trailer.

He heard the sound of rending metal and a hiss as the air brakes went out on the trailer, and suddenly the dashboard was lit up with half a dozen different panicky, flashing lights. It was trying to pull the tanker off the rig.

"*Fuck off!*" David shouted. He jerked the wheel back and forth, trying to shake it off, but all that did was cause the tanker to flick back and forth. He was actually *helping* the creature with every jerk of the wheel.

Just past the line of trucks, the grass ended in a burn line. The area surrounding the box was completely void of any plant life whatsoever, and the ground was scorched black. There were pools of what looked like either oil or blood in random spots around the crash site. Along one wall was a stack of bodies probably ten feet high. Scattered around the corpses were bones of all shapes and sizes, stripped clean to the white. (*Man's gotta eat!* David's fraying brain screamed at him. *Gotta eat meat! Meat is murder,* motherfuckers, *didn't you know that?*)

There were also piles of wiring, sheet metal, and shredded rubber tires around the ship, and small, cockroach-like creatures scuttling around, taking items from one pile and disappearing up into the Box. They had segmented, insectile legs and multi-jointed arms ending in oversized clawed hands. Their heads seemed to be turned around backwards, their necks twisted to accommodate the new shape that their bones had taken. Their faces were chitinous and rubbery, with small antennae-like protrusions sticking out of the sides of their skulls and above the brow ridge on their faces.

David watched them in horror, not wanting to believe his eyes. His brain was clicking badly and trying desperately to shut everything off. He could feel it, like the machine was about to break down and he was going to go completely batshit crazy. Just like he nearly did the first time he saw The Host coming up the road toward his sister's house. One of the scuttling bugs stopped on top of the pile of metal. A long stream of piss and blood streamed out of its tiny baby's penis, arcing out behind it like a naked cherub in one of those penny ponds with the Japanese koi in them, the ones that said *Please Don't Put Money in the Pond*, but people did anyway, because that's just what you did when you saw one of those ponds. Everyone wanted to be lucky. Paying for it wasn't out of the question.

But there was no luck for these cherubs. They'd run off at the sound of the Cube calling out to them, leaving their mother's arms and streaking across town as fast their rubbery baby legs could go. And when they got to the crash site, the Cube had special plans for them. Because they were babies, and their bones were soft. And their DNA was *softer still*, and easy to manipulate. The Cube had taken God's plan for these babies and dropped a big steaming pile of shit on the blue prints, then made paper airplanes out of the entire mess and reworked the children to better suit its ends.

And right now, at a little over twenty-five kilometres per hour, David was about to take a big steaming shit of his own. The trailer screeched behind him. From the sounds of it, the Gorilla back there had somehow managed to release the safety locks that kept the trailer attached to the rig. It didn't matter. They were close now, and getting closer by the moment. The cockroach babies scuttled about in a blind panic, like the rig was a flashlight and David had just pulled up a box in the cellar. David pulled the horn, one last roar, and the rig slammed the carcass of a little *S-10* pickup truck- *a baby truckling*, he used to tell Sarah when she was little. *It would grow up into a rig one day, if it got enough sun and water.* The rig shuddered and cast aside the body, and kept right on going. Outside, the sound of the Cube was fast and high, the panic squeals of a pig hanging from a hook by its feet. David adjusted the steering one last time. He pointed it right at the cube. He hit the gas.

And at the last moment, with less than fifty feet between the rig and the Cube, he kicked open the driver's side door and jumped.

He landed feet first on the ground, but that hardly mattered when you were doing close to forty km per hour. His feet touched the black earth and were instantly gone from under him, and he went crashing down on his face. He slammed his head into the ground hard enough for the world to stutter and freeze, and then he was over on his side, and rolling like a bag of shit dropped off a manure truck on the highway, rolling stupidly and leaking from a dozen holes at once. Something slammed into his back and doused him with gasoline; he gasped at breath that wouldn't come, and when it did he gagged and choked on fuel coming into his mouth and nostrils. He did his best to keep his arms tucked in, but there was too much force and too much happening at once, and several times he saw the Cube looming in front of him, growing larger with every rotation of sky and earth, and he realized sickly he was rolling toward the crash site still, and that the truck had ploughed into the side of the alien ship, carving out a side of it like taking a bite out of a big chunk of fudge when you were little at the fair behind Grampa's house.

The rig bit into that cube and scraped down the side of it, ripping alien metal away and leaving showers of sparks and gouts of flame behind it. Then the rig shuddered free and ploughed through the steaming, stinking pile of corpses stacked so neatly along one side, ready for consumption. The pile birthed a plague of flies on impact, and the rig sent pieces of townsfolk flying in all directions. It chewed some of the cockroach babies up in its grill and then staggered out into the grass beyond, mortally wounded. The Host fell upon it like a swarm of army ants, stabbing and pinching and pummelling in a futile attempt to bring it down. The air was thick with decay and bloated flies and gasoline. So much gasoline. The Cutters had severed the hoses to the tank, and fuel was pissing out both sides of the rig. They paid it no mind. The shrill whine from the Cube told them only one thing; destroy their attacker. Kill the truck. David could hear it in the noise, undulating like a lopsided washing machine filled with blankets:

WHUMPWHUMPWHUMPWHUMPWHUMP

David sat up. His back was on fire where he'd been struck by the hose, but the image of the Gorilla who'd had its face caved in by an errant nozzle made him think that perhaps he *had* bought a little luck, after all. He wiped his face with his hands and they came away covered in gasoline and blood. His head was killing him. The sound from the Cube had found a hole to get into his brain, and it was hitting him in rapid succession with spikes of jagged ice. The thought of a rose stem being pushed down into the Jell-O mush of grey matter in his skull came to him, and he found it quite fitting.

He stood up, fell down, and started to get up again. He managed to get to his knees and took a breather. Then he stood up for good this time. The pain washed over him like black water in the ocean, sickly, charcoal filled and frothing from petrochemicals. He swooned, took some deep breaths, wiped the gas and blood from his face with his shirt, and by then the black tide had receded enough that he could look around.

The Benelli was on the ground behind him. Just beyond that was one of the reeking pools that he'd seen from the rig. He'd thought they were filled with either oil, or blood. Now he wasn't sure it was either. It looked a little more like reddish brown brake fluid, and there were small black hoses running underground from the direction of the Cube. A filter of some kind, maybe, pumping fluid in with one hose and drawing it away with another. He could see the ripples of movement around the ends of the hoses. It was still doing its job, whatever it was. And then something moved in the murky depth of the pool and David scrambled for the shotgun.

Just how deep is *it?* David thought, but there never seemed to be enough time for answers in this new version of reality he'd slipped into.

This time, there *was* an answer.

The liquid darkened, and then in the middle of the pool a

shape coalesced, and as David watched in horror two long girlish arms, covered in red slime, appeared at the edge, grabbing for land.

David dropped to one knee. It *couldn't* be.

But it was.

Sarah pulled herself up out of the liquid like she was getting out of a swimming pool, by placing her hands on the edge of the ground and hopping up on her elbows. Then she leaned over, hooked one leg over the lip of the pool and pulled herself the rest of the way out. She was naked, and the liquid from the pool ran off her body and puddled around her like rust coloured shampoo. She was mostly unchanged, though, and David's heart throbbed in relief. She was a little thinner maybe, a little taller from the looks of it, but there were no other visible changes. No claws or saw-bone arms. No Gorilla fists or chest armour. David reached out to her.

Sarah turned toward him and shrieked. Her eyes had grown large and black, as though they'd dropped paint onto her eyeballs, and her mouth was now full of spindly, razor-sharp teeth. It looked like she had a mouthful of nails sticking through her gums; they pushed the old teeth out of the way and some of them were still dangling by soft tissue inside her mouth.

David staggered back away from her, but Sarah wasn't interested in him. Her head snapped toward the fuel truck, and she got to her feet and stalked toward it. Around them, in some of the other pools, more figures were emerging; half formed Gorillas with their soft flesh and ungainly, partially muscled arms, and Cutters with elongated arms red and lumpy from growing out new teeth. They acted as one, as

The Host did, their only thought to attack and damage the fuel truck as much as possible. Whatever was controlling them, it was pulling out all the stops. It was akin to sending out bee larvae to defend the hive from a wasp attack.

David looked at Sarah walking away from him and didn't think. He just reacted. He moved as fast as his battered legs would carry him, until he was within arm's reach of his little girl, and then he reached over her shoulder and snagged her around the throat in a chokehold. He jerked her back off her feet and started dragging her back toward the Benelli lying in the dirt. Sarah thrashed and shrieked; she clawed his arm to bloody ribbons and reached up behind her, long nailed fingers scrabbling for his face. He was able to duck her blows easily. Even in her state, she was still a child, and a small one at that. She was short like her mother was; and beautiful Percy, and David had often wondered if she'd get any taller. She was taller now, *a few inches taller*, but this was hardly the way David had hoped it would happen.

"Easy," David said to her. "Just be easy, girl." He was close to the shotgun now. Not much longer. Back at the fuel truck The Host had managed to flatten all the tires and were busy stripping the cab down. There were three Gorillas on top of the fuel truck, and David though he recognized one of them as the creature that had been trying to pull the trailer hitch apart. He couldn't be sure though. In a moment, it wouldn't matter. He picked up the shotgun and kissed Sarah on the back of the head. Then he threw her to the ground and planted a boot on her chest. Sarah hissed, her teeth chomping at the air and she clawed at his leg. Her nails ripped through the denim of his pant leg and sank into his flesh. He grimaced, and twisted his leg away from her, but she continued to claw at him and it hurt like hell. He'd have to do this fast, before she really started to hurt him.

David wiped the fluid Sarah was covered in from his face, brought the shotgun up to eye level, and took aim.

He pulled the trigger and the shotgun banged against his shoulder; a good, solid thump. Down near the Cube, one of the cutters in front of the gas truck suddenly began haemorrhaging blood out of its back. It lilted to one side, then turned and started sprinting toward David. The autoloader kicked the empty shell out the side of the Benelli and David was ready to fire again. He pointed the shotgun at the Cutter coming their way. It was in a direct line with the fuel truck. It threw its long arms out in front of it as it ran, making itself a smaller target in the process.

That was fine with David.

He took aim again, looking past the creature bearing down on him, and instead zeroing in on the mess of pipes and wires inside the box that had been exposed and damaged when the tanker hit it. They were arcing electricity and venting small plumes of fire. Sitting below it was a veritable pond of gasoline just waiting for an open flame.

David squeezed the trigger. *Gotta squeeze the trigger*, Nicky had said, *because if you pull on it the whole weapon goes out of whack and you lose your target. Always squeeze it. Never pull it. Kinda like your dick.*

The shotgun bucked. It missed the Cutter entirely, sailed over its head, and true on the mark, hit the exposed wiring and burning pipes inside the box. Exactly where David had wanted to place the shot. There was a flare of electric fire and the wires were hit with buckshot, and fire shot out of a half dozen new holes made by the shotgun. There was no flare up, though. No fire large enough dropped into the gasoline to ignite it. Once more the Benelli kicked out the empty round. David pointed the gun at the Cutter and pulled the trigger. The barrel clicked empty.

"Oh shit," David said, and then the Cutter was on top of him. He managed to put the shotgun between them as the creature hit him, full blast, attacking as the Gorilla had in the house. David tripped over Sarah and went down in a heap beside her, the wind knocked from his lungs and leaving him gasping for air.

The Cutter slashed at his head with hammer fist motions, and it was all David could do to deflect the attacks with the steel of his weapon. The teeth on its arms cracked and split from the force of the impact, and where they broke away, they bled freely. Within moments, the Cutter was swinging arcs of blood high into the air with every shot. It may as well have been swinging paintbrushes loaded with dull red paint. Sarah stood up and took off toward the fuel truck. At the last minute, David let go of the shotgun and reached out, grabbing her ankle in his fist and tripping her. The Cutter took the opportunity to strike, driving the shotgun and its own bone arm down into the soft meat of David's shoulder.

The pain of the wound and subsequent sawing motion by the Cutter as it withdrew its arm forced a scream of pain from David's lips, against his will. He let go of Sarah's ankle long enough to grab hold of the shotgun once more, and as the Cutter came in to finish David off, he snapped his weapon into the air. It caught the bone hard about halfway down what once might have been a forearm, and there was a loud lobster-shell crack and a spray of blood. The Cutter let loose a throaty, inhuman roar, and David planted the pistol grip stock alongside its head. The creature collapsed to the side, its skull fractured and bleeding horrendously from its ears and mouth.

David crawled out from under it and saw Sarah moving toward the fuel truck. She wasn't very far. She didn't run well on her new long legs. The muscles on her thighs and back were coated in goo and burnt grass from her time on the ground.

"*Sarah!*" David yelled, but his voice was sand in the wind. He ran after her, his legs screaming at him with every movement. As he ran up behind her again, his brain registered the fire that had broken out inside the Box. It looked like burnt rubber; it was sparkling and bright the way rubber burned, and it was dripping like melted wax out of the mass of wired and pipes above the gas. Exactly where he'd fired the shotgun.

The fire dripped down into the gas, and a moment later the area erupted in small blue flame. The Host were unaware of the event taking place, and they continued to attack the truck like angry hornets. Only at the last moment, as the blue fire licked up the fuel spilling out of the taps and disappearing inside the tanker, did they realize what was about to happen. It was a moment too late.

David reached Sarah just as the first rumble shook the ground, and he tackled her football style, around the waist. He threw himself on top her thrashing, naked body and covered their faces with his arms.

There was a crack as the world opened up and pure hell erupted. The tanker exploded back to front, incinerating The Host and all the cockroach babies in the area. It instantly dismantled half the Cube, vaporizing large parts of it into the atmosphere. The explosion caused a blast wave that knocked the rest of the Cube sideways, rendering it a useless, smoking hulk. The gasoline accelerated the fire and vapours lit the air on fire; a few hundred feet away David felt the skin on his back peel and begin to blister. The air was too hot to breathe, so he clamped a hand over his mouth and did the same to Sarah.

And then the air was filled with the roar of the explosion, and the fire reached up almost fifty feet into the sky, burning the Cube, The Host, everything. When David was finally able to look up, he had to shield his face from the heat and the brightness. It felt like he was standing next to a small sun.

When he looked around, however, he saw something that scared him even more.

The grass in the immediate area was drying out and catching fire. Within moments, the entire field would be ablaze. And it was moving toward them even faster, because the fuel hoses had painted a long wide strip of gasoline all the way from Percy's house.

David reached down and grabbed Sarah's limp form in his arms. He threw her over his shoulder and turned on his heel and started moving away from the fire. Quickly, as quick as his throbbing legs would carry him. His left knee was making an ugly, knuckle-cracking sound that he could hear from inside his body, and he couldn't seem to get it to go exactly where he wanted it to be. It might not last long like this, trying to run on uneven ground with his daughter across his shoulders, and a firestorm welling up directly behind him, but he made up his mind that it *would* last long enough. He wouldn't allow himself to be chewed up by a grassfire after destroying an alien ship in a crash site riddled with monsters.

The fire moved faster, though; it had its own ideas. And it wasn't trying to run on two bad legs and one *really* bad leg either. It was lapping at the back of David's legs before he was halfway to the tree line, and the flames practically *flew* along the path the fuel truck had taken. Within moments, David was high-stepping through thigh-high flames and trying his damndest not to scream out all his breath. He pushed the pain as far away from his thoughts as he could, put his head down, and sprinted the last hundred feet or so to the gravel road at the edge of town. He took four steps out of the grass, flopped Sarah down, and proceeded to roll on the ground like a lunatic trying to put the fire out on his pants.

He checked on Sarah, and she was breathing. She seemed all right. Her eyes and teeth were mutilated, however, but David wondered if it couldn't be fixed with some contacts and a lot of expensive dental care. She might be in braces by the time school rolled around in the fall. It wouldn't be so bad. His heart would ache for his sister and her wackjob husband, and the creature her baby son had become. For a long time. Maybe forever. Forever seemed fitting. After they came in here and swept everything under the carpet, he'd pay to have a nice gravestone for the three of them, somewhere he and Sarah could go to visit. But all that was in the future, and there was a lot of healing to do before that.

Sarah coughed, opened her eyes and looked at him. Her black eyes welled up, and then she put her hands out to him.

"*Daddy?*" she whimpered. "*I need you!*"

David went to her, cupped her head in his arms and held her, the way he did when she was a baby. She was suddenly aware of her nakedness, and she covered her body with her hands self-consciously.

"It's okay, sweetie," David said. "You're alright now. Everything is going to be alright." He looked back at the fire and sighed deeply, taking in the black smell of burnt grass and gasoline. He was beyond hurt. Beyond tired. But he was alive. They both were.

And that was good enough for now.

A column of military trucks, mostly personnel carriers, but also bio-hazardous waste trucks with men in hazmat suits and two cars full of scientists rumbled down the highway, away from a beautiful golden sunset and toward a very ugly black smudge on the horizon. They passed two figures on the side of the road, a man and a young girl, headed in the opposite direction, toward the sunset.

The man and the girl paid the trucks no mind. The man was limping badly and he was leaning on the girl for support. The girl was wearing clothes much too big for her, and much too hot in the summer sun. They walked on the shoulder of the highway, not looking up at the vehicles as they passed, simply staring at the road and holding each other as they walked.

When the final truck in the column stopped, the man and the girl stopped too. The man looked up at the vehicle, his face blistered and peeling from a terrible sunburn.

"Hey!" the driver of the truck yelled. "Hey you guys alright?"

"Fine," the man said, waving them off. "Just fine thanks."

"Yeah?" the man said. "Well, you don't *look* fine. You look fucked up. You sure you don't need a ride or something? Medical, maybe?"

"*HE SAID WE'RE FINE!*" The girl screeched, flashing her black gaze toward the truck.

"Holy fuck," the man said, recoiling like he'd been slapped. In the back of the truck, there was scattered laughter. "Hey, whatever you say. *Fuckin' wackos.*"

"Why the hell did you stop?" another man, in the passenger seat said. They were of similar size and colouring, and identical haircuts. "We're out of position now."

"I dunno, they looked hurt," the driver said. "Besides, you see that chick's face? She was fuckin' hot, dude."

"You're a sick asshole, Macintyre, you know that?" The man in the passenger seat said. "She was like twelve years old."

"Yeah, well," Macintyre said. "I didn't say I was gonna do her. I just said she was hot."

From behind them, someone banged on the roof of the truck.

"*Hurry the fuck up in there!*"

Macintyre hit the gas, and the truck started forward once more.

"This sure don't look like no fuckin' chemical spill," he said.

"You talk too much, Macintyre," the man in the passenger seat said.

"Just sayin'."

Behind them, on the road, the man and the girl had

stopped, looking back at the row of vehicles. The man cupped his hand over his eyes to shade out the sun.

"Think they'll find anything?" the girl said.

"They'll find *something,*" the man said, "but I'm not sure they'll know what it is."

"Come on, Dad," the girl said suddenly, taking his arm. "I don't want to be here if they decide to come back."

"That's a smart idea," the man said. He smiled, and saw his reflection in his daughter's liquid black eyes. "You're a bright girl."

The girl smiled, and leaned in for a quick hug. As they turned and continued to walk down the highway, he leaned in close and said, "You must take after your old man."

"If I'm lucky I will," the girl said. Her voice was slurred because of the new shape of her teeth. She put her arm around her father and squeezed, and they walked some more.

About the Author

JW Schnarr is an award-winning journalist originally from Calgary, Alberta. He is the author of the novel *Alice & Dorothy* and the former publisher of Canadian indie press Northern Frights Publishing. He is the editor/contributor of three anthologies, *Shadows of the Emerald City, War of the Worlds: Frontlines,* and *Timelines: Stories Inspired by H.G. Wells' The Time Machine.*

A member of the HWA and SF Canada, he can be seen lurking in places such as *Best New Zombie Tales Volume II* (Books of the Dead Press) where *Rue Morgue* magazine dubbed his story "Freshest Tale" of the anthology. He's also been spotted in *Andromeda Spaceways Inflight Magazine* and will be found in *Slices of Flesh* (Dark Moon Books) alongside the likes of Ramsey Campbell and Jack Ketchum. In 2012 he appeared alongside horror legend Clive Barker in *Torn Realities* (Post Mortem Press).

By day he works as a reporter and photographer for the *Claresholm Local Press* in Claresholm, Alberta where he makes his home with his awesome teenage daughter. The two of them often argue about who is going to do the dishes.

Look him up on Facebook, Twitter, Goodreads, or check out his blog at jwschnarr.blogspot.com.

NON-FICTION

Al Capone: Chicago's King of Crime, by Nate Hendley

Crystal Death: North America's Most Dangerous Drug, by Nate Hendley

Dutch Schultz: Brazen Beer Baron of New York, by Nate Hendley

Motivate to Create: a guide for writers, by Nate Hendley

The Organic Home Garden, by Patrick Lima and John Scanlan

Elephant's Breath & London Smoke: historic colour names, definitions & uses, Deb Salisbury, editor

Stonehouse Cooks, by Lorina Stephens

NON-FICTION COMING SOON

John Lennon: a biography, by Nate Hendley

Stephen Truscott, by Nate Hendley

Shakespeare & Readers' Theatre: Hamlet, by John Poulson

Shakespeare & Readers' Theatre: Romeo and Juliet, by John Poulson

Shakespeare & Readers' Theatre: Midsummer Night's Dream, by John Poulson

FICTION

Immunity to Strange Tales, by Susan J. Forest

Growing Up Bronx, by H. A. Hargreaves

North by 2000+, a collection of short, speculative fiction, by H.A. Hargreaves

A Subtle Thing, Alicia Hendley

Downshift, by Matt Hughes

Kingmaker's Sword, by Ann Marston

Mik Murdoch, Boy-Superhero, by Michell Plested

Things Falling Apart, by J.W. Schnarr

And the Angels Sang: a collection of short speculative fiction, by Lorina Stephens

From Mountains of Ice, by Lorina Stephens

Shadow Song, by Lorina Stephens

FICTION COMING SOON

88, by M.E. Fletcher

A Method to the Madness: A Guide to the Super Evil, Jeff Hite and Michell Plested, editors

Old Growth, by Matt Hughes

Stitching Butterflies, by Shermin Nahid Kruse

The Western King, by Ann Marston

Broken Blade, by Ann Marston

Cloudbearer's Shadow, by Ann Marston

King of Shadows, by Ann Marston

Sword and Shadow, by Ann Marston

Keylan's Story, by Ann Marston

A Still and Bitter Grave, by Ann Marston

Diamonds in Black Sand, by Ann Marston

Caliban, by Lorina Stephens

The Rose Guardian, by Lorina Stephens

www.5rivers.org

CPSIA information can be obtained at www.ICGtesting.com
Printed in the USA
LVOW082205180712

290640LV00001B/11/P

9 781927 400036